ALISTAIR MACLEAN'S CODE BREAKER

Alistair MacLean, who died on 2 February 1987, was the international bestselling author of thirty books, including world-famous novels such as *The Guns of Navarone* and *Where Eagles Dare*. In 1977 he was commissioned by an American film company to write a number of story outlines that could be adapted into a series of movies; two, *Hostage Tower* and *Air Force One is Down*, were, with Alistair MacLean's approval, published as novels by John Denis; these were followed with six by Alastair MacNeill, the highly successful *Death Train*, *Night Watch*, *Red Alert*, *Time of the Assassins*, *Dead Halt* and *Code Breaker*, and two, *Borrowed Time* and *Prime Target* by Hugh Miller.

Alastair MacNeill was born in Scotland in 1960. When he was six years old his family emigrated to South Africa, where he showed a growing interest in writing, winning several school competitions. He returned to Britain in 1985 to pursue a full-time writing career. As well as writing seven novels based on MacLean outlines he has written five novels under his own name. He lives in Sheffield.

Code Breaker is the eighth title in the UNACO serie

ALASTAIR MACNEILL

*Alistair MacLean's UNACO
Code Breaker*

HARPER

Harper
An Imprint of HarperCollins*Publishers*
77–85 Fulham Palace Road,
Hammersmith, London W6 8JB

www.harpercollins.co.uk
This paperback edition 2010
1

First published in Great Britain by
HarperCollins*Publishers* 1993

Copyright © HarperCollins*Publishers* 1993

Alastair MacNeill asserts the moral right to
be identified as the author of this work

A catalogue record for this book is
available from the British Library

ISBN: 978-0-00-647622-1

Typeset in Meridien by Palimpsest Book Production Limited,
Falkirk, Stirlingshire

Printed and bound in Clays Ltd, St Ives plc

Mixed Sources
Product group from well-managed
forests and other controlled sources
www.fsc.org Cert no. SW-COC-001806
© 1996 Forest Stewardship Council
FSC

FSC is a non-profit international organisation established
to promote the responsible management of the world's forests.
Products carrying the FSC label are independently certified
to assure consumers that they come from forests that are managed
to meet the social, economic and ecological needs
of present and future generations.

Find out more about HarperCollins and the environment at
www.harpercollins.co.uk/green

PROLOGUE

On an undisclosed date in September 1979, the Secretary-General of the United Nations chaired an extraordinary meeting attended by forty-six envoys representing virtually every country in the world. There was only one point on the agenda: the escalating tide of international crime. It was agreed to set up an international strike force to operate under the aegis of the United Nations Security Council, to be known as the United Nations Anti-Crime Organization (UNACO). Its objective was to 'avert, neutralize and/or apprehend individuals or groups engaged in international criminal activities'.* The envoys each nominated one candidate for the position of UNACO Director, with the Secretary-General making the final choice.

UNACO's clandestine existence came into being on 1 March 1980.

*UNACO Charter, Article 1, Paragraph 1C.

1

The two men were escorted briskly through customs at Lisbon's Portela Airport by a plain-clothes officer attached to the Special Forces Brigade, the élite Portuguese anti-terrorist squad. All formalities had been waived in advance, and a ground stewardess was on hand with their stamped passports and boarding cards once they reached the VIP lounge. The two men, Sergei Kolchinsky and Professor Abraham Silverman, were officially listed as members of a team of UNESCO scientists who had spent the last week on a fact-finding mission to Portugal. It was a cover. For the past four days Kolchinsky and Silverman had been in Lisbon to attend a top secret conference, hosted by the Special Forces Brigade, which had brought together all the leaders of Europe's anti-terrorist squads. Both men held key positions inside UNACO. Kolchinsky, a former major in the KGB, had been the Deputy Director at UNACO for the past three years, and Silverman, who was regarded by many of his peers as the world's leading cryptologist, had worked for the Israeli Intelligence Service, Mossad, before joining UNACO in the mid-Eighties. Inside the attaché case chained to Silverman's wrist were the minutes of the conference, as well as detailed information on UNACO which Kolchinsky had brought with him from New York. Silverman had coded all the documents personally and only he knew the key to decode the text . . .

The UNACO Director, Colonel Malcolm Philpott, had initially wanted one of the organization's élite Strike Force teams to accompany the two men to Lisbon, but the Portuguese authorities had insisted on using the Special Forces Brigade to protect all visiting delegates for the duration of the conference. In the event, Kolchinsky and Silverman had taken to their personal bodyguard, Lieutenant Carlos Pereira, from the start. His friendly, outgoing disposition was in stark contrast to the sombre and often presumptuous attitude of his superior, Major João Inacio, who had been in charge of security at the conference. Philpott and Inacio had both agreed that Pereira should be armed when he accompanied Kolchinsky and Silverman on the return flight to New York's JFK Airport, where one of the Strike Force teams would be on hand to meet the plane and escort the two men back to the United Nations. Inacio had made the necessary arrangements with the authorities to ensure that the three men would be given a special clearance through customs. Everything had gone according to plan ...

Kolchinsky declined the offer of coffee and, after Silverman and Pereira had left for the canteen, he took up a seat close to the window overlooking the runway. Taking a fresh packet of cigarettes from his pocket, he unwrapped it and lit one. He was in his early fifties with thinning black hair, doleful features, and what he regarded as the inevitable signs of middle-age spread for someone who'd spent much of his adult life stuck behind a desk. He had proved himself to be a brilliant tactician on joining the KGB, and although he'd attained the rank of major by the age of twenty-three, he'd become increasingly unpopular amongst his colleagues because of his often vociferous opposition to the brutal methods adopted by the KGB to suppress any form of anti-Communist sentiment. When he had finally exhausted his superiors' patience, he had been dispatched to the West as a military attaché, where he was to remain for the next sixteen years at a succession of Soviet embassies before being recalled to take up a senior post in the Second Directorate, which dealt with foreign intelligence, at the Lubyanka in Moscow. He had never settled on his return to Russia, though, missing the comforts that he'd grown accustomed to in the West, so he had been quick to accept the post of Deputy Director at UNACO when the position fell vacant.

Now his career had reached a crossroads. It had all come about after Philpott had suffered a heart attack earlier in the year, forcing him to take early retirement. Kolchinsky had been installed as the new Director, but he had struggled to cope with the extra pressures from the start, and matters had come to a head when an entire Strike Force team had been killed while on assignment in London. There had been immediate calls for his resignation and, although Kolchinsky had initially refused to buckle to the intimidation, he had become increasingly isolated amongst the politicians at the United Nations. Finally, realizing his position was untenable, he had tendered his resignation to the Secretary-General. Philpott had immediately been lured out of retirement and brought back as Director: his first task had been to persuade Kolchinsky to remain on at UNACO as his number two. Kolchinsky had agreed on the understanding that he would review the situation at the end of the year. That time had come. He'd already made up his mind before he'd left for the conference, but had wisely decided to keep it to himself until he got back. He still had some misgivings about his decision, but he'd learnt from experience always to follow his instincts. And deep down he knew he'd made the right choice . . .

He was on his second cigarette when Silverman and Pereira returned from the cafeteria. 'I'll be glad to get this off,' Silverman said, indicating the handcuff manacled to his wrist.

'Why don't you take it off until the flight's called?' Pereira asked. 'You're quite safe in here.'

'It comes off once I'm back at the UN,' Silverman replied brusquely. 'Not before.'

Pereira just shrugged, then looked around slowly until his eyes came to rest on the illuminated Christmas tree in the corner of the room. It seemed wasted in the first-class lounge. There wasn't a child in sight. And Christmas was essentially for the children as far as he was concerned. He had two sons of his own and he'd already managed to get Christmas Day off by swapping shifts with an unmarried colleague who'd wanted to attend a New Year's Eve party. He wasn't bothered about New Year's Eve parties any more – his family was all that mattered to him now.

'You're thinking about those two kids of yours, aren't you?' Silverman said, resting a hand lightly on Pereira's shoulder.

Pereira smiled. 'Yes, I was. Do you have any children, Professor?'

'I have a daughter in Israel. I'll be going out there early in the New Year to live with her.'

'Of course, this is your last assignment with UNACO. You retire at the end of the year. You must be looking forward to it.'

'Ask me that again this time next year and I'll be able to answer you more truthfully,' Silverman said with a resigned shrug. 'I'm sixty-four now. I've probably got another ten or fifteen years left in me if I take it easy and don't have any more trouble with my heart. That's a long time to be sitting around reflecting on life.'

'Are your family still in Russia, Mr Kolchinsky?' Pereira asked.

'What?' Kolchinsky said, looking round from the window. He smiled apologetically. 'I'm sorry, I was miles away.'

'I asked if your family were still in Russia.'

'My late wife's family live in Estonia. I don't have any other family.'

'Do you miss Russia?'

'Sometimes,' Kolchinsky replied vaguely, then gestured to the copy of the *International Herald Tribune* which was protruding from the side pocket of Silverman's overnight bag. 'Is that today's?'

Silverman nodded and handed the newspaper to Kolchinsky. Pereira took the hint and, looking across at the Christmas tree again, lapsed into a thoughtful silence.

It had been a relatively quiet shift for the three paramedics on duty at the airport that afternoon. Jaime Fernandes was beginning to regret that. To while away the time, they had played several hands of poker and, although the stakes hadn't been particularly high, he'd already lost enough money to incur the wrath of his wife once he got home. But he was now confident that he could repair some of the damage by winning the current pot on the table with the hand he was holding. His eyes flickered to his two colleagues. Augusto, the youngest of the three, had folded earlier; Luis, his best friend, who was sitting directly opposite him, looked up slowly at him.

'OK, let's see what you got, Jaime,' Luis said, tapping his finger impatiently on the table.

'Four of a kind,' Jaime announced triumphantly, splaying his cards on the table in front of him. 'Let's see you beat that.'

Luis stared at the cards then nodded to himself. 'Good hand, Jaime, but it still doesn't beat a straight flush.'

Jaime threw up his hands in despair and slumped back in the chair as Luis raked the winnings towards him.

The door opened behind Luis and a tall, commanding figure entered the room. He was wearing a maintenance overall and carried a tool box in his gloved hand. A second, shorter man with greasy black hair followed him into the room and closed the door behind him. He, too, was wearing an overall and carried a similar tool box.

'*Ola*,' Jaime greeted them with a smile. 'What's the problem?' he asked, then gasped in terror as he saw the tall man pull a silenced automatic from under his overall. He had no time to react further before the single shot ripped through his head. Augusto was still turning towards the two men when he too was dispatched with a single bullet through the head. In terror, Luis kicked his chair aside and darted towards a second door which led into the adjoining garage where the ambulance was parked. Two bullets thudded into his back, propelling him face forward into the wall, where his lifeless body slumped to the floor.

The shorter man glanced swiftly round the room then, finding the keys for the ambulance hanging above the control desk, followed his colleague through the interconnecting door into the garage. A third man was already waiting for them in the garage. The keys were tossed to him and he unlocked the back doors of the ambulance.

The taller man opened his tool box, dropped the automatic inside, and removed a cordless telephone. He dialled a number which was answered immediately at the other end. 'We're in,' he announced in Russian. 'Are you in place?'

'Yes, sir,' came the quick reply. 'I've got a perfect vantage point overlooking the runway. I'll be able to see Kolchinsky and Silverman as soon as they emerge from the terminal building.'

'We'll be ready,' came the curt reply, and the connection was severed. He placed the tool box in the back of the ambulance then, climbing in beside his colleague, he shouted in German for the driver to close the door behind them.

'It's just like the old days,' the shorter man said with a smile as he removed a Heckler & Koch MP5 sub-machine gun from the tool box at his feet.

The taller man said nothing as he pulled a black stocking from his pocket, tugged it over his face, then reached for the other sub-machine gun and placed it across his knees. He looked at his watch. It was almost time for the New York flight to be announced over the airport intercom . . .

Kolchinsky pulled up the collar of his overcoat as he stepped out into the cold night air, and he and his colleagues joined the stream of passengers already making their way towards the TAP Boeing 747 which was parked close to the terminal building. The conference had been taxing and Kolchinsky was looking forward to getting back home. He'd also be a lot happier once the attaché case that Silverman was clasping was safely deposited back at UN headquarters. An ambulance emerged from behind a row of warehouses and, with lights flashing, headed towards the stationary jet. Kolchinsky looked round sharply. He knew it was not usual to transfer a patient on to a plane while other passengers were still boarding, and a tremor of disquiet ran through him. He glanced at Pereira, whose eyes mirrored Kolchinsky's own uneasiness. The ambulance was heading directly for the line of passengers and, as a stray light scythed across the ambulance, Kolchinsky had a momentary glimpse of the driver, his features distorted underneath a black stocking mask.

He turned in alarm to Pereira, but their bodyguard was already unholstering his Astra pistol and yelling to the other passengers to get down.

The ambulance screeched to a halt and two smoke grenades were hurled out on to the runway. Passengers screamed in terror: some tried fleeing back through the dense smoke towards the terminal; others headed for the sanctuary of the plane. The ambulance was blocking any direct route back to the terminal building, so Kolchinsky opted to propel Silverman towards the mobile passenger stairs. Pereira was trying desperately to protect his charges, but it was impossible to pinpoint the vehicle or its occupants exactly in the dark and choking smoke. He heard a metallic crash as the back doors of the ambulance flew open, saw a flash through the grey from a sub-machine gun, then knew no more as two bullets pierced his heart, killing him instantly.

Kolchinsky watched in horror as Pereira's body hit the ground just in front of them. Galvanizing himself into action, Kolchinsky ordered Silverman towards the stairs, then stooped down to retrieve Pereira's fallen pistol. As he straightened up he saw to his horror a figure sprinting out of the swirling smoke; the man had already reached the foot of the stairs and was blocking Silverman's path. Kolchinsky raised the Astra but, before he could fire, Silverman suddenly stepped in front of the man and swung the attaché case at his head. The edge of the case caught him on the cheekbone; Kolchinsky heard his assailant's cry of pain as he stumbled back against the stairs, the Heckler & Koch spinning from his hand. Kolchinsky had the perfect shot as the man made a desperate grab for the sub-machine gun but, before he could fire, another pall of black smoke swirled up in front of him, obscuring his view. Kolchinsky cursed furiously under his breath and moved forward cautiously through the smoke, the pistol held at arm's length. The smoke dissipated as suddenly as it had appeared, and Kolchinsky saw that Silverman was now sprawled unconscious on the runway, a tranquillizer dart embedded in his neck.

Another man was crouched over Silverman: he looked up slowly at Kolchinsky, the dart gun still in his hand. 'Kill him,' he barked to his colleague in Russian.

That voice – Kolchinsky knew that voice! His finger froze on the trigger and, in that moment of hesitation, the second man ducked out from behind the ambulance, the Heckler & Koch raised to fire. Kolchinsky noticed the sudden movement out of the corner of his eye and was still turning when the bullet took him in the stomach. For a moment he felt unsteady on his feet and the pistol slipped from his numb fingers as a searing pain speared through his stomach. Then his legs buckled underneath him and he crashed to the ground.

He was barely conscious when the first police car shot past him in pursuit of the fleeing ambulance. A second police car pulled up beside him. He heard voices. Anxious voices. They sounded distant. Then nothing . . .

2

C.W. Whitlock paused outside the closed kitchen door and smiled to himself as he listened to his wife, Carmen, humming unevenly to the Michael Feinstein tape he'd given her for her last birthday. Normally she would have been glad of the company while she was cooking, but on this occasion he'd been given strict instructions to stay out. And he knew better than to argue ...

He went through to the lounge and poured himself a small whisky. Clarence Wilkins Whitlock was a handsome forty-four-year-old Kenyan with a light complexion and a neatly trimmed black moustache that he'd worn since his university days. After graduating from Oxford, he'd returned to Kenya and served for a short time in the army before being recruited by the Intelligence Corps where he'd remained for the next ten years, reaching the rank of Colonel. He had been one of Philpott's first field operatives at UNACO.

His six-year marriage had been far from idyllic. From the beginning Carmen had worried about his safety, but he'd constantly refused to trade his often dangerous field work for a desk job at UNACO, and it was only when she'd threatened to leave him that he'd reluctantly agreed to go over on to the management side. He had been appointed as Kolchinsky's deputy after Philpott was retired, and although it had improved relations at home, he had been desperately unhappy in his new position. So when Philpott had been reinstated as Director, Whitlock had immediately requested a transfer back to the field. This had been granted, and he had been reunited with his former Strike Force Three colleagues, Mike Graham and Sabrina Carver.

Carmen's reaction to the news had both surprised and unnerved him. He had expected to catch hell when he told her. But there had been no outbursts, no anger, no threats. Just a philosophical acceptance of his decision. He knew she must have been gutted by his decision, but she was obviously determined not to show it. He knew the back-lash would come, in time . . .

'Dinner will be ready in about fifteen minutes' time,' Carmen said, appearing in the doorway behind him. She was a Puerto Rican with shoulder-length black hair and a youthful beauty which belied her forty years. She crossed to where he was standing by the window of their seventh-floor Manhattan apartment watching the snow filtering down gently over an illuminated Central Park.

He slipped an arm around her shoulder as she nuzzled up against him. 'Am I allowed back into the kitchen yet?'

'No,' she replied with a grin. 'I've already told you. I'm preparing a special dinner for us. It's one of your favourite dishes. That's all I'm saying. So no peeking until it's on the table.'

'Isn't there anything I can do to help?' Whitlock said. 'I could set the table or open the wine –'

'It's all done,' she replied softly. 'You just enjoy the peace and tranquillity while you still can.'

'Don't remind me. My last day of freedom before your mother arrives from Puerto Rico tomorrow,' he said, rolling his eyes.

'That's a horrible thing to say,' Carmen said with a mock-reproving look. 'I know she's really looking forward to seeing all the family again. And it's her first trip back to New York since she flew up for our marriage.'

'As long as she doesn't make a habit of it,' Whitlock said

mischievously, already ducking out of the way of her playful punch.

'I'd better go and check on the food again,' she said, leaving the room.

He crossed to his favourite armchair, sat down, and was about to reach for the remote control to switch on the news when the telephone rang. He groaned to himself, got to his feet, and answered it.

'C.W.?'

'Evening, Colonel,' Whitlock replied, instantly recognizing Philpott's Celtic brogue.

'You're on a Code Red.'

Whitlock sat down slowly on the arm of the sofa and rubbed his hand despairingly over his face. A Code Red operation meant he was on immediate standby. It couldn't have come at a worse moment.

'C.W., are you still there?'

'Yes, sir, I'm still here,' Whitlock was quick to assure him.

'The briefing's in half an hour,' Philpott told him.

'I'll be there, sir.'

The line went dead.

Whitlock replaced the receiver and stood up. It was then he saw Carmen in the doorway. Her mouth was taut, her eyes cold and questioning. 'When?' was all she said.

'Straightaway,' Whitlock replied, grim-faced. 'I'm sorry, Carmen, I –'

'Spare it!' she snapped angrily. 'I should have guessed that something like this would happen.'

'You knew I was on standby over Christmas,' Whitlock said defensively, pulling on his jacket.

'You wouldn't have been had you still been the Deputy Director,' she shot back angrily. 'But you weren't even prepared to give it a chance, were you?'

'I stuck it out for as long as I could, but in the end I just couldn't come to terms with the idea of being stuck behind a desk for the rest of my life. It's not for me.'

'This is me you're talking to, C.W. Maybe you can fool your colleagues, but I can read you like a book. It's got nothing to do with being stuck behind a desk. It's all about growing old, isn't it? It's always been your greatest fear. That's why you jumped at the chance to return to the field. A last, desperate attempt to prove something to yourself.' She wiped a tear from the corner of her eye. 'You're not thirty any more, C.W. You have to know when to let go.'

'I've a briefing to attend,' Whitlock said brusquely.

'Then go to your briefing,' she yelled. 'But don't expect me to be here when you get back. If you can't start acting like a responsible father, then I'll manage without you.'

Whitlock's hand froze on the door handle. He looked round slowly at her. 'Father?'

She held his stare for some time before she finally spoke. 'I was going to tell you over dinner. At least that's how it was supposed to have turned out. I wanted to make it a night for us to remember. Well, it's certainly turning out that way, isn't it?'

Whitlock stared at her in disbelief. 'You mean I'm going to be a father?'

'Only if you're going to start acting like one,' came the sharp riposte.

Whitlock opened his mouth but found he couldn't speak. He held out his hands, palms upturned, and shook his head, still struggling to comprehend what she'd just told him. A slow grin spread across his face, but when he tried to embrace her she was quick to push him away.

'You've got a briefing to attend, remember?' she said caustically.

'Carmen –'

'We'll talk about it when you've got the time to spare,' she cut in sharply, then turned on her heels and disappeared back into the kitchen.

Whitlock was about to go after her but he checked himself. Damn Philpott and his briefing. With a last, desperate glance

14

in the direction of the kitchen, he reluctantly let himself out·
of the apartment.

'You're not going out dressed like that?'

'No,' Sabrina Carver replied as she pulled a New York
Giants peaked cap from her pocket and tugged it firmly over
her head. 'There. Now I'm ready.'

George Carver eyed his daughter's clothes disapprovingly.
'Those jeans are far too big on you. And that leather jacket
looks as if it's been crumpled in the bottom of your wardrobe
for the past six months.'

Sabrina grinned. 'It's called fashion, Daddy.'

George Carver shrugged helplessly and went back to his
crossword. For the last three years George and Jeanne Carver
had come up from Miami to spend Christmas with Sabrina
at her small Manhattan apartment. It gave them a chance
to see their daughter, and to take in some of the top
Broadway shows that they would otherwise have missed
in Florida. He could remember a time when Sabrina would
have accompanied them to all the shows. Now she rarely
went anywhere with them. Not that it surprised him. She
had her own life with her own friends and, like her mother,
was also very headstrong and fiercely independent. He
looked up at her. She was perched on the edge of the couch,
using the remote control to flick absently through the television channels. He smiled to himself. Yes, very much in
the mould of her mother ...

Sabrina was a strikingly attractive twenty-eight-year-old.
Her shoulder-length blonde hair was tinted with auburn high-
lights, and her near-perfect figure was kept so by aerobics
classes three nights a week. A black belt in karate, she also
taught self-defence to women twice a month at a commu-
nity centre in the Bronx. She had a degree in Romance
languages from Wellesley College and, after completing her
post-graduate work at the Sorbonne, she had joined the FBI,
mainly due to her father's influence in government circles,

15

where she had graduated top of her year and proved to be one of the finest shots ever to have attended the academy. But a growing resentment amongst some of her peers, who felt her father was pulling strings to advance her career, had made her position untenable, forcing her to resign. The Director had then forwarded her dossier to Philpott as a possible recruit for UNACO. She was accepted immediately, this time completely on her own merit. She was still the only female field operative in the organization.

'Where are you going tonight?' George Carver finally asked, putting down the newspaper.

'Fat Tuesday's,' Sabrina replied. 'It's a jazz club over on Third Avenue.'

'She's going with Mike Graham,' Jeanne Carver said, entering the room. Her accent still bore the traces of her French upbringing.

'It's no big deal,' Sabrina replied quickly. 'Mike's my partner. We both happen to like jazz.'

'And football,' Jeanne Carver added with a knowing smile as she sat down beside Sabrina. 'You used to hate football. Now suddenly you're a big fan of the New York Giants. The same team that Mike supports, *n'est-ce pas?*'

'I've been to Meadowlands a couple of times with Mike to watch them play,' Sabrina replied defensively. 'Read into that what you want, *Maman*, but as far as I'm concerned, he's nothing more than my partner. Period.'

'Are we finally going to get to meet him over Christmas?' Jeanne Carver asked.

'No, why?' Sabrina rolled her eyes and handed the remote control to her mother. 'Watch some television, *Maman*. I'll see you both in the morning.'

As she turned to leave the apartment, the telephone rang. Sabrina was quick to answer it, and when she replaced the receiver moments later her face was grim. 'That was Colonel Philpott,' she told her parents. 'I'm on standby. The briefing's in half an hour.'

'So much for the jazz club,' George Carver said with a philosophical smile.

'So much for Christmas,' Sabrina retorted with a resigned shrug then, picking up her car keys, she left the apartment.

It was two years since Mike Graham's wife and son had been murdered. Although he felt that he'd finally come to terms with their deaths, he knew the real test still lay ahead – Christmas Day. He'd spent the previous Christmas with his mother in California, but this year she'd gone to stay with her brother and his family in Australia. This time he was alone . . .

As was his custom every Wednesday, he'd travelled down to New York from his home in Vermont to place fresh flowers on their graves in the cemetery situated close to their old apartment block in Murray Hill. On his return to the hotel he'd found a note from Sabrina tucked underneath the door inviting him to Fat Tuesday's with her that evening. He would be glad of the company . . .

It was snowing lightly when he emerged from the hotel. Digging his hands into his pockets, he quickened his pace as he made for the nearest subway. The train arrived shortly after he reached the platform; as he stepped into the carriage he noticed that it was barely half full, which was surprising for that time of night. At least it meant he could sit down . . .

Graham was a youthfully handsome thirty-eight-year-old with an athletic physique and tousled, collar-length brown hair. A talented sportsman at school, he'd captained both the football and basketball teams in his final year before going on to UCLA where he'd graduated with a degree in Political Science. He'd then signed up as a rookie quarterback with the New York Giants, the team he'd supported since childhood, but a month later he had been drafted into Vietnam where he'd sustained a shoulder injury which had put an end to his promising football career. He had been transferred to a CIA base in Vietnam where his leadership qualities were quickly recognized by his superiors and, on his return to the United States, he had been recruited for Delta, the élite anti-terrorist squad.

Eleven years later he had been promoted to team leader of Squadron-B. His first mission had been to take a team of five men into Libya and destroy a known terrorist base outside Benghazi. As they had been about to close in on the base, news had reached him that his wife, Carrie, and five-year-old son, Mikey, had been aducted by three masked men outside their Murray Hill apartment. He had known it was a ploy to force him to withdraw. He had refused to back down and, although the base had been destroyed, the two main targets, Salim Al-Makesh and Jean-Jacques Bernard, had managed to escape. Despite a massive nation-wide hunt by the FBI, no trace of his family had ever been found. He had been retired from Delta at his own request and his dossier had been forwarded on to Philpott who had offered him a post at UNACO.

On a recent assignment he'd finally come face to face with Bernard, the man he'd held responsible for the disappearance of his family. It was then he'd finally discovered the truth. Bernard had been working for Robert Bailey, the deputy director of the CIA, at the time of the kidnapping. Bailey had regarded Bernard as too valuable an asset to lose, and had set up the abduction of Carrie and Mikey from Langley to give Bernard time to escape before the Delta unit closed in on the base. Having discovered from Bernard where the bodies of Carrie and Mikey were buried, Graham had had the remains exhumed and reburied side by side in the grounds of the church where he and Carrie had been married. They were finally at rest . . .

The train pulled into the next station and the doors opened. Graham was immediately aware of the two youths who got in at the far end of the carriage – skinheads dressed in torn jeans and studded leather jackets. One spat on the floor then, grabbing hold of the rail above his head, leaned closer to his friend and whispered in his ear. They both grinned salaciously as their eyes went to a pretty brunette sitting further down the carriage. The doors closed and the train began moving. The two youths made their way down the carriage until they were standing directly in front of her. She glanced up nervously at them then focused her eyes on the floor.

'What's your name, sweetheart?' one of the youths said, leaning over her.

She tried to get up but the second youth quickly pushed her back down. 'Now that isn't friendly. What's your name?'

'Please, I . . . do not want trouble,' she stammered nervously in a German accent.

'We got a piece of foreign here, Joe,' the first youth said with a twisted grin.

Joe sat down next to her and ran his fingers through her hair. She jerked her head away but he grabbed her chin between his thumb and forefinger, forcing her to look at him. 'What's wrong, babe? Aren't I your type?' He gestured to his friend who was still leaning over her. 'How about Matt? Is he your type?'

She looked round in desperation but nobody held her pleading stare. Matt laughed derisively. 'Welcome to New York, sweetheart. Lesson number one of the subway. Nobody helps nobody. You're on your own. So why not relax and enjoy the ride.'

Graham watched with growing dismay. Where the hell were the subway cops? Or the Guardian Angels? He didn't want to get involved in case it drew unnecessary attention to himself and the organization but, as he looked round the carriage, he knew that nobody else would go to her aid. The kid was right. On the subway you were on your own. Suddenly one of the youths slipped his hand under her sweatshirt. When she tried to push him away, the second youth opened a switchblade inches from her face and pressed the tip of the blade against her throat. She stopped struggling and closed her eyes tightly as the youth's hand continued to wander under her sweatshirt.

Graham cursed furiously under his breath. It had gone on long enough. He got to his feet and approached the two youths.

The smile faltered on Matt's face. 'What you looking at, man?'

'Leave her alone,' Graham said sharply.

Joe looked up slowly at Graham. 'Well, well. We got us a regular Bernie Goetz here. You'll back off if you know what's good for you, mister, otherwise you're gonna get hurt.'

Matt stood up slowly, a twisted grin on his face, switch-blade extended towards Graham; at the same time Graham was grabbed from behind by the second youth, and his arms pinned to his sides. Graham snapped his head back viciously, and his assailant screamed out in pain, stumbling backwards before dropping to his knees, his hands cupped over his shattered nose. Now Matt lunged at Graham, slashing wildly with the switchblade, but Graham countered with a forearm block, locking his other hand around the boy's wrist, twisting it violently and forcing him off balance. He used his foot to whip Matt's legs from under him and, as he landed heavily on the ground, Graham slammed his heel down viciously into Matt's groin. The switchblade fell from Matt's fingers as he screamed in agony, his hands clamped over his groin. Graham picked up the switchblade and looked down at the other youth who was still slumped against the door, his bloodied hands covering his face. Satisfied he wouldn't have any more trouble from either of them, Graham pocketed the switchblade and sat down beside the terrified girl.

'You OK?' he asked gently.

She nodded through her tears. 'Thank you.'

'You want to press charges against these bas . . . these guys?'

'I want no trouble,' she replied, shaking her head.

'Wise move,' Graham said. 'It's not worth the trouble.'

'I get off here,' she said anxiously as the train slowed down.

Graham waited until she had alighted before bundling the two youths out on to the platform. A policeman hurried over to where the two men lay and looked to Graham for an explanation.

'I was doing your job for you!' Graham snapped angrily. 'If you had a cop on the train none of this would have been necessary.'

'What happened?' the policeman demanded.

Graham told him.

'Where's the woman now?' the policeman asked.

'She couldn't wait to get off the train,' Graham replied. 'Can you blame her?'

Radioing for a patrol car, the policeman signalled to the train driver that he could leave; seconds later the train had disappeared into the tunnel.

'I'll need a few details from you,' the policeman said, pulling a notebook from his pocket. 'Name?'

'Michael Green,' Graham replied, using one of his UNACO aliases.

'Address?'

Graham gave him a fictitious UNACO address. He knew UNACO would stonewall any further investigation, but he also knew that he was going to catch hell from Philpott for getting involved in the first place. He didn't regret it though. Not for a moment . . .

The policeman asked him a few more questions, then closed his notebook. 'We'll be in touch if we need to talk to you again.'

Graham watched impassively as two uniformed policemen arrived. After a brief word with their colleague, they hauled the two youths to their feet and led them away. 'Well, if that's all, I'm meeting a friend in twenty minutes,' Graham said, looking at his watch. 'And this time I'll take a cab.'

'Say,' the policeman shouted after Graham. 'You did a good job on those two grunges. Where did you learn to handle yourself like that?'

'I watch a lot of cop shows on TV,' Graham retorted as he made his way towards the steps leading up to the street level.

'Excuse me,' a female voice called out behind him as he reached the foot of the steps.

He looked round. He estimated her to be in her mid-thirties. Tall, slender figure; long red hair pulled away from an attractive face and tied in a ponytail at the back of her head.

'You dropped this on the train,' she said, holding out a wallet towards him.

He instinctively patted his pocket. His wallet wasn't there. 'Thank you,' he said with a smile, taking the wallet from her.

'It fell out of your pocket when you tackled those two skinheads on the train.'

'Thank you again. I didn't even notice it was gone.'

'My name's Katherine Warren, I'm a reporter for the *New York Sentinel*,' she told him. 'I'd like to do an article on you for the paper. There's nothing the public love more than a subway vigilante.'

Graham's mind was racing. A reporter. He had to get away from her. Fast. But without causing suspicion. He feigned a quick smile. 'That's very kind of you, but I'm not looking for publicity. Hell, it was just a spur of the moment thing.'

'You're not a cop, are you?' she asked. 'Only you seemed to know how to handle yourself back there.'

'No, I'm not a cop,' he replied with a chuckle. 'Just another concerned citizen, that's all.'

'Were you ever in the military?'

'I'm actually running rather late ...' Graham stopped abruptly when his bleeper suddenly went off. He was quick to silence it. 'You'll have to excuse me. Thank you again for returning my wallet.'

Graham hurried up the steps and disappeared out on to the street before she could say another word. Katherine Warren smiled to herself. She sensed she was on to something. Why had he told the cop that his name was Michael Green when the credit cards in his wallet were in the name of Michael Graham? Who was he really? And what was he hiding? She was determined to find out. Zipping up her blouson, she decided to follow him. Discreetly ...

Having talked to Philpott on the telephone, Graham hailed a cab and told the driver to take him to the United Nations building. Once there he showed his pass to a security guard in the Dag Hammarskjöld Plaza and was allowed to continue. He took the lift to the twenty-second floor and walked to an unmarked door at the end of the corridor. He fed a code into the bell-push on the adjacent wall and there was a metallic click as the door unlocked. He entered a small, sparsely furnished room; the door locked automatically again behind him. Three of the walls were papered in a light cream colour; the fourth wall was constructed of teak slats, incorporated into which were two seamless sliding doors which could only be activated by miniature sonic transmitters. The door on the right led into the soundproofed UNACO Command Centre where teams of analysts worked around the clock monitoring the ever-changing developments in world affairs. The door on the left, which led into the Director's private office, was open.

Sabrina, who had monitored Graham's arrival on the video screen in Philpott's office, appeared in the doorway and beckoned him into the room.

'Where's the Colonel?' Graham asked, noticing that she was alone in the office.

'He's in the Command Centre,' she replied, gesturing to a door behind Philpott's desk. 'I'm to call him when we're all here.'

Graham sat down on the nearest of the two black leather sofas. 'Has he told you anything about this Code Red?'

She shook her head and moved to the percolator in the corner of the room. 'Want a coffee?'

'Yeah, I could use one after what happened tonight,' he replied.

Sabrina poured him a coffee, added milk and sugar, and handed the mug to him. 'What do you mean, *after what happened tonight*?' she asked suspiciously, sitting down beside him.

He recounted the events on the train, including his brush with Katherine Warren.

'The Colonel's going to blow a fuse when he finds out, especially if this reporter decides to pursue the story,' she said. 'You know how he feels about field operatives bringing unnecessary attention on UNACO.'

'What the hell was I supposed to do?' he snapped angrily, getting to his feet. 'Nobody else was going to lift a finger to help her.'

'Hey, I'm behind you all the way,' she said quickly, trying to diffuse the sudden tension. 'I'd have done the same, you know that.'

'Yeah, I know. I'm sorry. I guess I'm still a bit wound up. That reporter really threw me.' Graham gestured to the video monitor. 'C.W.'s here.'

Sabrina dialled the number for the Command Centre on one of the telephones on Philpott's desk. It was answered immediately by the duty officer. 'Would you let Colonel Philpott know that Strike Force Three are here for the briefing.'

Whitlock had already decided against telling his colleagues that Carmen was pregnant – at least not until he'd had a chance to talk to her properly. He could understand her anger

24

and frustration, but he couldn't afford to let it affect him, not while he was on a Code Red assignment . . .

The door behind the desk slid open. Philpott entered the room and used a miniature transmitter to close the door again behind him. A fifty-six-year-old Scot with gaunt features and thinning red hair, Philpott limped heavily on his left leg, the result of a wound incurred in the last days of the Korean War. Leaning his cane against the side of the desk, he sat down and opened the folder in front of him.

'Sir, there's something I need to tell you before you start the briefing,' Graham said, casting a quick glance in Sabrina's direction.

Philpott looked up slowly from the folder. His face was drawn and there were heavy bags under his eyes. 'Well?'

Graham explained in detail what had happened on the subway earlier that evening, then braced himself for Philpott's anger.

It never came. Instead Philpott rubbed his eyes wearily and made a couple of notes on his desk pad. 'I'll stonewall any enquiries at this end should the need arise.'

Graham and Sabrina exchanged suspicious glances. This wasn't like Philpott. Why was he taking it so calmly?

'Under any other circumstances you'd have found yourself carpeted for blatantly disregarding a UNACO directive by bringing unnecessary attention on yourself and the organization,' Philpott said in answer to their quizzical looks. 'But right now we're facing the most serious Code Red UNACO has ever had to deal with. And as the most experienced team in this organization, I need you there at the very heart of the operation.' He turned his attention back to the folder in front of him. 'Sergei's been in Portugal for the past four days as the official UNACO representative at a top secret meeting of the leaders of Europe's anti-terrorist squads. The only other people at the UN, apart from Sergei and myself, who knew about this meeting were the Secretary-General and Professor Abe Silverman, who'd accompanied

Sergei to Lisbon to encode all the documents as an added security precaution. Two hours ago three masked men shot and killed the duty paramedics at Lisbon Airport and used the ambulance in an attack on Sergei and Professor Silverman as they were preparing to board a flight back to New York. Their bodyguard, an officer of the Portuguese Special Forces Brigade, was shot and killed when he tried to intervene. Sergei took a bullet in the stomach. He's alive but in intensive care.'

'Will he be all right, sir?' Sabrina asked anxiously.

'The doctors say the next twenty-four hours will be critical. We can only wait and see. I've arranged with the Special Forces Brigade to have a twenty-four-hour guard mounted outside his hospital room in case his attackers should return to try and finish the job.'

'Do you anticipate that, sir?' Sabrina asked.

'I would doubt it, but we can't afford to take any chances.'

'What happened to the Professor?' Whitlock asked.

'Professor Silverman was drugged and bundled into the back of the airport ambulance which the three assailants had used to approach the aeroplane. They fled before the airport's own security police arrived on the scene. The ambulance was later found abandoned in woodlands close to the airport, but there was no sign of either Professor Silverman or his abductors.

'Professor Silverman had an attaché case secured to his wrist. In it were two folders which contained, amongst other sensitive documents, a coded list of the ten Strike Force teams as well as details of all major operations carried out by UNACO personnel over the last five years.'

Sabrina sat forward, her hands cupped over her face, her eyes riveted to an imaginary spot on the carpet. She finally lowered her hands and exhaled deeply. 'And if the kidnappers were to apply enough pressure, they could force Professor Silverman to decode the folders for them.'

'And if he did, the decoded documents could then be

used to settle personal scores against the organization,' Graham hissed angrily.

'Which is why it's imperative that we find his abductors before they can use the information against us,' Philpott said.

'You sound as if you're resigned to the fact that they'll break Silverman, sir,' Whitlock said.

'I am,' Philpott replied matter-of-factly. 'As you know, Professor Silverman suffered a heart attack last year. He now has to take tablets for angina attacks. I doubt it would take much to break him.'

'Why the hell was Silverman carrying the case in the first place?' Graham demanded. 'Surely it would have been more prudent to have had Sergei carry it?'

'In retrospect, it might have been more prudent,' Philpott agreed tersely. 'But that's not the issue right now, is it?'

'Do we have anything to go on, sir?' Sabrina asked, breaking the lingering silence.

'Yes, there is one clue. A box of matches was found under the driver's seat in the ambulance. A set of prints were lifted from it but they didn't match up to any of the airport's paramedics. We put the prints through our computer and came up with the name Heinrich Berger. He's been an enforcer for a Marseilles gangster called Emile Jannoc for the last two years, but the word on the street is that he no longer works for Jannoc. I'm not convinced though.'

'Why do you say that, sir?' Whitlock asked.

'Six months ago Christian Jannoc, Emile's younger brother, was killed in a gun battle in Marseilles' Old Port. Emile Jannoc swore at the funeral to avenge his brother's death.'

'I still don't see the connection, sir,' Whitlock said.

'Strike Force Eight had been working undercover in Marseilles to try and crack the Jannoc firm. They were caught up in the gun battle in which Christian Jannoc was killed. Ballistics tests subsequently proved that the bullet which killed Jannoc wasn't fired from any of Strike Force Eight's weapons, but we still had to abort the operation and pull them out.'

'And somehow Jannoc's found out that one of the UNACO teams was involved in the firefight and he now holds the organization responsible for his brother's death,' Graham concluded.

'But he obviously doesn't know which Strike Force team was in Marseilles at the time, which is why he needs details of the operation,' Sabrina added.

'Why don't we pull him in?' Graham demanded.

'Because we don't have a shred of evidence to link him to the incident at the airport,' Philpott told him. 'We have Berger's prints on a matchbox. But Berger supposedly left Jannoc's employ over three months ago. And even if we were able to make a connection between Berger and Jannoc, it wouldn't necessarily bring us any closer to finding either Professor Silverman or the folders. If anything, it could push the folders even further underground. And we can't afford to do that. Who knows where they may land up in the future?' Philpott shook his head. 'No, we don't touch Emile Jannoc, at least not until we've got the folders back safely.'

'How would Jannoc have known about the conference in Lisbon, sir?' Whitlock asked. 'You said it was classified top secret.'

Philpott sat back in his chair. 'That's been gnawing away at the pit of my stomach ever since I received word of what happened in Lisbon tonight. It's obvious that he was tipped off about it. And it's my guess that his source had to be someone inside this organization. None of the delegates knew what the Professor was carrying in the attaché case. But you let me handle that. You've got quite enough to occupy your minds as it is.'

'So how are we going to approach the operation, sir?' Graham asked.

'You and Sabrina are going to Lisbon,' Philpott replied,

taking two manila envelopes from the folder and handing them to Graham and Sabrina. Inside was a résumé of the assignment, which was to be destroyed after reading; airline tickets; confirmation of hotel accommodation; a brief character sketch of their contact, and a sum of money in escudos. 'Your contact in Portugal will be Major João Inacio, a senior officer in the Special Forces Brigade. Call him the moment you get there. It's imperative that we work as closely as possible with the Portuguese authorities on this one.'

'Yes, sir,' Graham replied, getting to his feet.

'I know it's your necks on the line if these folders are decoded and fall into the wrong hands,' Philpott said. 'But it's no use seeing it as a vendetta. You have to approach it in a disciplined and professional manner.'

Graham knew Philpott's comments were directed at him. He remained silent.

'Where do I come in, sir?' Whitlock asked.

'I'll explain that in a moment,' Philpott replied, then turned to Graham and Sabrina. 'I want regular reports from you. At least twice a day. Now go on, you've got a plane to catch.'

'Yes, sir,' Graham said, following Sabrina from the room.

Philpott took the third manila envelope from the folder and handed it to Whitlock. 'You're going undercover in Marseilles. Jacques Rust is already on his way to Paris from our European HQ in Zürich. You'll rendezvous with him there and he'll brief you in full.'

'I understand, sir,' Whitlock said, standing up. 'When do I leave?'

'There's a flight out of New York bound for Paris later this evening. You're already booked on it.'

Whitlock stood up. 'What happens if we don't find the folders before they're decoded?'

'Just make sure you do,' Philpott replied, closing the folder. 'That's all, C.W.'

*   *   *

'That's him,' Katherine Warren said, spotting Graham through the night-vision binoculars. 'Can you get a good shot of him?'

'Yeah,' came the confident reply.

Katherine Warren had tailed Graham as far as the United Nations building, then, after paying off the cab driver, she'd called the night editor at the *New York Sentinel* and told him to send her a photographer right away. They now sat in the front of the photographer's car which was parked discreetly opposite the United Nations building.

'Hey, who's that?' the photographer said as Sabrina emerged from the building behind Graham. He whistled softly to himself. 'Jesus, she's some looker, isn't she?'

Katherine Warren focused the binoculars on Sabrina as she caught up with Graham and gestured towards her champagne-coloured Mercedes Benz 500 SEC parked nearby. They made their way towards it.

The photographer took several pictures of them, including one of the car, then lowered the camera. 'What now?'

'We follow them.'

'Who's the woman?' the photographer asked again as Sabrina started up her car.

'I've no idea,' Katherine Warren replied, lowering the binoculars. 'At least not yet. But with those kind of looks she's certainly going to add a bit of spice to the story.'

'If there is a story,' the photographer corrected her.

Katherine Warren traced her tongue lightly across her lips and a faint smile touched the corners of her mouth. 'There's a story all right. It's just a question of finding it. And that's exactly what I intend to do.'

3

Jacques Rust had been confined to a wheelchair for the past two and a half years. He didn't regard himself as handicapped, though, and was quick to admonish those who made the mistake of treating him as such. It had happened to him earlier that morning when he'd arrived at the hotel in Paris. His personal driver, who always accompanied him on foreign trips, had assembled his portable wheelchair and positioned it beside the open back door. He knew better than to offer to help Rust into the wheelchair, but as Rust had begun to manoeuvre himself from the back seat into the wheelchair, the doorman had hurried forward to help him. He knew these Samaritans meant well, but all they were doing was making him feel inferior. And that's what made him so angry . . .

Rust moved to the window of his hotel room and looked out over the Parisian skyline. He was a forty-two-year-old Frenchman with short black hair and sparkling blue eyes which offset his rugged features. He had spent fourteen years with the French *Service de Documentation Extérieure et de Contre-Espionnage*, before joining UNACO where he and Whitlock had been paired off together. When the Secretary-General had sanctioned a move by Philpott to increase UNACO's field operatives from twenty to thirty, Sabrina had been brought in to join them and form the original Strike Force Three.

31

Six months later, Rust and Sabrina had been on a routine stake-out at the Marseilles docks, where they were working undercover to bust an international drugs ring operating between Algeria and France, when they had come under fire from the smugglers. Rust had covered Sabrina's retreat, but when he'd tried to go after her he had been hit in the spine, leaving him paralysed from the waist down. Philpott, who had always had a great admiration for Rust's abilities, offered him the position as head of UNACO's European operation, based in Zürich. Rust had been there now for eighteen months, and had already turned down the chance to return to New York as UNACO Director when Philpott had been forced to take early retirement. He had no wish to leave Zürich and, with his insight into European politics and his vast network of contacts across the Continent, his decision hadn't surprised many of his colleagues. Jacques Rust *was* UNACO's European connection.

There was a knock at the door. Rust wheeled himself across the room to answer it and was surprised to find Whitlock standing in front of him. 'I wasn't expecting you here for at least another hour.'

'I can always come back later if you want,' Whitlock replied with a grin.

'Come in,' Rust said genially, gesturing Whitlock into the room. He closed the door and turned the wheelchair round to face Whitlock. 'You're looking well, *mon ami*. How are things with Carmen?'

'Could be better,' Whitlock replied with a sigh as he sat down. 'This will be the third Christmas in a row that I've been away from home. She's not too happy about it.'

Rust nodded grimly. 'I can believe it. But then it goes with the job, doesn't it?'

'Try telling that to Carmen.'

'You should really think about starting a family, C.W. It would certainly help to bring you and Carmen closer together.'

'Possibly,' Whitlock replied.

'Definitely,' Rust replied. 'And I know you'd both make great parents.'

Whitlock gave a nonchalant shrug. He hoped it looked convincing. Rust was a close and trusted friend but he couldn't tell him that Carmen was pregnant. Not yet. Getting to his feet, he moved to the window then turned back to face Rust. 'The Colonel said you'd brief me about this under-cover job in Marseilles.'

Rust picked up his attaché case, opened it, and removed a folder. 'How much do you already know?'

'I read Jannoc's file on the flight over here. That's it. You're to fill me in on the details of the assignment.'

Rust took a photograph from the folder and handed it to Whitlock. 'His name's Frank Royce. Or perhaps I should say *was* Frank Royce. He was killed in a car crash ten days ago.'

'And I'm to assume his identity?'

Rust nodded.

Whitlock studied the photograph. 'Well, at least we're the same colour,' he said at length. 'I suppose that's a start.'

'You don't need to worry about any facial similarities: nobody will recognize you anyway.'

Whitlock handed back the photograph. 'So tell me a bit about this Frank Royce.'

'He was thirty-eight at the time of his death. Born in London. Orphaned at the age of two. He joined the army from school but was cashiered a year later for striking an NCO. He then went to Africa where he made a name for himself as a mercenary. He had the reputation as a hard man but he always fulfilled his contracts. Ironically he was killed on his first visit back to the UK in ten years when his car was hit by an articulated lorry outside London. He had no close friends, so his death went virtually unnoticed. There's a more detailed account of his life in the folder. Memorize it: you may need to fall back on some of the information at a later stage. It's the perfect cover for you.'

'To do what?' Whitlock asked, sitting on the bed.

'To infiltrate Jannoc's organization and find out where he's holding Abe Silverman.'

'But according to Jannoc's file, he only hires ex-legionnaires to work for him,' Whitlock was quick to point out. 'Was Royce ever in the French Foreign Legion?'

'No, but that can only be to your advantage,' Rust replied. 'You won't be recognized by any of his men.'

'And how exactly am I supposed to get Jannoc to change his tune suddenly after all these years?'

Rust took another photograph from the folder and handed it to Whitlock. 'That's his eleven-year-old daughter, Mathilde. I'm sure he'll be very grateful when you thwart an attempt to kidnap her later today. Perhaps even grateful enough to take you on when he finds out you're looking for work.'

'Kidnap?' Whitlock said suspiciously.

Rust nodded. 'We know from a source in Marseilles that Mathilde Jannoc's going to a friend's birthday party today. A bodyguard will take her to the party this afternoon and wait for her there until it finishes. That should be around eight tonight. The kidnappers will strike when he takes her home again.'

'How do you know about the kidnapping?'

A knowing smile crept across Rust's face. 'Because I arranged it.'

'I should have guessed it would be something like that,' Whitlock said.

'Emile Jannoc has a lot of enemies, especially in and around Marseilles. That's why he assigns a bodyguard to accompany his daughter wherever she goes. She's his Achilles' heel. And his enemies know that. There's already been an attempt to abduct her a few months ago. That's where I first got the idea for the kidnapping. I've already recruited a couple of ex-cons in Nantes to do the job.' Rust handed Philpott two mugshots from the folder. 'That's them. Sebastian Ronnet and Pierre Mensel. Both are particularly nasty pieces of work, with form as long as your arm. There is one snag, however.

They're under the impression that I'm the middleman for an anonymous Marseilles gangster out to settle a score with Jannoc.'

'Which means they think the kidnapping's for real,' Whitlock concluded. 'So when I show, they're not going to give in without a fight. Is that it?'

'It's the only way I could be sure of getting them to trust me,' Rust replied with an apologetic shrug. 'But you won't have any trouble dealing with them, C.W. They're just a couple of heavies, that's all.'

'Will they be armed?'

'I gave them strict instructions not to carry guns. It was part of the deal.'

'Why don't I feel reassured?' Whitlock retorted. 'Surely the bodyguard will be packing?'

'I would be very surprised if he wasn't, but Mensel and Ronnet have been around a bit, they can handle themselves, especially if they use the element of surprise to their advantage.' Rust closed the folder and handed it to Whitlock. 'Your flight to Marseilles leaves in a couple of hours.'

'And what if Jannoc doesn't hire me?'

'Just make sure he does because, if he was behind the incident in Lisbon last night, and I personally believe he was, then he'll know where Abe Silverman's being held. And that means he's our one real chance of getting those folders back before they can be decoded.' Rust replaced the folder in the attaché case. 'The Colonel wants you to liaise with me. I'll be flying back to Zürich later this afternoon. Make sure you keep me posted.'

'I will,' Whitlock promised.

'And C.W.,' Rust called out after Whitlock as he crossed to the door, 'good luck.'

'Why have I got a feeling I'm going to need it?' Whitlock replied ruefully, closing the door again behind him.

*   *   *

Major João Inacio was at the airport to meet the flight which brought Graham and Sabrina to Lisbon. He was a tall man in his late forties, a veteran of campaigns in both Mozambique and Angola where he had served with the marine unit, *Corpo de Fuzilieros*, before his transfer to the élite Special Forces Brigade.

'I have a car waiting outside to take you to your hotel,' Inacio said in faultless English, gesturing towards the main doors.

'Is there any change in Sergei's condition?' Sabrina asked as they headed for the exit.

'Mr Kolchinsky's condition remains unchanged,' Inacio told her. 'He's still in a coma in the intensive care unit.'

The driver jumped out from the unmarked white Mercedes when Inacio emerged from the terminal building. Taking Graham and Sabrina's hand luggage, he placed it in the boot before climbing back behind the wheel and starting the engine.

'The Altis Hotel,' Inacio instructed him brusquely before turning round in the passenger seat until he could see Graham and Sabrina behind him. He removed a small plastic bottle from his jacket pocket. 'This was found on the runway, close to where Professor Silverman was abducted.'

Graham took it from Inacio and felt a knot tighten in the pit of his stomach as he read the label on the side of the bottle. Glyceryl Trinitrate. A prescription for the tablets Silverman used to combat the angina attacks he'd been suffering since his heart attack the previous year. Graham handed the bottle to Sabrina.

She read the label, grim-faced, then looked anxiously at Graham. 'These were Professor Silverman's lifeline. He always carried them on him wherever he went.'

'And he's not going to last long without them,' Graham said.

'He may already be dead,' Inacio said, breaking the sudden silence.

Graham and Sabrina didn't reply. They knew he could be right.

'It could actually be to our advantage if he were already dead,' Inacio said matter-of-factly. 'Because, without him, his abductors won't be able to decode the folders. And that would put them right back to square one again, wouldn't it?'

Silverman woke to find himself on an uncomfortably narrow bed in the corner of a dark room. The only light came from the corridor, filtering through the small grille in the metal door. As he tried to sit up, a sharp pain speared through his head. He inhaled sharply through gritted teeth, then slowly lowered his head back on to the threadbare palliasse. He closed his eyes again and massaged the back of his neck gently until he felt the pain begin to subside. He lay motionless for several minutes on the bed before raising his head gingerly off the palliasse again. The pain was still there, but not as intense as before. He swung his legs on to the floor, then sat forward, his head in his hands, his mind racing back over the events which had led to his abduction.

He could still see Pereira spinning grotesquely as the bullets thudded into his chest. It had been the first time he'd actually seen someone shot. And it was true what his colleagues both at Mossad and UNACO had told him: you see it almost as if it were happening in slow motion. He also remembered seeing Kolchinsky fall to the runway. Though he hadn't even heard a shot that time, with all the panic and confusion going on around him. Then there had been the sharp pain in his neck. The tranquillizer dart. He winced when he touched the bruise on his cheek where his face had struck the ground. It was still tender. He couldn't remember anything after that. He had no doubts why he had been abducted. To decode the folders in the attaché case which had already been removed from his wrist. But where was he? And how long had he been unconscious? He had to find out.

His eyes were now accustomed to the semi-darkness and

he looked around him slowly. He was obviously in some kind of prison cell which was empty apart from the bed. He got to his feet and moved cautiously to the door. Shielding his eyes against the glare of the naked bulb which hung outside the door, he peered through the grille. The corridor was deserted. He could see more cell doors but, judging by the stifling silence all around him, he assumed they weren't occupied. That suited him perfectly. A plan began to take shape in his mind.

He banged his fist against the door and immediately grimaced as the hammering reverberated through his head. But if his plan were to have any chance of success, he had to lure one of his guards into the cell. With that in mind he continued to pound on the door until he heard the sound of approaching footsteps. Moments later a shadow fell across the door grille.

'What do you want?' a voice enquired in a thick German accent.

'A glass of water. My throat's dry.'

Silverman heard his guard walk off down the corridor. When he returned he used a key card to activate the cell door. He held a Heckler & Koch MP5 sub-machine gun in one hand, the cup of water in the other. 'You will sit on the bed,' he ordered, gesturing with the barrel of the sub-machine gun.

Silverman crossed to the bed and sat down. 'Where am I?' he demanded as his captor placed the plastic cup in the centre of the floor.

'That does not concern you,' the man replied tersely.

'It does when I'm being held against my will!' Silverman shot back, getting to his feet.

Immediately the Heckler & Koch was swung round on Silverman. 'You will stay where you are,' the man snapped in his halting and heavily accented English.

'You won't kill me,' Silverman said defiantly, hoping his sudden injection of false bravado was convincing enough to mask his inner fear. 'You need me. Why else would you have gone to all the trouble of kidnapping me?'

'I will not kill you,' the man agreed. 'But if you try to escape, I will shoot you in the legs. Then you will not walk again. *Verstehen?*'

'And how am I going to escape with you pointing that machine gun at me?' Silverman snorted, then gestured to the cup on the floor. 'Can I have the water now?'

His guard nodded, and Silverman picked up the cup, taking a sip of the water. 'Where are your cronies?' he asked casually.

'Cronies?' The word was clearly unfamiliar to the German.

'The rest of your little team,' Silverman explained sharply.

'They will come back later. Then you will work.'

'Like hell –' Silverman suddenly clutched his chest and the cup fell from his fingers. He slumped on to the floor, his breathing ragged and uneven. 'Pills. I need my pills. Please, give me my pills,' he gasped.

The German stood hesitantly in the doorway, clearly unsure of what to do, suspecting a trick but unwilling to ignore Silverman in case his pain was genuine. If Silverman were to die while the Russians were away, he'd have a lot of explaining to do. Closing the door, he crossed to where Silverman lay on the floor.

'Please, help me,' Silverman whispered through clenched teeth. 'My pills. I need my pills.'

The sub-machine gun was trained on Silverman as the guard crouched down beside him and turned him over on to his back. He loosened Silverman's tie and, as he did so, Silverman grabbed his shirt. A trail of saliva dribbled from the corner of his mouth. Silverman opened his mouth to speak and the German instinctively leaned closer to try and hear. Silverman brought his hand up fast, gouging his thumb savagely into the guard's eye. Howling in agony, the man stumbled back, his hand clutched over his face. He was still fumbling with the Heckler & Koch when Silverman lashed out with his foot, taking his legs from underneath him. The German fell heavily, the sub-machine gun clattering to the floor. Silverman moved fast, grabbing it and bringing the butt down viciously on to the side of the man's head, knocking him out. Rummaging through the unconscious man's pockets, Silverman found the vital key card and hurried out into the corridor. Looking round quickly to make sure he was alone, he used the key card to close the door again behind him. The metal door at the end of the corridor wasn't locked. He emerged into a large hall and, wiping the sweat from his eyes, tried to fathom out which of the numerous corridors leading off it would bring him out at the main entrance. He picked his way carefully through the discarded crates littering the floor until he reached the other side. Pausing again to get his bearings, he noticed that one of the corridors wasn't lined with cells but led to a second security door, which was closed. All the other corridors were partitioned off by only a single security door. Gripping the key card excitedly, he made his way down the corridor to the security door and activated it. Three wooden doors, all closed, led off from the black and white tiled corridor. Ignoring them, he crossed to a third security door and slipped the card into the lock. There was the customary metallic click and the door slid open. He stepped tentatively through the doorway and slowly looked around him . . .

A sudden pain speared out from the centre of his chest and he cried out in agony as it quickly spread up to his throat and across his back. He stumbled back into the corridor, his hands gripped tightly over his chest. Pills. Where were his pills? Did the guard have them? He doubted it: clearly the German had been anxious to keep him alive. Even if he did, Silverman knew he'd never make it back to the cell in time. He couldn't move. Everything was becoming blurred. He felt cold. So cold.

Another sharp pain pulsed through his chest, forcing him

to his knees. It seized him in a grip of excruciating agony for several seconds before a merciful darkness finally enveloped him and he slumped forward on to the floor, his sightless eyes staring vacantly at the key card which lay inches away from his outstretched hand.

It had come as a great relief to Graham and Sabrina when Inacio had announced at the hotel that he didn't intend to act as their chaperon while they were in Portugal. He had given them a number which they could call, day or night, if they needed him. Philpott had obviously had a quiet word with him before they arrived, knowing they preferred to work alone. It suited them perfectly . . .

After a quick change of clothes, they met up again in the foyer, both armed with the Beretta 92 automatics that Inacio had given to them before he left the hotel. Graham also had the keys for the white Ford Sierra which Inacio had arranged to be left for them outside the hotel. The only clue they had to work on was the box of matches found in the ambulance: a white box with the wispy blue silhouette of a woman on its cover which had originated from a wine bar, *A Azul Senhora*, the Blue Lady, situated on the Rua de São Pedro in the Alfama, the Old Town.

The Rua de São Pedro was a tourist trap in summer with its *tabernas*, restaurants, and seemingly limitless number of street vendors peddling their trinkets and curios to gullible foreigners with more money than sense. At this time of year, though, there was little sign of tourist activity on the street. Most of the shoppers were locals, out in search of last-minute Christmas presents. As Graham parked the car outside the *taberna*, a hopeful vendor hurried over to the car, but Graham was quick to dismiss him. They descended a flight of stairs into the bar.

The lone barman looked up from the newspaper he was reading. 'We are not open yet,' he said curtly, then turned his attention back to the sports page.

'We don't want a drink,' Graham said, taking a photograph of Berger from his jacket pocket and placing it on the counter. 'Have you ever seen this man in here before?'

The barman picked up the photograph. He immediately shook his head. 'No.'

'Take another look,' Sabrina said to him in Portuguese. 'He would probably have been in here sometime in the last few days.'

The barman's eyes lingered on Sabrina. 'Who are you?' he demanded, feeling more comfortable in his native tongue.

'We're friends of his,' she told him. 'He was supposed to meet our plane at the airport this morning. He didn't show and now he seems to have disappeared. We know he was here recently because when he last phoned he told us about the place. Are you sure you haven't seen him?'

The barman studied the photograph more carefully then shook his head and handed it back to her. 'I haven't seen him.'

'Hey, let me see that,' an American voice said behind them.

Graham and Sabrina looked round at the youth standing at the foot of the stairs. He was in his early twenties with a rich tan, sun-bleached hair and a gold sleeper in his left ear. He gave them a warm smile and crossed to where they were standing. 'The name's Ricky Hardin. I work here. You've got to excuse Luis, he only turns on the charm when he sees the colour of your money.'

The barman grunted, then picked up his newspaper and moved further down the counter.

'You're a long way from home,' Sabrina said to Hardin.

'I came out here for the summer. I liked the country so I stayed on. This place is strictly for the tourists: that's how I got the job.' Hardin gestured to the photograph in Sabrina's hand. 'Let's see that.'

She handed the photograph to him.

He pursed his lips thoughtfully then shook his head. 'Sorry, I don't know him. You sure he was here?'

'Sure,' Graham said.

'Tell you what,' Hardin said, appraising Sabrina more closely. 'Why don't you give me your number and I'll be sure to call if he shows.'

'You can call me at the Altis Hotel. The name's Graham.'

Hardin smiled. 'Well, if you'll excuse me, I've still got to restock the bar before we open.'

Graham pocketed the photograph and headed back towards the stairs.

'Your boyfriend?' Hardin asked Sabrina as she turned to follow him.

'Yes,' she replied with a grin as she went after Graham.

'Lucky bastard,' Hardin muttered, then noticed that Luis had lowered his newspaper and was staring coldly after them. He picked up a leaflet from the counter and hurried after them. 'Hey, wait up,' he called out, catching up with them at the foot of the stairs. 'We're having a Christmas Eve party here tonight. If you show this pass at the door before ten o'clock you'll get in for free.'

'No, thanks,' Graham replied.

'That guy's been here,' Hardin whispered, then pressed the leaflet into Sabrina's hand. 'Go on, take it,' he said loudly.

'When?' Graham asked.

'We can't talk here,' Hardin hissed. 'I'll meet you at your hotel later today. Say four o'clock this afternoon. But the info will cost you a grand. American.'

'What?' Graham retorted. 'We don't have –'

'No money, no deal,' Hardin retorted, then stepped back and gestured to the leaflet in Sabrina's hand. 'Starts at eight. It's going to be one hell of a bash. Hope to see you guys later.'

Sabrina followed Graham up the stairs and out into the street. 'What do you think?'

'He obviously knows something,' Graham conceded.

'But then so does the other guy. You could smell the fear on him.'

Sabrina nodded. 'I also got the feeling he was hiding something.'

'And with some luck Hardin will be able to tell us what it is,' Graham said, unlocking the driver's door.

'What now?' she asked, looking at him across the roof of the car.

'There's nothing we can do until we've spoken to Hardin. He's our only lead right now. Let's just hope he's worth his money.'

Larry Ryan was on the telephone when Katherine Warren knocked and peered around the door. He gestured for her to enter his office and pointed to the chair in front of his desk. Ryan, in his mid-forties, had a distinguished journalistic career behind him. After serving as a deputy editor on both the *Miami Herald* and the *Washington Post*, he had been recently appointed the new editor of the *New York Sentinel*.

He had been married to Katherine Warren's younger sister Louise, a popular children's TV presenter on network television, for the past eight years. A year ago, much to their delight, Katherine had started to date one of his best friends, a fellow journalist, Mark Randall, whom she had met when they were colleagues at the *Washington Post*. Two months later Ryan had been the best man at their wedding. But the marriage had quickly turned sour. Randall had wanted children. Katherine had wanted a career. Whereas Louise had automatically sided with her sister, Ryan had found himself caught in the middle. But secretly he'd agreed with her. She was one of the best reporters he'd ever known and he wanted her to stay on at the *Post*. It had come to a head when her father died, and she had requested a transfer back to New York to be closer to her mother. Randall had stayed behind in Washington. The marriage was over.

Ryan put the receiver down. 'That was your little sister

on the line, Katy. She sends her love. I'm to remind you that you're expected for drinks at the house tonight.'

Ever since she was a child, Katherine had always insisted on being called by her full name. No Kates or Kathys. It had to be Katherine. Yet Ryan had always called her Katy and, for some reason she didn't quite understand herself, she'd never minded it coming from him. But he was still the only exception to her rule.

'I haven't forgotten, but I'm not sure I'll be there.'

'What does that mean?' Ryan asked suspiciously. 'You know Louise has had this planned for the last six months. She'll be real disappointed if you don't show.'

'I think I'm on to something big, Larry. Really big.'

Ryan sat back, his hands clasped behind his head. 'I'm listening.'

Katherine explained about the incident involving Graham on the subway the previous evening.

'So the guy didn't want to get involved with any further enquiries,' Ryan deduced. 'That's why he gave the cop a false name. You can't blame him after all the publicity involved in the Bernie Goetz case.'

'There's more, Larry,' Katherine said, then went on to explain about Graham's visit to the United Nations. She removed an envelope from the folder in her lap and tossed it on to the desk. 'These were taken outside the UN last night.'

Ryan opened the envelope and slowly sifted through the photographs until he came across one of Sabrina. 'Who's the looker with the cute ass?'

'I thought she might interest you,' Katherine said with a faint smile. 'I tailed them to JFK where they caught a flight to Portugal. When I got home I faxed a couple of the photographs through to a spook at Langley who owes me a few favours.'

'And?' Ryan asked, his interest now stimulated.

'They're both on file there,' she said, handing him a sheet of paper. 'My contact faxed this back to me this morning.'

Ryan read through it carefully then looked up at her. 'It's incomplete.'

'That's what I thought when I first read it. So I got in touch with him again. All information on Graham after he was retired from Delta, and on Carver after she left the FBI, has been classified top secret.'

'Can't he access it?'

'He hasn't got the necessary clearance, and he's a fairly senior man in the CIA.'

'So whatever they're up to, it's well under wraps. Do you think they're working for the Company?'

Katherine stood up and moved to the window. 'I doubt it. I rang the UN after the fax came through this morning. Graham's listed as an adviser on foreign policy to the US Ambassador. Carver's listed as a French translator at the General Assembly. Perfect disinformation, given their backgrounds.'

'What are you getting at?' Ryan asked.

Katherine turned to face Ryan. 'I think they may be with UNACO.'

Ryan lit a cigarette and drew thoughtfully on it. 'If it exists,' he said slowly.

'That's what I intend to find out. If they are on some assignment, I want to know about it. It would make one hell of a story, wouldn't it? An ultra-secret anti-crime organization working out of the UN. And we'd have the exclusive.'

Ryan picked up a photograph of Sabrina. 'She's something else, isn't she?'

'Her face alone would sell the story. It would be the scoop of the year. What do you say, Larry?'

Ryan took another drag on his cigarette. 'I want proof that UNACO really exists. I also want proof that Graham and Carver work for UNACO. Because, without that, we don't have a story. There's no way I'll run it on circumstantial evidence, and at the moment that's all we've got. Bring me results and I can promise you that your name will be on the lips of every editor in this country.'

Katherine grinned at him. 'You can count on it, Larry.'

'Do you want to take any back-up with you?'

'No, I'll work with Ed Miller. He's an old friend who's now working freelance around Portugal and Spain. He's got a house in Lisbon. We can handle it by ourselves.'

'Miller?' Ryan said with a frown. 'He's that gay journalist Mark took a swing at at your wedding reception, wasn't he?'

'I should have realized then what an asshole I was marrying,' Katherine said bitterly.

'Is this Miller reliable?' Ryan asked.

'More reliable than anyone on this paper,' Katherine shot back. 'What's it with you, Larry? Have you got a problem with the fact that Ed's gay? Is that why you have to question his abilities as a journalist?'

Ryan held up his hands defensively. 'Come on, Katy, you know me better than that. I don't give a damn whether he's gay or straight, I just want to know if he can handle himself if the going gets rough out there. And if we are dealing with UNACO, it could get very rough if they think we're on to them.'

'Ed's covered wars in places like Nicaragua, El Salvador, and more recently in Bosnia. You can't get much rougher than that, can you?'

'OK,' Ryan replied, quickly deciding to change tactics. 'Do you want anything done from this end?'

'I've already got someone making a few discreet enquiries about UNACO around the different intelligence agencies. What I am going to need is cash.'

'Draw what you need from the slush fund, I'll sign for it.' Ryan leaned forward, his arms resting on the desk. 'I expect a story out of this, Katy. And a damn good one at that. Don't disappoint me.'

'I won't.'

'What are you going to do about flight reservations? You don't have a hope in hell of getting seats on a plane on Christmas Eve. Do you want me to pull a few strings for you?'

'No need,' Katherine replied, holding up an airline ticket. 'I knew you couldn't pass up on a good story, so I pulled a few strings of my own this morning.'

Ryan gave her a wry smile. 'What time's your flight?'

'Eleven. I'm already packed and ready to go.'

'Then why are you still here?' Ryan asked, stubbing out his cigarette.

'Thanks, Larry,' Katherine said, crossing to the door.

'Oh, and Katy?' Ryan waited until she looked round at him. 'Merry Christmas.'

'I've got a feeling it will be,' Katherine said with a knowing smile as she closed the door behind her.

Graham was quick to answer the telephone when it rang.

'Graham, it's Hardin.'

'You're late,' Graham snapped, looking at his watch.

'I had to make sure I wasn't being followed,' came the reply. 'Have you got the money?'

'I've got it,' Graham shot back irritably.

'Good. I'll be in the alley at the back of the hotel in five minutes.'

The line went dead.

Graham called Sabrina's room and they agreed to meet up in the foyer. Tucking the Beretta into his shoulder holster, he pulled on a baggy leather jacket, zipped it up, then slipped the money into his pocket and took the lift to the foyer. Sabrina was already there. The skies were dark and overcast when they emerged from the hotel; the rain wasn't far off. They made their way cautiously to the alley at the back of the hotel where a waiter was stuffing several cardboard boxes into one of the large metal bins opposite the back door. He eyed them suspiciously, then disappeared back into the hotel.

Hardin appeared at the far end of the alley, his hands dug deep into the pockets of his black blouson. He looked around slowly then walked towards them. 'Let's see the money,' he said on reaching them.

48

Graham took the money from his pocket and fanned it with his thumb. 'Now you've seen it, let's hear you earn it.'

Hardin pulled a packet of cigarettes from his pocket and lit one. 'Who are you guys? Feds or something?'

'Just tell us what you know,' Graham snapped impatiently.

Hardin shrugged and took another drag on the cigarette. 'Last week I dropped by at the bar to pick up my wages. At first I couldn't find Luis –'

'The guy who was there today?' Graham cut in.

'Yeah, Luis Caldere. He owns the place. He's a complete bastard but the job pays well. That's why I've stuck it out this far. Anyway, I hear voices coming from inside the bar. Only it wasn't supposed to be open at that time of the day. We only open at night during the week. So I'm about to go through to check it out when I suddenly hear Luis' voice. And he's angry. He's shouting something about a kidnapping. Well, that's when I stop dead in my tracks. I ain't about to go walking in on Luis when he's talking like that. So I look through the one-way mirror behind the bar. There's three of them sitting at a table. Luis was facing the bar. And the guy in the photo was sitting next to him. He had a foreign accent: German I think. I couldn't see the third guy. He was sitting with his back to me but, judging by his accent, I'd say he was local.'

'Did you hear what they were saying?' Sabrina asked.

'I caught bits of the conversation,' Hardin replied. 'They were discussing having someone kidnapped here in Lisbon. The name was Silver, or something like that. Luis wasn't going to be involved in the actual kidnapping, I don't think, but it seemed that the guy in the photograph would be driving the getaway car. I got the impression that he wasn't too happy about it.'

'Did they say where they were going to take the victim after the kidnapping?' Sabrina asked.

Hardin shook his head. 'That's all I heard. I got out of

there when Luis stood up and came round behind the bar. I don't know what he wanted, but I wasn't about to stick around to find out. This has got something to do with that incident at the airport a couple of days ago, hasn't it?'

'Why didn't you go to the police if you knew about the kidnapping?' Graham asked, ignoring the question.

'Hey, I've already had a couple of brushes with the local cops since I've been here. I don't want any more aggro from them. And anyway, they won't pay me for info. I got to live, you know.'

'Is that all you can tell us?' Graham asked.

'Isn't it enough? Now you can pull in Luis and sweat him. That's what you want, isn't it?'

'Which would put you out of a job,' Sabrina said suspiciously. 'A job that pays well.'

Hardin gave her an indifferent shrug. 'I've been here for eight months now. It's time to move on.' A faint smile touched the corners of his mouth. 'And that grand will help to pay for my flight back to the States.'

'What can you tell us about Luis Caldere?' Graham asked, holding up the money.

Hardin tugged the money from Graham's hand and counted the bills. 'Married with a couple of kids. Both as obnoxious as their father. He used to be a soldier, or so he claims. That's about all I know. We don't socialize much outside work.' He pocketed the money then pointed a finger at Graham. 'And don't expect me to corroborate any of this in court. I only came here to steer you in the right direction and pick up a bit of cash for my trouble. It's up to you guys to get the evidence yourselves. As far as I'm concerned, this conversation never took place. I'm sure we understand each other. Merry Christmas.'

'I don't think he realizes he's playing in the big league now,' Graham said disdainfully after Hardin had gone.

'Well at least he was cheap at the price,' Sabrina said.

'I'd rather he'd asked for more. At least then we'd have

known we weren't dealing with some bloody amateur. And that's what makes him so dangerous. He's likely to shout his mouth off to anyone for the right price.'

'We could get Inacio to pull him in,' Sabrina suggested.

'That could alert Caldere,' Graham replied then, taking Sabrina's arm, steered her back towards the hotel as a few spots of rain began to fall.

'What do you suggest we do?' Sabrina asked as they entered the hotel foyer.

'Nothing – at least not until we've checked out Caldere. If Hardin's right, he could be our link to the kidnappers.' Graham gestured to the lift. 'Come on, I want to call Inacio and get a run-down on our friend Luis Caldere.'

'What did you find out about this Caldere?' Philpott asked after Graham had finished relating the day's events to him over the telephone.

'He spent fifteen years in the Portuguese armed forces and he's a veteran of the colonial wars in both Angola and Mozambique. He left the marines three years ago and bought the wine bar. He's married with two kids and lives in the city.'

'So he has no links with Jannoc or the Foreign Legion?' Philpott asked.

'Not that Inacio's aware of, sir,' Graham replied. 'Do you want us to bring him in?'

'No, it could push the folders even further underground if, as I suspect, he's only a small player in the overall operation. He's probably involved on a need-to-know basis only. No, the best thing to do at the moment is to keep him under surveillance. He could lead you to Berger, or one of the other kidnappers. Then you can move in.'

'We'll have to bring Inacio in on it, sir,' Graham said reluctantly.

'He may be a pain, Mike, but he's still damn good at his job,' Philpott reminded him. 'He's your contact over there, use him. I know he'll give you his full support.'

51

'Yes, sir,' Graham replied. 'Is there any news of Sergei?'

'He's still in a coma. I've told the hospital to call you the moment there's any change in his condition. That way you can get over there right away.'

'How's the search going for our mole, sir?'

'I've whittled the investigation down to a shortlist of five heads of department,' Philpott replied. 'They're the only ones who could have possibly known about the conference. I still find it hard to believe that any one of them could be responsible for this treachery.'

'The leak had to originate from somewhere, sir,' Graham said.

'You let me worry about that. Call Major Inacio and have him put both the wine bar and Caldere's house under twenty-four-hour surveillance. But it must be discreet. Caldere's our only link to the kidnappers at the moment. We can't afford to scare him off.'

'I'll get on to it right away, sir,' Graham assured him.

'Keep me posted, Mike,' Philpott said, and the line went dead.

Marseilles is served by the international airport at Marignane, seventeen miles north of the city. Whitlock had flown into the airport earlier that morning, then taken the bus through to the Gare St Charles, Marseilles' central railway station, where he'd collected a hold-all from one of the lockers. Inside were a pair of old jeans, a sweatshirt, a pair of scuffed boots and a thick herringbone overcoat; clothes that Rust had felt would add authenticity to Whitlock's cover as Frank Royce. After changing in a cubicle in the men's toilets, Whitlock had deposited the hold-all, which now contained his own clothes, back in the locker. He'd studied the local map carefully on the plane, and now knew exactly where Mensel and Ronnet intended to intercept the car carrying Jannoc's daughter back from the party. An abandoned farmhouse on the outskirts of town. He had decided against using a cab to get there. Frank Royce had been almost penniless when he'd died and, intent on keeping up the deception, Whitlock had taken a bus as far as he could then completed the remainder of the journey on foot.

It had gone six-thirty by the time he finally reached the farmhouse. He did a quick reconnoitre of the area, then trudged the fifty yards up the muddy driveway to the front door. He winced as the door squeaked open, then crossed to the broken bay window which looked out over the road. According to Rust's dossier, Mensel and Ronnet would park in the driveway, where they intended to wait for Jannoc's personal metallic gold BMW 850i to drive past the farmhouse. It was a perfect spot, hidden from the road by the row of gnarled oaks on either side of the gate. Finding an old, rusted tin drum in the kitchen, Whitlock returned with it to the lounge and, inverting it, sat down by the window to await the arrival of Mensel and Ronnet.

An hour passed. A biting mistral wind had whipped up outside, scything through the broken windows around him, and, despite his thick overcoat, Whitlock was now bitterly cold. He buttoned the coat up to the collar and dug his hands deep into the pockets to try and keep them warm. What a way to spend Christmas Eve! Carmen and her mother would probably be sipping egg-nog in front of the TV set; the smell of roasting turkey would be wafting out from the kitchen. He cursed angrily under his breath. Get your mind back on the job. But within seconds he was thinking about Carmen again. She had been ever-present in his thoughts since he left New York. Carmen and their baby. The guilt had been intense at times, like a stabbing pain at the back of his mind. It had angered him – he had nothing to feel guilty about. UNACO was his life. And now the organization was facing its most serious challenge to date . . .

His thoughts were interrupted by the sound of an approaching engine. He peered cautiously through the window and saw the black Mercedes turn into the driveway. He ducked out of sight as the Mercedes approached the farmhouse: for one horrible moment he thought it was going to pull up in front of the window, but it turned round and headed back down the driveway again. It stopped a few yards short of the gate. The engine and lights were switched off. The passenger door swung open and the man Whitlock recognized as Pierre Mensel climbed out of the car. He was wearing a peaked cap tugged down over his unkempt, shoulder-length black hair. His partner, Ronnet, passed him a lighted cigarette through the open door, then Mensel picked up something from the dashboard which, at first, Whitlock couldn't make out. When Mensel attached it to his belt, Whitlock realized that it was a two-way radio. So that was how they intended to spring the trap. Mensel would take up a position close to the road and radio through to Ronnet when the BMW came into view. A sudden thought flashed through Whitlock's mind. What if Mensel and Ronnet intended to ignore Rust's instructions and make their move nearer town? But the more Whitlock thought about it, the more illogical it sounded. Neither Ronnet nor Mensel knew Marseilles, which had been one of the main reasons why Rust had chosen them in the first place and, judging by their dossiers, he doubted either man had the ability or the intelligence to put together an alternative plan. They were huskies, not draughtsmen.

Whitlock waited until Mensel had gone then, leaving the farmhouse, made his way cautiously through the undergrowth to within thirty yards of the Mercedes. He crouched down behind a tree and checked the dial of his luminous watch. It had already gone seven forty-five. Pulling up the collar of his overcoat and turning his back into the wind, he settled down to wait again.

It was another twenty minutes before the Mercedes coughed into life. Whitlock was immediately alert and, scrambling to his feet, he watched the Mercedes creep forward, its lights still off, until it reached the gate and stopped. Moments later Whitlock saw the lights of an approaching car illuminate the deserted road in front of the gate. Why was Ronnet waiting? He knew the plan: cut out in front of the car, and force the bodyguard either to stop or to swerve off the road. The engine grew louder as the car drew ever closer to where the Mercedes was lying in wait like some cunning black feline, ready to pounce on its unsuspecting prey. But still the Mercedes remained motionless. Then Whitlock saw the bonnet of the sleek metallic gold BMW 850i through the trees. It was then that he knew what Ronnet was about to do.

The BMW was ten yards away when Ronnet gunned the engine and the Mercedes shot forward through the gate, ploughing into the side of the BMW. The momentum of the impact slewed the BMW in an ungainly spin and it finally came to rest facing the direction from which it had originally come. The driver's door had taken the full force of the impact; the bodyguard, still harnessed by his safety belt, lay slumped over the wheel with blood streaming down his face from the gash above his eye. Mathilde Jannoc had been sitting in the back and appeared to be fumbling with her safety belt when Mensel reached through the shattered driver's window, unlocked the back door, and wrenched it open. Releasing the safety belt, he pulled her roughly from the back of the car, and dragged her screaming towards the Mercedes.

Whitlock, who had reacted instantly to the collision, sprinted from his concealed position in the undergrowth. He was already at the gate when Ronnet pushed open the back door for Mensel. Both men had their backs to him. Mensel shoved Mathilde Jannoc into the back seat, but when he tried to get in beside her, she reached up and raked her nails savagely down the side of his face. Whitlock heard Mensel's howl of pain as he clutched at his face, but Ronnet was quick to reach over and grab her arm when she tried to flee. Whitlock had almost reached the car when Mensel saw him and shouted to Ronnet. But the warning came too late. Whitlock tackled him and the two men fell to the ground. Whitlock flinched as Mensel caught him on the bridge of the nose with a flailing hand, then kicked out at him with his foot, catching Whitlock painfully in the ribs and momentarily knocking the wind out of him. Mensel scrambled to his feet and Whitlock looked up to see him pulling an automatic from his jacket pocket but, before he could fire, Whitlock lashed out with his foot, taking Mensel's legs from under him. Mensel stumbled back against the side of the car; by the time he'd regained his footing, Whitlock had taken cover behind the BMW. Mensel wiped the blood from his cheek and advanced on the BMW.

'Leave him,' Ronnet shouted angrily after Mensel. 'We've got to get out of here before someone comes along.'

'He could finger us,' Mensel retorted without looking round.

'Get in here and look after the brat!' Ronnet snarled as he continued to struggle with the feisty girl.

Mensel cursed furiously, then hurried back to the Mercedes and got in beside Mathilde Jannoc. The car pulled away, heading in the direction of the city.

Whitlock had tried unsuccessfully to open the driver's door of the BMW but it was jammed, buckled out of shape by the force of the collision. He waited until the Mercedes had sped away, then hurried round to the other side of the car and opened the back door. He managed to free the harnessed bodyguard and pushed him unceremoniously into the passenger seat. He found a holstered Sig P225 automatic under the man's jacket and, pocketing it, climbed behind the wheel and gritted his teeth anxiously as he reached for the gear lever. If the engine was damaged, he could forget about going after the Mercedes. The whole exercise would have been in vain. He slipped the gearstick into first and gave a deep sigh of relief when the car responded to the controls. Pressing the pedal to the floor, he sped off in pursuit of the Mercedes. His only fear now was that he wouldn't be able to catch up with it before it reached the first of the residential areas on the outskirts of the city. He could ill-afford a gun battle in some built-up area, especially on Christmas Eve when there would be plenty of people on the streets. But at least he knew from the map that the old road continued for some miles before it merged with the A50 which led directly into the centre of Marseilles. He had to intercept them before they reached that . . .

Despite the damage to the bodywork, the car still handled well under Whitlock's excellent guidance. Less than a minute later he picked out the Mercedes in his headlights but, as he narrowed the distance between the two cars, although he could see Mensel and Ronnet, there was no sign of the girl. Had she been knocked out to stop her struggling? The thought was quickly dismissed when Mensel leaned out of the back window and fired at the BMW. Whitlock ducked instinctively, but the bullet was well wide of the car. He assumed that the car would be protected by bulletproof windows, but he wasn't about to let his guesswork be put to the test. He waited until Mensel leaned out of the window again, then switched the lights to bright and, touching the accelerator, rammed the BMW into the back of the Mercedes. Mensel was jerked forward, and Whitlock saw his head crack against the angle of the door pillar. Whitlock immediately pulled out into the opposite lane but, as he drew abreast of the Mercedes, Ronnet unholstered his automatic and aimed it at the BMW. Swinging the wheel violently, Whitlock struck the Mercedes broadside on, forcing Ronnet to discard the pistol as he struggled to regain control of the wheel. Again Whitlock nudged the BMW against the Mercedes, forcing Ronnet to take evasive action to prevent the car from leaving the road. Seizing his opportunity in the confusion, Whitlock fired three bullets at the nearest tyre.

One scored a direct hit and the Mercedes immediately veered away from the BMW as Ronnet fought with the wheel. The Mercedes skidded off the road and came to a shuddering halt only yards away from a row of trees. Whitlock spun the BMW around in a one-hundred-and-eighty-degree turn and, training the headlights on the Mercedes, slipped out of the passenger door moments before the first bullet thudded into the side of the BMW.

Whitlock peered cautiously around the side of the car. He could see Ronnet slumped over the steering wheel, his face streaked with blood. The windscreen was shattered and Whitlock guessed that Ronnet had been thrown forward when he trod on the brakes. Mensel appeared to have abandoned the Mercedes and was presumably crouched behind the car. But what about the girl? He still couldn't see her. If anything had happened to her . . .

Another bullet hammered into the BMW. Whitlock lay flat on his stomach and peered under the car, hoping to catch a glimpse of Mensel's feet. He couldn't see anything. Then a movement caught his eye: Mensel was trying to manoeuvre himself around to the other side of the Mercedes. Whitlock wet his chapped lips and, holding the automatic in both hands, squeezed the trigger. Mensel screamed out in agony as the bullet smashed into his ankle. Whitlock was on his feet in an instant and ran the short distance to the back of the Mercedes. Crouching down behind the boot, he gripped the automatic tightly in both hands and pivoted round sharply. Mensel had his back to him, one hand clenched over his bloodied ankle, the other still holding the automatic.

'Drop the gun!' Whitlock ordered in French.

Mensel swung the automatic on Whitlock who shot him twice in the chest. Mensel was punched back against the car before slumping to the ground. Whitlock approached Mensel cautiously and checked for a pulse. There was none. He tossed Mensel's pistol into the undergrowth, then opened the back door of the Mercedes and found Mathilde Jannoc wedged down between the front and back seats, her hands manacled and a strip of plaster secured over her mouth. Her eyes were wide and fearful, her cheeks streaked with tears. Whitlock gave her a reassuring smile and was about to lift her out of the car when he heard the sound of an approaching helicopter in the distance. When it came into range he saw to his horror that it bore the insignia of the police on the side of the fuselage. A powerful spotlight was trained on the ground, and within seconds it had settled on the Mercedes. Whitlock squinted upwards but couldn't see the occupants behind the glare of the spotlight.

'Throw down the gun and move away from the car with your hands in the air,' a voice barked at him in French through a speaker on the undercarriage of the helicopter.

Where had the helicopter come from? Had someone raised the alarm? Whitlock knew there would be time for questions later. It would be pointless for him to try and make a break for it in the BMW. He had to take Mathilde Jannoc, and there was no way she would go with him voluntarily. He also knew that the whole operation would be in jeopardy if he were to be taken into custody. How could he meet Emile Jannoc if he were stuck behind bars? Suddenly it looked as if all the careful planning had been in vain.

'I said throw down the gun and move away from the car with your hands in the air,' the voice barked again.

He reluctantly tossed the gun to the ground and, stepping away from the car, slowly raised his hands in the air.

4

Katherine Warren was one of the first passengers to disembark from the TAP 747 after it landed at Lisbon's Portela Airport. On clearing customs she collected her suitcase and made her way out on to the packed concourse. She noticed Ed Miller straightaway, distinctive as always in a crowd with his shiny bald pate, loud plaid jacket and cheroot tucked into the corner of his mouth. They had been friends for more years than she could remember.

'How was the flight?' he asked, kissing her lightly on the cheek.

'Tedious,' she replied. 'Did you manage to find me any accommodation?'

'I thought that, as we'd be working odd hours, it would be best if you stayed at my place,' Miller told her. 'I've made up the spare room for you.'

'Perfect,' she replied. 'And how are our roving duo?'

'They've been busy,' Miller replied, then went on to explain about their trip to the wine bar and their subsequent meeting with Hardin at the back of the hotel.

'Did you manage to overhear anything that was said in the alley?' she asked as they reached his car.

'I couldn't risk getting within earshot in case I was seen,' Miller replied with a dejected shrug. 'I had to have all my wits about me just to ensure that they didn't know they were being followed. These two are pros, Katherine.'

'And you're sure they didn't know you were on to them?' she asked.

'I'm sure,' Miller was quick to reassure her.

'So what did you find out about this Hardin?'

'Only that he's an American working his way around Europe, picking up jobs here and there to keep him in pocket.'

'I think it's about time I met him,' she said.

'It just so happens that there's a Christmas Eve party at the wine bar tonight.' He indicated the leaflet on the dashboard. 'That gets us in for free, as long as we're there before ten.'

Katherine looked at her watch. 'That give me just enough time to change into my party dress.'

Miller smiled, then started the engine and headed for the exit.

Katherine Warren drew admiring looks in her figure-hugging black dress as she and Miller crossed the street to the wine bar. The doorman, who had the physique of a seasoned bodybuilder, looked up reluctantly from her stockinged legs to take the leaflet from Miller then, stepping aside, opened the glass door to allow them to enter.

Katherine looked around slowly. The catchpenny decor was obviously aimed at the tourist trade. She could imagine that it would be packed in summer. A parquet had been laid in the corner of the room, and a handful of middle-aged customers were dancing to some mind-numbing disco song that she hadn't heard since the Seventies.

Miller touched her arm. 'What do you want to drink?'

'Let me get the drinks,' she replied. 'I want a word with our friend. I assume that's him with the sun-bleached hair and the earring?'

Miller had briefed her on both Hardin and Caldere, and he nodded in affirmation. 'I'll get us a table.'

'As far away from the dance floor as possible,' Katherine said, screwing up her nose disdainfully as another dated track boomed out from the loudspeakers. 'What are you drinking, Ed?'

'A glass of their house wine. It's the only good thing about this place.'

Katherine waited until Hardin had finished serving a customer before approaching the bar. Another man – Caldere, she assumed – suddenly appeared from the open doorway behind the counter and made towards her but, to her relief, Hardin quickly cut in front of him, giving him a conciliatory smile on reaching her first. Caldere eyed him coldly then crossed to the other end of the counter to serve another customer.

'What can I get you?' Hardin asked, leaning towards her.

'You're from LA, right?' Katherine said, wagging a finger at him.

'Yeah, how did you know that?' Hardin replied.

'I recognized the accent. My ex-husband's from LA.'

'Right,' Hardin said, nodding his head. 'So where you from?'

'New York, born and bred.'

'Yeah?' Hardin reached under the counter and brought out a badge similar to the one he was already wearing on his waistcoat. He handed it to her: the wispy blue silhouette of a woman on a white background. 'There you are: a memento of the place. You can take it back with you to the Big Apple.'

'Thanks,' Katherine said, pinning it to her dress.

'By the way, the name's Ricky Hardin.'

'Katherine Warren,' she replied, shaking his extended hand.

'Is that your boyfriend over there?' Hardin asked, looking across at Miller.

'No, he's just a business associate,' she replied. 'But he does recommend your house wine.'

'So do I,' Hardin said with a grin. 'Two glasses?'

Katherine nodded. 'And have one yourself.'

62

'Thanks.' Hardin returned moments later with two glasses of the house wine and placed them on the counter in front of her. 'If you're not doing anything later, maybe we could meet up somewhere? What do you say?'

'That sounds like a great idea,' she replied. 'Then you can tell me what you told those two Americans when you met them at the back of the Altis Hotel this afternoon.'

The smile faltered on Hardin's face. 'I don't know what you're talking about,' he stammered.

'Don't worry, I'm not the law,' she was quick to reassure him then, taking one of her business cards from her bag, handed it to him. 'In fact, I could make it worth your while to talk to me.'

'You're a journalist?' Hardin said suspiciously.

'That's what it says on the card. Well, what do you say?'

'Why do you want to know –'

'That's not important,' she cut in quickly. 'How much did they pay you?'

'A couple of grand,' Hardin replied, trying his luck.

'I'll double it. Then you tell me, word for word, what you said to them. But if I find out later that you've been holding out on me, I'll see to it that my colleague makes life very difficult for you here in Portugal. Do we have a deal, Mr Hardin?'

'Sure,' Hardin replied, then glanced across at Caldere who was serving a customer at the far end of the counter. 'We can't talk here. Do you know Lisbon?'

'Where do you want to meet?' Katherine retorted crisply.

'Outside the Santa Apolonia Station; it's not far from here.'

'What time?'

Hardin checked his watch. 'We don't close till one. Let's say two-thirty to be on the safe side. And have the money ready.'

'I'll have it,' she told him, then peeled off a couple of notes and tossed them on to the counter. 'Enjoy your drink.'

Hardin watched her cross to the table. He began clearing empty glasses from the counter. The telephone rang. He lifted it out from under the counter and answered it.

'Caldere?' the voice demanded.

'No, I'll get him for you,' Hardin said in Portuguese then, cupping his hand over the mouthpiece, called Caldere to the phone.

Caldere took the receiver from Hardin and, putting his finger to his ear to block out the blaring music, screwed up his face as he struggled to hear what was being said to him. He finally replaced the receiver and returned the telephone to its position under the counter. 'Leave those, I'll do that,' he snapped as Hardin continued to clear the glasses from the counter. 'It is not busy at the moment; take the rubbish outside.'

Hardin went into the back room where three bulging refuse bags were stacked beside the door. He unlocked the door, grabbed the bags, and emerged out into the alley. The wind bit through his thin nylon shirt as he hurried over to the nearest metal bin and tossed the bags inside. He slammed the lid closed and was about to hurry back to the bar when a shadowy figure suddenly emerged from behind one of the bins. His face was partially obscured by a black fedora but, as he stepped away from the bin, his features were illuminated by the security light above the back door. Hardin didn't know him, but he did notice a dark, discoloured bruise on his right cheek. The man slowly removed his gloved hands from his pockets. In one hand was a Walther P88 automatic, a silencer already attached. Hardin wanted to run. The door was only feet away but his legs felt like lead. He tried to speak but fear had frozen his voice. The man's face remained expressionless as he raised the Walther and shot Hardin twice through the heart.

Unscrewing the silencer, the man slipped the automatic back into his shoulder holster. As he turned to leave, he found his path blocked by the doorman and for the first time a faint smile touched his lips. Flexing his fingers, he moved towards the menacing figure standing in the mouth of the alley. The doorman lunged at him, swinging a wild punch at his head, but the man blocked the punch easily with his forearm, and brought his elbow up savagely into the doorman's ribs. The doorman cried out in pain as he doubled over. He was still raising his head when the man delivered a hammering rabbit punch to the side of his head. He was unconscious before he hit the ground. The man brushed his hands together, then emerged from the alley and made for a Ford Escort which was parked nearby.

Inacio had called Graham the moment he'd heard about Hardin's murder. He was standing at the entrance to the alley when Graham and Sabrina arrived on the scene. 'It looks like a professional hit,' he said, watching as a forensics team continued to scour the alley for clues. 'Two bullets through the heart. Death would have been instantaneous.'

'Didn't your surveillance team see anything?' Graham demanded.

Inacio shook his head. 'Nothing, but then they were parked at the end of the street.'

'What about the doorman?' Graham asked. 'Couldn't he give you a description of the gunman?'

'He already has, but it's very hazy to say the least,' Inacio replied. 'He said that the alley was dark and that the gunman was wearing a hat pulled down over his forehead to obscure his face.'

'Could it have been Caldere?' Graham suggested.

'He had the motive, had he known that Hardin spoke to you earlier today,' Inacio agreed. 'But there are witnesses who'll verify that he was in the bar all the time. And anyway, the killer was seen driving away in a red Ford Escort.'

'Licence number?' Sabrina asked.

'The plates were blacked out with masking tape,' Inacio told her.

'Which leaves Berger, or one of the team that abducted Silverman,' Graham said. 'Perhaps our friend Hardin knew more than he was letting on.'

'That is a possibility,' Inacio replied. 'I've already put an APB out on Berger, but I still believe that Caldere is our best chance of getting to him. There's already a twenty-four-hour surveillance on Caldere, as you requested. With some luck he'll try and contact Berger. And when he does, we'll move in and arrest them both.'

'Don't do anything without first contacting us,' Graham said.

'My men may have to move fast,' Inacio told him. 'There may not be time to contact you.'

'Then they'd better make time,' Graham retorted. 'It's our necks on the line here. You don't do anything without first clearing it with us. Is that understood?'

Inacio bit back his anger, but he knew better than to argue. His orders were to assist UNACO in every possible way. 'I understand,' he said tersely, then excused himself and disappeared down the alley.

'Ease up, Mike,' Sabrina said once Inacio was out of earshot. 'It's not going to do any good if you antagonize the guy. This is his turf and his people. We need him on our side.'

'Yeah, sure,' Graham retorted without much conviction, then took the car keys from his pocket. 'Come on, let's go. There's nothing more we can do here.'

'Let's just hope C.W.'s having more luck in Marseilles than we're having here,' she said as they got into the car and headed back to the hotel.

Whitlock had been in police custody for the past four hours. As he sat dejectedly on the bed in the corner of his cell, he realized that there was now little chance of him being released, even on bail, without the intervention of either Rust or Philpott. But he also knew that, if he were to contact them, it would blow his cover. He had hoped, somewhat optimistically, that Jannoc might have pulled some strings to get him out, if only to hear his side of the story, but the chances of that happening were diminishing with each passing hour. Not that it surprised him. Jannoc would have his informers inside the police force who would already have briefed him on the statement Whitlock had made earlier in the evening. He'd spent almost two hours in a small, windowless room with two detectives who'd fired a barrage of questions at him in French, desperately trying to find contradictions in his answers. But he hadn't been rattled. He'd explained it exactly as it had happened and stuck resolutely to his cover story. His lawyer, a surly character who obviously resented having to work on Christmas Eve, had been of little use to him, and Whitlock had just been grateful to get back to his cell where he could sit quietly and compose his thoughts. He knew it would only be a matter of time before the detectives came back to grill him again . . .

He didn't hear the approaching footsteps above the drunken voice which had been shouting incessantly from the adjoining cell for the last half-hour. Only when the key was inserted into the lock did he look up. The door opened and a uniformed policeman entered the cell. Whitlock's eyes went to the figure who appeared in the doorway behind the policeman. Whitlock estimated him to be in his early forties and well over six feet tall. His skin was bronzed and leathery and a jagged scar ran from the corner of his mouth down to his chin. He nodded to the policeman then stepped into the cell. The policeman retreated and stood outside the door, his back to the cell.

'Frank Royce?' the man asked.

'That's right,' Whitlock replied, getting to his feet. 'Who are you?'

'*Parlez-vous français?*'

'With some difficulty,' Whitlock replied truthfully.

'It is all right, I will speak English. My name is Saisse. Fabien Saisse. I work for Monsieur Emile Jannoc.'

Whitlock knew the name from Rust's dossier. A former NCO in the French Foreign Legion, he was now Jannoc's right-hand man, or, as Rust had put it more succinctly in the dossier, 'Jannoc's personal enforcer'.

'The girl's father?' Whitlock said, feigning surprise.

Saisse nodded. 'That is right. Monsieur Jannoc has asked me to apologize for the delay in obtaining your release, but he had to make some phone calls to arrange it. You will come with me now. Monsieur Jannoc would like to see you.'

'Has he posted bail for me?' Whitlock asked as they left the cell.

'It was not necessary,' Saisse replied.

'I don't understand,' Whitlock said with a frown.

'The police will not be pursuing the case. That is all you need to know.'

'What?' Whitlock shot back in amazement. 'Christ, Jannoc's daughter was almost kidnapped tonight. And now you say that the cops aren't going to do anything about it? It doesn't make any sense.'

'You do not need to know any more!' Saisse snapped, glaring at Whitlock.

Whitlock fell silent and, collecting his personal possessions from the desk sergeant, followed Saisse to a white BMW which was parked outside the police station. It didn't surprise him that Jannoc had managed to bury the case with such ease. According to his file at the Command Centre, Jannoc was known to have senior contacts within the various branches of the city's public offices. Bribery and blackmail obviously had their advantages, Whitlock thought bitterly to himself. He knew Rust would see to it that the French authorities conducted their own investigation into any irregularities once the operation was over. That, at least, gave him some peace of mind.

'I believe you are a soldier?' Saisse asked, breaking the silence.

'Yes.'

'A mercenary?'

'Sometimes,' Whitlock replied.

'Where did you fight?'

'Ethiopia. Sudan. Chad. Basically anywhere where they needed another gun.'

'And what are you doing in Marseilles?' Saisse asked, glancing at Whitlock's reflection in the rear-view mirror.

'Looking for a passage back to Africa. I've spent almost all my money just getting here from London. That's why I look such a mess. Christ, I haven't eaten in over twenty-four hours.'

'How will you get back to Africa if you have no money?'

Whitlock knew Saisse was testing him, probing for answers he could check at a later stage. 'I can work my passage on a ship bound for the north African coast. I've done it before. Crewmen get drunk, or arrested, at this time of year. I'll go down to the docks after Christmas and see who's looking for crews. It shouldn't be too difficult.'

'No, it is not difficult,' Saisse replied, giving the impression he'd done it all before. 'Why were you at the farm-house? It has been empty for years.'

'It wasn't the last time I was here. It used to be a bed-and-breakfast place. I was quite surprised when I got there and found it derelict. Whatever happened to Madame Noiret?'

Saisse's eyes flickered towards Whitlock again. 'She is dead. Two years now.'

'I'm sorry to hear that. I liked her. I can't say the same about her cats though. She must have had about thirty of them in all. All strays.'

'I remember the cats,' Saisse said with a dismissive gesture of his hand. 'How long had you been at the farm?'

'I arrived this morning. Like I said, I'm almost broke so

I thought, what the hell, I'll just bivouac there until after Christmas. Well, that was the idea – until what happened tonight.'

Saisse asked Whitlock to explain, in his own words, his part in thwarting the attempt to kidnap Mathilde Jannoc earlier that evening. After feigning some exasperation at going through it all again, Whitlock obliged. Occasionally Saisse interceded with a question to clarify a point but, in general, he remained silent, listening impassively as Whitlock recounted the details to him, so that by the time they reached their destination he had a much clearer picture of what had actually happened.

Le Boudin was one of the most popular nightclubs in the city. Situated on the waterfront in the Vieux Port, its brightly lit façade illuminated the rows of yachts rocking gently in the waters of the harbour. Saisse parked in an alley at the side of the nightclub.

'Does Jannoc own this?' Whitlock asked, getting out of the car.

'*Le Boudin* is one of Monsieur Jannoc's clubs. He has several in the city.'

'*Le Boudin*?' Whitlock mused as Saisse used a miniature transmitter to activate a side door. 'That's the marching song of the French Foreign Legion, isn't it? What's the significance?'

'Monsieur Jannoc was an officer in the *Légion Etrangère*,' Saisse replied, ushering Whitlock through the door and closing it again behind him. 'He still has close ties with the *Légion*. All his staff are ex-legionnaires and he regularly entertains the officers from the Bas-Fort Saint-Nicolas, the *Légion Etrangère*'s recruiting office here in Marseilles.'

'So you were in the Legion as well?' Whitlock asked, following Saisse up a flight of stairs.

'I was a *sergent* in the *Police Militaire*,' Saisse replied.

'I've heard about you guys. You hunt down the deserters, don't you?'

Saisse paused at the top of the stairs. 'There are many crimes in the *Légion Etrangère*: the most serious is desertion. It was an honour to be chosen to track down these cowards and take them back to the *citadelle* to face a court martial.'

'I guess that's one way of looking at it.'

'You would not understand, Royce. You were a mercenary. Your allegiance is to money. My allegiance was always to the *Légion*.'

'So why aren't you still chasing these so-called cowards around Africa?' Whitlock asked, holding Saisse's icy stare.

'That is not your concern!' Saisse snapped indignantly.

Whitlock could understand Saisse's reluctance to venture an explanation. He knew from Rust's dossier that Saisse had served three years in a military prison for beating a deserter to death with a spade. On his release, he had been stripped of his rank and thrown out of the Foreign Legion.

Saisse led him to a door further down the corridor which opened on to a beautifully decorated bathroom, complete with a sunken bath and jacuzzi. 'You can bath here. Then you will meet Monsieur Jannoc. I will have clothes sent to you. When you are ready, press the bell beside the sink and someone will come and show you to Monsieur Jannoc's office.'

'I'm overwhelmed by the hospitality,' Whitlock said with a hint of sarcasm, but then added truthfully, 'I'll be glad of a bath though.'

'You are hungry?'

'Damn right,' Whitlock replied.

'I will send you food with the . . .' Saisse trailed off abruptly when a figure emerged from the lift at the end of the corridor.

Whitlock had to quickly check his disbelief when he looked round at the tall, commanding figure striding purposefully towards them. Colonel Nikolai Zlotin, reputed to be the most decorated officer in the history of the élite Soviet Special Forces unit, *spetsialnoye nazhacheniye*, or *spetznaz*. There wasn't a field operative at UNACO who wasn't familiar with every detail of Zlotin's life. Some even unashamedly regarded him as their role model. Whitlock knew from the computer records that Zlotin was a forty-three-year-old Ukrainian, but his cropped brown hair was now beginning to grey at the temples and the deep lines creasing his rugged, weatherbeaten face gave him an older, more distinguished appearance than had been evident in the photographs of him currently on file at UNACO's Command Centre in New York.

'We need to talk,' Zlotin said brusquely to Saisse in French, one of eight languages Whitlock knew he spoke fluently.

'I have some business to attend to,' Saisse said sharply to Whitlock, then led Zlotin back to the lift.

Whitlock closed the bathroom door behind him and sat down on the edge of the sunken bath. It was obvious that Saisse already knew Zlotin, judging by his expression when he'd first seen him. But was Zlotin involved in the kidnapping of Abe Silverman? Had he been one of the three masked men at the airport? If so, why was he in collusion with a gangster like Jannoc? Was he working on assignment for *spetznaz*? Or was he now freelance? And did Jannoc and Saisse even know that Zlotin was a Colonel with the Russian Special Forces?

Whitlock rubbed his hands over his face. Suddenly there were so many questions that needed to be answered. He'd contact Rust after he'd met with Jannoc. It was essential that he find out as much as he could about the situation before filing his report. Draping his overcoat over the chair in the corner of the room, he ran the water for his bath. He needed time to collect his thoughts.

'What are you doing here?' Saisse hissed at Zlotin, closing the door to Jannoc's personal office behind him.

'I'll discuss that with Jannoc when he gets here,' Zlotin replied tersely.

'Does Monsieur Jannoc know you're here?'

'I didn't see him when I arrived, but I told one of the doormen to let him know that I was here,' Zlotin replied, slowly taking in the six Abstract Expressionist paintings which had been positioned equidistant from each other on the three beige-coloured walls. The fourth wall, behind the large antique walnut desk, was made up of a two-way mirror which was hidden behind a set of Venetian blinds. Zlotin stared at the nearest painting for some time trying to read something – anything – into it, but finally gave up with a sad shake of his head. He could never see the attraction in a series of swirls and lines which looked as if they had been slashed across the canvas in a fit of temper. To him, that wasn't art. 'Are they originals?'

'Of course,' Saisse snapped back indignantly.

'It seems that selling heroin to teenagers does have its advantages after all.'

'I'd watch my tongue if I were you, Zlotin,' Saisse snapped, stabbing a finger in his direction.

The door opened and Emile Jannoc entered the room. Dressed in a tuxedo and black tie, Jannoc was a short, thickset man in his late forties with black hair which was combed back from a pock-marked face and secured in a ponytail at the back of his head. He crossed to the desk, sat down in the swivel chair, and lit himself a cigarette. 'You were told never to come here. Why have you blatantly disregarded my orders?'

'Silverman's dead,' Zlotin replied bluntly.

'Dead?' Jannoc retorted in disbelief. 'What happened?'

'It seems that he died of a heart attack while trying to escape. And he almost succeeded as well.'

'Why wasn't he in his cell?' Jannoc demanded angrily.

'He was when my colleagues and I left him. Berger was supposed to have kept an eye on him while we were away. Silverman managed to lure Berger into his cell, overpower him, then make his escape. We found Berger locked in the cell on our return.'

'Where's Berger now?' Jannoc asked.

'Dead,' Zlotin replied contemptuously. 'I executed him after he'd told us what had happened. I will not tolerate that kind of incompetence from anyone under my command.'

'He wasn't under your command, you bastard,' Saisse snarled, moving threateningly towards Zlotin. 'He was one of us. The best man I had. That's why I agreed to let you use him in the first place. He took his orders from me, not from you.'

'If he was the best man you had, this organization must be in a lot of trouble,' Zlotin retorted disdainfully.

'I've taken just about all –'

'Sit down, Fabien!' Jannoc snapped.

Saisse glared furiously at Zlotin, then returned to his chair and sat down.

'Had Silverman decoded any of the documents before he died?' Jannoc asked, turning back to Zlotin.

'No.'

'So we're right back to where we started.' Jannoc banged his fist angrily on the desk. 'Now I'll never know the truth about my brother's death. This whole operation has been a complete waste of time and money, hasn't it?'

'On the contrary,' Zlotin replied. 'I drew up a contingency plan after our first meeting to cover for an eventuality like this. I see no reason why it can't work.'

Jannoc stubbed out his cigarette and sat forward, his hands clasped on the desk. 'Go on.'

'As I'm sure you're already aware, Silverman taught at the Sorbonne for several years before he was recruited by the Israelis. In that time, several brilliant students passed through his hands. Two in particular, Gunther Auerbach and Alain Fisier, went on to become leading cryptologists in their individual fields. Both men are now regarded by their peers as being as good as their mentor. Dr Auerbach is the head of cryptology at the University of Leipzig and Professor Fisier holds the same post at the Sorbonne. They're probably the only two men alive capable of breaking Silverman's personal code.'

'And you're suggesting that we use them to decode the UNACO folders?' Jannoc asked.

'They would need an incentive. Auerbach is a widower, but he does have a teenage daughter. Fisier has a wife. I'm sure they could be persuaded to help us if we were holding the two women as additional hostages.'

Jannoc wet his lips excitedly. 'It could just work, couldn't it? Do you know where Auerbach and Fisier are at the moment?'

'Not off-hand, but it won't take long to find out,' Zlotin replied.

'It could take them weeks to break the code,' Saisse said to Jannoc. 'We don't have that much time. We know that UNACO has two of its operatives in Lisbon. They've already been to Caldere's wine bar –'

'Only because Berger left a box of matches in the ambulance with his fingerprints on it,' Zlotin cut in sharply. 'Don't worry, they'll be given a deadline to decode the folders. And they'll be left in no doubt at all as to what will happen if they don't make that deadline.'

'Then do it,' Jannoc told him. 'And this time I want results.'

'This time you'll get them,' Zlotin assured him.

'What do you know about these two agents UNACO have sent to Lisbon?' Jannoc asked. 'Could they be a threat to the operation?'

'Of course they'll be a threat,' Zlotin shot back. 'They're professionals. UNACO only recruit the best. The woman I don't know. But I know a lot about her partner, Mike Graham. Ex-Delta, the American anti-terrorist unit. He's good. Headstrong and very tenacious. We'll have to watch him closely.'

'Why not just kill him?' Jannoc asked.

'They would only send in someone else to replace him,' Zlotin said. 'No, it's better the devil you know. And I can use that to my advantage if I'm to keep him chasing shadows. But if he does become too much of a nuisance, he'll be dealt with accordingly.'

There was a knock at the door.

'*Entrez*,' Jannoc called out.

A head popped round the door. 'I have Monsieur Royce outside. I believe you wish to see him, Monsieur.'

Saisse held up a hand in apology to Jannoc. 'I meant to tell you that I'd picked up Royce from the police station, but it slipped my mind when Zlotin showed up. I'm sorry.'

'Ask Monsieur Royce to wait outside. I'll see him shortly.'

The door closed again.

'Who's Royce?' Zlotin asked.

Jannoc explained about the attempt to kidnap his daughter earlier that evening, then had Saisse brief him on what he'd learnt from Whitlock in the car on the way to *Le Boudin*. 'What do you make of him?' he asked once Saisse had finished.

'I'm not sure,' Saisse replied. 'It strikes me as being too much of a coincidence him being at the farmhouse at that time. I could be wrong, of course.'

Jannoc nodded thoughtfully, then asked Saisse to show Whitlock into his office. When Whitlock entered, Jannoc immediately rose from behind his desk and shook his hand. 'It's a pleasure to finally get to meet you, Mr Royce,' Jannoc said, switching to English. 'I can't begin to thank you for what you did tonight. I am for ever in your debt.'

Saisse shook his head sadly to himself as he resumed his seat. He should have known that Jannoc wouldn't take a blind bit of notice of any criticism he had of Royce. The man had saved his precocious little brat from two bumbling kidnappers, and that was all that mattered to him. Mathilde had always been Jannoc's Achilles' heel. She got whatever she wanted whenever she wanted it. She'd even managed to turn Jannoc against his own wife. Saisse had seen the bruises on Brigitte's face on more than one occasion when she'd dared to criticize Mathilde. Saisse knew Mathilde would be Jannoc's downfall. She would eventually destroy him. And he was damned if he was going to wait around to see it happen.

'I think you've already repaid the debt by getting me out of jail,' Whitlock replied with a quick smile. 'I still don't know how you managed to convince the police to drop the case. You must have some clout in this town.'

'I called in a few favours,' Jannoc replied with a modest shrug. 'I'm a very prominent businessman here in Marseilles, Mr Royce. I can't afford this kind of adverse publicity. It could give others ideas, if you see what I mean?'

Whitlock could see exactly what Jannoc meant. If Mathilde was ever abducted it would leave Jannoc vulnerable to the kidnappers' demands, and if that were ever to reach the press, other would-be kidnappers would be encouraged to have a go as well. Open season for his rivals . . .

Jannoc removed Whitlock's passport from the desk drawer and handed it back to him. 'You're free to leave the country whenever you want.'

'What will happen to the surviving kidnapper?' Whitlock asked, pocketing the passport.

'He will be dealt with once he's released from hospital. I will see to that.' Jannoc clapped his hands together. 'But that needn't concern you. Would you care for a drink?'

'Bourbon, if you have it,' Whitlock replied, remembering Royce's favourite drink.

Jannoc poured out a double shot of bourbon and handed it to Whitlock. 'Fabien tells me you're a mercenary. You were never with the Foreign Legion, were you?'

'No, but I knew a few legionnaires when I was in Africa,' Whitlock replied.

'Whereabouts in Africa did you fight?' Zlotin asked, his English as perfect as his French.

'This is a business colleague of mine,' Jannoc was quick to say, gesturing to Zlotin, but not mentioning him by name.

'I spent a year in Chad. I did a couple of tours in the Sudan. I've also seen action in Ethiopia and Somalia. Hell, basically anywhere where there's been a war in the last twelve years.'

'Sounds like you've been around a bit,' Zlotin said.

'I guess I have,' Whitlock replied. 'It's all I know. That's why I'm going back again. Hopefully I'll be able to work my passage on a freighter out of Marseilles. They're always looking for crewmen after Christmas.'

'Leave that to me, I'll see that you get to Africa,' Jannoc told him.

'That would be a great help,' Whitlock said.

'It is the least I can do,' Jannoc replied then, putting his arm around Whitlock's shoulders, walked him to the door. 'It goes without saying that you will be my guest until you leave for Africa. I'm having a small party downstairs. A few friends and business associates. Why not join them? I'll be along shortly. Fabien will show you the way.' He waited until the two men had left, then opened the blinds. The two-way mirror looked out over the packed dance floor. He watched Saisse and Whitlock descend a flight of stairs and disappear into the bar. Then he turned back to Zlotin. 'What do you make of Royce?'

'I hadn't really thought about it,' Zlotin replied. 'Why do you ask?'

'We're going to need a replacement for Berger.'

'Are you suggesting Royce?' Zlotin said in surprise. 'He's an outsider.'

'He's also a professional, and if he were offered the right kind of financial incentive, he'd do as he was told, no questions asked.'

'It's too risky.'

'Not if he's eliminated after the operation's completed. That way there can be no comebacks, can there?'

'We don't know anything about him.'

'We've both got contacts who could have a complete

dossier on him by the morning.' Jannoc moved to his desk and sat down. 'Berger and Saisse were the only two men in my organization who knew about the operation at Lisbon Airport. Saisse is my second-in-charge. I need him here. Royce, on the other hand, doesn't know anything about the operation, and if he were to conveniently disappear once the folders have been decoded, nobody would be any the wiser. I think it's worth a try.'

Zlotin thought for a moment then nodded in agreement. 'Very well. I'll have one of my *spetznaz* colleagues check him out tonight. If he is on the level, and can prove that he is Royce, then I'll use him.'

'And if not?' Jannoc asked.

'Then I'll kill him. Either way, Royce is a dead man.'

Malcolm Philpott sat grim-faced in the back of the Mercedes as it threaded its way carefully through New York's early evening traffic. In contrast to the last-minute shoppers hurrying from store to store in search of that elusive present, Christmas was the furthest thought from his mind. He'd spent the last ten hours in his office collating the information he'd gathered over the past couple of days in his attempt to track down the mole in the organization. Having begun the morning with a shortlist of five names, he'd whittled it down to two by the afternoon. By early evening he was certain he knew the identity of the mole, but was still awaiting a fax to confirm his worst suspicions. Only then could he make his move . . .

He'd still been awaiting the fax when he'd received a telephone call from Jacques Rust to brief him on Whitlock's latest report. They'd speculated on why Nikolai Zlotin, the most decorated officer in *spetznaz* history, would be working in league with a Marseilles gangster. Was he on some shadowy assignment, sent by a group of militant hard-liners out to discredit UNACO? Although it made little sense, it certainly couldn't be discounted. Or had he turned his back on his country, disgusted at the fragmentation of a nation once regarded as the greatest military power in the world? Whatever the reason, Philpott wanted answers and he knew just the man who could provide them for him.

The Mercedes turned into West Fifty-seventh Street and the driver, unable to find a parking space, double-parked outside the Russian Tea Room before climbing out of the car and opening the back door for Philpott.

'I won't be long,' Philpott told him. 'Wait for me here.'

'Yes, sir,' the driver replied, touching his cap.

Philpott entered the restaurant and was immediately approached by the *maître d'hôtel*. 'Good evening, sir. May I help you?'

'Yes, I'm looking for Ambassador Zhorev,' Philpott told him. 'I believe he's dining here tonight?'

'Yes, sir, he is. Are you with his party?'

'No, I'm not, but it's imperative that I speak with him. Would you tell him that Colonel Philpott's here?'

'The Ambassador is hosting a party –'

'Just tell him that I want to see him now,' came the curt riposte.

The *maître d'* bowed stiffly and disappeared through the doorway behind him, returning moments later with a short, plump man in his early fifties. Anatoli Zhorev, a vociferous opponent of old-style Communism, had been the Russian Ambassador to the United Nations for the past seven months. He waited until the *maître d'* was out of earshot before addressing Philpott. 'Is there a problem, Malcolm?'

'You could say that. We need to talk.'

'This is a very inconvenient time,' Zhorev told him. 'I am entertaining friends here tonight.'

'I wouldn't have come unless it was important. You know that.'

'Very well, what is it?' Zhorev asked with a hint of irritation in his voice.

'Not here,' Philpott replied, looking around him. 'My car's

outside. We can talk more privately there. Unless, of course, you'd prefer to discuss Nikolai Zlotin in public.'

Zhorev's face suddenly went pale and, swallowing nervously, he gestured towards the doors behind him. 'I will make the necessary apologies to my guests,' he said quietly. 'Please excuse me.'

When he returned, the two men walked silently from the restaurant. The driver opened the back door for them, then climbed behind the wheel and looked to Philpott for instructions.

'Just keep driving around the block,' Philpott told him, then activated the soundproof window between the front and back seats. 'I've never seen you so rattled, Anatoli. I think you'd better tell me what's going on.'

Zhorev wet his dry lips and stared at his hands which were clenched tightly in his lap. 'Has Zlotin become involved in a UNACO operation?' he asked softly without looking up at Philpott.

'Yes,' Philpott replied. 'But that's all I can say at the moment. It's classified.'

'I knew something like this would happen,' Zhorev hissed angrily. 'I told them but they would not listen to me. No, they had to cover it up.'

'You're not making any sense, Anatoli!' Philpott snapped exasperatedly. 'What had to be covered up?'

'May I?' Zhorev asked, indicating the miniature drinks cabinet in front of them.

'Of course,' Philpott replied, gesturing absently towards the mahogany cabinet.

Zhorev poured himself a whisky and gulped it down. 'Have you ever met Zlotin?'

'No.'

'I knew him well. Not by choice, I assure you, but because he was in charge of the *spetznaz* garrison in Kalinin at the same time that I was mayor of the town. In fact, he arrived within days of my taking office. Naturally we disagreed on

81

almost everything. He was born in the Ukraine but always regarded himself as a Russian, first and foremost. Never a Ukrainian. He believed strongly that the country should remain as one nation, not a fragmented union of autonomous states. He also prided himself on being a fiercely patriotic Communist. He hero-worshipped Stalin and despised the likes of Gorbachev and Yeltsin. That gives you some insight into the kind of man we are dealing with here.'

'So, in other words, he turned his back on his country when all his beliefs came to nothing,' Philpott concluded.

'If it were only that simple,' Zhorev replied. 'Zlotin became a vociferous outspoken critic of Gorbachev's new policies, but he was only one of many within the military who opposed the liberal use of *glasnost, perestroika* and *demokratizatsiya*. At the time Gorbachev did not have the foresight to stamp down on these militant dissidents. Well, as you know, it all came to a head when Gorbachev's Vice President, Gennady Yanayev, and his co-conspirators – amongst them the Defence Minister, General Dmitri Yazov – attempted the ill-fated putsch in August 1991. It was only then that we, the pro-democracy members of the Politburo, found out that Nikolai Zlotin was more than just another voice in the crowd. He was Yazov's man in *spetznaz*. Had Yanayev's nerve held under the scrutiny of the world's press, the outcome could have been very different. Zlotin made it clear from the outset that his troops would deploy anywhere they were needed. And that included the streets of Moscow and St Petersburg where the majority of the pro-democracy rallies were being held. But fortunately Yanayev panicked and Zlotin was never called on to back the putsch with force. By the time Zlotin realized the situation had turned against the conspirators, it was too late to do anything about it. The streets of Moscow and St Petersburg had already been secured by troops loyal to Gorbachev. Zlotin and his two adjutants, Major Viktor Rodenko and Captain Valentin Yemenkov, were arrested, along with several other senior *spetznaz* officers who had supported the failed putsch. Rodenko and Yemenkov, like Zlotin, were both highly decorated *spetznaz* officers. They were tried and found guilty of treason. All three were stripped of their ranks and sentenced to twenty-five years imprisonment.

'The convoy taking them to the military prison on the outskirts of Moscow was ambushed by a gang of masked men. None of these men have been apprehended, so we can only assume that they were fellow *spetznaz* soldiers sympathetic to the cause. Zlotin, Rodenko and Yemenkov escaped. My government immediately put a lid on the whole affair. A news blackout was imposed and the subsequent investigation by the police and the military was undertaken in complete secrecy. It had been hoped to rearrest them without any of this ever reaching the West. We have already posted senior army officers to all our embassies around the world with strict instructions to find these men and bring them home.'

'Why the secrecy, for God's sake?' Philpott demanded.

'My government were desperate to play down the military's involvement in the attempted putsch. If the West thought there was still some kind of internal power struggle going on between the military and the politicians, it could have harmed future negotiations between my government and Western leaders.'

'There's more to it than that, isn't there?' Philpott asked, noticing the uneasy expression on Zhorev's face.

'Yes,' Zhorev replied. 'We have received some disturbing information within the last few days from more than one reliable source inside *spetznaz* that Zlotin may be planning another putsch. He had talked of it before his arrest and we know there are still many hard-liners in the military who would willingly support him.'

'But surely your government's anticipated that and would now be able to counter any threat with enough firepower of its own?' Philpott said.

'How would you counter a nuclear bomb secreted some-where in your own country?' Zhorev asked, holding Philpott's stare.

'Good God,' Philpott replied, ashen-faced. 'But how would he smuggle a nuclear device into the country without it being detected?'

'Why take the risk when there is already weapon-grade plutonium for sale on the Russian black market?' Zhorev nodded when he saw the look of horror on Philpott's face. 'With so many nuclear devices now spread amongst the fragmented states it was inevitable that a percentage, small as it may be, of weapon-grade plutonium would eventu-ally find its way on to the black market. And with enough plutonium in his possession, Zlotin could realistically hold any government in the world to ransom.'

'Why were UNACO not informed of this before?' Philpott demanded.

'If UNACO had been told, then every intelligence agency in the world would have had to be told as well. It would have certainly destroyed the credibility of my government. That is why it had to be kept under wraps. But now that Zlotin has transgressed the law outside my country, I feel it is necessary to break the silence. We cannot continue with this deception any longer. We have *spetznaz* officers who know Zlotin better than any of your people. I think it would be a good idea for us to pool our resources. I know my superiors would agree to a joint operation. After all, it may be our only chance of catching him.'

'Out of the question,' Philpott shot back angrily. 'We'll handle this ourselves.'

'Malcolm, I think you should reconsider –'

'Keep your people out of it, Anatoli, or you can be sure I'll see to it that every intelligence agency in the world will know about our little conversation here tonight. You can deny it all you want, but I've got it down on tape. And if you think I won't release it, just try and call my bluff.'

'I gave you this information in good faith, Malcolm,' Zhorev snapped indignantly.

'You gave me this information because your back's to the wall. You're clutching at straws and you know it. I'm disappointed in you, Anatoli. Whatever happened to *glasnost*? Or do you only use that term to charm the foreign press?'

'I had my orders,' Zhorev retorted brusquely.

'You can be sure I'll be taking this up personally with the Secretary-General first thing in the morning. Christmas Day or not, I'll make sure he knows just what we're up against here. A conspiracy of silence from the Kremlin.' Philpott flicked on the intercom switch in front of him. 'Jerry, take the Ambassador back to the restaurant. We wouldn't want his guests to be kept waiting any more than was absolutely necessary.'

5

Christmas Day

Graham woke at six o'clock that morning. Not that he'd slept much the previous night. There had been a party in a neighbouring room which had gone on until the early hours of the morning. The noise had been enough to disturb a light sleeper like himself. But he hadn't complained. He knew he wouldn't have got much sleep anyway with the uncertainty over the missing UNACO folders and the thoughts of Carrie and Mikey which had continually washed over his subconscious throughout the night. Turning over in bed, he reached for the photograph of Carrie and Mikey which he'd removed from his wallet the previous evening, and placed it on the bedside table. The last photograph he'd ever taken of them. He traced his finger lightly over Carrie's face, then smiled gently as he looked at Mikey in his favourite New York Giants sweatshirt, a football tucked under his arm as he grinned mischievously at the camera. 'Merry Christmas,' he said softly, then replaced the photograph on the table.

He climbed out of bed and changed into his tracksuit, then spent the next forty-five minutes going through his daily exercise routine before heading for the shower. Twenty minutes later he was dressed in a pair of jeans and a sweatshirt and, after phoning room service for a Continental breakfast and a copy of the *International Herald Tribune*, he slumped down on the bed, positioned a pillow behind his back and switched on the television set. He flicked absently through the channels, chose a current affairs programme even though he didn't understand a word they were saying, and tossed the remote on to the bed beside him.

There was a knock at the door. Palming his Beretta from under his pillow, he slipped it into the back of his jeans, then moved to the door and peered through the spyhole. It was Sabrina. He opened the door and gave her a wry grin. 'You're up bright and early. I thought you never surfaced before eight-thirty unless under great duress?'

'Christmas Day's always been an exception,' she replied, entering the room. 'I guess I'm still a kid at heart.'

'Some Christmas this is turning out to be,' Graham snorted, closing the door behind her.

'I've had better,' she agreed with a smile, then kissed him lightly on the lips. 'Merry Christmas, Mike.'

'Yeah, you too,' he replied, placing the Beretta on the bedside table. 'I've already ordered down for some breakfast. You want me to order for you as well?'

'Sure.'

He ordered another Continental breakfast to the room and, after he'd replaced the receiver, found Sabrina standing in front of him, a small gift-wrapped present in her upturned palm. 'We said no presents this year, Sabrina. We agreed to donate some money to UNICEF instead.'

'It's only a little present,' she said with a coy smile. 'It's nothing much, believe me. Go on, open it.'

Graham shook his head despairingly and unwrapped the paper. Inside was an oblong-shaped box containing a Swiss-made Mauser Officer's pocket knife. The olive-green handle held a stainless steel main blade, skinning knife, saw blade, screwdriver, bottle opener and corkscrew.

'I remember you telling me last week when we were on manoeuvres in Virginia that you'd lost your Swiss Army knife,' she said to him. 'And, knowing you, it would have taken you ages to get round to replacing it. There's an inscription on it.'

He turned it around in his hand until he found the inscription. *To Mike – a true friend. Love Sabrina.* 'That's great, thanks,' he said with an awkward shrug to hide his obvious discomfort.

She grinned. 'Try not to lose this one as well.'

There was another knock at the door. They exchanged suspicious glances. It couldn't be room service, not that quickly. Tucking the Beretta into the back of his jeans again, Graham crossed to the door and looked through the spy-hole. He stepped back in surprise. 'It's Jacques,' he called out to Sabrina, and opened the door to allow Rust to wheel himself into the room.

'What are you doing here?' she asked, greeting Rust with a kiss on the cheek. 'We weren't told you were coming.'

'Did you really want me to call you at three in the morning to tell you I was on my way to Lisbon?' Rust opened his attaché case, removed two envelopes, and handed one to each of them. 'Not much of a Christmas present, I'm afraid.'

'It's not much of a Christmas,' Sabrina replied, then held up the envelope. 'What's inside?'

'A copy of the faxes the Colonel sent through to me earlier this morning. He asked me to deliver them to you in person. They are for your eyes only. You'll understand why once you've read them.'

They opened the envelopes and read the faxes in silence. Graham was the first to finish. He crossed to the window then looked round anxiously at Rust. 'Have the Kremlin confirmed Zhorev's allegations?'

Rust nodded. 'Yes. The Colonel spoke personally to the Russian President last night. It's all true.'

'Then we're in trouble. Big trouble.' Graham shook his head to himself then sat down on the edge of the bed. 'It's the nightmare scenario, isn't it? Only now the nuclear device won't be in the hands of some two-bit terrorist group. We're talking about one of the most astute and brilliant tacticians ever produced by the Russian militia. He's an anachronism in modern Russia, a throwback to the Cold War era, and that's what makes him all the more dangerous. Who the hell ever said that patriotism was a virtue?'

'You became something of an expert on Zlotin when you were at Delta, didn't you?' Rust asked him.

'Yeah, I spent over ten years studying the man and the soldier. Not that there's much to differentiate between the two. I guess that's what makes him so good. But I did discover one chink in his armour. Zlotin's an ideologist. His whole life's been an obsessive crusade to further the aims of Communism. And this zealous fanaticism has been his one weakness. It's made him predictable.'

'What do you know about Rodenko and Yemenkov?' Rust asked.

'I saw a copy of Rodenko's psychiatric report when I was at Delta. It had been smuggled out of the country by a defecting *spetznaz* officer. According to the report, a military psychiatrist diagnosed Rodenko as psychotic when he was first recruited by *spetznaz*. Any other Special Forces unit would have dumped him straightaway on the strength of that report alone, but it seems that several senior *spetznaz* officers regarded him very highly and had the report buried and the psychiatrist sworn to silence. They were obviously right, to a point, because he went on to become one of the most decorated officers in the history of the unit. But at the same time he was also responsible for some of the most inhuman atrocities imaginable against women and children while serving in Afghanistan. He was never reprimanded, so obviously his superiors were prepared to overlook the darker side of him. He's not in Zlotin's league when it comes to tactics and strategies, but in his own way he's just as dangerous.'

'And Yemenkov?' Sabrina asked.

Graham shook his head. 'I've never heard of him, but then the Colonel did say in his fax that Yemenkov was only in his late twenties. He's obviously one of those officers who came to prominence in Afghanistan. But the mere fact that

Zlotin holds him in such high regard makes him just as dangerous as the others.'

'The Russians have agreed to provide us with detailed dossiers on all three men,' Rust said. 'So once they arrive we'll have a clearer picture of Yemenkov.'

'What do you make of this theory about Zlotin using the money he'd get for selling the folders to buy enough weapon-grade plutonium to force the Russian government to concede power back to the Communists?' Sabrina asked Graham.

'I think it's a very real possibility,' came the reply.

'But it would never work, surely he realizes that?' Rust said. 'Even if the Russian government were to give some ground, the people would never stand for it.'

'We're dealing with fanatics here, Jacques,' Graham replied. 'Zlotin, Rodenko and the group of faceless Communists back in Russia who're actually pulling the strings. All fanatics. They believe that what they're doing is right for the country and they'll stop at nothing to carry out their plans. We've seen it before. The Japanese kamikaze pilots in the Second World War. The Lebanese terrorists of the Seventies and early Eighties. The Shi'ite Muslims in Iran and Iraq. They were all prepared to die for the cause. And I believe that if they did manage to get their hands on enough weapon-grade plutonium to make a nuclear device, they'd actually go ahead and detonate it if the government failed to meet their demands. That's the level of fanaticism we're dealing with here.

'Having said that, I don't think they'd necessarily have to buy the weapons-grade plutonium and build the device from scratch,' Graham continued. 'In fact, I'd say it's quite feasible that they could get their hands on more than one nuclear device from sources inside the country.'

'I don't follow,' Sabrina said.

'I do,' Rust said, wagging a finger at Graham. 'What you're saying is that, now that the old Soviet Union's fragmented into a myriad of smaller, independent states, there are stockpiles of dormant nuclear weapons just waiting to fall into the wrong hands.'

'Rumour has it some already have,' Graham told him.

'So if the Communists were to buy several devices and strategically locate them around the country, it would give them a much stronger hand when it came to negotiating with the authorities,' Sabrina said.

'If there were to be any negotiations,' Graham said. 'What if a nuclear missile were fired deliberately from, say, Georgia into Russia? The Russians would immediately retaliate, but instead of targeting Georgia, their missile lands in neighbouring Armenia. Armenia would then retaliate. And it could go on until half a dozen warheads had been detonated across the country within a very short space of time. But the individual governments wouldn't have ordered the reprisals; those would have been carried out by rebels who already had the nuclear weapons in their possession. The individual heads of government would almost certainly be amongst the casualties – the rebels would have seen to that – and that would invariably lead to chaos and confusion across the country.'

'And from the ashes, Communism would rise again,' Rust deduced. 'It's a neat scenario, Mike, but hardly original. A case study from the pen of a KGB officer, if I'm not mistaken? Only for "Communism", read "Dissident elements within the Soviet Union". I remember reading a translated version of it when I was still with the *SDECE*. How to attack the belly of the Bear from inside the beast itself. It was a good idea in theory, but no more than that.'

'That's because you read it when Russia was still one country, not a fragmented division of little states squabbling over the spoils of independence. But it wasn't written by a KGB officer. It was written twenty years ago by a young Special Forces officer during an examination in military theses at the Lenin Komsomol Higher Airborne School in Ryazan. His name was Lieutenant Nikolai Zlotin.'

'I had no idea that was Zlotin's work,' Rust said in amazement.

'So if he's as predictable as you say he is, Mike, it's quite feasible that that may be his plan of action once the warheads are in place,' Sabrina said to Graham.

'It depends on how much influence he has with his superiors,' Graham replied. 'If he's been given a free hand to conduct the military operation, then he's likely to fall back on a plan he's confident would work. And unfortunately this particular one fits the bill perfectly.'

There was a knock at the door. Sabrina answered it and a room service waiter brought the two Continental breakfasts into the room. Rust declined her offer to order him breakfast, having already eaten on the UNACO flight from Zürich, and settled for coffee instead. She found another cup in one of the drawers and poured one for him.

'If Zlotin's been planning this operation for as long as the Russians would have us believe, then he must have made the first move to get Jannoc interested in some kind of deal which would be beneficial to both of them,' Graham said once the waiter had left the room.

'Which begs the question of how he could have known that UNACO were involved in the operation which eventually led to the death of Christian Jannoc,' Sabrina concluded.

'Exactly,' Graham agreed. 'And although it's possible that he could have found out in advance about the anti-terrorist conference here in Lisbon, how could he have known that UNACO would be attending it as well?'

'I see what you're getting at,' Rust said after a moment's thought. 'I know the Colonel's still investigating the possibility of a mole inside the organization. If he does unmask the culprit, then we should know the answer to those questions.'

'Perhaps,' Graham said without conviction.

'You think it unlikely?' Rust asked.

'It's not that, Jacques,' Graham replied. 'It's something that's been bothering me ever since I read the fax. Frankly,

I don't buy this alliance between Jannoc and Zlotin. It just doesn't ring true.'

'Go on,' Rust prompted when Graham fell silent.

'What I don't understand is why he would team up with someone like Jannoc unless he had an ulterior motive which would somehow benefit his cause. Jannoc and his ilk are anathema to Zlotin. The capitalists of the world. And in Jannoc's case, a corrupt capitalist into the bargain. It strikes me as a very uneasy alliance indeed.'

'But surely if Jannoc were going to pay him handsomely for his part in the operation, he could use that money to further the cause,' Rust said.

'We're talking weapons-grade plutonium here, Jacques. It'll cost him millions if he wants to buy enough of it to pose a serious threat to the stability of the Russian government. And I hardly think Jannoc's going to pay him *that* handsomely, do you?'

'So you think Zlotin intends to double-cross Jannoc and keep the folders once they've been decoded?' Sabrina concluded.

'It's the only way he'd benefit from it. That way he can sell the folders to the highest bidder and you can be sure there won't be a shortage of them willing to pay for revenge.'

'It's a valid point, Mike,' Rust said after some thought. 'But at the moment your only concern is to find those folders.'

'You're very optimistic that we're going to nail these bastards,' Graham said, helping himself to another cup of coffee.

'I know the consequences if we don't,' Rust replied sombrely.

'Point taken,' Graham said gruffly.

'Have you heard any more news from C.W.?' Sabrina asked, breaking the sudden silence.

'Nothing since his last call to tell me about Zlotin,' Rust replied. 'If he should try and contact me again tonight, I've told the duty officer at Zürich HQ to have him ring me here at the hotel. But he did say when we last spoke that he didn't know when he'd be able to call in again.'

The telephone rang. Graham and Sabrina exchanged glances, both with the same thought in mind, and he quickly reached out a hand to answer it.

'Is that Mr Graham?' a tentative voice asked.

'Speaking,' Graham replied suspiciously, and shook his head at Sabrina. It wasn't Whitlock. 'Who is this?'

'This is Dr de Sousa. I was asked to contact you the moment Mr Kolchinsky regained consciousness.'

'When did he come round?'

'In the last few minutes,' de Sousa replied.

'I'm on my way,' Graham told him.

'You won't be able to see him for long, you understand. He's still very weak. Ask for me when you arrive at the hospital. Dr Eduardo de Sousa.'

'Thank you, doctor,' Graham said, replacing the receiver. He turned to face the others. 'Sergei came out of his coma in the last few minutes. I'm on my way over there now.'

'I'm coming with you,' Sabrina said, getting to her feet.

'One of us needs to stay here in case something crops up,' Graham told her.

'I'll stay,' Rust offered. 'I've got a few calls to make anyway.'

'Thanks, Jacques,' Sabrina said, crossing to the door. 'I'll get my jacket from my room. I'll see you downstairs in the foyer, Mike.'

'Yeah,' Graham replied absently, then slipped the Beretta into his holster and secured it at the back of his jeans.

'Send Sergei my regards and tell him I'll drop by at the hospital later to see him,' Rust said, watching Graham pull on his leather jacket.

'Will do,' Graham replied, closing the door behind him.

Katherine Warren stifled a yawn and poured herself a coffee from the thermos flask on the seat beside her. She added the contents of a sachet of powdered milk to the coffee, then cursed under her breath when she realized there wasn't any sugar. Miller didn't take sugar; he'd prepared the coffee and sandwiches the previous night. She took a sip, wrinkled up her nose at the bitter taste, then reached for the last of the sandwiches in the plastic container on the dashboard and bit into it.

She had been sitting in the car opposite the Altis Hotel for the past two hours. It was the perfect vantage point for her to watch both the entrance to the hotel and the off-ramp leading from its car park. If Graham or Carver tried to leave the hotel, she would see them. Her only concern was to stay awake for the next three hours, at which time Miller had promised to relieve her. She'd only had a couple of hours' sleep since arriving in Lisbon the previous day. And she was beginning to feel it. But that couldn't be helped. She was determined to get her story . . .

She was still furious that they'd left the wine bar so quickly after she'd spoken to Hardin the previous evening. But, as Miller had pointed out, they had no way of knowing what was going to happen within minutes of their departure. It was scant consolation. As it was, they had gone to the rendezvous at the Santa Apolonia Station but of course Hardin hadn't showed; it was only when they'd driven to the wine bar that they had discovered what had happened. If only she'd stayed to finish her drink. Then she'd have been the first journalist on the scene of the murder, instead of having to rely on Miller to get all the relevant information from second-hand sources. It had been totally demeaning. She knew Hardin's murder was somehow related to the story she was doing on Graham and Carver. But were they involved? Somehow she doubted it. The doorman's description of the killer didn't fit Graham. It was more likely that Hardin had been silenced by the opposition. But who were the opposition? If only she could find that out, it would add further credibility to her article. It could also be extremely dangerous, but that only gave her renewed confidence in herself. She worked best under pressure when the adrenalin was pumping through her body. But she also knew the value of being discreet because, if they were dealing with UNACO, and she now believed they were, then the slightest whiff of the press would certainly see Graham and Carver on the first plane back to the States. And that would kill the story.

She poured the coffee back into the thermos flask and was busy screwing the lid back on when she noticed the white Ford Sierra emerge from the car park. Graham was driving. Sabrina sat beside him. Katherine waited until the car had passed her then, starting up the engine, pulled out into the road and tailed them at a discreet distance.

Dr de Sousa met Graham and Sabrina in the hospital's reception area, then ushered them into the lift and pressed the button for the third floor.

'How is Mr Kolchinsky?' Graham asked once the lift doors closed.

'Considering that he was on a life-support machine only twenty-four hours ago, I'd say he was doing remarkably well,' de Sousa replied. 'I must admit there were moments during the operation that we thought we might lose him. But he's obviously a fighter.'

'Yeah, he is,' Graham replied, giving Sabrina a knowing smile.

'How long will he have to stay in hospital?' Sabrina asked.

'It's still a little early to say for sure, but unless he suddenly suffers a relapse – and I'd have to say that's now highly unlikely – I'd anticipate he'd be here for another week or so.'

The doors parted and they stepped from the lift. The two armed guards, seated outside a door at the end of the corridor, immediately challenged them. De Sousa tapped the identity badge on his white jacket. Graham and Sabrina produced the Special Forces Brigade passes which Inacio had issued to them on their arrival in Lisbon. The guards resumed their seats.

'I can only allow you five minutes with Mr Kolchinsky,' de Sousa told them. 'He's still very weak. You'll be able to stay longer the next time you come.'

'Thank you, doctor,' Sabrina said, then followed Graham into the private ward.

Kolchinsky lay motionless in the bed, an intravenous drip attached to his arm. His face was pallid, his eyes closed. For an anxious moment they both thought he had lapsed back into unconsciousness but, as they neared the foot of the bed, his eyes flickered open and a weak smile touched the corners of his dry lips.

Sabrina pulled up a chair and took Kolchinsky's hand gently in hers. 'How are you feeling, Sergei?'

'I've felt better,' Kolchinsky replied softly.

'It's good to have you back with us, buddy,' Graham said. 'But I've got to tell you, you've had us all worried these last couple of days. It looked at one point as if you were negotiating a one-way ticket to Valhalla.'

'I'll go when I'm ready, Michael, not before,' Kolchinsky said, his eyes flickering to where Graham was standing behind Sabrina's chair. 'Could I have some water?'

Sabrina poured a little water into a glass from the jug on the bedside table and put the glass to his lips. He took a sip, then reached up a shaky hand and pushed the glass away from his mouth.

'I recognized one of the men who attacked us at the airport,' Kolchinsky told them.

'Nikolai Zlotin?' Sabrina said.

'Yes,' came the surprised response. 'Have you caught him?'

'Not yet,' Graham replied, but decided against elaborating on the case. There would be time for that later.

'What happened to Abe?'

'He was kidnapped by Zlotin and his cronies,' Graham said.

'We don't know where he's being held, but we're working on it.'

'And the folders?'

'Also taken,' Graham said.

'What would *spetznaz* want with the folders?' Kolchinsky asked.

'There isn't time to explain it all now, Sergei,' Sabrina said gently. 'But I promise we'll come back later and brief you in full.'

Kolchinsky suddenly squeezed Sabrina's hand. 'You've got to find Abe. He's a sick man. He won't hold out long under pressure.'

'We'll find him, Sergei,' Sabrina assured him, then eased her hand gently from his grip and stood up.

Kolchinsky closed his eyes again, seemingly exhausted by their short visit. She glanced at Graham, who indicated the door. They left the room and walked silently to the lift.

'Sergei's always maintained that he never met Zlotin while he was with the KGB,' Graham said, entering the lift and pressing the button for the ground floor. 'So how could he have been so sure it was Zlotin at the airport? According to the eyewitness reports, Zlotin and his team were wearing black stocking masks over their faces.'

'Maybe he recognized Zlotin from one of the stills we have of him on computer,' Sabrina said.

'Yeah, sure,' Graham said sarcastically. 'Would you have recognized him under a stocking mask?'

Sabrina just shrugged, stepping quickly from the lift when they reached the ground floor.

Graham grabbed Sabrina's arm. 'OK, what's going on?'

'What do you mean?' she said, her eyes instinctively flickering towards a nurse who was emerging from the adjoining lift.

'I know when you're holding out on me, Sabrina. You always avoid eye contact. What is it?'

She waited until the nurse was out of earshot before answering. 'Sergei has met Zlotin before, but not when he was with the KGB. The Colonel wanted to recruit Zlotin for UNACO. Sergei held three lengthy meetings with Zlotin in the space of a fortnight to try and convince him to come over to us, but each time Zlotin refused even to consider the idea. He wouldn't leave *spetznaz*. So Sergei returned to the US empty-handed. As far as I know, Zlotin's the only person ever to have turned down a position with UNACO.'

'Why isn't any of this mentioned in Zlotin's dossier?' Graham demanded. 'And how the hell do you know about it?'

Sabrina stared at her feet for some time before looking up at Graham again. 'Zlotin was the Colonel's initial choice to replace Jacques after he was retired from Strike Force Three. When he couldn't persuade Zlotin to leave *spetznaz*, he recruited you instead. Apart from Sergei and the Colonel, C.W. and I were the only others at UNACO who knew about the Zlotin episode. The Colonel was desperate to play it down, not only to save face, but also to spare you any embarrassment, especially as you were regarded by your former colleagues at Delta as being an expert on *spetznaz*, and on Zlotin in particular. So C.W. and I were sworn to secrecy.'

'Why didn't you tell me this before?' Graham hissed angrily.

'Because it wasn't important, that's why,' came the sharp riposte.

'Yeah, well, I can understand why the Colonel wanted Zlotin,' Graham said. 'He's the best there is.'

'I'd say that was a matter of opinion, wouldn't you?' she replied, looking directly at Graham.

The implication wasn't lost on him. 'Come on, let's go,' he said gruffly, and headed for the exit.

They walked in silence to the car and, as Graham unlocked the driver's door, he noticed the sole occupant in the Audi Quattro parked nearby. He looked away quickly and got in behind the wheel.

'Mike, what is it?' Sabrina asked when she saw the anxiety etched on Graham's face.

'Remember I told you about the reporter in New York who wanted to write an article about me?'

'You mean after the incident on the subway?' she asked.

'Yeah. Well, she's sitting in a blue Audi back there.'

'Are you sure it's her?'

'Of course I'm sure it's her!' came the indignant reply.

Sabrina's brow furrowed anxiously. 'Are you going to confront her?'

'No,' Graham replied quickly. 'That would only make things worse.'

'What do you suggest we do then?' she asked.

'We go back to the hotel as normal. Let's hear what Jacques has to say about it.'

'This is all we need!' Rust snapped irritably after Graham had told him about Katherine Warren. 'How could she possibly have known you were out here?'

'I did go straight to the UN from the subway,' Graham replied after a moment's thought. 'She could have tailed me.'

'Didn't you check?' Rust snapped.

'Of course I checked,' Graham retorted, stung by the insinuation that he hadn't followed standard UNACO procedures. 'She was probably in a cab. Christ, there are thousands of cabs on the streets of New York at that time of night. If she kept her distance, how could I possibly know she was tailing me?'

'Hey, are you two going to carry on bickering like this, or are we going to try and minimize the damage that's already been done?' Sabrina demanded, her eyes flickering between the two men.

Rust gave a resigned sigh and looked across at Graham.

'Sabrina's right. This isn't getting us anywhere. I'll call the Colonel and get his reaction. He may even decide that you're both a liability now and take you off the case, I don't know. It's entirely up to him.'

Graham helped himself to a bottle of mineral water from the mini-bar and crossed to where Sabrina was standing by the window.

'Jacques was wrong to have a go at you like that,' she said softly, glancing round at Rust who had his back to them as he spoke to Philpott on the telephone.

'We're all on edge at the moment,' Graham replied, taking a sip from the bottle. 'Hell, he may be right though. I failed to pick up on her and now we've got to deal with the situation as best we can.'

'In that case, we're both guilty,' Sabrina said, staring down into the street below. 'She obviously tailed us to the airport as well. How else could she have known that we were coming out here? And I certainly didn't notice anyone following us when we drove to the airport.'

'It's no use worrying about that now,' Graham told her. 'What's done is done. At least we know she's here and that means we can take the necessary precautions to avoid her in the future.'

'If we're still on the case after Jacques gets off the phone,' she reminded him.

'You're still on the case,' Rust said behind them. 'We have to assume the worst, which is that this Katherine Warren suspects that the two of you are with UNACO. Replacing you with another Strike Force team would only give credence to her suspicions. We mustn't let her know that we're on to her or it could blow the whole operation wide open.'

'Can't the Colonel pull some strings back home to get her off our backs?' Sabrina asked.

'That could do more harm than good right now,' Rust told her. 'If she was pulled off the story, the paper could decide to run a piece on what she'd already uncovered on the two of you. It may be nothing, but we can't afford to take that chance.'

'But the longer she's allowed a free rein, the more evidence she'll be able to accrue for her article,' Sabrina said.

'Not necessarily,' Rust replied. 'You're both listed as bona fide UN employees, Mike as an adviser on foreign policy to the US Ambassador, and you as a translator at the General Assembly. And, according to your UNACO legends, you see quite a bit of each other outside work. So even if she did observe the two of you leaving the UN together, that in itself isn't particularly suspicious. You were at the UN after receiving a telephone call to say that a mutual friend of yours, Sergei Kolchinsky, a member of UNESCO, had been shot in what appeared to have been a motiveless attack at Lisbon Airport. You flew out here to see him. That's the story we'll put out should there be any enquiries. So it's imperative that you continue to visit Sergei on a regular basis to give credibility to your cover story.'

'Warren's sure to have the hotel under surveillance,' Graham said. 'So how do we give her – or whoever's watching the hotel at the time – the slip when the need arises?'

'You can use the Sierra when you visit Sergei, and have another car parked in a side street to use when you're on official business. I'll ask Major Inacio to have one of his men deliver it as soon as possible.'

'Why not just bring in another team to head the assignment and use us as decoys?' Sabrina asked.

'We would have, had we not known that Zlotin was involved,' Rust replied. 'But Mike knows Zlotin better than anyone at UNACO, and his insight into Zlotin's character could just give us the edge when we need it most.'

'I hope I don't disappoint you, Jacques,' Graham said from the window. 'He's one of the best in the business.'

'So are you,' Rust replied. 'And that's why we need you right here. You're our only real chance of getting to Zlotin. Remember that.'

'It's ironic, isn't it?' Sabrina said, breaking the lingering silence. 'We could get the folders back intact and the organization could still be compromised if Warren were to publish an article about us.'

'I think Colonel Philpott might have something to say about that,' Rust replied, allowing himself a faint smile of satisfaction. 'He always seems to have an ace up his sleeve to deal with these kinds of situations. And, knowing him, he'll play it when they least expect it.'

At that moment Philpott didn't have an ace to deal with Katherine Warren. He'd come to realize soon after taking charge at UNACO that the use of legal action to enforce the organization's clandestine existence could be both a costly and time-consuming exercise and, with that in mind, he'd recruited four ex-FBI men whose task it was to rake up the indiscretions and, at times, illegal activities of those individuals Philpott regarded as a threat to the organization. Although they were officially listed as part of UNACO's disinformation bureau, they quickly became known amongst the field operatives as the 'Dirty Pool'. All material gathered by them was invariably backed up with sworn affidavits or, where possible, compromising photographs which would be produced whenever the organization's stability was threatened. As yet, UNACO had never been compromised. And Philpott intended to keep it that way. One of the team's main targets were the editors of influential newspapers both at home and abroad. And as the editors changed, so the team had continually to revise and update their material. They had had enough on the former editor of the *New York Sentinel* to keep him off their backs. But so far they had nothing on Larry Ryan. Philpott had called them in that morning to find something – anything – on either Ryan or Katherine Warren that could be used if the need arose. He was well aware it was Christmas Day and that all four men had families, but Rust's call had forced his hand. He had to act, fast . . .

The car turned off the Interborough Parkway in Queens,

continued for another two hundred yards, then came to a halt in front of a metal gate. The hoarding next to the gate warned ominously: UNSAFE STRUCTURES. DANGEROUS. KEEP OUT! The driver used a transmitter on the dashboard to activate the gate, and it closed automatically again behind the car. Half a mile later, they reached what appeared to be a derelict complex consisting of half a dozen buildings. The driver pulled up in front of a row of lock-up garages on the edge of the complex and, using a different frequency, activated one of the doors. He drove into the garage and the door closed again behind them. Then he programmed a code into the transmitter – the code was changed each morning – and the floor began to descend on a powerful hydraulic press until it locked into place fifty feet below ground level. They were in UNACO's Test Centre, which had been specially built underground to ensure maximum security. It housed all UNACO's ballistic, forensic and research departments; a spacious gymnasium where field operatives were obliged to spend a minimum of five hours a week practising intensive unarmed combat; and a modern, high-tech firing range where field operatives were constantly assessed on their ability to use the latest weaponry on the market.

Philpott got out of the car and the driver immediately engaged gears and drove off towards the parking bay. A tall, bald-headed figure emerged from the lift and strode purposefully towards Philpott. Major Neville Smylie, a former SAS officer who had served with distinction in Malaysia, Oman and Northern Ireland, had been head of the Test Centre since it first opened in the early Eighties. He was a dour Englishman with little time for humour, and although he wasn't particularly liked by the field operatives, they all had the greatest respect for him as a soldier. His criticisms, which were always taken seriously, had saved lives in the past. Philpott had known Smylie since Malaysia and, although he was loath to admit it, he had never really taken to the ex-SAS man either.

'Morning, Malcolm,' Smylie said in his clipped public school accent, hand extended. 'I wasn't expecting you here today.'

'I could say the same about you,' Philpott replied, shaking Smylie's hand. 'It's Christmas Day, for God's sake. Why aren't you at home with Sheila and the family?'

'I've got a few things I wanted to clear up here this morning. I told Sheila I'd be back in time to carve the turkey for lunch. What about you? What brings you over here at such short notice?'

'Business,' Philpott replied. 'It's about the attack on Abe and Sergei at Lisbon Airport two days ago.'

'How is Sergei?' Smylie asked.

'He came round early this morning. The doctors are confident that he'll make a full recovery.'

'That's wonderful news,' Smylie said without sounding very convincing.

'I didn't come over here just to tell you that,' Philpott assured him. 'There's something else I wanted to discuss.' He hesitated before continuing. 'I've always suspected that someone inside the organization tipped off the attackers about the conference in Lisbon. It's the only way they could have known that Abe was carrying sensitive folders in his attaché case.'

'And you suspect someone here in the Test Centre?' Smylie retorted in amazement.

'Yes. I've conducted a thorough investigation on my own and I'm now satisfied that I know the identity of the mole. I asked him down here this morning on the pretext of needing some information from him.'

'Who is it?' Smylie queried.

Philpott removed a folder from his attaché case and showed Smylie the name on the cover.

'I don't believe it,' Smylie said in disbelief.

'Neither did I when I first discovered who it was,' Philpott replied. 'I certainly wouldn't have come here today unless I was sure of my facts. The evidence is conclusive as far as I'm concerned.'

'I see,' came the numb reply.

'I'd like to use your office if I may?'

'Yes, of course,' Smylie replied, gesturing to the lift behind them.

They descended to the second level of the complex and stepped out into a drab concrete passage which was lined on either side by a row of unmarked metal doors. Behind each door was a soundproofed room where UNACO personnel used the latest high-tech equipment to aid them in their specialist fields in the continuing struggle against international crime. The two men walked to the door at the end of the corridor and Smylie activated it with a miniature transmitter in his pocket. They entered the room and Smylie closed the door again behind them.

Smylie's military background was self-evident by the numerous framed black-and-white photographs which lined three of the walls. All were memories of his SAS campaigns, from Korea through to Northern Ireland. The fourth wall was reserved for a sheathed sword, bearing the regimental insignia on the handle, which had been presented to him by his colleagues when he'd resigned his commission to take up the post at the Test Centre.

Philpott sat down behind the mahogany desk and dialled an internal number. He spoke briefly into the handset then replaced it and looked up at Smylie. 'Have a guard posted outside the door. I'll let you know when I'm through in here.'

'Of course,' Smylie replied, then turned on his heels and strode from the room.

Philpott closed the door then turned his attention to the folder in front of him. He still found it hard to accept that someone he'd held in such high esteem could have turned against UNACO in the way he did. Especially a head of department at the Test Centre. Professor Marcel Toure had been in charge of UNACO's ballistics department for the past three years. Philpott felt betrayed. And very angry . . .

A light began flashing above the door, indicating that someone had pressed the bell outside. Philpott looked at the monitor on the desk as a closed-circuit television camera panned the figure standing in the corridor. His fists clenched tightly on the desk at the sight of Toure, but he was quick to check his emotions and used the transmitter to activate the door.

'Morning, Malcolm,' Toure said with a cheerful smile as he entered the office. 'Compliments of the season to you.'

'Sit down,' Philpott replied, struggling to contain his anger.

Toure eased himself into the nearest armchair, the smile still in place. 'Your call was very mysterious this morning, Malcolm, but naturally I came down right away. You mentioned on the phone that you wanted some information. What is it exactly you're after?'

'What can you tell me about Emile Jannoc?' Philpott asked, his eyes riveted on Toure's face.

'Jannoc?' came the hesitant reply, the smile suddenly gone. 'Yes, I remember him now. I was called on to testify at his trial. He was up for murder. It must be a good five years ago now.'

'And your testimony was crucial in getting him acquitted, wasn't it?'

'The gun I was sent for testing wasn't the same one that was used in the murder. I despise Jannoc and his kind as much as the next person, but I was under oath. I had to tell the truth.'

'The detective leading the investigation claimed after the trial that the gun sent to you *was* the actual weapon used in the murder. He seemed to think that the gun was somehow substituted for another while it was in your care.'

'Yes, I remember that,' Toure replied with a quick shrug. 'He was desperate for a conviction and, when he didn't get it, he made this outrageous accusation against me. A police investigation subsequently exonerated me of any kind of collusion with the defence.'

Philpott removed a sheet of paper from the folder and placed it on the desk in front of Toure. 'Those are the findings of the investigation. As you say, you were exonerated of any blame. Do you remember who led the investigation?'

'No, not offhand. What is this all about, Malcolm?'

'The investigation was led by a Captain Alain Laroux of the Paris *Sûreté*,' Philpott replied, ignoring Toure's question. 'That's his signature on the document. Earlier this year Laroux was jailed for police corruption. It came out at his trial that for the last eight years he'd been taking bribes from several leading underworld figures, including Emile Jannoc.'

'I had no idea,' Toure replied, his face suddenly pale.

'I'd say that would throw considerable uncertainty on the findings of this report, wouldn't you?' Philpott said, gesturing to the paper on the desk.

'You're not suggesting that I was in league with Jannoc and Laroux?' Toure said, swallowing nervously.

Philpott took a fax from the folder and placed it beside the other sheet of paper. 'This came through late last night. It's from my opposite number in the Paris *Sûreté*. A signed confession from Laroux naming you as the person who switched the guns before Jannoc went to trial.'

'That's insane,' Toure shot back. 'He'd say anything to get his sentence reduced.'

'The police didn't make any deals with him,' Philpott replied. 'He made this statement voluntarily. But it didn't end there, did it? Jannoc had you by the short hairs and he used you several times after that to get inside information for him, didn't he?'

'I don't know what you're talking about, Malcolm,' Toure said, traces of desperation now filtering into his voice.

'I couldn't care less whether you and Laroux conspired to pervert the course of justice in France or whether you subsequently took bribes from Jannoc for favours provided,' Philpott snapped angrily. 'My only concern is with UNACCO.

You sold us out, Marcel. You told Jannoc about the conference in Lisbon, didn't you?'

'Malcolm, I don't –'

'Didn't you?' Philpott thundered, thumping his fist angrily on the desk.

Toure sat forward, his face buried in his hands.

'What really sticks in my throat is the fact that Abe Silverman was your friend. And you repaid his friendship by handing him over to Jannoc. I only hope the money was worth it.'

Toure looked up slowly, close to tears. 'I swear I didn't know this was going to happen, Malcolm. He promised me that Abe wouldn't be harmed. He said that nobody would be harmed. I was gutted when I heard what had happened in Lisbon.'

'I'm sure you were,' Philpott shot back disdainfully.

'I didn't want any part of it, Malcolm, but Jannoc threatened to expose me if I didn't do exactly as he said.' Toure raked his hands through his hair. 'I had no choice. I have a family. I had to protect them from any scandal.'

'It's a bit late for that now,' Philpott said bitterly.

'What's going to happen to me?' Toure asked, as if it were the first time he'd really contemplated the consequences of his treacherous actions.

'That depends on you. If you co-operate fully with the investigation, it would certainly be in your favour.'

'I'll co-operate,' Toure replied despondently. 'What do you want to know?'

Philpott removed a micro-cassette player from his attaché case and placed it on the desk between the two men. He switched it on. 'I'm going to ask you a few questions now. You'll be questioned in more detail later today by two senior UNACO officials here in the Test Centre. You have the right to have a lawyer present at this or any subsequent cross-examination. Do you wish to call a lawyer?'

Toure shook his head.

'Please answer the questions verbally,' Philpott said, indicating the micro-cassette player.

'I don't want a lawyer at the present time.'

'Very well. How many times have you passed information about UNACO on to Jannoc since you arrived here at the Test Centre?'

'This was the first time, I swear it.'

'When did he first contact you here at UNACO?' Philpott asked.

'I don't remember the exact date offhand, but it was within days of his brother's funeral.'

'What did he want from you?'

Toure sat forward, his eyes staring forlornly at the carpet. 'He'd found out from an informer that one of the Strike Force teams had been responsible for killing his brother. At first he wanted me to find out which of the teams was in Marseilles at the time. I told him that all information about field operatives, including their identities, was classified and known only to a handful of senior UNACO officials. As far as I know, I've never even met a field operative.'

'What did he say then?'

'It didn't make any impression on him. He wanted the names of those responsible and I was to get them for him. So in desperation I bugged Abe's office. I knew that in his line of work, he'd have to know the names of the individual members of the Strike Force teams.'

'Offices are swept for bugs every morning,' Philpott said. 'How did you secrete the bug without it being detected?'

'I had to remove it every night before I went home and replace it again the next morning after the office had been swept for devices. It was far from satisfactory, but it was the best arrangement I could come up with at such short notice.'

'And that's how you found out about the conference in Lisbon?'

Toure nodded. 'Yes. I heard Abe discussing it on several

different occasions with Sergei on his scrambled line. I passed the information on to Jannoc and he must have decided that stealing the folders was his one way of finding out who killed his brother.'

'Did he discuss the plan with you?' Philpott asked.

'All he told me was that he intended to get hold of the folders while Abe was in Lisbon, but I had no idea how he intended to get them. Had I known . . .'

'You were about to say?' Philpott prompted after Toure fell silent.

Toure shifted uncomfortably in his chair. 'I didn't know that Sergei would be shot or that Abe would be abducted. I swear I didn't know.'

'I don't buy that, Marcel,' Philpott retorted bluntly. 'It doesn't take much intelligence to realize that the folders would have been useless to Jannoc without Abe to decode them for him. Jannoc needed Abe just as much as he needed the folders.'

'I didn't mean any of this to happen, Malcolm,' Toure said softly. 'But I had no choice. You must understand that.'

'Save your pleas for the judge,' Philpott said, switching off the micro-cassette player. 'He might take a more sympathetic view.'

'You won't let any of this reach the press, will you?'

'Of course not. Any trial involving UNACO is always held in camera. You know that, you've testified at enough of them in the past.' Philpott activated the door and gestured for the guard to enter. 'Take Mr Toure to one of the interview rooms. Nobody is to see him unless authorized by either Major Smylie or myself. Is that understood?'

'Yes, sir,' came the curt reply.

Toure shrugged off the guard's arm and got to his feet. He had only taken a couple of steps towards the door when he stumbled forward and had to grab on to the nearest chair to prevent himself from losing his balance. The guard grabbed Toure's arm to steady him and, in that instant,

Toure wrenched the Heckler & Koch pistol from the guard's holster and stepped away from the door, the pistol levelled at Philpott.

'Put the gun down, Marcel,' Philpott said calmly. 'You're in enough trouble as it is. Don't make it any worse for yourself.'

Toure turned the pistol on the guard when he took a step towards him. 'I don't want to hurt either of you, but I will if you come any closer. I have the gun and that gives me the advantage, no matter how much training you've had in unarmed combat. Don't force me to kill you.'

Philpott gestured for the guard to back off. 'You know you'll never get out of here, Marcel. So why don't you just put the gun down and we'll forget this incident ever happened.'

'I want you both to walk out of here,' Toure said, his eyes flickering between the two men. 'Do it!'

Philpott picked up his cane and came round from behind the desk. 'Marcel, it's not worth –'

'Spare it, Malcolm,' Toure cut in quickly. 'There's no turning back. Not now.' He gestured to the door. 'Out. Both of you.'

Philpott nodded to the guard; the moment they emerged into the corridor the door closed behind them. Both men looked round. Toure had sealed himself inside the office.

'Get Major Smylie,' Philpott barked at the guard. 'And tell him to bring his spare transmitter.'

The guard ran to a wall-mounted telephone further down the corridor and had Smylie paged. When he returned he found Philpott staring at the door, his face grim. There was no way that either man could communicate with Toure – all the rooms in the complex were sound-proofed for added security.

When Smylie emerged from the lift he hurried over to where the two men were standing. 'What's going on?' he demanded breathlessly.

Philpott explained the situation briefly to him. Smylie glared furiously at the guard for allowing himself to be taken so easily, then handed the transmitter to Philpott and pulled the Browning from his holster.

'I've got a feeling you won't need that,' Philpott said, noticing the automatic in Smylie's hand.

'We can't take any chances,' Smylie replied, moving to the side of the door.

Philpott activated the door and Smylie swivelled round, fanning the office with the Browning. He slowly lowered the pistol. Toure had shot himself through the roof of the mouth. The bullet had penetrated his brain and exited through the back of his head, embedding itself in the blood-splattered wall behind him. Smylie already knew that Toure was dead, but went through the motions anyway to check for a pulse. He looked up slowly at Philpott and shook his head.

'Get the duty medic down here right away,' Philpott said to the guard who hurried from the room.

'Look,' Smylie said, indicating the micro-cassette player clenched in Toure's outstretched hand.

Philpott prised it from Toure's fingers. It was still running. He switched it off and spooled back the tape until he found the section where he'd finished questioning Toure. Sitting down behind the desk, he placed the micro-cassette player in front of him and listened impassively to Toure's last words.

'Malcolm, I realize just how much damage I've caused to the organization, but I swear I never knew it would come to this. I know that if I were ever to stand trial, it would only bring shame and disgrace on my family. My wife is a proud and honest woman. She would be heartbroken if she ever discovered what I'd done, especially as it was for nothing more than financial gain. And my daughter is in her last year at Columbia University. I don't want her to carry the stigma of my crimes with her for the rest of her life. That's why I've chosen this way out. Now there can be no trial. I know I've betrayed your trust, Malcolm, and you have every right to be bitter towards me, but I can only leave it to your conscience to decide whether you feel it necessary to tell my family the truth behind what happened here today. I know you'll do what you think is right.'

Moments later the sound of a shot rang out. Philpott switched off the micro-cassette player and sat back in the chair.

'Are you going to tell his wife?' Smylie asked.

'No,' Philpott replied after a moment's thought then, reaching for his cane, got to his feet and moved to the door. 'Have my driver paged, will you? I've got a feeling I've got a long day ahead of me.'

6

Whitlock was awake within seconds of the telephone ringing. He sat up in bed, switched on the bedside lamp, and lifted the receiver to his ear.

'Royce?' a voice barked.

'Yes,' Whitlock muttered, rubbing his eyes wearily. He picked up his watch from the bedside table. It was five-thirty in the morning. 'Who is this?'

'Jannoc,' came the reply. 'Get dressed. I've got a business deal that might just interest you.'

'At this time of the morning?' came the incredulous reply.

'Are you interested or not?' Jannoc snapped.

'Sure I'm interested,' Whitlock replied, now fully awake. 'What kind of deal?'

'We'll discuss it further in my office. I'll send Saisse to your room in, say, ten minutes to bring you to my office. OK?'

'Sure,' Whitlock replied.

The line went dead.

Whitlock's mind was racing. A business deal? Jannoc had obviously had him checked out and his legend had held firm. It didn't surprise him. Philpott always covered every eventuality. But what kind of deal? That intrigued him. Was Jannoc going to offer him a job in his organization? It seemed the most likely answer. Doing what? Would it allow him to gain access to Jannoc's office and plant the miniature bugs Rust had given him in Paris? It was all idle speculation, he was quick to remind himself. He wouldn't know what Jannoc had in mind until he'd actually spoken to him.

He got out of bed, took a quick shower, and had almost finished dressing when there was a knock at the door. Pulling on his sweater, he went to answer it.

'You are ready?' Saisse demanded. 'Monsieur Jannoc is waiting for you.'

Whitlock followed Saisse to a lift. There were no buttons to control it, only a slot to admit a key card. Saisse slipped the disc into the aperture and, moments later, the lift arrived. He indicated for Whitlock to enter, then stepped in after him and used the key card on a second slot inside the lift. A control board lit up. He pressed the button for the penthouse.

The doors opened on to Jannoc's personal office, but it was Zlotin who sat behind Jannoc's desk, engrossed in the contents of the fax he was reading. Jannoc sat in an armchair, a cup of coffee in one hand. Saisse pulled a Heckler & Koch P7 automatic from his shoulder holster as Whitlock stepped into the room, using it to indicate a wooden chair in the middle of the room.

'What the hell's going on?' Whitlock demanded, looking towards Jannoc for an explanation.

'Sit down,' Jannoc replied, gesturing towards the chair with his free hand.

Whitlock fought back a wave of anxiety that swept over him as he crossed to the chair and sat down. Had his cover been blown? If it had, why hadn't they just descended on the bedroom while he was still asleep? Why go to the trouble of waking him and having him brought to Jannoc's office? No, the more he thought about it, the less likely it seemed. UNACO were probably the best in their field when it came to providing legends for their operatives. Nothing was ever left to chance. He decided his best bet was to go on the offensive. Not only would it be in character for Royce, but it would also help to mask his own uncertainty of the events unfolding around him. 'I want to know what's going on here. Christ, I'm hauled out of my bed at five-thirty in the morning on the pretext of discussing some business deal, and when I get here I have a gun waved at me and I'm ordered to sit in the middle of the room like some criminal under interrogation. What the hell's going on?'

Zlotin looked up slowly at Whitlock. 'You told Jannoc on the phone that you were interested in the business deal he intends putting to you. Am I right?'

'I'm always interested in business deals, especially if they pay well,' Whitlock shot back.

'I'm sure you'll find the remuneration more than generous, even for someone like you,' Zlotin replied disdainfully. 'But before we do take you on, we need to be sure you are who you claim to be.'

'What are you talking about? I'm Frank Royce. Who the hell do you think I am?'

'As I said, we have to check out your credentials. That's why Jannoc and I made separate enquiries about you last night. Jannoc has a contact in Africa, I have a contact in Russia.' Zlotin tapped the two faxes on the table in front of him. 'The details came through earlier this morning.'

'And?' Whitlock challenged. 'Did I check out to your satisfaction?'

'Frank Royce certainly exists, there's no doubt of that,' Zlotin replied. 'Both faxes contained roughly the same information on him. But then that kind of information isn't hard to come by. What I was really after was a photograph, one that's been authenticated by a reliable source. That's the only way I'll be convinced you are Royce.'

'If your contacts did their homework properly, then you'd already know I don't pose for the camera. I've always kept a low profile. I've found it helps me to stay alive that little bit longer.'

'There is a photograph,' Zlotin told him, the satisfaction evident in his voice. 'I was hoping it would have been sent

117

through by the time you got here, but we're still waiting for it.'

Whitlock's eyes narrowed uncertainly. 'Where did it come from?'

'It was found in the military archives at Ryazan.'

Ryazan? Home of the *spetznaz* military academy. How did a photograph of Royce turn up there?

'You look puzzled,' Zlotin said, watching Whitlock carefully. 'But if you are Royce, you'll have nothing to worry about, will you?'

'I'm worried all right,' Whitlock retorted, knowing his only chance now was to improvise. 'I told you, I don't pose for the camera. And to the best of my knowledge the only photograph of me in existence is the one taken when I joined up with the British Army. So how the hell did that come to fall into Russian hands?'

'It's not your army photograph,' Zlotin replied. 'All I know is that it was supposedly taken somewhere in Africa. The details will be faxed through with the photograph.'

Well, at least it wasn't the army photograph. That was some consolation. He'd never have been able to talk his way out of that. But if it were a photo taken somewhere in Africa, he could try and wing it for a while by insisting that it was obviously a case of mistaken identity. Not that he expected Zlotin to believe him, but at least it would give him a few extra seconds to extricate himself from the net that seemed to be tightening around him. Saisse was the closest to him. And his weapon was drawn. If he could get to Saisse and disarm him . . .

'You can leave now if you want,' Jannoc said, entering the conversation for the first time. 'Nobody will stop you. There's a freighter bound for Algiers later this afternoon. All I need to do is pick up the phone and you'll have your passage to Africa. It's entirely up to you.'

Whitlock knew if he walked out now it would be tantamount to admitting that he wasn't Royce. He'd never leave the room alive. And even if he were allowed to leave, what use would he be to UNACO on a freighter bound for Algiers? No, he'd have to take his chances. 'What if I'm not in this photo?' he demanded, going back on to the offensive again, knowing his bravado was all he had left going for him.

'Then we'd just have to find out who you really were, wouldn't we?' Zlotin replied, reaching for the cup of coffee at his elbow.

'You save some kid's life and this is the thanks you get for it,' Whitlock said, shaking his head to himself. 'Christ, I wish I'd never come to Marseilles now.'

'As I said to you before, if you are Royce you've nothing to worry about,' Zlotin assured him.

'And as I keep telling you, I don't pose for the camera. So if some snap-happy war correspondent's taken a photo of someone else and mistakenly attributed it to me, then I'm going to have a hell of a job trying to explain my way out of it. That's hardly fair, is it?'

'You can still leave,' Saisse said, gesturing to the lift.

You'd like that, wouldn't you? Whitlock had sensed from the outset that not only did Saisse dislike him, he also didn't trust him one little bit. And he knew Saisse would like nothing better than to put a bullet in him as soon as his back was turned. All he needed was Jannoc's consent . . .

'I'll take my chances,' Whitlock replied, holding Saisse's cold stare. 'I've got a feeling the money could be pretty good around here after all this has been sorted out. It had better be, or you can be sure I'll be taking that freighter to Algiers.'

Zlotin swivelled his chair round when the fax machine started up behind him. Whitlock felt a drop of sweat seep out from under his hairline and trickle down the side of his face. He glanced up at Saisse who was leaning against the desk, the automatic held loosely in his hands in front of him. Saisse never took his eyes off him. Whitlock tensed himself, ready to spring at Saisse if the need arose . . .

Zlotin picked up the faxed copy of the photograph, studied it at length, then dropped it on to the desk in front of Whitlock who slowly, almost reluctantly, looked down at it. His first reaction was that of surprise. Then he had the sudden desire to laugh out loud as the relief flooded over him. The photograph depicted him sitting against a rock with the members of Strike Force Nine. It had been taken by Sabrina when the two units had been on manoeuvres at UNACO's secret camp in the backwoods of Pennsylvania. He remembered it well. Graham had sprained his ankle in a bad fall earlier in the day, and he'd been laid up at base camp while the others had continued the exercise without him. What was most remarkable was the condition of the original photograph. It was dog-eared and creased as if it had been carried in a wallet for some length of time. It had all the trademarks of Philpott's handiwork. Obviously Philpott had assumed that Zlotin would check up on him and had the photograph planted in the archives as a precaution. But how had he managed it at such short notice?

'You look surprised,' Zlotin said, watching him carefully.

'I am,' Whitlock replied truthfully. 'I'd forgotten all about this until now. It sure takes me back.'

'According to the accompanying text, the names of your three colleagues are printed on the back of the photograph. Who are they?'

Whitlock had to think fast. Was Zlotin calling his bluff or had their names been written on the back of the photograph to add authenticity to his cover? And if so, what names? The real names of his colleagues in Strike Force Nine? Or aliases that all field operatives were given for undercover work? But each operative had three aliases, together with passports in those names. And he certainly didn't know all the aliases used by Strike Force Nine. No, it had to be their real names. Or did it? There was only one way to find out . . .

'That's Simon Houchen, Dietmar Reuter and Johnny Ellis,' Whitlock announced, pointing to each face in turn.

Zlotin's face remained impassive as he got to his feet and crossed to the lift. He paused and looked round at Whitlock. 'Jannoc will brief you on the terms of the deal. If you're in, we leave in an hour. Just make sure you're ready.'

Jannoc waited until Zlotin had followed Saisse from the room then moved to the desk and sat down. He glanced at the copy of the photograph, nodded to himself, then placed it to one side. 'The terms of the deal are very simple. You'll be paid thirty thousand pounds to work on an assignment with the Russian. Half up front, the balance once you've completed the operation. It shouldn't take any more than four or five days at the most. You'll be directly under his command and you'll be expected to carry out his orders without question. As an experienced soldier, you shouldn't have any difficulty with that. The assignment will be on a need-to-know basis and the Russian will brief you later on what he feels you should know.'

Whitlock's face gave away nothing, but behind the disciplined mask he could barely contain his excitement. The most he had dared to hope for was some kind of work at the club. That way he could have kept tabs on Jannoc. Now, out of nothing, he had the chance to get himself into the very heart of the operation. Finally, a break. And how they needed it! But it was essential to remain in character and that meant he had to think and act like Royce. After several seconds he stood up, dug his hands into his pocket, and paced the room as if in deep thought. He finally looked at Jannoc again. 'I need to know more than you've told me before I can come to a decision.'

'Those are the terms, Royce. If you don't like them, there's always that freighter bound for Algiers later today. It's entirely up to you.'

Whitlock realized he was now treading a very fine line indeed. Royce would naturally be suspicious of such vague terms, but at the same time he could ill-afford to hold out for too long for fear of losing out altogether. He had to know when to give in. 'Who is this Russian? I don't even know his name.'

'And it'll remain that way unless he chooses to tell you,' Jannoc retorted.

'How can you expect me to give you an answer without knowing anything about the operation? Granted, thirty grand is a hell of a lot of money, but I've got to know what I'm supposed to do for it. You'd want to know more if you were in my shoes, wouldn't you?'

'You'll be part of a team guarding some prisoners. That's all I can tell you.'

'Where?' Whitlock pressed.

'Don't push your luck, Royce. I can always find someone else to go in your place. Now, are you in or out?'

'Count me in,' Whitlock replied at length. 'I've put my life on the line for a lot less than that before.'

Jannoc removed a sealed envelope from his pocket and tossed it on to the desk. 'Fifteen thousand up front, as agreed.'

Whitlock slit open the envelope and checked the money. 'You could have drafted in one of your own men to work with the Russian and it wouldn't have cost you a penny. So why offer it to me?'

'Because I think you're the best man for the job. I had you checked out last night. You've got a good record as a professional soldier in Africa. Not only that, you've also seen more action than any of the men I've got working for me. That certainly swung it in your favour. As they say, there's no substitute for experience.'

'I hope I won't disappoint you,' Whitlock said, pocketing the envelope.

'So do I, for your sake.'

'What's that supposed to mean?' Whitlock replied suspiciously.

'The Russian's not as convinced about you as I am, but as I'm the one calling the shots, he's had to go along with my judgement. If you carry out his orders to the letter, you'll have no trouble from him. Cross him, and he'll kill you.'

'Now you tell me,' Whitlock retorted.

'You're a professional soldier, Royce, you know how to take orders. Just make sure you do as he says, and you'll be thirty grand richer by the end of the week.'

Whitlock pondered Jannoc's words then managed a wry smile. 'Yeah, I think I can manage that.'

'I'm sure you can,' Jannoc replied, reaching for the telephone to call Saisse and have him escort Whitlock back to his room.

Whitlock waited for several minutes after Saisse had left, then opened the door of his room and peered cautiously into the corridor. It was deserted. He slipped out, closing the door silently behind him, and moved to the stairs. It was imperative that he contact Rust to brief him on the latest developments; there was no knowing when he'd get another chance. He made for the payphone near the first-floor bar where Saisse had taken him the previous evening. The bar was closed and the adjoining corridor deserted. Pausing to look around him again, he lifted the receiver and dialled the number of UNACO's European headquarters in Zurich but was told by the duty officer that he could contact Rust in Lisbon. Whitlock, who was already running low on coins, gave the duty officer the number of the payphone and asked him to have Rust call him back as soon as possible. He didn't have long to wait for Rust's call and was quick to outline what had happened in Jannoc's office that morning.

'And you're certain he used the term "prisoners"? Plural?' Rust asked once Whitlock had finished talking.

'I'm certain.'

There was a thoughtful pause on the other end of the line. 'If it is their intention to bring in another cryptologist,

123

or more than one for that matter, it implies that something could already have happened to Abe,' Rust concluded at length.

'That had crossed my mind,' Whitlock agreed. 'Look, Jacques, I've got to go. I'm risking my neck as it is by calling you from here. I don't know when I'll next be able to call. It'll all depend on circumstances.'

'I understand. Take care, *mon ami*.'

'You can count on it.'

Whitlock replaced the receiver and made his way back to his room. He opened the door and found Saisse standing by the window, looking out over the Old Port.

'Where have you been?' Saisse demanded, turning away from the window.

'I went for a walk,' Whitlock shot back, knowing he would have to go straight on to the offensive if he was going to talk his way out of this one. 'What's it got to do with you anyway?'

'I told you not to leave your room,' Saisse snapped.

'Correction, you told me not to leave the club,' Whitlock was quick to point out. 'And I made sure I didn't. Satisfied?'

'You are very sure of yourself,' Saisse said, standing face to face with Whitlock. 'Over-confidence can be a dangerous weakness.'

'I'll bear it in mind,' Whitlock retorted icily. 'Now if you've quite finished spying on me, I'm sure you can find your way out by yourself.'

'You may have won over Monsieur Jannoc, but there is still something about you that I do not trust. I cannot put my finger on it yet, but when I do the Russian will be the first to know.' Saisse smiled coldly as he opened the door. 'I am sure you will bear it in mind, *Mister* Royce.'

Whitlock sunk on to the bed after Saisse had left the room and exhaled deeply, his eyes riveted on the door. He knew UNACO had done everything possible to ensure his legend was impenetrable. But if Saisse decided to dig deep enough, there was always the chance he'd uncover something to discredit the legend. It had happened to other field operatives in the past. He knew the risks of undercover work. They all did. But it was scant consolation if you were exposed. How many times had Carmen begged him to get out of the field before something happened to him? Was she right; was he pushing his luck that little bit further every time he undertook another assignment? He'd always maintained that you made your own luck in any given situation. Luck which could continue indefinitely, or run out at any time.

Was his luck about to run out?

'That's brilliant news,' Sabrina exclaimed excitedly after Rust had explained about Whitlock's latest call from Marseilles. 'But how did the Colonel manage to place the photograph in the *spetznaz* archives at such short notice?'

'We've had a man in *spetznaz* for the last six years now. A senior officer known only to the Colonel, Sergei and myself. Not only was he able to plant the photograph in the archives last night, he also had the necessary authorization code to backdate it on the computer to make it look as if the entry had been made around the time the photograph was supposed to have been taken. There's no way Zlotin's contact could have known that it was a plant.'

Sabrina looked across at Graham who was standing by the window, staring pensively down into the street below. 'What's on your mind, Mike?'

'Zlotin's obviously in trouble.' Graham said at length.

'Why do you say that?' Rust asked when Graham didn't venture an explanation.

'It's always been one of Zlotin's principles to work only with those who've gained his trust. And believe me, it takes one hell of a lot to win him over. As I'm sure you already know, he had his own élite commando unit within *spetznaz*, and those he recruited were carefully monitored for months in advance, either by himself or by one of his senior officers, before being offered a position in his unit. That's why it seems to be totally out of character for him to have recruited someone he only met last night. And that can only mean one thing. Something's obviously happened to force him to make some changes at the last possible moment. The clue could be in what Jannoc said to C.W. about him having to guard some prisoners. It's my guess that Abe Silverman's dead. We knew it could happen if he didn't get his medication in time. Now Zlotin has to draft in a replacement – perhaps even more than one, which would account for Jannoc's use of the term "prisoners" – if his plan is to have any chance of succeeding.'

'But those folders were in Abe's own personal code,' Rust was quick to point out. 'Nobody else knew how to break his code. That was the whole point of the exercise.'

'Leaving Zlotin to improvise as best he can.'

'Of course,' Sabrina said, snapping her fingers. 'He'll bring in someone who thinks like Abe. Someone who's worked with him.'

'Or someone who's been taught by him.' Graham added. 'It's my guess he'll bring in two, maybe three, of the world's foremost cryptologists to try and break the code. And he'll only concentrate on those who've either worked with, or been taught by, Abe Silverman.'

'You could be on to something here, Mike,' Rust said after a moment's thought. 'I'll get on to the Colonel right away and have the Command Centre come up with a short-list of names for us to work on. In the meantime you two have got a little errand to carry out.'

'What?' Graham replied suspiciously.

'When I rang the Colonel to tell him about C.W., he felt it would be in our best interests now to bug Caldere's office at the wine bar. If Zlotin or any of his cronies do try and contact Caldere, it may be our only source of information if C.W. has no way of contacting us again once he teams up with the Russians.'

126

'But won't the place still be swarming with cops?' Graham asked.

'I spoke to Major Inacio a short time ago, and he told me that the forensic team finished their work in the alley earlier this morning. The alley is still cordoned off and there's a policeman on duty there.'

'OK, so how the hell are we supposed to get into the building without being seen?' Graham demanded.

Rust took a set of keys from his pocket and handed them to Graham. 'The Special Forces Brigade found these in Hardin's flat last night before the local police got there. They're duplicate keys for the wine bar. One of the keys will open the one door which is out of sight of the alley where Hardin was killed. It's the only way you'll be able to enter the building without being seen.'

'It's very risky, Jacques,' Sabrina said.

'Not if you're not seen, it isn't.' Rust removed a couple of two-way radios from his attaché case and handed them to Graham. 'One of you will have to act as a look-out while the other goes into the bar. I don't foresee any difficulties, but should anything crop up, I want you both to pull out straightaway. There's to be no confrontation with the local police. Is that understood?'

'Sure,' Graham replied. 'So what will we be using to bug Caldere's office?'

'One of our standard CG-11s,' Rust replied, handing the miniature listening device to Graham. It was no bigger than a match-head and was sealed in plastic wrapping.

'What about bugging the phone?' Graham asked, pocketing the device.

'The Special Forces Brigade will deal with that later today,' Rust told him. 'They can run a tap on the line from outside the building. As I said, it's unlikely that Zlotin would try and get in touch with Caldere over the phone, but we still have to be prepared for any eventuality.'

'So why don't the Special Forces Brigade bug the office

as well?' Sabrina asked. 'If there was any trouble with the local cops, they could pull rank and that would be an end to it.'

'The Colonel wants Caldere's office searched and we'd both feel better if one of you were to check it out rather than leaving it to the Special Forces Brigade. As you already know, we're taking a battering at the UN right now as it is over the lost folders, so if we were to find something that was instrumental in solving the case, it would certainly be in our favour when it came to answering our critics.'

'Who'll monitor the bug once it's in place?' Graham asked.

'The Special Forces Brigade. They'll report directly to Major Inacio and he'll pass any relevant information on to me.'

'So where is Caldere at the moment?' Sabrina asked.

'At home with his family. He's not due to open the bar again until later this afternoon. So that gives you plenty of time to check the place out.' Rust watched them cross to the door. 'And remember what I said. No confrontation with the local police. Get out the moment there's any hint of trouble.'

They returned to their own rooms, picked up their Berettas and shoulder holsters, and met up again in the foyer. They exited through a side door and made their way to where a blue VW Passat had been left for them in one of the streets at the back of the hotel by a member of the Special Forces Brigade earlier in the morning. Sabrina took the keys from her pocket and climbed behind the wheel. Graham looked around slowly and, satisfied that they hadn't been followed, got in beside her. Using a detailed map of the streets immediately surrounding the hotel, they were able to double-back on to the main road without being seen from the front of the hotel. Sabrina drove to the Old Town and parked within sight of the wine bar.

'There's the cop,' Graham said, indicating the uniformed policeman who was standing in front of the official police cordon which still sealed off the alley. 'Hell, he's just a rookie. He can't be much more than twenty.'

'I bet he's thinking of all the other places he'd rather be on Christmas morning,' Sabrina said with a smile.

'You just make sure you keep your eye on him,' Graham said, reaching for the door handle. 'And call me if he decides to go walkabout.'

'And where do you think you're going?' Sabrina asked.

'That's a dumb question,' Graham shot back.

'Not if you're thinking of going into the wine bar, it isn't. Jacques wants Caldere's office searched, doesn't he?'

'Yeah. So?'

'Since when could you read Portuguese?' she said, her eyebrows raised questioningly. 'Because everything in Caldere's office is going to be in Portuguese, isn't it?'

Graham cursed angrily under his breath and slumped back in his seat. Then, taking the keys and the sealed CG-11 from his pocket, he handed them to Sabrina. 'We need to maintain radio contact with each other. It's best if you initiate the calls. Say every five minutes just to make sure everything's going according to plan.'

'Agreed.'

'Good luck,' Graham called out after her as she climbed out of the car.

She crossed the road and, glancing towards the policeman, allowed herself a faint smile of satisfaction when she noticed him absently scuffing the ground in front of him with the toe of his boot. With her baggy clothes, her hair piled up under a peaked cap and a minimal application of make-up, she wasn't attracting the normal lascivious glances she was used to getting from members of the opposite sex. Her little ploy had worked. Slipping unnoticed around the side of the wine bar, she found herself in a narrow alleyway. It was deserted. Pausing to slip on a pair of leather gloves, she took the keys from her pocket and checked the type of lock on the door. It could be any one of half a dozen keys on the bunch. Inserting the first key, she tried to turn it. Nothing. She tried the second and third with the same result. The fourth didn't even fit into the keyway. The fifth key turned out to be the right one. Easing open the door she slipped inside, quickly closing it again behind her. She found herself in a carpeted passage leading to a pair of swing doors that wouldn't have been out of place in a Wild West saloon. The doors opened on to the games room. But she knew that already, having seen a hastily sketched layout of the premises which had been left in the car for them. Taking the sketch from her pocket, she found her bearings and, entering the games room, made for a flight of stairs on the opposite side of the room. Reaching the top of the stairs she moved carefully down the hallway until she found a wooden door with the words *Luis Caldere – Gerente*, written on it in gold lettering. Again she had to try several different keys before finding the one to open the door.

If Caldere's desk was anything to go by, the man didn't regard neatness as a particular priority in life. Files and folders, interspersed with loose memos and invoices, were strewn haphazardly across the desk. The remains of a half-eaten slice of pizza had been dumped beside the overflowing ashtray, and a chipped coffee cup stood precariously on the edge of the desk. Her eyes went to a framed photograph in the centre of the wall behind the desk. It depicted a grinning Caldere with his arm around some bemused man in a tuxedo. She took the CG-11 listening device from her pocket and carefully removed it from its plastic wrapper. Then, after replacing the wrapper in her pocket, she looked slowly around the room, deciding on the best place to conceal the bug. She discounted several possibilities, including the pen stand and the artificial plant on the filing cabinet behind the desk, and finally chose to secrete it inside one of the plugs which lined the wall to the right of the desk. She took a Swiss Army knife from her pocket and, crouching down beside the plugs, eased the nearest one from its socket. It took her less than a minute to open the plug, fit the tiny device inside, and close it again.

Moving to the desk, she began to sift through the loose papers, careful to leave them exactly as she'd found them. Reaching the bottom of the pile, she found that they'd been dumped on top of an open diary. She bit her lip as she eased the diary out gently from underneath the invoices, then scanned the scrawled handwriting hoping to discover something which could be beneficial to the case. Most entries seemed to be appointments – a name with a time bracketed behind it. Several of the names cropped up regularly. All were Portuguese names. She assumed they were either reps or fellow club owners but, taking no chances, she photographed each of the pages in turn with the miniature camera which was standard issue for every field operative. She'd reached the last fortnight in the diary when she found a single name scrawled diagonally across the page with what she assumed to be a telephone number beneath it. The name was unmistakable. *Berger*. She quickly photographed the page then turned to the next page. Again Berger's name appeared, this time with the word *meio-dia*, midday, in brackets behind it. It had to be an appointment. Nothing for the next three days. Then, on the following page, was written *Saisse – Aeroporto 4.45 P.M.* A telephone number was written in brackets underneath it. She photographed the page. There were two more references to Berger, both with *meio-dia* in brackets after the name, and one further reference to Saisse which was accompanied by the same telephone number as before. She placed the diary carefully on the desk and contacted Graham on the two-way radio.

'Have you planted the bug?' Graham asked.

'Yes. I've also found his diary.'

'And?' Graham prompted.

'It contains references to Saisse and Berger. I've already photographed the relevant pages. I'll go through the desk next. Any activity out there?'

'Nothing,' Graham replied. 'The kid hasn't moved since you left. How long do you think you'll be in there?'

'It's hard to say,' she replied. 'It just depends if I find anything worth further investigation.'

'OK, but keep me posted. Over and out.'

Sabrina replaced the diary exactly where she'd found it, then searched through the drawers of the desk. There was nothing of any significance in any of them. Then, taking out each of the drawers in turn, she checked to see if anything had been taped underneath them. Again she drew a blank. Moving to the metal filing cabinet in the corner of the room, she found that the first two drawers contained bundles of dog-eared invoices secured with elastic bands. The bottom drawer, however, was locked. She checked Hardin's keys and found one that slotted into the keyway. Unlocking the drawer, she pulled it open. Her eyes instinctively went to the automatic pistol which lay on top of a battered journal. The magazine was already in the breech. Moving the pistol to one side, she lifted out the journal and leafed through it slowly. Inside were figures detailing the takings for each day over the past three months. That was of no use to her. She sifted through a pile of folders. They, too, were work-related. Then, lifting the bottom folder, she found a small red book which had been wedged underneath it. Inside were dozens of names, the majority of which were accompanied by an address and a telephone number.

'Sabrina, come in. Over,' Graham's anxious voice suddenly came over the radio.

She immediately unclipped the radio from her belt. 'What is it, Mike?'

'Trouble,' came the reply. 'The kid's just had a call over his radio and now he's making his way towards the door you used to get into the joint. It's time to get out of there.'

'I've just found Caldere's address book. I need time to photograph it.'

'Forget it,' came the terse response. 'If the cops have been

132

tipped off that there might be someone inside the building, they're going to be down here in no time at all after what happened to Hardin last night. Remember what Jacques said, we're not to get involved with the local cops. Now get the hell out of there.'

'Where's the cop now?' she asked, locking the drawer again behind her.

'He's standing within sight of the door. It's my guess he's waiting for the back-up to arrive. And from where he's standing he seems to have all the possible exits covered. You're going to have to leave through one of the doors on the other side of the building. I'll try and distract his attention long enough for you to slip out of the alleyway unnoticed. I'll pick you up on the next block.'

'Understood,' she replied.

'Call me once you're in place.'

'Roger, will do. Over and out.' She clipped the radio back on to her belt and looked from the address book in her hand to the closed drawer in front of her. 'What the hell,' she said to herself, and slipped the book into her pocket. Getting to her feet, she checked that she'd left the office exactly as she'd found it, then hurried out into the corridor, locking the door again behind her. Consulting the layout diagram again, she made her way back down the stairs into the games room but, instead of retracing her steps out into the corridor, she scrambled nimbly over the bar counter and through a door which led into a small kitchen. There were two possible exits. The door to the left led into the main bar room where she and Graham had first encountered Hardin and Caldere. The other door led out into the alleyway where Hardin had ultimately met his death. She moved to the second door. Although it had double bolts on the inside, both had been left unlocked to allow the police access to the building the previous night. She unclipped her radio and put it to her lips. 'Come in, Mike. Over.'

'You in place?' came the response.

'Yes. Is the cop still standing by the other door?'

'Yeah. He's not going anywhere. Give me thirty seconds then get the hell out of there.'

'Roger, will do. Over and out.'

Graham took a map of the city from the glove compartment, then climbed out of the car and crossed the street to where the policeman was standing. 'Excuse me,' he called out. 'Do you speak English?'

'Yes, I do,' came the hesitant reply.

'That's a relief,' Graham replied with a grin. 'I seem to be hopelessly lost. I need to get to the Altis Hotel. Can you help me?' He noticed the policeman's eyes flicker the length of the street. 'I am in a bit of a hurry. It's only that I got into Lisbon this morning and I was supposed to meet my wife and my son at the hotel an hour ago. I don't even have the number to call them. I'd really appreciate it if you could show me on the map the quickest way to get to the hotel.'

The policeman reluctantly took the map from Graham and opened it out.

'Thanks,' Graham said, purposely turning away from the alley. 'The thing is, I've got all the Christmas presents in the trunk. I brought them up from New York. My boy's only five. He hasn't had any presents yet and look at the time already. My wife's going to kill me, she really is.'

'We are here,' the policeman said, pointing out the road on the map. Tracing his finger across the map, he found the location of the hotel. 'The hotel is there.'

'You're joking,' Graham shot back, feigning a look of horror. 'I'm miles away. How the hell did I manage to end up here? Which is the quickest way to get there?'

A movement caught the policeman's eye and he swung round, already reaching for his holstered revolver as Sabrina emerged from the alleyway. '*Parar!*' he snapped, ordering her to stop.

She froze at the sight of the revolver levelled at her. Her

eyes instinctively went to Graham, who found himself in a dilemma. If he disarmed the policeman, it would only complicate matters even further. But if Sabrina were arrested, Rust and Inacio would need to do a lot of explaining to get her off a charge of breaking and entering.

Suddenly a car screeched to a halt beside Sabrina and two men jumped out. Both wore lightweight suits and were armed with Heckler & Koch automatics. The policeman hurried forward to confront them. Graham watched apprehensively as one of the men extended an ID card towards the policeman, who immediately came to attention and saluted him. The second man pushed Sabrina up against the car, removed the Beretta from her shoulder holster, then took a pair of handcuffs from his pocket and, twisting her arms behind her back, snapped them over her wrists. He opened the back door and gestured for her to get into the car. Once she was inside, he climbed in beside her and the door was closed behind them. The first man took the young policeman to one side, spoke softly to him, then got behind the wheel and started up the engine again.

Graham quickly returned to his car. Who were the two men? Plain-clothes cops? Now what was he supposed to do? Rust had specifically impressed upon them not to get involved with the local police, so under the circumstances there was nothing Graham could have done to have prevented Sabrina's arrest. All he could do now was tail them and report back to Rust once they reached their destination.

The car pulled away from the wine bar. Graham went in pursuit, but was careful to remain at a safe distance to avoid any unnecessary complications to an already convoluted situation. Once out of sight of the wine bar, the car turned off the road and disappeared through a gate leading on to a deserted building site. Graham's heart began to pound. If they were plain-clothes cops, why had they gone in there? And if they weren't, who were they? He knew Sabrina's life could be in danger. He had to get to her, fast.

Parking the car, he jumped out and made his way cautiously towards the wooden fence surrounding the building site. Then, easing the Beretta from his shoulder holster, he hurried towards the gate, his body doubled over to prevent him being seen from the other side of the fence. On reaching the gate he swivelled round, the Beretta extended in both hands to fan the area in front of him.

The car was parked fifty yards from where he stood, the driver seated behind the wheel. Sabrina, who was still handcuffed, stood beside the car. The second man stood directly behind her. All three had their backs to Graham. The man slipped his hand into his pocket and withdrew Sabrina's Beretta, then reached out his other hand towards Sabrina's manacled wrists.

'Drop the gun!' Graham commanded, the Beretta now trained directly on the man's back. 'Drop it and step away from her. Do it now.'

The man glanced over his shoulder then tossed the Beretta on to the ground before slowly raising his hands above his head.

'Who are you?' Graham demanded.

'Captain Morales, Special Forces Brigade,' came the reply. 'I was about to remove your partner's handcuffs when you arrived. As you can see, I already have the key in my hand.'

Graham and Sabrina exchanged suspicious glances.

'Put the key on the hood of the car,' Graham ordered. 'And you, in the car. Get out slowly with your hands where I can see them.'

The driver got out of the car, his hands held away from his body. 'I can assure you that we are with the Special Forces Brigade. We both have ID on us. In our pockets.'

'You just keep your hands where I can see them,' Graham said, picking up the key and unlocking the handcuffs.

Sabrina retrieved her automatic. 'Let's see your ID. Both of you. Take them out slowly and place them on the hood of the car. Very slowly.'

The two men gingerly removed their ID cards and placed them on the hood. Sabrina studied them both and, satisfied that they were genuine, slipped the automatic back into her shoulder holster. 'Sorry about that, but you could have saved yourselves all that trouble if you'd shown me these in the car.'

'Our main priority was to get you away from the wine bar as quickly as possible,' Morales replied, pocketing his ID card again. 'We intended to identify ourselves after we'd removed the handcuffs and returned your gun to you.'

'How did you know I was in there?' Sabrina asked.

'All police calls are monitored from our headquarters,' Morales replied. 'It's standard procedure. As I'm sure it is in your organization as well. The police received a call from a resident in a block of flats overlooking the wine bar who claimed to have seen an intruder entering the building. Fortunately, Major Inacio had already been informed by one of your superiors that you were going in to plant a bug and check out the place for clues. It was then just a question of intercepting you before the local police got there. That's why we had to get you away as quickly as possible. The police will be there by now, but once Major Inacio has contacted his opposite number in the CID, they will be called off. Caldere will never know that any of this ever happened.'

'How did you manage to get there so quickly?' Graham asked suspiciously.

'We were only parked at the end of the street. As you know, we've had the wine bar under constant surveillance for the past two days. So if this Russian, or any of his men, should try to make contact with Caldere, we'll know about it straight away and be able to react accordingly.'

'And what exactly does "react accordingly" mean?' Graham asked.

Morales shrugged. 'That would be for Major Inacio to decide.'

'No, it wouldn't,' Graham shot back. 'It would be for us to decide. This is our case, not yours. We call the shots. You'd do well to remember that.'

'You are in our country,' the other man retorted behind Morales. 'You'd do well to remember that.'

Morales snapped angrily at the man in Portuguese then gave Graham a conciliatory smile. 'We realize that this is your case. All I meant was that Major Inacio, in consultation with your superiors, would advise us on what to do. That's all.' He turned to Sabrina. 'Did you find anything of any importance in the wine bar?'

'I didn't get the chance to have a proper look,' Sabrina replied. 'But I did manage to check through his diary. It contained references to both Berger and Saisse, two of Jannoc's men. I've photographed the relevant details. Naturally we'll forward a copy of the film on to Major Inacio once it's been developed.'

'We'd appreciate that. Well, if you'll excuse us, we must get back to the wine bar. Our shift doesn't end until later this afternoon.'

'Thanks for bailing me out back there,' Sabrina said, shaking Morales' extended hand.

'Not at all,' Morales replied then, nodding in Graham's direction, returned to the car. Moments later the engine coughed into life and the car arced in a semi-circle before disappearing out through the gate.

'Nice move, Sabrina,' Graham snapped, turning on her. 'The diary was all we had to go on. Couldn't you have at least waited until the film had been checked by one of our lab teams before shouting your mouth off about it? We don't need to offer the Special Forces Brigade everything we find. They're only our contacts here in Portugal, not our partners. Try and remember that next time.'

'No, it isn't all we've got to go on!' Sabrina retorted sharply, pulling the address book from her pocket. 'This should throw up far more information about Caldere's contacts than the diary ever could, so perhaps you'd better hang on to it just in case I get the sudden urge to hand it over to the Special Forces Brigade as well. Go on, take it. Take it.'

Graham stared at the book in Sabrina's extended hand, then sighed deeply and sat down on a pile of bricks behind him. 'I'm sorry, I didn't mean to go off at you like that. It wasn't called for.'

She sat down beside him. 'We're all on edge at the moment, Mike. It wouldn't be natural if we weren't.'

'The only difference is that, like C.W., you've always been able to keep a lid on your emotions. I've never been able to do that and I invariably end up speaking my mind, irrespective of who gets hurt in the process.'

'I've got a thick skin,' she said with a wry smile. 'Well, I should do after all the flak I've taken from you since we've been working together.'

Graham sat forward, his arms resting on his knees, and cast a sidelong look at Sabrina. 'It's just me letting off steam. It's nothing personal, you know that.'

'It was when you first joined UNACO. You were well pissed off about having to work with a female partner, and that's why you'd go out of your way to knock me at every opportunity. Whether it was on a personal or a professional level, it didn't matter to you, just as long as you were scoring points off me. We had some feisty exchanges in the early days, didn't we?'

'You almost make it sound as if you miss all that,' Graham said.

'Hardly,' came the quick reply. 'But at least some good's come out of it. We've learnt a lot about each other since then, and now we've got the best partnership going in UNACO. The end's obviously justified the means, and I for one don't regret any of it.'

'Yeah,' Graham muttered.

'Are you going to expound on that?' she asked.

'Come on, we're wasting time here,' Graham said gruffly, getting to his feet. 'We've got work to do.'

Sabrina smiled to herself. Some things hadn't changed in all the time she'd known him. He always got defensive and would invariably change the subject if he felt a particular conversation was becoming too personal for him to deal with. She regarded it as a compliment that he wouldn't discuss the merits of their partnership any further ...

'What's so funny?' he demanded, noticing the faint smile on her lips.

'You,' she replied, standing up and brushing the dust off the back of her jeans.

'What the hell's that supposed to mean?'

'You're never prepared to commit yourself on personal issues, are you? You always have to sidestep them by changing the subject. Contrary to what you may think, Mike, openness isn't a sign of weakness, especially when you're amongst friends.'

'We can discuss the merits of our partnership some other time, assuming of course that there's still a partnership left to discuss after all this is over. But right now we've got more important things to worry about, like getting that film developed and taking a closer look at the address book you found in Caldere's office.'

'So let's go,' Sabrina replied.

'There's just one thing you seem to have overlooked in your haste to take that address book from Caldere's office,' Graham said as they walked back to the car. 'Once Caldere discovers it's missing, he's going to smell a rat, isn't he?'

'Not if the police tell him that a duplicate set of keys for the wine bar were found in Hardin's flat last night,' she replied, then gestured to the car keys in his hand. 'Do you want me to drive back to the hotel?'

'I'm back,' Ed Miller called out as he entered the house. Closing the front door behind him, he went through to the

140

kitchen where he found Katherine Warren poring over a folder on the table in front of her, a pen in one hand, a cup of coffee in the other.

'Who's watching the hotel?' she asked without looking up.

'A local reporter called Damas. He owes me a few favours.'

'Is there anyone in this town who doesn't owe you a few favours?'

'One or two, but I'll get round to them.' Miller placed two pizza boxes on the table. 'It's the nearest I could get to Christmas lunch. At least they've got turkey in them.'

'That's great,' she said absently, then sat back in her chair and tossed the pen on to the table. 'What did you tell this local reporter about Graham and Carver?'

'Nothing. That's what you wanted, wasn't it? All I did was give him one of the photos so that he'd be able to recognize them. I told him to tail them if they leave the hotel and report their final destination to me. We can take it from there.' Miller sat down and indicated the folder on the table. 'What have you got there?'

'I've been doing a little homework while you were staking out the hotel,' she told him. 'I've found out the name of the man Graham and Carver went to see at the hospital this morning.'

'Sergei Kolchinsky?'

'How did you know that?' Katherine asked in surprise.

'I also did a little homework this morning,' Miller replied with a smile. 'I made a few discreet enquiries on my car phone. It helped to alleviate the boredom. So, what did you find out about Kolchinsky?'

'That he was a senior member of a UNESCO team out here on a fact-finding mission,' she replied. 'I went to the hospital but nobody seemed to know anything about his condition or why he'd been admitted there in the first place. I didn't want to push it in case word got back to Graham or Carver that someone had been snooping around the hospital. The last thing we need to do is put them on their

141

guard. We have to play this close to the chest, at least until I've got enough evidence to confront them about their involvement with UNACO.'

'You want some evidence? I assume you've heard about the supposedly unprovoked attack two days ago by three masked men at Lisbon Airport on a group of passengers about to board a flight to New York?'

'Of course, it was in all the papers back home. The authorities put it down to left-wing terrorists out to cause maximum embarrassment to the government in the run-up to the general election next month. What's this got to do with Kolchinsky?' She suddenly sat forward, her eyes riveted on Miller's face. 'Was he one of those wounded in the attack?'

'He was the *only* one wounded in the attack,' Miller corrected her.

'Tell me everything you know, Ed,' she said, taking a micro-cassette player from her handbag which was draped over the back of the chair.

Miller placed his hand lightly on hers to prevent her from switching it on. 'Let me just say at the outset that the only reason my source agreed to co-operate was because I have in my possession some photographs which would not only ruin his career, but also his marriage as well. Neither his wife nor any of his police colleagues know about his penchant for young boys. I told him that his identity would remain anonymous and I intend to keep my word. Let's just get that straight before we continue.'

'I don't give a damn about his perversions, Ed, I just want to know what he told you,' Katherine said, switching on the machine.

'You can be a real cold-hearted bitch at times, you know that?'

'It comes with the job,' came the terse reply. 'So what did he tell you?'

Miller took a pack of cigarettes from his pocket and lit one. 'The story that the attack was carried out by local

142

terrorists was given to the press by the Special Forces Brigade, the Portuguese anti-terrorist squad. They took over the case from the local CID, but not before my source had received a preliminary report from one of his senior officers at the scene of the crime. According to the report, four men were killed, including three paramedics; one wounded and one abducted. It had all the signs of a very professional operation. Certainly not the random attack of a group of militant terrorists.'

Katherine wet her lips excitedly. 'What happened to Kolchinsky?'

'He took a slug in the stomach. It was touch and go whether he'd survive, but the operation was a success and the doctors are now confident he'll make a full recovery.' Miller inhaled on his cigarette and blew the smoke up towards the ceiling. 'But this is where it gets really interesting. The Special Forces Brigade named the dead passenger as Carlos Pereira, a local businessman. The name was genuine enough, but not the occupation. Lieutenant Carlos Pereira was a member of the Special Forces Brigade. He was travelling to New York with Kolchinsky and another man called Abe Silverman.'

'And Silverman was the one who was kidnapped?' Katherine concluded.

Miller nodded. 'He's also listed as a member of UNESCO. That's all my source could find out about him. Or so he claimed. Silverman was travelling on an Israeli passport, so I called a couple of journalists I know in Tel-Aviv. One had never heard of him. The other, an expert on the Israeli intelligence services, told me that Silverman had been head of Mossad's cryptology department for several years back in the Eighties.'

'So if Silverman is working for UNACO, he could have been carrying some coded documents back to New York,' Katherine concluded. 'That would certainly account for the bodyguard, wouldn't it?'

'Which would mean that whoever carried out the attack was specifically after him,' Miller added. 'Because, without him, those coded messages would be useless. And that's why he was abducted. They needed him to decode the documents.'

'So UNACO send Graham and Carver out here to find Silverman before he's coerced into decoding the documents,' Katherine said. 'This is dynamite, Ed. But it's all just speculation at the moment. That's why we need to get a copy of the report forwarded to your source before the CID are taken off the case,' Katherine replied, switching off the cassette player.

'I've already told you, Katherine, he's not to be involved,' Miller was quick to remind her. 'As a fellow journalist, you know the importance of protecting the identities of your informers.'

'None of my informers are paedophiles,' Katherine retorted. 'Christ, Ed, you despise his kind just as much as I do.'

'Didn't you say a few minutes ago that you didn't give a damn about his perversions?' Miller said, holding her stare.

'You'd better decide now where your true loyalties lie, Ed,' Katherine shot back angrily. She held up a hand and smiled gently at him. 'I'm sorry, I didn't mean to snap at you like that. It's just that I feel like a muzzled donkey who's got a carrot dangling in front of its nose.'

'Interesting metaphor,' Miller said, stubbing out his cigarette. The telephone rang. 'Excuse me,' he said, then disappeared out into the hall to answer it.

Katherine slumped back in her chair and rubbed her hands slowly over her face. She knew Miller was right to protect the identity of his informer. But she also knew that the newspaper wouldn't risk printing hearsay from an anonymous source. She had to get the report to back up her story. Getting to her feet, she crossed to the fridge and helped herself to a Diet Pepsi. As she closed the door behind her, she noticed Miller's jacket draped over the washing machine in the corner of the room. She knew he never went anywhere without his black address book which was crammed full of the names of his many contacts around the world. She found the book in the inside pocket of his jacket and slipped it into her folder. When he returned to the room he was smiling contentedly to himself.

'You look like the cat who's just drunk the last of the cream,' she said, tossing the empty can into the bin.

'That was an old colleague of mine, Igor Kolanin, the deputy foreign editor of *Pravda*. I rang him this morning to ask him to see what he could dig up on our friend Kolchinsky.'

'And?' Katherine prompted.

'Kolchinsky's ex-KGB,' Miller replied, sitting down. 'He left the KGB a few years back to take up a new position outside the organization. Only nobody seems to know exactly where he went. It seems that information's classified.'

'Just like Langley's information on Graham and Carver,' Katherine said.

'Which would seem to tie them all in with UNACO,' Miller concluded.

'Not without that report it can't.'

'I've already told you, I'm not prepared to divulge the name of my informer,' Miller told her.

'I understand that. But it doesn't stop me from going after him, does it?'

'And how exactly do you intend to do that when you don't even know his name?'

Katherine opened the folder and held up the address book. 'It's my guess that your informer's name's somewhere in here. I'll call all the local numbers if I have to until I find him. That wouldn't be too good for business, would it?'

'You'd do it as well, wouldn't you?' Miller hissed.

'This isn't just any story, Ed. This is the kind of story that comes along once in a lifetime. I want it. And I'm damned if I'm going to lose the chance of getting the proof I need to print it because you want to protect the identity of some perverted bastard who should have been thrown in jail years ago.'

'You're a fine one to talk about morals at a time like this. You're screwing me just for the sake of a story. Doesn't our friendship mean anything to you?'

'I'm a fine one to talk about morals, am I?' Katherine said sarcastically, sitting forward, her arms resting on the table. 'What about your little coup when you were a foreign correspondent in El Salvador? You had the army tipped off about a rebel camp so that when they arrived you were already in place to photograph the action. Only the camp contained women and children, not gun-toting rebels. How many innocent lives were lost as a result of your anonymous tip-off?'

'You know damn well that I didn't know there were women and children in there,' Miller said, wiping the back of his hand across his clammy forehead. 'It's something I will have to live with for the rest of my life. Christ, I should never have told you about it.'

'Your secret's safe with me,' she replied. 'We're two of a kind, Ed. That's probably why our friendship's lasted this long. We respect each other but we'd also cut each other's throat for a good story. And don't say you wouldn't have pulled one over on me if the roles had been reversed. I know you too well for that.'

'This is going to cost you, Katherine Warren,' Miller said, levelling a finger at her. 'What can you offer me that's worth sacrificing my top CID contact?'

'How about your name as co-correspondent of an exclusive on the front page of the *New York Sentinel*? That's something you've never had before, is it?'

'His name's Captain Antonio Gonzalez. But let me deal with him. I've got more clout with him.'

'Be my guest,' Katherine replied, then got to her feet

and crossed to the door. 'You don't mind if I use your phone, do you? I'd better call Louise and wish her a Merry Christmas otherwise she'll never forgive me.'

'Carry on,' Miller replied, gesturing towards the door with a flick of his hand. 'By the way, how is your little sister?'

'She's well pissed off with me right now because I'm not celebrating Christmas with the rest of the family. Then again, she always was far more family-orientated than me. That's probably why her marriage has lasted so long. My little maternal sister.'

'Send her my love, will you?'

'Sure,' came the reply.

'Oh, and don't forget to wish Larry a Merry Christmas from me as well,' Miller called out after her as she disappeared through the swing door.

Katherine's head popped round the door and she held up the micro-cassette player. 'I've got a feeling it will be, once he's heard this. Come to think of it, I doubt he'll get a better present for a very long time to come.'

7

Zlotin executed a perfect landing on the runway, taxied the twin-engined Piper Navaho to within fifty feet of a row of hangars, then closed down the engine. He unbuckled his safety belt and opened the cockpit door. 'Wait here,' was all he said to Whitlock before alighting from the aircraft and disappearing into the nearest hangar, closing the door again behind him.

Whitlock removed his safety belt and cursed in exasperation. If only he knew where they were. Zlotin had announced on leaving Marseilles that he'd filed a flight plan to Munich, but two hours into the flight he'd contacted Munich's Riem International Airport and announced that they were experiencing engine trouble and would be putting down as quickly as possible to check out the problem. Zlotin had assured Munich air traffic control that he would contact them as soon as he was airborne again. But Zlotin hadn't put down. Instead he'd changed course and reduced altitude to avoid detection on the radar scanners. Whitlock had tried several times to determine their new destination, but all his enquiries had been met with the same silence. He'd finally given up asking, knowing he'd find out, in time . . .

Now, as he looked around, Whitlock could see that they had obviously landed at an abandoned airfield. Weeds had sprung up between the cracks in the runway and graffiti had been sprayed on the sides of the disused hangars.

To his right was the tower, now little more than a hollow shell with shattered windows and a door which hung grotesquely from a single, rusted hinge. Like the hangars, it too was covered in graffiti.

When Zlotin emerged from the hangar he crossed to the aircraft and peered up at Whitlock through the open cockpit door. 'OK, you can come out now.'

'I'm not moving until I know where the hell we are and what the hell we're doing here!' Whitlock shot back.

Zlotin pondered Whitlock's outburst for a moment then gave a shrug. 'You'll find out soon enough,' he acknowledged. 'We're in Leipzig. This airfield used to belong to the East German militia before the Wall came down.'

'That's half the question answered,' Whitlock said defiantly.

'We're here to pick up a couple of passengers,' Zlotin told him.

'So where are they?' Whitlock asked. 'In the hangar?'

'No, we'll have to fetch them ourselves.'

'Why do I get the feeling that they don't know we're coming?' Whitlock said, climbing from the cockpit.

'Don't worry, they won't give us any trouble,' Zlotin said, leading the way back to the hangar.

'Who are they?' Whitlock asked.

'Their names wouldn't mean anything to you.'

'Try me,' Whitlock replied.

Zlotin paused at the door, his hand resting lightly on the handle. 'Professor Gunther Auerbach and his eighteen-year-old daughter, Lisl.'

Whitlock pursed his lips thoughtfully, then shrugged. 'No, I can't say the names mean anything to me.'

'I didn't think they would,' Zlotin replied.

Whitlock's mind was racing. Although he had never met Gunther Auerbach, he'd certainly heard of him. A former East German chess champion at the age of fourteen, Auerbach had already been targeted as a future recruit for the ubiquitous East German intelligence service when his father, a senior officer in the Ministry for State Security, had been exposed as a double agent working for the CIA. Auerbach and his mother had been smuggled out of the country by an underground movement within hours of his father's arrest. He was never to see his father again. After graduating with a doctorate in cryptology from the Sorbonne, he had been recruited by the West German intelligence service, the BND, and went on to become the youngest ever section chief of its specialist codes and ciphers department, a post he held for the next seventeen years until the Berlin Wall finally came down. It was then that he chose to turn his back on the world of espionage and returned to his home town of Leipzig with his daughter, Lisl, where he accepted a position as head of the university's cryptology department.

Whitlock knew there were those within Western intelligence circles who regarded Auerbach as a better, more adaptable cryptologist than Silverman. Although Whitlock was in no position to compare the two men, he did know that Auerbach was without question one of the world's leading cryptologists. And if Zlotin needed to bring Auerbach into play, then it meant that something must already have happened to Silverman . . .

'Royce!' Zlotin barked from the doorway. 'Get in here.'

Whitlock was quick to follow Zlotin into the hangar. A figure stood in the shadows behind the Ford hatchback which was parked at the other end of the hangar, his hands dug into the pockets of his knee-length overcoat, his face partially obscured under the rim of a black fedora.

'Who's that?' Whitlock asked, indicating the man.

'He's my contact here in Leipzig,' Zlotin replied. 'One of the few East Germans I can still trust.'

'Why doesn't he come out of the shadows?' Whitlock asked, lowering his voice as they neared the car.

'You don't need to whisper, he doesn't understand English,' Zlotin said. 'He won't take any unnecessary risks because, like many of his colleagues, he's had to go to ground since the Wall came down.'

'What was he? Stasi?'

'Military intelligence,' Zlotin replied, then crossed to the man and spoke softly to him in German. The man took a set of car keys from his jacket pocket and handed them to Zlotin, who unlocked the driver's door before looking across at Whitlock. 'Come on, let's go. We don't have much time.'

Zlotin started up the car and drove out of the hangar on to a road which ran through the heart of the deserted air base before joining a slip road further on which brought them out on to the main highway leading into Leipzig.

'A Russian with contacts in the old East German military intelligence?' Whitlock mused, trying to see how much he could draw out of Zlotin. 'You also knew your way around that base back there, which would imply that you've been here before. What are you? GRU? KGB?'

Zlotin cast a sidelong look at Whitlock. His expression gave nothing away. 'I told you back in Marseilles, who I am is not important. You'd do well to remember that.'

'This is crazy,' Whitlock shot back in exasperation. 'I'm hired to work with you and I still don't even know your name. It's a bit damn much, you know.'

'And I intend to keep it that way.'

'OK, I get the message,' Whitlock said tersely.

'Good. Now maybe we can dispense with the small talk.'

'Can I ask a question about the operation, or is that also regarded as "small talk"?'

'You can ask,' Zlotin replied, his voice implying that there wouldn't necessarily be an answer at the end of it.

'For whatever reason, we're going to kidnap this professor and his daughter and take them back to the plane. You've already filed a flight plan to Munich so you'll have to land there to allay any suspicions. And that means we'll have to clear customs, even if it is your intention to fly out straight away again. So what are you going to do about our two passengers? If you dope them, you'll have some explaining to do once we land, but if you don't, what's to stop them from raising the alarm once we reach customs?'

'It's a good question,' Zlotin replied at length.

'Do I get an answer?'

'You'll find out soon enough,' was all Zlotin would venture.

Whitlock shrugged helplessly and lapsed into a silence which lasted until they pulled up in front of a small, red-brick house on the outskirts of the city. Zlotin opened the glove compartment and removed a Walther P1 automatic and a silencer.

'Do I get to carry?' Whitlock asked.

'No,' Zlotin replied bluntly, pocketing the automatic. He climbed out of the car and strode up the narrow pathway to the front door. Whitlock kept close behind him. Zlotin knocked sharply on the door then turned to Whitlock. 'I'll do all the talking. There's no need for you to say anything. And when I give you an order, I expect it to be carried out without question. Is that understood?'

'Perfectly,' Whitlock replied curtly.

A bolt was drawn back from inside the house and the door swung open. Whitlock estimated the girl to be no older than sixteen, with short blonde hair which framed a pleasant rather than attractive face.

'You must be Lisl,' Zlotin said in German, giving her a friendly smile.

'Yes, that's right,' she replied hesitantly.

'Your father's told me a lot about you,' Zlotin said. 'We work together at the university. I was in the neighbourhood so I thought I'd drop by and wish him a Merry Christmas.'

'He'll like that. Please, won't you come in?' she said.

Zlotin gestured to Whitlock. 'This is an old friend of mine. He's out here on holiday from the States. You don't mind if he comes in as well, do you?'

'No, of course not,' she replied with a smile in Whitlock's direction.

'Thank you,' Zlotin replied, indicating for Whitlock to enter first.

'My father's in the lounge,' she said, closing the door behind them. 'He won't have heard the door. I bought him a tape of Handel's "Messiah" for Christmas and he's been listening to it on his headphones all morning. He loves classical music.'

'And you don't, judging by the tone of your voice,' Zlotin said, following her to a door further down the hall.

'Not really,' she replied, entering the room.

Gunther Auerbach was sitting in an armchair in front of the fireplace, slippered feet extended towards the open fire, head tilted back, eyes closed. The only movement was the rhythmical tapping of his finger on the arm of the chair. She shook him gently. Opening his eyes, he reluctantly removed the headphones to hear what she was saying. He got to his feet but his smile faltered when he saw the silenced automatic in Zlotin's hand. Lisl shrank back against her father, who slipped a protective arm around her shoulder without taking his eyes off the pistol. 'Who are you?' he demanded, looking from Zlotin to Whitlock. 'What do you want?'

'Who we are isn't important,' Zlotin replied in German, taking a step towards them. 'What we want is a little of your time. Three days at the most. That's all.'

'What is it you want me to do?' Auerbach asked suspiciously.

'That will become apparent in due course,' Zlotin said.

'You're Russian, aren't you?' Auerbach said, and noticed Zlotin's eyes narrow fractionally in surprise, confirming his suspicions.

'You're very perceptive, Professor, but then I'm forgetting that while you were with the BND you worked closely with several defectors from both the KGB and the GRU.'

'So which one are you? KGB or GRU?' Auerbach asked, the disdain obvious in his voice.

'Neither,' Zlotin snapped irritably, then looked at Lisl

who was still pressed against her father, her eyes wide and uncertain. 'Miss Auerbach, would you come here please?' he said softly, his free hand extended out towards her.

'No,' Auerbach shot back, his grip tightening around her shoulders. 'Your business is with me. Leave Lisl out of it.'

'In her own way, your daughter's just as important to us as you are,' Zlotin told him. 'I have no intention of harming her, unless you force my hand. It's your choice, Professor.'

'It's all right, Papa, I'll do as he says,' Lisl said softly, then slipped out from under her father's protective arm and crossed to where Zlotin was standing.

Zlotin took a small, cigar-shaped metal case from his pocket and handed it to Whitlock. 'Open it,' he said in English.

Whitlock unscrewed the top. Inside was a hypodermic syringe, the tip of the needle protected by a plastic cover. When he removed the syringe from the case he noticed that it was filled with a clear, colourless liquid.

'You and your father will be coming with us,' Zlotin said, addressing Lisl Auerbach. 'But for security reasons, I'm not able to disclose our final destination, other than to say that it'll take several hours to reach by plane. During the flight I wish to discuss certain matters with your father which, again for security reasons, I would prefer you didn't hear. That's why I prepared this sedative before we came here. It'll take effect within half an hour and you'll be asleep for an hour at the most. Please, would you roll up your sleeve?'

'No, Lisl,' Auerbach shouted, moving towards her.

Zlotin touched the barrel of the automatic against Lisl's head. 'You're beginning to test my patience, Professor. As I've already explained to your daughter, the sedative is quite harmless. If I'd really wanted to kill her, don't you think I'd have done so already? Now why don't you sit down before I do something we'll all regret?'

'Do as he says, Papa,' Lisl said, fighting back the tears.

Auerbach sat down slowly in the chair behind him, his eyes riveted on the syringe in Whitlock's hand.

'Do it,' Zlotin snapped at Whitlock. 'And make sure you find a vein.'

Whitlock found the vein in the crook of her arm and gently inserted the tip of the needle into her skin, releasing the liquid into her bloodstream.

'You've got five minutes to get both your passports and to pack some clothes into a hold-all,' Zlotin said to her then turned to Whitlock. 'Go with her. Watch her. And make sure it's only clothes she brings with her.' He closed the door behind them then turned back to Auerbach. 'Now that your daughter's out of the room, I can tell you what was really in the syringe.'

'What have you done to her, you bastard!' Auerbach shouted, jumping to his feet.

'Nothing, as long as you co-operate with us,' Zlotin replied calmly. 'And I would suggest you keep your voice down, Professor. I'm sure you wouldn't want to alarm your daughter unduly. Well, at least not yet.'

'What exactly was in the syringe?' Auerbach asked anxiously, the fear and uncertainty etched on his face.

'It contained a lethal virus which has been developed over several years at a secret military laboratory in Russia. There's only about a dozen of us who even know of its existence. The incubation period is roughly seventy-two hours. The first symptoms are a slight fever, a loss of appetite, restlessness and a certain degree of disorientation. In fact, symptoms similar to those encountered in rabies. If left untreated, the virus will go on to attack the central nervous system. I've actually seen a man die from this particular virus. It was quite horrific. His body went into violent spasms and he bit off his tongue, broke both arms, and snapped his spinal column before finally lapsing into a coma. He was dead within three hours of the first symptoms appearing.' Zlotin watched as Auerbach sank back into the chair, his face buried in his hands. 'Don't worry, Professor, there is an antidote. So all you have to do is to complete your work for us within the specified deadline and the antidote will be administered to your daughter. It's as simple as that.'

Auerbach's head suddenly snapped up, his eyes blazing. 'And if not, you'd stand by and let her die.'

'I certainly wouldn't be responsible for her death, Professor. You would. I'd remember that if I were you.'

'You bastard,' Auerbach snarled, lunging at Zlotin.

Zlotin sidestepped the clumsy challenge and, grabbing Auerbach's arm, twisted it violently behind his back and ran him face first into the wall. 'The clock's ticking, Professor. Every second you waste brings the deadline that little bit closer.'

'I'll do whatever you want,' Auerbach conceded, his resolve finally broken.

'That's very commendable, Professor,' Zlotin replied, releasing the pressure on Auerbach's arm. 'There is a sedative built into the virus, so don't be alarmed when your daughter sleeps it off on the plane. As I said, the virus itself won't take effect for another three days. I'll leave it entirely up to you whether you decide to tell her about the virus or not.'

'I'll tell her,' Auerbach said quickly. 'Lisl and I have never had any secrets from each other.'

'Good. It'll solve a lot of problems for both of us. You see, we'll have to clear customs at Munich and Madrid before we reach our final destination. The reason I mention this is because you or your daughter may try to alert the authorities at either airport and have us arrested. It's a chance we have to take but I should warn you, I'm not carrying the antidote on me, and I can assure you that even the most eminent toxicologist in his field couldn't come up with an equivalent antidote in the time that would be left to save your daughter's life. I'm now your daughter's only realistic chance of coming out of this alive. I'd bear that in mind if I were you, Professor.'

'I told you, I'll do whatever you want,' Auerbach said bitterly.

The door opened and Lisl entered the room, a hold-all in her hand. Whitlock was close behind her. 'We're ready,' he told Zlotin.

'Our car's parked outside, Professor,' Zlotin said, gesturing to the door. 'After you.'

Auerbach put his arm around Lisl's shoulder and led her from the room.

'My colleagues will have completed their part of the operation and should be on their way back to base camp by now,' Zlotin said to Whitlock, slipping the automatic back into his pocket. He allowed himself a rare smile of satisfaction. 'Yes, it's all going according to plan again.'

'You make it sound as if you've been experiencing some difficulties,' Whitlock said, hoping to discover what had happened to Silverman.

'We had a temporary setback,' was all Zlotin would say.

'What kind of setback?' Whitlock probed.

'That doesn't concern you,' Zlotin snapped abruptly then opened the front door. 'Shall we go, Professor? I'm sure you'll be wanting to start your work as soon as possible, won't you?'

Viktor Rodenko and Valentin Yemenkov hadn't completed their part of the operation. In fact, nothing seemed to be going according to plan. All they had been required to do was to drive the twenty miles from Porto to the picturesque seaside resort of Vila do Conde where, according to a reliable *spetznaz* source still loyal to Zlotin, Dr Alain Fisier and his wife, Marie, were spending a fifth successive Christmas at their time-share villa. Fisier had been head of the cryptology department at the Sorbonne in Paris for the past seven years and, although a highly respected cryptologist in his field, he hadn't been Zlotin's first choice to partner Auerbach. Zlotin had initially wanted to bring in two other cryptologists: one a Briton who had worked extensively for MI5, the other an American affiliated to the CIA; but the difficulty in getting

157

them to Portugal, together with the amount of time that would have been wasted in the process, had forced him to reconsider his options. And because of Fisier's current proximity to their base camp, as well as the fact that he'd studied, albeit briefly, under Silverman at the Sorbonne, he was the obvious choice from the remaining cryptologists on Zlotin's shortlist. With that in mind, Zlotin had given orders for Fisier and his wife to be brought back to the base camp as quickly as possible.

Rodenko and Yemenkov had set out early that morning in the second-hand car Zlotin had bought when they had first arrived in Lisbon. Both had been confident of reaching Vila do Conde within the hour, but neither of them had bargained on the series of mishaps that were to plague their short journey. A flat tyre outside Porto, a broken fanbelt at Matosinhos and, finally, an overturned lorry which had completely blocked the highway into Vila do Conde for three hours. They finally reached Vila do Conde four and a half hours after leaving Porto . . .

The Fisiers' villa was one of a group of thirty situated on a hillside on the outskirts of the city. The scenery was breathtaking. To the north was the small fishing village of Azurara, its flotilla of wooden-hull vessels lying dormant in the tranquil harbour waters; to the south lay Vila do Conde with its wide, expansive beaches and rugged coral reefs.

'A view like this back home could only have been seen from one of the President's summer dachas,' Yemenkov said in awe, looking slowly around him. A twenty-nine-year-old Georgian with boyish features and cropped blond hair, he had been one of the most promising officers to have emerged from the Afghan war: many within the military had seen him as a natural successor to Nikolai Zlotin. He had the temperament, the courage and, when necessary, the ruthlessness of the man he'd idolized since childhood. He'd been tipped as a future *spetznaz* commander at the very least. Perhaps even a defence chief in the Politburo. But that had been before the coup. Now Valentin Yemenkov had been stripped of his rank and discarded by his superiors as an anachronism of the old-style Communism the new Russia wanted to bury for ever. At his court-martial he'd been called a disgrace to his country. But Yeltsin's Russia wasn't his country. Not any more . . .

Rodenko gazed around him but, unlike Yemenkov, he wasn't impressed by what he saw. A Lithuanian, he was twelve years Yemenkov's senior, with greasy black hair and cold, dispassionate grey eyes set deep into a rough, weather-beaten face. He'd started to grow a beard since arriving in Portugal, and the coarse stubble, together with the discoloured bruise under his left eye which he'd received when Silverman had hit him with the attaché case at the airport, only added to his menacing features.

He purposely slammed the car door behind him, jolting Yemenkov out of his reverie. 'I hate to interrupt your sightseeing, but we do have a job to do. And we're already running well behind schedule.'

Yemenkov was used to Rodenko's sarcasm, but he knew better than to talk back to him. He'd witnessed incidents over the years of cocky junior officers rising to the bait and responding to Rodenko's mocking sarcasm, only to be stripped naked in front of their peers, often at gunpoint, and beaten mercilessly until they lost consciousness. It was Rodenko's own way of dealing with insubordination. Yet in all the time Yemenkov had known him, Rodenko had never once been carpeted by his superiors for his brutal methods of enforcing discipline amongst his men, and this had only added to his reputation as one of the most feared and hated officers in the history of the unit. Yemenkov had never liked Rodenko as a person, but he'd always had the greatest respect for him as a soldier. Yet both he and Zlotin knew that this wasn't the same Viktor Rodenko who'd fearlessly led his men against the Mujahedin in Afghanistan. He'd been devastated by his arrest after the timid collapse of the attempted coup d'état, finding it inconceivable that many of his former *spetznaz* colleagues could have turned against him in the way they did. Then, to make matters worse, he'd started drinking since they'd arrived in Portugal three weeks earlier to prepare for the operation. Yemenkov knew that Zlotin was already worried that Rodenko could ultimately become a liability to the success of the operation. He also had no doubt in his mind that, despite the friendship which existed between the two men, Zlotin would have no hesitation in killing Rodenko if the need arose . . .

Rodenko rapped sharply on the front door then stepped back, his right hand curled around the Makarov pistol in his jacket pocket. He tapped his foot impatiently then cursed angrily and knocked again on the door. 'Where are they?' he snapped irritably at Yemenkov.

Yemenkov cupped his hands on either side of his face and peered through the lounge window. 'Nobody in there,' he announced, shaking his head. 'And the room looks spotless. You'd expect empty glasses or newspapers to be lying around, especially on Christmas Day. I don't think they're here.'

'I suppose we shouldn't really be surprised after everything else that's happened to us today,' Rodenko shot back angrily.

Yemenkov looked up when a bald-headed man appeared on the balcony of the adjoining villa, still tying his bathrobe around his ample waist.

'You lookin' for the doc, mate?' the man called out in a Yorkshire accent.

Like Zlotin, Yemenkov was fluent in several languages. 'Yes, that's right,' he replied. 'It doesn't look as if they're in. Do you know if they've gone out?'

'They've gone caravanning,' came the reply. 'Left yesterday. Said they'd be gone for a few days. He asked me and the wife to keep an eye on the place for them. You friends of theirs?'

'Yes,' Yemenkov replied. 'Do you have any idea where they went?'

'Somewhere up north, that's all the doc said. We were well surprised when he told us they were going caravanning. They're hardly the most adventurous couple in the world, are they?'

'Yes, I know what you mean,' Yemenkov replied with a chuckle. 'That's why we came round today without bothering to call first. We just naturally assumed that they'd be in.'

'Sorry, mate, but it looks like it's been a wasted trip.'

'Strangely enough, we were thinking of travelling up north ourselves for a few days between now and the New Year. Who knows, we might even bump into them. Do you know what kind of car they were driving?'

'It was a blue Capri. I should know, he had me tinkering with the engine the day he hired it.'

'Well, thanks for your help,' Yemenkov said, giving the man a wave. 'Sorry to have troubled you.'

'No trouble. Do you want me to tell the doc you were here?'

Yemenkov shrugged. 'Like I said, we're heading up north ourselves in the next couple of days. If we don't see them, we'll give them a ring when we get back. Thanks anyway.'

The man watched them retreat back down the path to where their car was parked, then looked round at his wife who had been standing out of sight of the balcony.

'Why did you lie to him?' she asked, frowning suspiciously. 'The car wasn't blue, you know that.'

'And it wasn't a Capri either,' the man replied, brushing past her into the lounge. He crossed to the sideboard and jotted a number down on the front page of the morning paper.

'Joe, what are you doing?' she demanded.

'Making a note of the registration number of their car before I forget it,' came the reply.

'What for, for God's sake?' she asked in amazement. 'First you lie about the make and the colour of the car, and now

161

you're writing down registration numbers. What's got into you?'

'You didn't see those two blokes down there, did you?'

'No, I only heard a voice,' she replied. 'It sounded pleasant enough to me.'

'He was foreign – I couldn't place the accent. But it was his mate who worried me. He was a right vicious-looking bastard. Christ, he looked like he'd been living rough for the last few days.'

'Next you're going to tell me you think they were villains or something,' she said sarcastically.

'There was something about them I didn't like, OK?' he snapped defensively. 'And the doc did ask us to keep an eye on the place for him, remember?'

'If you're that worried, why don't you call the cops and let them check out these two characters for themselves? It's worth it if it's going to put your mind at rest.'

'What am I supposed to tell them? That two guys were looking for our neighbours? They'd hardly take me seriously, would they? No, forget it.' He moved back to the sliding door then looked round at his wife again. 'But if they show their faces around here again, I will call the cops. I swear I will.'

Graham made no attempt to shake off the tail when they drove to the hospital that afternoon. It was the same car Katherine Warren had used to follow them earlier in the day, but this time there was a man behind the wheel. They didn't recognize him but, judging by his inexperience in the art of pursuit, they guessed that he was pretty new to the job. On reaching the hospital, they found that the car park was already packed; it was only a stroke of good fortune which allowed them to get a space close to the main entrance. To their amusement, their hapless pursuer was still driving around in circles in search of a parking space when they entered the foyer. They took the lift to the third floor and, showing their ID badges to the new duty officers

162

on guard in the corridor, they were allowed into Kolchinsky's ward.

Although his face was still pale, and dark sacs arced underneath his bloodshot eyes, Kolchinsky was now sitting up in bed.

'How are you feeling, Sergei?' Sabrina asked. 'You certainly look a lot better than you did this morning.'

'I feel a lot better. I'm still a bit weak but I suppose that's only to be expected considering I've been in a coma for the last forty-eight hours. Oh, and before I forget, Merry Christmas.'

'You too, Sergei,' Graham replied, pulling up a chair and sitting down.

'I assume from the tone of your voice that you haven't brought good tidings with you?' Kolchinsky said.

'C.W.'s our only real chance of cracking the case now,' Sabrina told him. 'And we don't even know where he is at present. The last we knew was that he'd been recruited by Zlotin in Marseilles. After that, nothing.'

'Yes, so I heard,' Kolchinsky said. 'I was on the phone to the Colonel in New York a few minutes ago. He briefed me on the latest developments. So it seems that not only do we have Zlotin and company to contend with, we've also got some meddlesome journalist out to splash UNACO's name across the front page of the *New York Sentinel*.'

'And so far the "Dirty Pool" haven't come up with anything that could be used to force her to drop the story,' Graham said with a disgruntled shake of his head. 'The last we heard the Colonel had told them to change tactics and focus their attention on Larry Ryan, the new editor of the *Sentinel*. He's married to Warren's sister. Hopefully they can dig up something on him. If not, Sabrina and I are going to become the most reluctant front-page celebrities in the history of journalism, and there won't be a damn thing that we can do about it.'

'They'll find something,' Kolchinsky assured him. 'They

always do. UNACO's continued existence is testament to that.'

'I guess,' Graham said without much conviction in his voice.

'Did you get anything useful from Caldere's address book?' Kolchinsky asked.

'It's still being analysed at Zürich HQ, but so far they haven't come up with anything significant,' Sabrina replied. 'Most of the names are contacts Caldere's made in the licensing trade since he took over the wine bar. And the entries in the diary were just as predictable. There was a telephone number next to Saisse's name, but it turned out to be a private line at *Le Boudin*, Jannoc's main casino in Marseilles. Another dead end.'

'I don't think it's a lost cause by any means,' Kolchinsky announced after a thoughtful silence. 'With C.W. on the inside and Michael's knowledge of Zlotin's psyche, we're still in with a good chance of getting the folders back intact.'

'You also know a bit about Zlotin, Sergei,' Graham said, getting to his feet and crossing to the window. 'And you've got one big advantage on me. You've met him in person.'

Kolchinsky looked to Sabrina, who nodded guiltily. 'He knows about the Colonel's attempt to bring Zlotin to UNACO. I had to tell him, Sergei.'

'Well, I'm glad it's finally out in the open,' Kolchinsky said. 'And if it's any consolation to you, Michael, I was opposed to the idea from the start.'

'It's water under the bridge, Sergei,' Graham said, peering down into the car park. He couldn't see any sign of the car which had tailed them from the hotel. 'What did you make of him when you met him in Moscow?'

'He was very arrogant,' Kolchinsky replied. 'It was my first impression of him and he did nothing in the subsequent meetings to change that opinion. I made it quite clear to the Colonel after the first meeting that I didn't think Zlotin was suitable for UNACO. But you know how stubborn the Colonel can be when he's determined to press ahead with something. He made it equally clear to me that he wanted Zlotin brought in as Jacques' replacement. To be fair to the Colonel, he'd been sent a very impressive dossier on Zlotin by his opposite number in *spetznaz*. I think he was swayed by that, together with all the praise that had been heaped on Zlotin by the Politburo over the years. In theory, Zlotin's the model soldier. Disciplined, fearless and ready to carry out an order without question. But when I met him, I found the man and the myth two very different people indeed. I think this case proves the point.'

'Yeah,' Graham was quick to agree.

'There is something else I wanted to discuss with you,' Kolchinsky said at length. 'As I said earlier, I spoke to the Colonel before the two of you got here. He'd just got off the phone to the Director of the Russian Intelligence Service – what was the old KGB. The Russian authorities are very worried about the possible repercussions if Zlotin, Rodenko and Yemenkov were ever returned home to complete their prison sentence.'

'What exactly are you saying, Sergei?' Graham asked, eyeing Kolchinsky suspiciously.

'You're going to have to kill them once our files have been recovered,' Kolchinsky replied, holding Graham's unflinching stare.

'And what if they choose to surrender?' Sabrina asked.

'It doesn't matter,' Kolchinsky said. 'They can't be allowed to return to Russia.'

'What's this all about, Sergei?' Graham demanded. 'You've always been a stickler for the rules. You're forever preaching passages from the UNACO Charter to any Strike Force team that steps out of line. The Charter states quite categorically that in the line of duty any field operative may respond with force if force is used against them. That doesn't include killing a suspect in cold blood.'

'And since when have you ever gone by the rules?' Kolchinsky snapped.

'Sure I break the rules,' Graham retorted. 'But I've never killed an unarmed suspect. Never.'

'I know, and I never meant to imply that you had. But please, at least hear me out.' Kolchinsky paused to marshal his thoughts before continuing. 'In the event that Zlotin, or his colleagues, were arrested and handed back to the Russians, there's every chance that they would be sprung again soon after they landed on Russian soil. Last night a crack *spetznaz* unit deserted from the barracks at Ryazan. It's believed to be under the direct command of Major Petr Koslov –'

'Koslov?' Graham cut in quickly. 'That's Zlotin's brother-in-law. But he's always been regarded as a liberal. He was one of the first within the military to publicly denounce the August coup and back Yeltsin's stand against the conspirators. What are you suggesting now, Sergei – that he's been in league with the hard-liners all along?'

Kolchinsky nodded. 'The authorities have found certain incriminating documents which tie him in with Zlotin. They now seem to think that Koslov's stand during the attempted coup was a set-up to make sure that he'd be certain of retaining his rank within the military if it failed.'

'And in doing so, Zlotin and the hard-liners would still have a reliable contact inside *spetznaz*?' Sabrina concluded.

'That's how it looks,' Kolchinsky agreed.

'So Koslov could have been behind the attack on the convoy taking Zlotin, Rodenko and Yemenkov to the military prison on the outskirts of Moscow?' Graham said.

'He could certainly have masterminded it, but he was actually in Georgia when the convoy was attacked.'

'The perfect alibi.' Graham moved to the foot of the bed. 'What was the Colonel's reaction to the Russians' idea of using us to do their dirty work for them?'

'Naturally he rejected it out of hand. He had to of course.

UNACO are a strictly non-political organization. If he'd agreed to their demands and the truth had then come out we'd have been seen as little more than freelance assassins working for a foreign power. The whole concept of UNACO would then have been in jeopardy. And that would have done nothing to enhance our already tarnished reputation amongst many of the diplomats at the United Nations.'

'And he's right,' Graham said.

'Sure, if you're going to play it by the rule book,' Sabrina said, looking at Graham. 'But what if we hand Zlotin over to the Russians only to have Koslov spring him again? Not only would all our hard work have been in vain, but it would also give Zlotin another chance to plan some new way of bringing the Russian government to its knees. You were the one who said we were dealing with fanatics who would stop at nothing to carry out their plans. And in this case those plans could result in the loss of hundreds of thousands of innocent lives. To hell with the rule book, Mike. I'd gladly put a bullet in him if I thought it would save just one innocent life in the process.'

'And if he was unarmed?' Graham said.

'Then he'd be a fool, wouldn't he?' she replied coldly.

'Yeah, I guess he would,' Graham replied, still stunned by Sabrina's outburst. It wasn't like her to react like that. She'd always been the pragmatic half of the partnership. How often had she acted as his conscience by talking him out of doing something rash which would have put him in contravention of the UNACO Charter? Now the tables had turned. Suddenly he was the one defending the Charter. The irony certainly wasn't lost on him. But was she right?

The bleeper on Graham's belt suddenly went off. He was quick to silence it before picking up the telephone on the bedside table and ringing Rust at the hotel.

'I've just had a call from Major Inacio,' Rust told him. 'He's got an important lead. He wouldn't elaborate further over the phone. He's on his way over to the hotel now to brief me. I want you and Sabrina back here as soon as possible.'

'We're on our way, Jacques.'

'How's Sergei?'

Graham glanced at Kolchinsky. 'He's a lot better. Actually, we've just had an interesting little chat with him these past few minutes. I'll tell you about it when we get back to the hotel.'

'I look forward to it,' Rust replied. 'Send Sergei my regards and tell him I'll be over when I get the chance.'

'I'll do that.'

'Oh, and Mike? No mention of C.W. in front of Inacio. I don't see any reason why Inacio should have to know about him. Well, at least not yet.'

'You won't have any arguments from me on that score,' Graham replied. 'The less the Special Forces Brigade know about this whole operation, the better it'll be for all concerned.'

'I thought you might see it that way,' Rust replied. 'I'll see you two shortly. Bye.'

The line went dead and Graham replaced the receiver. 'We're wanted back at the hotel,' he explained to Sabrina and, turning to Kolchinsky added, 'Jacques sends his good wishes.'

'What's going on?' Sergei asked him.

Graham shrugged. 'Not sure,' he said, 'but no doubt Jacques will fill you in when he comes to see you.'

'We'll drop by again when we can,' Sabrina promised Kolchinsky, then followed Graham to the door.

'You could bring me something to read the next time you come,' Kolchinsky called out after them. 'A man can only read the *International Herald Tribune* so many times, you know.'

'How about a copy of the UNACO Charter?' Graham said, looking round at him.

'I think I'd prefer a few magazines, Michael.'

'We'll sort something out, Sergei, don't worry,' Sabrina

said as she followed Graham out into the corridor. 'You think I was wrong to back Sergei in there, don't you?'

'Did I say that?' Graham shot back. 'Come on, Jacques is waiting for us at the hotel.'

She grabbed his arm as he turned to go. 'You're my partner, Mike. Talk to me. Tell me what you're thinking.'

'I'm thinking that we've got a briefing to attend at the hotel,' he said, pulling his arm free from her grasp. 'Now let's go.'

'You know I'm right,' she called out after him as he strode briskly down the corridor.

He didn't look round at her until he'd reached the lift. 'Are you coming or not?'

'Sure,' she replied in exasperation, and hurried towards the lift.

Inacio had already briefed Rust and left the hotel by the time Graham and Sabrina returned from the hospital.

'So what was this important lead you mentioned on the phone?' Graham asked once Rust had ushered them into his room.

'The local police in Vila do Conde, a small tourist resort north of Porto, received a call earlier today from a woman who told them that two men had been asking after the couple who were staying in one of the neighbouring time-share villas. It seems she'd only contacted the police to get some peace and quiet because her husband had been going on all morning about how suspicious one of the men had looked to him. The police told her to call again if the two men should return and it was left at that. An hour later a team from the Special Forces Brigade arrived in Vila do Conde to check on Dr Alain Fisier, the head of cryptology at the Sorbonne, who was on holiday there with his wife. He was one of the cryptologists on the list I circulated this morning to all Special Forces units around the world.'

'And it turns out that the two men were looking for Fisier?' Sabrina concluded.

Rust nodded. 'The English couple have already been interviewed by the Special Forces Brigade and the husband has positively identified both Rodenko and Yemenkov from photographs. He's sure they were the two men he saw this morning.'

'Where is Fisier now?' Graham asked.

'He and his wife went caravanning a couple of days ago. Their present whereabouts are unknown. An APB's been put out on them as well as on the Russians' car. The Special Forces Brigade have already sent another team to the area to help in the search for the Fisiers. It's imperative that we get to them before the Russians do, especially in the light of the news I received from Zürich a few minutes ago. Another name on my list was Professor Gunther Auerbach, formerly head of cryptology with the old West German intelligence agency, the BND. He and his daughter were seen by neighbours leaving the house in Leipzig with two men earlier today. One was described as tall with cropped brown hair and a distinctive military bearing. The other was black with a neatly trimmed moustache and wearing glasses.'

'Zlotin and C.W.?' Graham said.

'It has to be,' Rust replied. 'Zlotin's obviously decided to bring in Auerbach and Fisier to crack Abe's codes.'

'Which means Abe must already be dead,' Sabrina said.

'Why else would Zlotin bring in two more cryptologists, unless Abe were either already dead or certainly incapable of working on the codes?' Rust concurred.

'At least it'll give us more time,' Graham said. 'Auerbach may be regarded as one of the world's leading cryptologists, but even he wouldn't be able to make any sort of headway with the coded folders for some time, even if he did have Fisier to help him. If, in fact, he *can* break Abe's codes. There's no guarantee that he will. That's obviously why Zlotin's taken

Auerbach's daughter as well. It'll give Auerbach an added incentive to break the codes.'

'And the more we disrupt Zlotin's plans, the more time we'll have to get the folders back before they can be decoded,' Rust told Graham. 'I want you and Sabrina to co-ordinate the operation at Vila do Conde. The Special Forces Brigade will fly you there. One of their helicopters is being refuelled as we speak. It'll be ready for take-off by the time you reach the airport. It's imperative that we find the Fisiers before the Russians do. Not only would it thwart Zlotin's plans if we did so, it would also give us the drop on Rodenko and Yemenkov so that, when they did show, they would be walking straight into a trap. And getting those two in custody would be a serious setback for Zlotin. I wouldn't expect either of them to break under interrogation, not with their training, but at least they would be out of the way, leaving Zlotin completely isolated. That's when he might make a mistake, and we could be ready to pounce the moment that happened.'

'It's a good idea in theory,' Graham said, shooting a dirty look in Sabrina's direction. 'As long as one of us doesn't kill them before they can be taken into custody.'

'I don't believe it,' she snapped, throwing up her arms in frustration. 'We were talking hypothetically at the hospital, that's all.'

'Well that's not how I read it,' Graham shot back.

'Wait a minute,' Rust cut in before Sabrina could answer, his hands held up towards them. 'One moment we're rationally discussing the case, and the next moment you're at each other's throats. Can someone tell me what's going on?'

'It's a difference of opinion, that's all,' Graham replied with a shrug.

'I'd never have guessed,' Rust retorted sarcastically. 'Now will one of you tell me what this is all about?'

Sabrina told Rust what Kolchinsky had told them.

'So that was the "interesting little chat" you were talking

about when I phoned you at the hospital?' Rust said to Graham.

'Yeah,' he replied.

'Sergei had no right to tell you about Koslov,' Rust snapped angrily. 'That information was for senior UNACO personnel only. Colonel Philpott, Sergei and me. Nobody else, especially not the two of you.'

'Why not?' Sabrina asked.

'As Sergei pointed out, the Colonel balked at the very idea of using UNACO to settle personal scores for the Russians. And he certainly didn't want to put either of you in any sort of a predicament that could have interfered with the way you approached the case. But, thanks to Sergei's indiscretion, you're now at loggerheads with each other. I can understand why he did it, but that's still no excuse. He should have known better. To be honest I'm a little surprised that the Colonel told him about Koslov in the first place. I wouldn't have. In fact, I won't be telling him anything about the case when I see him and I would prefer it if you were to do the same.'

'Why?' Sabrina said in surprise. 'He's the Deputy Director of UNACO, Jacques. He has a right to know what's going on.'

'As far as I'm concerned, he's now the Deputy Director in name only,' Rust replied. 'What I'm about to tell you is off the record. Nobody at UNACO apart from the Colonel, Sergei and I know about this. If it were ever to get out that I'd told you, I'd have a lot of explaining to do.'

'You know us better than that, Jacques,' Graham said.

'Sergei was offered the Directorship of the Russian Intelligence Service a couple of days before he came out here for the conference. He told the Colonel he'd give him an answer when he returned to New York, but the Colonel knows as well as I do that there's no way he'll pass up on it. He's never really been happy at UNACO since the Colonel returned to take over as Director again. He felt that his authority had been undermined when the Secretary-General accepted his resignation, and he only agreed to stay on as the Colonel's number two until the end of the year. He'd probably have taken early retirement if this offer hadn't come up. So you see, he'll finally be going home after all these years; that's all he'll be thinking about now.'

'Will you take his place in New York?' Graham asked.

'No, I'll be staying on in Zürich. I feel I can be of more use to UNACO there than I would be as the Colonel's number two.'

'Will C.W. be offered the position again?' Sabrina asked.

'I honestly don't know, *chérie*,' Rust replied with a shrug, then gave her a knowing smile. 'And even if I did know, I wouldn't tell you. I've already told you far too much as it is.'

'Thanks for explaining the situation to us, Jacques,' Graham said.

'Bear it in mind the next time you want to update Sergei on the case,' Rust said. 'Don't get me wrong, I think the world of him, but the fact still remains that he'll almost certainly be on his way back to Moscow within the next few weeks to take up a position as the new head of the RIS, which is, after all, a rival intelligence agency.'

'Don't worry, we'll just rehash what he already knows the next time we see him,' Graham assured him.

'He could still get the info from the Colonel,' Sabrina said.

'I'll have a word with the Colonel,' Rust said. 'Once he knows that Sergei purposely leaked the Koslov story to you, he might be a bit more wary about what he tells him in the future.'

'Well, we'd better get going,' Graham said, standing up and moving to the door.

'Sabrina?' Rust called out as she followed Graham to the door. 'You're a member of an international strike force unit, and as such you're expected to be completely objective and impartial in your approach to any given assignment. Do you think that we're not all well aware of what could happen if Zlotin or either of his colleagues were sprung again once they're back on Russian soil? But if we start acting as judge, jury and executioner then we'll have become no better than them. Contrary to what some of the African and Asian Ambassadors at the UN believe, we're not freelance assassins who are above the law. Don't give them extra ammunition to use against us, not when our standing at the UN is already at an all-time low. It would actually be to our advantage to bring them in alive, if at all possible. Then they can be handed over to the Russians, preferably on neutral territory, who can then do what they want with them. Frankly, I hope they shoot the bastards on the spot. But whatever they decide to do, our hands will be clean. And at the end of the day, that's all that really counts, isn't it?'

'I read you, Jacques,' Sabrina said.

Graham put his hand lightly on Sabrina's arm. 'I'd like nothing better than to put a bullet in Zlotin the first chance I got, but I'm damned if I'm going to do the Russians' dirty work for them. Not only that, it would also reflect badly on UNACO which, as Jacques rightly pointed out, isn't exactly the most popular organization at the UN right now. We have to put UNACO before our personal feelings. Remember that.'

'I know,' she said softly.

Rust smiled to himself. 'I never thought I'd see the day when the last UNACO rebel actually stood up for the principles of law and order. You must be slipping, Mike.'

'Yeah? I just hope Zlotin's foolish enough to try and pull a gun on me, because that would automatically give me the right to defend myself. Nothing would give me greater satisfaction than to send that bastard back to Moscow in a body bag.' Graham opened the door. 'Come on, Sabrina, we've got a plane to catch.'

Rust stared at the door for some time after they had left, then reached for the telephone to call Philpott in New York.

* * *

Katherine Warren replaced the receiver and was about to reach for her notebook on the table beside her when she heard the front door open. 'Is that you, Ed?' she called out.

'Yeah, who else would it be?' Miller retorted from the hallway. Moments later he poked his head around the lounge door. 'You weren't expecting anyone else, were you?'

She shook her head. 'Did you get to see the charming Captain Gonzalez?'

'Of course,' Miller replied, removing his overcoat and tossing it over the back of the nearest chair. 'He suddenly became very co-operative when I offered to show his wife and daughter some of the photographs I had with me. I don't think he thought it was a very good idea, especially not on Christmas Day.'

'Did he give you the report?' she asked, wetting her lips excitedly.

'I told you, he was very co-operative,' Miller replied, removing the folded report from the inside pocket of his overcoat. 'It makes fascinating reading, but you won't understand a word of it until I've had a chance to translate it for you.'

'Well, it'll give you something to do after we get back from the hotel.'

Miller stopped as he was about to pour himself a bourbon from the bottle on the sideboard and looked round suspiciously at her. 'Why are *we* going to the hotel? It's your shift next. I'm only on again at midnight.'

'Change of plan. I had a very interesting chat with your colleague, Damas, while you were out. It seems he'd gone into the hotel to buy some cigarettes, when who should emerge from the lift but our intrepid double act, Graham and Carver. But instead of heading for the car out front they disappeared through a side door. Damas went after them just in time to see them driving off in a blue Passat which had been parked out back. He flagged down a taxi and followed them to the airport, but he couldn't find out where they were headed. That's when he called me.'

175

'So if they had a car out back it means they're on to us,' Miller concluded as he poured himself a small measure of bourbon.

'It certainly looks that way,' she replied. 'Graham must have seen me, possibly at the hospital. It's the only possible explanation I can come up with at the moment.'

'So what happens now?'

'We bring in a couple more of your colleagues to keep up the pretence that we're still watching the white Ford out front. We've only been using the one car, so Graham and Carver won't have any trouble spotting it parked outside the hotel. We'll use a second car to keep an eye on the Passat. They're obviously using the Passat for business and the Ford to visit Kolchinsky at the hospital.'

'So by taking the Ford to the hospital, they're making out that the only reason they're in Lisbon is to visit Kolchinsky. It's a neat trick.'

'And it's imperative that we let them believe that they've got one over on us,' Katherine said. 'We can certainly use it to our advantage in the long run, especially if we can now keep tabs on them while they're on the case. Any pictures would only add further credibility to our story.'

'So why are we going to the hotel?'

'Damas said he'd pick up a hire car and meet us at the back of the hotel in an hour's time. We'll have to work out where best to park the car so as not to miss them when they next use the Passat.'

'If they're not at the hotel right now, we could search their rooms. I've got a miniature camera, so anything we found could be photographed and replaced exactly as we'd found it. They'd never even know we'd been there.'

'If they already know we're on to them, they're sure to have taken precautions to guard against us doing just that. Microphones, perhaps even a hidden camera to monitor anyone entering their rooms while they were out.'

'But that's where we've got the edge on them. After all,

they are only supposed to be out here visiting Kolchinsky in hospital. If we were to conceal our faces, they may suspect it was us, but I hardly think that their superior at the UN is going to ring up Larry Ryan at the *Sentinel* and complain about it, do you?'

'If they thought for one moment that we'd been in their rooms, they'd know immediately that we'd found out about the second car at the back of the hotel. How else would we have known that they weren't in the hotel?' She shook her head. 'No, let them think we're still stumbling about in the dark. It can only be to our advantage.'

'Point taken,' Miller reluctantly conceded. 'I just hope all this cloak-and-dagger stuff is worth it in the end. If UNACO know we're on to them, then they're going to pull out all the stops to prevent the story from being published. I'm just surprised that we've been allowed to track Graham and Carver for so long.'

'Of course UNACO know we're on to them, but the last thing they'd want right now is publicity. That would only jeopardize the case Graham and Carver are working on at the moment.' She smiled to herself. 'You can be sure that there are already moves afoot back at the UN to have my exposé intercepted the moment Graham and Carver return to New York, but unless UNACO intend to take out some kind of injunction against the *Sentinel*, which I would very much doubt anyway as it would only heap even more publicity on to them, then this story's going to be the scoop of the year and there isn't a damn thing they can do about it. That's the beauty of it, Ed. They're in a no-win situation, and that's something we can exploit to the full. And believe me, I intend to do just that.'

The helicopter carrying Graham and Sabrina put down on a football field close to the small police station in Vila do Conde where the Special Forces Brigade had set up their own Command Centre to co-ordinate the search for the Fisiers.

A police car was on hand to drive them to the station; when they arrived they were shown to the room where a familiar face was on hand to greet them.

'Captain Morales, isn't it?' Sabrina said, shaking the extended hand.

'Yes, it's good to see you both again.'

'You guys sure get around,' Graham said. 'I thought you and your partner were supposed to be staking out Caldere's joint in Lisbon.'

'Major Inacio pulled me off the stake-out an hour before our shift was due to end and sent me up here as your liaison officer. Being single does have its disadvantages, especially at this time of year.'

'Don't worry, it's the same for us,' Sabrina said, gesturing to Graham. 'We always seem to be on standby over Christmas as well. I guess it just goes with the job.'

'What have you got for us?' Graham asked.

'I've got a dozen men working in conjunction with the local police checking all known caravan sites within a fifty-mile radius of the town, but as yet there haven't been any positive sightings of either the Fisiers or the Russians,' Morales replied, perching on the edge of the table by the door. 'Twenty minutes ago the car the Russians were using was found abandoned in a side street close to the Fisiers' villa, but so far no vehicles have been reported stolen in that area: with it being Christmas Day, the owner may not even realize it's gone for another couple of days yet.'

'If, in fact, the Russians did steal another vehicle,' Graham said thoughtfully.

'What do you mean?' Morales asked.

'Zlotin may have been forced to amend his original plan at short notice, but that doesn't mean he'll be any less meticulous in the way he carries out those changes,' Graham told him. 'It's my guess that they would have had a second car parked somewhere close to the villa anyway as additional back-up in case of an emergency. And knowing that their car had been seen by one of the neighbours, they took no chances and switched to the second car. And it goes without saying that they'll already have devised an escape plan to bring into play as soon as they've snatched the Fisiers. Nikolai Zlotin never leaves anything to chance. Never.'

'You think a lot of this Zlotin, don't you?' Morales said to Graham.

'I respect his ability as a fellow soldier, if that's what you mean,' Graham retorted.

'*Capitão?*' a voice called out from behind a computer terminal at the far end of the room.

'*Sim?*' Morales replied.

'*Telefone.*'

'*Quem e?*' Morales asked, reaching for the telephone on the table behind him.

'Sergento Branco,' came the reply.

Morales lifted the receiver to his ear and moments later grabbed the pointer off the table and crossed to the map on the wall. He used it to find Branco's position on the map and circled the area in red. Then, after barking a series of orders down the line, he hung up and turned back to Graham and Sabrina. 'We've found them,' he announced excitedly.

'Who?' Sabrina asked.

'Dr Fisier and his wife,' Morales replied. 'I've got two men with them now. They'll stay with them until we get there.'

'Where exactly are they?' Sabrina asked.

Morales gestured to the map behind him. 'At a small caravan park close to the village of Ponte de Lima. It's about thirty miles north of here.'

'Any sign of the Russians?' Sabrina asked.

'Not as yet,' Morales replied. 'But you can be sure they can't be too far behind. There are only so many caravan sites in the area. Their neighbour had the good sense to mislead them about the colour and make of the car the Fisiers were driving, but that will only throw them off for a while. That's why we've got to get Dr Fisier and his wife

179

out of there as quickly as possible. I would suggest we use the helicopter to airlift them from the caravan site.'

'Where will they be taken?' Sabrina asked.

'We have a safe house in Santiago,' Morales told her. 'They can stay there until this is over.'

'So what are we waiting for?' Graham demanded, heading for the door.

Morales issued a string of orders to his men, then hurried after Graham and Sabrina. He caught up with them outside the police station. 'Come on, that's my car over there,' he said, gesturing to a white Ford parked on the opposite side of the street.

By the time they reached the football field, the pilot had already been briefed over the radio and was ready for take-off. They ran, doubled-over, to the helicopter, and scrambled inside. Morales was still closing the door behind him when the helicopter began slowly to lift away from the ground.

'How much further is it?' Graham asked, tapping Morales on the shoulder.

'It's not far now,' Morales replied. 'Two, three miles at the most. We'll soon be able –'

'Capitão, olhar!' the pilot cut in sharply, pointing into the distance.

At first Morales couldn't see what the pilot was pointing at, but the moment the helicopter cleared the woodland directly ahead of them they all saw the thick black smoke in the distance. He instinctively knew it was coming from the caravan site but, as the helicopter drew nearer, he realized that it wasn't a fire as he'd initially thought. The smoke wasn't spiralling upwards as it would from flames; it was diffusing out over a wide area and blanketing the caravan site in a tenebrous cloud.

'Smoke grenades,' Sabrina said, peering through the window at the pall of black smoke beneath them.

'It's still fairly thick,' Morales added, gesturing for the

pilot to take the helicopter down. 'That means the Russians may still be there.'

'No chance,' Graham snapped behind him. 'You couldn't see your hand in front of your face down there. The Russians aren't going to work in those conditions. Those smoke grenades were left to disorientate your people so that they wouldn't be able to give chase. No, the Russians have already gone, you can be sure of that.'

The radio on the seat beside Morales suddenly crackled into life. 'Branco to helicopter, do you read me, over?' a voice shouted breathlessly in Portuguese. 'This is Branco to helicopter, do you read me, over?'

Morales grabbed the radio and was quick to identify himself. 'What happened down there?'

'The Russians caught us by surprise, sir,' came the despondent reply. 'We didn't even see them until they smashed the windows and threw a smoke canister into the caravan. Dr Fisier and his wife panicked and fled the caravan. We tried to go after them, but we came under fire the moment we tried to open the door. We couldn't move, we were pinned down. A car pulled up outside the caravan and the Fisiers were bundled into the back seat, but by then we couldn't get in a clear shot at the Russians because of all the smoke.'

'So they got away?' Morales hissed.

'Yes, sir.'

'Didn't you at least try and follow them?' Morales demanded angrily.

There was a pause before the answer came. 'They sabotaged our car, sir. The wheels were shot out and the radio destroyed. That's why we couldn't contact you until now.'

'So where are you calling from now?' Morales demanded.

'The local police got here a short time ago. I'm using one of their radios.'

'This gets better by the minute. What make of car were the Russians driving?'

'It was a red Mazda, sir,' came the reply, and Morales was given the number of the licence plates. 'They made for the slip road which joins up with the 203. That's when we lost sight of them. The 203 leads to the coast.'

'How long ago was this?'

'Not five minutes ago, sir.'

'At least that's something,' Morales snarled sarcastically. 'I want you and Corporal Villarta to return immediately to the police station in Vila do Conde and I expect your written reports to be on my desk by the time I return. Is that understood?'

'Yes, sir,' came the sullen reply.

'Over and out.' Morales turned to look at Graham and Sabrina behind him. 'It's the worst possible news, I'm afraid.'

'Your guys lost the Russians. Yeah, we know.' Graham noticed the surprise on Morales' face. 'Sabrina speaks Portuguese. She translated the gist of the conversation for me.'

Morales' eyes flickered towards Sabrina. 'Then you'll also know that we have the make and the licence plates of the car the Russians are using.'

'Yeah,' Graham replied. 'The local cops are already here, so let them get on with the job of evacuating the area. And now that you know your guys are all right down there, our best bet now would be to stay up here and track those bastards from the air.'

Morales nodded in agreement, and the pilot immediately pulled the helicopter away from the caravan site. Knowing the Russians already had a five-minute head-start on them, Morales ordered the pilot to follow the route of the 203 then, using his radio, contacted Lieutenant Degas, his deputy at the command centre in Vila do Conde, and explained what had happened. He gave orders for an APB to be put out on the red Mazda, for two more helicopters to be scrambled as quickly as possible to assist in the search, and for another Special Forces team to be sent to the caravan site to liaise with the local police.

'If these Russians are as smart as you say they are, they could already have switched cars again,' Morales said to Graham, replacing the radio on the seat beside him.

'Not unless they've either stolen or hijacked one since leaving the caravan site, and I very much doubt that they would want to waste any more time than was absolutely necessary,' Graham replied. 'You've got to remember that they already knew the location of the Fisiers' villa before they actually went there. That way they were able to plan their escape route in advance. But when they found that the Fisiers weren't at the villa, that would have thrown them. They've had to improvise since then by scouring the caravan sites in the area in the hope of finding the Fisiers before we did. So there's no way that they could have come up with an alternative plan if they didn't know where the Fisiers were up until a short time ago.'

'I see your point,' Morales said. 'So if you are right, and they have already devised an escape route from Vila do Conde, then surely they'll revert back to it now that they've got the Fisiers?'

'Wouldn't you?' Graham replied with a questioning look.

'How's the fuel situation?' Morales asked the pilot.

'We've still got about an hour of fuel left,' came the reply. 'Do you want me to stay on this course, sir?'

Morales nodded. 'If Mr Graham's right about this escape plan, then the Russians will be on their way back to Vila do Conde by now.'

'It would seem the most logical move,' Graham said. 'And stick to the main road; the Russians won't risk chancing some short-cut in case they end up lost. That's the last thing they'd want with the authorities already breathing down their necks. They know it'll only be a short time before the whole area's crawling with police.'

The helicopter followed the contours of the road as it

weaved its way through the countryside, over the small village of Deão and on to the coastal town of Viana do Castelo where the 203 melded into the EO1 motorway. The pilot banked the helicopter sharply southwards until they were directly over the motorway. He checked the fuel gauge. They still had forty minutes of flying time left; by the time that had expired, other helicopters would have been scrambled and could continue the search. Like the others, the pilot was concerned that they hadn't come across the Mazda yet. If the Russians did only have five minutes' head-start on them, and if they had stuck to the main roads, then the helicopter should already have come across the car by now. But then there were a lot of *ifs* . . .

The radio on the seat crackled into life again. 'Degas to Captain Morales. Come in.'

Morales picked up the radio. 'Morales here.'

'Return to the caravan site immediately.'

'What's happened?' Morales demanded of his deputy.

'We can't talk over the radio, sir. There's every possibility that this conversation's being monitored by the Russians. You'll be briefed in full once you reach the caravan site.'

Morales waited until Sabrina had translated the dialogue to Graham, then looked round at them, his eyes narrowed uncertainly. 'The only way the Russians could monitor the conversation is if they had one of these radios with the code frequency already punched into it. And if they had taken one of the radios, why didn't Branco mention it earlier?'

'Are you sure that is Degas?' Sabrina said, indicating the radio in Morales' hand.

'It certainly sounds like him,' Morales replied.

'It's easy to disguise a voice over the radio,' Graham said.

The radio crackled again. 'Degas to Captain Morales. Are you there, sir?'

'I'm still here,' Morales replied quickly, then released the button again to prevent them from being heard at the other end. 'What are you suggesting? That the Russians somehow overheard my conversation with Degas earlier and now one of them's impersonating him to send us on some wild-goose chase?'

'According to his file, Yemenkov speaks several languages fluently, including Portuguese,' Graham pointed out.

'If they are monitoring your frequency, they'll already know that there's a chopper on their tail,' Sabrina added. 'And knowing that they can't possibly outpace us, they create a diversion instead to give them that extra time they would need to make good their escape. It makes sense.'

Morales thought for a moment, then put the radio to his lips. 'How do I know this really is Lieutenant Degas?'

There was a moment's pause. 'You circled Ponte de Lima in red on the map here in the Command Centre when Branco rang to say that he'd found Dr Fisier and his wife.'

Satisfied that it was Degas, Morales gave the order for the pilot to turn the helicopter around and return to the caravan site.

Most of the smoke had dissipated by the time they reached the caravan site, and the pilot was able to put down on a section of the approach road which had already been sealed off by the local police.

Morales was the first out of the helicopter. He hurried over to where two of his men were waiting for him. They spoke at length and Morales' face was grim as he approached Graham and Sabrina who were now standing clear of the rotors, their hands dug into their pockets against the icy wind which had whipped up within the last hour.

'Well?' Graham asked.

'Branco and Villarta are dead,' Morales replied, pulling a packet of cigarettes from his pocket. Graham and Sabrina shook their heads when he held it out towards them. 'They were found in the caravan. Both had been shot through the back of the head.'

'So it was Yemenkov, and not Branco, who radioed through to you earlier?' Graham said.

Morales nodded, then pushed a cigarette between his lips, cupped his hands around his lighter, and lit it.

'Why, what would the Russians have to gain by . . .' Sabrina trailed off as the truth suddenly dawned on her. 'There never was a red Mazda, was there?'

'Actually there is,' Morales corrected her. 'It's still parked in the berth opposite the Fisiers' caravan. The Russians took another car from the caravan site which the police have since found abandoned a few hundred yards from here. Of course there was no sign of either the Russians or the Fisiers.'

'The Russians had obviously left their own car there to ensure that it wouldn't be seen from the caravan site,' Graham said. 'They must still have been here when we arrived in the helicopter, so Yemenkov impersonated Branco and sent us off on a wild-goose chase, leaving them with plenty of time to make good their escape.'

'That's not all,' Morales said. 'It seems that Yemenkov, again masquerading as Branco, called the local police soon after the smoke grenades went off and told them not to respond to any calls from the caravan site as the Special Forces Brigade were already dealing with the incident themselves.'

'And he told us that the local cops were already here when we arrived,' Graham hissed. 'So by playing one off against the other he made sure that both the Special Forces Brigade and the local cops would stay away from the caravan site, at least until they were well clear of the area.'

'Lieutenant Degas has already arranged for roadblocks to be set up along the main highway to Vila do Conde,' Morales said.

'By the time the roadblocks are in place the Russians will be long gone,' Graham told him.

'You have to give them credit for ingenuity,' Sabrina said, albeit grudgingly. 'They certainly had us going, didn't they?'

'They took us for a ride in every sense of the phrase,' Graham snorted in disgust.

Morales took a long drag on his cigarette, then exhaled the smoke up towards the dark, overcast sky. 'I'm going to be lucky to keep my commission by the time Major Inacio's through with me.'

'You're not the only one who's going to be dodging the flak, buddy,' Graham said despondently. 'We've blown our one real chance of nailing these bastards, and that puts us right back to square one again.'

'Is there anything you particularly want to see here?' Morales asked, gesturing around him. 'If not, we'd better get back to Vila do Conde and report in to our superiors.'

Graham looked at Sabrina who shook her head. 'There's nothing we can do here,' he replied.

Morales held out his hands, palms upturned, as the first spots of rain began to fall. 'I think we're in for a storm.'

'Yeah, in more ways than one,' Graham retorted gloomily, hurrying after the others as they made for the helicopter.

8

'How much further to go?'

'Not far now,' Zlotin replied as Whitlock entered the bridge behind him.

Whitlock had to grab on to the handrail beside him as another wave crashed over the deck. 'I'll be glad to get my feet back on terra firma again,' he said through gritted teeth.

'You're not comfortable on the water, are you?'

'Not when I'm in the middle of a storm, I'm not,' Whitlock replied testily.

'This is nothing,' Zlotin said indifferently. 'It's only a squall. It'll blow itself out within an hour.'

'You sound like you're used to these kind of conditions,' Whitlock said, easing himself down on to the padded bench at the back of the wheelhouse.

Zlotin eyed Whitlock coldly in the reflection of the rain-streaked window. 'Did you come up here for anything in particular?'

'I came topside to shoot the breeze, that's all,' Whitlock replied defensively.

'I'm really not interested in your small talk, Royce,' Zlotin retorted angrily. 'So unless you have something relevant to say, I suggest that from now on you keep your mouth shut and your mind on your work.'

From a personal point of view, Whitlock could think of no better arrangement, but it was imperative that he stay in character at all times and Royce, whose suspicious nature had only ever been surpassed by his avarice, would have wanted to find out anything he could about the mysterious Russian.

Whitlock shrugged. 'I was just trying to be friendly, that's all.'

'You weren't hired for your companionship,' Zlotin snapped back.

'So what exactly was I hired for?' Whitlock demanded, his eyes boring into the back of Zlotin's head. 'All Jannoc mentioned was something about guard duties. So who exactly am I guarding? The professor and his daughter? Is that it?'

'You'll find out soon enough,' was all Zlotin would say.

Whitlock fell silent and, as he listened to the rain outside, fleeting droplets tapping rhythmically on the illuminated windows before being swept away in the wake of the wind, he found his mind drifting back slowly over the past twelve hours.

They had left Leipzig soon after midday, and Zlotin had flown them on to Munich's Riem Airport, their destination on the original flight plan from Marseilles, where Zlotin had filed a report explaining about the so-called 'engine trouble' which had caused their late arrival at the airport. An engineer had been dispatched to check the engine as a matter of routine, had naturally found nothing amiss, and they had been given the necessary clearance by air traffic control to continue on their journey. Six hours later they had touched down at Madrid's Barajas International Airport, where they had again been required to clear customs. Then, after the Piper Navaho had been refuelled, they had taken off on a two-hour flight to Portugal's second largest city, Porto, where Zlotin had arranged in advance to have a hire car waiting for them at the airport. The storm clouds had already been gathering ominously overhead when Zlotin had driven them to Matosinhos, a small coastal town five miles north of Porto, where a sleek forty-foot motor cruiser, *A Agua Bruxa*,

The Water Witch, was berthed. Zlotin had hired it in Lisbon shortly after arriving in Portugal.

Having taken the wheel, Zlotin had dispatched Whitlock below to keep an eye on the Auerbachs. The two prisoners had sat together on one of the upholstered banquettes, occasionally exchanging words but never once acknowledging Whitlock who had taken up a position at the foot of the stairs.

He'd watched Lisl Auerbach carefully, trying to detect any signs of stress but, apart from the occasional smile at her father, her face had remained expressionless as she'd stared impassively at her feet. He could only marvel at the resolve and equanimity of this sixteen-year-old in the face of such adversity. He could still picture the moment when her father had taken her aside at the abandoned airstrip in Leipzig and told her about the lethal virus. She hadn't broken down or become hysterical as he'd expected her to do. Instead she'd hugged her father tightly, then taken his hand and walked with him silently to the waiting aeroplane. It was then that Whitlock had realized just how special the bond actually was between father and daughter. It had made him feel strangely uncomfortable, an intruder on a family's private grief. What made it all the harder to accept was the fact that there was nothing he could do to help or to reassure them, at least not for the time being . . .

'We're here,' Zlotin announced, his voice snapping Whitlock out of his thoughts.

Whitlock scrambled to his feet and crossed to where Zlotin was standing. At first he couldn't see anything in the darkness, but suddenly the bow lights danced uneven shadows across the towering rock face directly ahead of them. It seemed to have loomed out of nowhere, and he instinctively took a step backwards as if fearful that the motor cruiser was about to be dashed against it. 'You're a bit close, aren't you?' he said, quickly regaining his composure.

Zlotin cast a sidelong glance at Whitlock. 'The lights distort the actual distance between us and the rock face. There's still plenty of room to manoeuvre in to dock.'

'Dock?' Whitlock said incredulously. 'Where the hell are you going to dock? That's just a sheer rock face ahead of us.'

'It's the same on all sides,' Zlotin told him. 'But there is a cavern on the eastern side of the island. That's where we'll be docking.'

A bolt of lightning sheared across the darkness, momentarily illuminating the dark, forbidding façade. Whitlock leaned closer to the window and looked up in awe at the sheer size of the rock face in front of them.

'One thousand four hundred and twenty-eight feet,' Zlotin said, as if reading Whitlock's thoughts before turning the wheel into the path of an oncoming wave. 'It's quite magnificent, isn't it?'

'How do you know its exact measurements?' Whitlock asked, grabbing on to the handrail as the motor cruiser rose then dipped sharply again in the turbulent waters.

'I was able to get hold of the original blueprints of the prison which was built there in the Fifties. The height of the four rock faces was included in the plans.'

'There's a prison built on the island?' Whitlock shot back in amazement.

'Not on it, inside it. The centre of the rock is hollow. The prison was known as *A Fortaleza*. The Fortress. The name speaks for itself. It was closed down in the Eighties after a fire swept through part of the building. It's perfect for us though.'

Whitlock found himself nodding in agreement. 'Ingenious. But how did you find out about it in the first place?'

'That doesn't concern you,' Zlotin retorted sharply, then jerked his thumb towards the hatchway behind him. 'Bring the Professor and his daughter up here. We'll be docking shortly.'

When Whitlock returned to the saloon he found Auerbach standing in front of one of the windows, staring absently into the darkness. He knew Auerbach had seen

191

him in the reflection of the window, but the German made no attempt to acknowledge his presence in the room. Lisl was still sitting on the banquette, her hands clasped in her lap, her eyes downcast.

'OK, time to go,' Whitlock announced from the foot of the stairs. He knew they both understood English, having already established that in Leipzig. In fact, Auerbach spoke it fluently from his years with the BND.

'Where are we?' Auerbach asked without looking round.

Whitlock knew it would be best to leave the explanations to Zlotin. That way there could be no misunderstandings. He decided to play it safe and fell back on one of Zlotin's own lines. 'You'll find out soon enough.'

'I want to know now!' Auerbach retorted.

'I don't think you're in any position to make any demands, do you?' Whitlock shot back. 'Now let's go.'

'I said –'

'And I said let's go!' Whitlock cut in sharply, then crossed to where Auerbach was standing and levelled a finger of warning at him. 'You'd be well advised to do as you're told, Professor.'

Auerbach glared at Whitlock then brushed past him, grabbed the hold-all from under the table, and strode briskly to the stairs where he paused to look back at his daughter who was still sitting hesitantly on the banquette. 'Lisl, *komm*,' he snapped, gesturing her towards him.

She shot Whitlock a withering look, then got to her feet and followed her father up on to the bridge.

Whitlock exhaled deeply and slowly rubbed his hands over his face. He knew he'd only been staying in character, but he still hated himself for it. Quick to remind himself that he was a professional with a job to do, he pushed any feelings of guilt from his mind and made his way back up on to the bridge. Only then did he realize that the motor cruiser was already inside the cavern.

He moved to the nearest window and took in his

extraordinary surroundings. He estimated the cavern itself to be at least two hundred feet wide, twice that in length and another hundred feet to the tip of the rugged, arched roof. A metal landing stage, which was beginning to rust from the years of neglect, spanned the length of one of the walls. A metal door, which was built into the rock face, slid open, and Yemenkov, dressed in a black shell suit, hurried down the metal steps and on to the landing stage.

'Throw him the mooring rope,' Zlotin said to Whitlock as the cruiser bumped gently against one of the fenders secured against the side of the dock.

Whitlock scrambled out on to the deck and was immediately aware of Yemenkov's eyes following him as he made his way across to the mooring rope. Picking it up, he heaved it over the side of the boat. Yemenkov tethered the rope to a bollard, then stepped back and gave a thumbs-up sign to the bridge. Zlotin waited until Whitlock had put out the gangplank then ushered the Auerbachs from the bridge and down on to the landing stage.

'Keep an eye on them,' Zlotin told Whitlock as he crossed to where Yemenkov was waiting for him.

'I'm glad now that we took the helicopter,' Yemenkov said, gesturing to the boat behind him. 'It looks pretty rough out there.'

'I've been through worse,' Zlotin replied with a dismissive shrug. 'Are Dr Fisier and his wife here?'

Yemenkov nodded. 'We brought them in about an hour ago.'

'You should have been back this afternoon,' Zlotin said suspiciously. 'What happened?'

'It's a long story, sir, and it involves UNACO.'

'Let's get the Auerbachs to their quarters, then you can brief me in full,' Zlotin told him.

Yemenkov looked across at Whitlock. 'Who's the new face, sir?'

'Berger's replacement,' Zlotin told him. 'His name's Royce.'

'Another legionnaire?' Yemenkov asked.

'No. It's also a long story. Where's Major Rodenko?'

'He's in his quarters, sir,' Yemenkov replied, looking down nervously at the floor.

'What is it?' Zlotin demanded. 'Captain, look at me when I'm talking to you!'

Yemenkov raised his eyes reluctantly. 'He's been drinking, sir.'

'Where did he get it from?' Zlotin demanded.

'He bought it on the mainland, sir,' Yemenkov answered hesitantly.

'You know I gave strict orders that no more alcohol was to be brought on to the island. Why didn't you stop him?'

'With all due respect, sir, Major Rodenko is my superior and I had no authority to question his actions,' Yemenkov replied stiffly.

Zlotin patted Yemenkov on the arm. 'You're a good soldier, Valentin. Show Professor Auerbach and his daughter to their quarters then report back to me.'

'What about Royce?' Yemenkov asked.

'Take him with you. Let him see the place for himself.'

'Yes, sir,' came the reply.

'Oh, and Valentin? Royce doesn't know our names. Let's keep it that way, shall we?'

'Yes, sir,' Yemenkov replied, hurrying away to carry out his orders.

Zlotin used a key card to activate the metal door, which opened on to a dimly lit corridor. Passing through a second door, Zlotin entered the inspection hall. A dozen wings led off from the circular hall, each housing a hundred and forty cells. He made straight for the wing where the Russians had set up their own quarters, entering the only illuminated doorway in the long, deserted corridor. Rodenko was sitting on one of the beds, his back against the wall, his knees drawn up to his chest, a bottle of vodka held loosely in his hand.

'Welcome back, *tovarisch*,' Rodenko said with a grin when Zlotin appeared in the doorway. 'Come in and sit down.'

Zlotin crossed to the bed, yanked the bottle out of Rodenko's hand and hurled it against the opposite wall. 'I will not tolerate insubordination of any kind, especially from a senior officer who should know better.'

Rodenko stared at the shattered bottle, then got to his feet and crossed to the door. He shook his head to himself then turned back to Zlotin. 'I brought one bottle back with me from the mainland. One lousy bottle, that's all.'

'I don't care whether you brought back one bottle or a whole crate; the fact remains that you disobeyed a direct order,' Zlotin shot back angrily. 'What's happened to you in these last couple of weeks, Viktor? You were always a stickler for the rules. You used to carry out orders without question and you were always the first to crack down on any hint of insubordination amongst the junior officers. This isn't the same Viktor Rodenko I've known for the past twelve years.'

'You're the one who's clinging to the past, Nikolai, not me. You know very well that you don't have the authority to pull rank on me any more. The court martial stripped us of our rank and threw us out of the army. There's no way back from that.'

'So what you're saying is that, although I can't pull rank on you any more, it's still all right for you to pull rank on Yemenkov when it suits you, is that it?' Zlotin retorted sharply.

'I do it to humour him, that's all. And even that's now beginning to wear thin.'

'You were as much in favour of the putsch as the rest of us. You can't deny that.'

'I don't deny it,' Rodenko told him. 'But my reasons for supporting it were very different from yours. I've been a card-carrying member of the Communist Party for as long as I can remember, but that still doesn't make me an ideologist. I never have been. You of all people should know that. I've always been a career soldier. The military was my life and I saw that threatened by Gorbachev's reforms. That's why I backed the putsch. You, on the other hand, always regarded the military merely as an extension of your political beliefs. And that's where we differ, Nikolai. You, and Yemenkov for that matter, still believe there's a future for Communism in Russia, and you'll stop at nothing to turn the clock back again to the days of the Cold War. I don't hold with those views, not after what I witnessed during the attempted putsch. The people would rather have died than let the old-style conservatives back into power again. That's when I realized that I had no future in the new Russia. Communism's dead, Nikolai. It's dead.'

'It's strange that this should all come out now. I didn't hear you complaining when we devised the plot to use Jannoc to get us out of Russia.'

'What was the alternative? Turn it down and spend the next twenty-five years in some freezing Siberian jail? You're damn right I didn't complain about it.' Rodenko paced the cell floor then stopped in front of Zlotin. 'When we got Jannoc to spring us, it was on the understanding that we would undertake a job for him, for which we would be paid half a million dollars in cash. It was only when we got to Portugal that you announced your own little amendment to the plan.'

'So what you're saying is that you're in this purely for your share of Jannoc's money?' Zlotin asked.

'Yes,' Rodenko replied bluntly. 'I've got no intention of ever going back to Russia again. At least with my share of the money I've got a chance to start over in another country. I'm sorry if I've disappointed you, Nikolai, but I've been in this for myself right from the start.'

Zlotin stared thoughtfully at his feet before looking up slowly at Rodenko. 'Why have you waited until now before telling me this?'

'I was actually going to wait until after Jannoc had paid

us before telling you, but this whole façade's finally forced my hand.'

'What façade?' Zlotin asked.

'The two of you, but Yemenkov in particular, have been playing at soldiers ever since we got here. If it's not you barking out orders then it's Yemenkov, with his Colonel Zlotin this, Major Rodenko that. It's driving me mad, Nikolai.'

'That's because we are still soldiers,' Zlotin told him.

'Not any more we're not, and you know it.'

'Perhaps not in your eyes, but I know I speak for Captain Yemenkov when I say that neither of us recognized the validity of the court martial which chose to convict us of treason.'

'That's crazy, Nikolai,' Rodenko shot back.

'Hear me out!' Zlotin thundered.

'Is that another of your orders, *sir*?' came the sarcastic riposte.

'No,' Zlotin replied calmly. 'You've had your say, Viktor, I think it's only fair that I now have mine.'

'Go on,' Rodenko said gruffly, knowing that Zlotin was right.

'I agreed to Jannoc's demands, not because I saw it as a way out of Russia, but rather as a way of giving something back to my country. I make no secret of my intention to, as you put it, "turn the clock back again to the days of the Cold War". And you know as well as I do that those sentiments aren't just confined to a few hard-liners in the military. There's a growing support for a change right across the country. Whatever else was wrong with the old Communist regime – and I'm the first to admit that it had its faults – at least it guaranteed the people work, housing and fixed low prices. Yeltsin's government has brought with it a plague of unemployment, poverty and homelessness. Not only that, there's been civil war in virtually every state that chose to break away from Moscow since the signing of the Union of Sovereign States treaty. Russians are killing each other every day over the spoils of independence. How can that be justified?'

'It's the choice they made, Nikolai,' Rodenko reminded him.

'It's the choice they made at the time,' Zlotin corrected him. 'But as they continue to bury their dead, I know that many of them are already having second thoughts about the price they're paying for this new democracy.'

'Now you know why I've stayed clear of political ideology all these years,' Rodenko said. 'There's just no clear-cut solution to politics. There never is, and there never will be.'

'So what will you do with yourself after this is over?' Zlotin asked. 'I can't see you opening a delicatessen in some Parisian side street.'

'Neither can I,' Rodenko replied with a smile. 'Good military advisers are in short supply in Africa. There's always some corrupt dictator who'll pay good money for someone with my knowledge and expertise.'

'Until he's ousted by another corrupt dictator,' Zlotin said disdainfully.

'Then I'll just renegotiate my contract with his successor. As I said, military advisers are in short supply over there.' Rodenko peered out into the corridor when he heard the sound of approaching footsteps. It was Yemenkov and Whitlock. 'Who's that with Yemenkov?'

'Berger's replacement,' Zlotin replied.

'Another of Jannoc's clowns?' Rodenko snorted in disgust.

'Not this time. I'll tell you about him later, but for the moment just remember that he doesn't know who we are. So no names in front of him.'

'That suits me fine,' Rodenko replied.

Moments later Yemenkov appeared in the doorway. 'We've secured the prisoners in their quarters, sir.'

'Good,' Zlotin said. 'I'll speak to Professor Auerbach and Dr Fisier shortly, but before that we have a few things to discuss amongst ourselves. Come in, Captain.'

'Thank you, sir,' Yemenkov said, entering the cell.

'Ah, Royce,' Zlotin said when Whitlock followed Yemenkov into the room. 'Have you been shown around the prison?'

Whitlock nodded. 'Your buddy gave me the guided tour.'

'He's a captain in the Russian armed forces,' Zlotin snapped. 'You will refer to him by his rank in future.'

'He's a captain in *spetznaz*,' Whitlock retorted. 'Why don't you just say it?'

Yemenkov swallowed nervously as he felt Zlotin's eyes on him. 'I didn't tell him anything, sir,' he stammered in Russian. 'I swear I didn't tell him anything.'

Zlotin held up his hand to silence Yemenkov then looked at Whitlock. 'Why do you say that?'

'You're fluent in French, German and English. As far as I'm aware – and correct me if I'm wrong – the only branch of the Russian armed forces which teaches their soldiers foreign languages is *spetznaz*.'

'There's more to you than meets the eye, Royce. Yes, we are all officers of the élite *spetznaz* unit.' Zlotin gestured to Rodenko. 'This officer holds the rank of major and I the rank of colonel.'

'Three *spetznaz* officers holed up in an abandoned prison on an island somewhere off the Portuguese mainland?' Whitlock said, looking at each face in turn. 'This gets more intriguing by the minute. So what exactly am I doing here? If you needed another pair of hands, why not bring in one of your own people?'

'All you need to know is that you're here to replace a colleague who very carelessly allowed a prisoner to die while in his care.'

Whitlock knew the prisoner had to have been Abe Silverman. It didn't come as any surprise to know that he was dead. It just confirmed what UNACO had suspected for some time . . .

'So what exactly did happen to my predecessor?' Whitlock asked.

'He was executed,' Zlotin replied, as if it were unimportant. 'But we have more pressing matters to discuss. As you'll already have seen, Miss Auerbach and Mrs Fisier have been housed in a separate wing to the cryptologists. They will be your responsibility, leaving us free to concentrate our attention on Professor Auerbach and Dr Fisier.'

'What do these responsibilities entail?' Whitlock asked.

'General guard duties, that's all. You'll also be expected to prepare all meals for them while they remain here on the island. We've put together a makeshift kitchen in the cell next to yours. It's small, but perfectly adequate for your needs. They will be allowed out of their cells twice a day, once in the morning and once at night.'

'Who controls the locks for the cell doors?' Whitlock asked.

'We do. You'll find that the only cells in operation are the ones that are actually in use. It took some time to rewire the circuit board. All the interconnecting doors are operative, and the three of us carry key cards which allow us access to the various wings within the prison,' Zlotin told him. 'There's no need for you to have a key card as you'll have no reason to leave your wing.'

'And what if I need to contact you?'

'We all carry two-way radios,' Zlotin replied. 'You'll be issued with one in due course.'

'What about weapons?' Whitlock asked. 'I noticed that the captain's carrying a 9 mm Makarov in his shoulder holster. Is that standard issue around here?'

'For us, yes,' Zlotin replied.

'Don't I get to carry?' Whitlock shot back.

'I hardly think you'll need a pistol to guard a grandmother and a teenage girl, do you?' Zlotin said scornfully.

'You don't trust me, do you?'

'Trust needs to be earned, Royce,' Zlotin replied.

'If you don't trust me, why did you hire me?'

'I didn't hire you,' Zlotin reminded him. 'Jannoc did. Just remember that.'

'In other words, if I step out of line like my predecessor, you won't have any qualms about putting a bullet in me and dumping my body in the ocean,' Whitlock said.

'I'm sure we could come up with something a little more original than that,' Zlotin replied. He got to his feet and took Rodenko to one side. 'Show Royce to his quarters then report back to me. I should still be with Fisier and Auerbach by the time you get back.'

'I don't like that son-of-a-bitch one little bit, Nikolai,' Rodenko said, glancing across at Whitlock. 'He's too damn cocky for his own good.'

'I'm sure you'll have come up with an original way of dealing with him before we leave here,' Zlotin said, patting him on the arm.

Rodenko smiled coldly. 'You can count on it.'

'Oh, and on your way over there, pick up a two-way radio from the stores and give it to Royce.'

Rodenko nodded then crossed to the door. 'Royce, come with me,' he snapped at Whitlock. The two men left the room.

Yemenkov watched Zlotin slump down on the edge of the bed and cup his hands over his nose and mouth, his eyes fixed on the broken bottle in the corner of the room. 'Sir, are you all right?' he asked anxiously.

There was no reply.

'Colonel Zlotin?' Yemenkov said, moving closer to the bed.

Zlotin looked sharply up at Yemenkov, his brow furrowed. 'What did you say?'

'You looked worried, sir,' Yemenkov said softly. 'Is everything all right?'

'Everything's fine,' Zlotin replied quickly then, rubbing his hands over his face, he shook his head. 'No, everything isn't fine. Major Rodenko won't be returning to Russia with us once this is over.'

'I don't understand, sir,' Yemenkov said.

'He's decided to leave once the folders have been decoded

and Jannoc's delivered the money to us. He'll probably go to Africa as a military adviser.'

'Will you try and stop him, sir?' Yemenkov asked.

'You mean would I shoot him for desertion?'

'Would you, sir?' Yemenkov asked suspiciously, having already witnessed Zlotin execute fellow officers for desertion when they served together in Afghanistan.

'No,' Zlotin said at length.

'I understand, sir.'

'No, I don't think you do. This has got nothing to do with friendship.' Zlotin got to his feet and moved to the door before wheeling round to face Yemenkov. 'Major Rodenko saved my life in Afghanistan. Not only that, he almost died in the process. Did you know that?'

'No, sir, I didn't,' Yemenkov replied guiltily.

'It happened during the Kunar Offensive of '85. I was hit in the leg by shrapnel from a Mujahedin mortar as we were closing in on Barikot. I was left stranded in no man's land with constant Mujahedin gunfire strafing overhead. Major Rodenko broke cover, ran at least a hundred yards to where I lay, and carried me back to safety. Only then did he let on that he'd been hit. In fact, he'd been hit four times in all. Twice in the stomach, once in the back and once in the shoulder. And not only was he still conscious and totally coherent, he also insisted, at gunpoint, that the medics treat me first. He lapsed into a coma shortly after that and it was only the skill of one of our field doctors that saved his life.' Zlotin's eyes flickered across to the broken bottle again. 'You shoot cowards for desertion, Valentin, and whatever else is wrong with Major Rodenko, he's certainly not a coward.'

'I know that, sir,' Yemenkov replied.

'We've both been concerned about Major Rodenko's sudden change of character since we arrived in Portugal, but what he told me tonight obviously goes a long way towards explaining it. I thought it only right that you should know, if only to put your own mind at rest. But it's imperative that you keep this to yourself. No mention of it to Major Rodenko.'

'That goes without saying, sir,' Yemenkov replied crisply.

'Well, I think it's time we went to see Professor Auerbach and Dr Fisier, don't you?'

Alain Fisier jumped to his feet when the door slid open and Yemenkov entered the cell. 'What's happened to my wife?' he demanded. 'What have you done with her?'

'I can assure you that your wife's quite safe,' Zlotin replied in French, appearing in the doorway behind Yemenkov. 'It's a pleasure finally to get to meet you in person, Dr Fisier. I've read most of your papers over the years. Very enlightening, especially to a layman like myself.'

'Who are you?' Fisier snapped, taking a step towards Zlotin.

'I'm in charge here,' Zlotin told him.

'That doesn't answer my question,' Fisier retorted indignantly.

'I'm afraid that's the only answer you're going to get.' Zlotin gestured to the chair behind Fisier. 'Please, sit down.'

'Listen to me, you bastard, I want to see my wife. Now!'

Yemenkov grabbed Fisier's arm, twisted it viciously behind his back, and forced him down on to the chair. 'When you're told to do something, you do it,' he hissed into Fisier's ear. 'Do I make myself understood?'

Fisier nodded his head vigorously, his face creased in pain. Yemenkov released his grip and Fisier immediately pulled his arm to his stomach and began gingerly massaging his aching wrist.

Auerbach glared at Yemenkov then looked across at Zlotin. 'You've made your point,' he said, speaking French for Fisier's benefit. 'Now maybe you'll tell us what exactly it is you want of us.'

Zlotin nodded to Yemenkov who retrieved Silverman's

case from the corridor and placed it on the table in the middle of the room. Zlotin unlocked the case and opened the lid. 'In here are two leather-bound folders, the contents of which have been written up in code. Your job, gentlemen, is to break that code.'

'And if we refuse?' Fisier shot back.

'Then you'd be condemning your wife, and Miss Auerbach, to a very slow and agonizing death. What's more, you'd both be on hand to watch them die. Is that really what you want, Doctor?'

Auerbach put a restraining hand on Fisier's arm; the Frenchman appeared to be about to try and lunge at Zlotin. 'Let it go, Alain,' he said softly.

Fisier slumped back dejectedly in his chair. 'What kind of inhuman bastards are you?' he said in a soft, emotional voice.

'I have no more wish to see your wife die than you do, Doctor,' Zlotin replied. 'It would mean that you'd failed to break the code.'

'Do you already have the antidote for the virus here on the island?' Auerbach asked.

'Yes, and as I told you in Leipzig, it will be administered once I'm satisfied that you've broken the code,' Zlotin replied.

'How do we know you'll keep your word?' Auerbach asked.

'You don't,' Zlotin replied bluntly. 'But I don't see what other choice you have, do you?'

Auerbach looked at Fisier. 'We'll have to go along with it, Alain, it's the only chance Lisl and Marie have of coming out of this alive. We have to do it, if only for them.'

'I know,' Fisier agreed sombrely.

Auerbach looked up at Zlotin. 'We'll need to know what kind of situation these codes were developed for before we can actually start working on them.'

'They're top secret files from the United Nations Anti-Crime Organization,' Zlotin replied.

'Dear God,' Auerbach muttered, his face suddenly drained of colour.

'I always thought this UNACO was a myth,' Fisier said to Auerbach.

'That's what they've always wanted the outside world to believe, but I've had dealings with their cryptology department when I was still with the BND . . .' Auerbach suddenly trailed off and looked up sharply at Zlotin. 'Of course, now it's all starting to make sense. Abe Silverman's head of cryptology at UNACO, and both Dr Fisier and I were pupils of his at the Sorbonne. That's why you brought us here, isn't it?'

'Abe Silverman's with UNACO?' Fisier said in surprise. 'I thought he'd retired after leaving the Israeli Mossad.'

'More UNACO disinformation,' Auerbach told him.

'Professor Silverman *was* head of cryptology at UNACO,' Zlotin corrected him.

'What do you mean *was*?' Auerbach said suspiciously.

'Professor Silverman's dead. That's why we were forced to bring in you and Dr Fisier at this late stage.'

'You killed him, didn't you?' Auerbach said in horror.

'No, actually he suffered a heart attack. You're right, of course, you were brought here because you've both studied under him. Especially you, Professor. You were regarded as Silverman's protégé at the Sorbonne, weren't you?'

Auerbach got to his feet and crossed to the table where he picked up one of the leather-bound folders and leafed through it. 'We may have studied under Abe, but that doesn't mean a damn thing when it comes to decoding this. I know Dr Fisier will agree with me when I say that Abe Silverman was without question the foremost authority on cryptology in the past thirty years. We could spend a month on these folders and still be no closer to breaking his code.'

'You don't have a month,' Zlotin told him. 'You have about sixty hours left before the effects of the virus begin to take effect on your daughter.'

'This is madness,' Fisier cried out, jumping to his feet, but Yemenkov was quick to step in front of him before he could make towards Zlotin. 'Gunther's right, it could take months for us to break the code. And you expect us to do it in sixty hours? For God's sake, be realistic. We'll need more time.'

'I would suggest you work in shifts,' Zlotin said, ignoring Fisier's impassioned outburst. 'Say eight hours on, eight hours off. But I'll leave that entirely up to you. You should find everything you need in here. There will always be one of us on duty in the adjoining cell so if you should need anything else, or more importantly, if you should break the code, just shout.'

'We need more time,' Fisier implored in desperation.

'Sixty hours is all the time your wife has, Doctor. You both come highly regarded; now's your chance to prove your worth.' Zlotin took a sheet of paper from his pocket and placed it on the table. 'I've written down the names of the three members of UNACO that I already know of. The Deputy Director, Sergei Kolchinsky, the head of their ballistics department, Professor Marcel Toure, and one of their field agents, Michael Graham. You may have heard of Kolchinsky, Professor.'

'I only ever dealt with Abe Silverman,' Auerbach told him. 'I never knew the names of any of their personnel. It's the way UNACO always operated. Total secrecy at all levels.'

'Pity,' Zlotin said.

Auerbach picked up the paper then met Zlotin's eyes. 'What are you going to do with the folders if we do manage to decode them? Sell them?'

Zlotin glanced at his watch. 'You're wasting time, Professor. You only have sixty hours left, remember?'

Yemenkov removed the two folders from the attaché case, placed them on the table, then closed the case again and carried it from the room.

Zlotin moved to the door then looked round at the two men. 'I'm sure you've both already realized the futility of trying to escape, but just in case you were thinking about plotting some elaborate way of getting off the island, I wouldn't bother if I were you. You wouldn't get very far without one of these,' he said, holding up his master key card. 'Then, of course, you'd have to find the antidote for the virus before you could leave here. It would just be a waste of valuable time. Good night, gentlemen.'

Zlotin emerged from the cell and Yemenkov inserted his key card into the slot on the wall adjacent to the door. The door slid shut.

'Why didn't you tell them about Graham's partner, Sabrina Carver?' Yemenkov asked as they walked down the corridor.

'Auerbach was head of cryptology with the BND for seventeen years,' Zlotin said, inserting his key card into the slot to activate the door which led into the cell he'd converted into his own personal quarters. 'He must have known about the joint operations which were carried out by UNACO and the BND in that time. And that would mean he'd also have known the names of the UNACO personnel involved in those operations.'

'And he said he only knew of Silverman,' Yemenkov said, following Zlotin into the cell.

'Exactly,' Zlotin replied, sitting on his bunk. 'If they do break the code, there's always a possibility that Auerbach may try and change some of the information in the folders. I'm not saying he will, but we can't afford to take that chance. So if he gives any name other than Carver as Graham's partner, then we'll know he's been tampering with the contents of the folders. I also know the names of two other field operatives who joined UNACO from *spetznaz* in the Eighties, so I'll be able to cross-check anything relating to them with our contact in Moscow.'

'Would you like a coffee, sir?' Yemenkov asked, gesturing to the small butane gas cylinder in the corner of the room.

'Yes, thank you,' Zlotin replied.

'Make that two, Valentin,' Rodenko said from the doorway. 'Royce is in his quarters.'

'Sit down, Viktor. I want to know exactly what happened when you crossed swords with UNACO this afternoon.'

'I think it would be best if Valentin were to tell you,' Rodenko said, sitting on one of the wooden chairs. 'After all, he's the one who masterminded our escape.'

Yemenkov finished making the coffee, then recounted the events of the afternoon to Zlotin, who listened in silence, the mug of hot coffee held tightly between his hands.

'They're getting closer every time,' Rodenko said once Yemenkov had finished speaking. 'We need to deal with them before it's too late.'

Zlotin took a sip of his black, sugarless coffee, then sat forward, his elbow resting on his knees. 'It's too dangerous,' he said at length.

'Not if we set a trap for them, sir,' Yemenkov joined in.

Zlotin looked across at Yemenkov. 'So you agree with Major Rodenko?'

'Yes, sir, I do,' Yemenkov replied. 'Next time we might not be so lucky.'

'That's my point exactly,' Zlotin said.

'What do you mean, sir?' Yemenkov asked.

'Graham's the best there is, I don't need to tell you that,' Zlotin said. 'I don't know much about Sabrina Carver, but if she's Graham's partner, then she must be good. He wouldn't be working with her if she wasn't up to scratch.'

'You don't think we could take them, is that it?' Rodenko said tetchily.

'I don't know, and that's why I don't think it's worth tempting fate.'

'Yemenkov and I could take them out,' Rodenko said sharply, bristling indignantly at the thought that he could be considered inferior to a couple of UNACO operatives, especially as one of them was a woman.

'I can't afford to put you both on an operation like this,' Zlotin replied. 'If something were to go wrong –'

'Nothing would go wrong,' Rodenko cut in.

'Would you let me finish my sentence, Viktor?' Zlotin hissed angrily.

Rodenko sat back stiffly in his chair, his arms folded across his chest, but said nothing.

'If something were to go wrong, I couldn't complete this operation by myself.' Zlotin shook his head. 'No, it's not worth the risk when we're this close to our deadline.'

'Sir, if Graham and Carver do manage to track us down in the next couple of days, then all our hard work will have been for nothing,' Yemenkov told him. 'But if we can take them out now, that would seriously disrupt the whole UNACO operation. The UNACO hierarchy would have to assemble another team, brief them, and send them out here to replace Graham and Carver. That would take up valuable time; UNACO are working against the clock just as much as we are. We have to take the initiative, sir. We owe it to our colleagues back home who are depending on us to complete our part of the operation successfully.'

'You remind me very much of myself when I was your age, Valentin,' Zlotin said. 'I was never afraid to stand up to my superiors if we had a difference of opinion, even if it meant risking a charge of insubordination. You mentioned something earlier about a trap. Do you have something specific in mind?'

'Yes, sir, and it would only involve one of us,' Yemenkov told him.

'Then let's hear what you have to say,' Zlotin said. 'And if I think it'll work, I'm prepared to go along with it.'

9

Graham was awake within seconds of the telephone ringing. He switched on the bedside light and picked up the receiver. 'Hello?' he said, reaching for his watch. It was 3.30 A.M.

'Is that Graham?' a voice enquired.

'Yeah, who's this?' Graham demanded suspiciously.

'Luis Caldere. You remember me?'

'Sure, from the wine bar,' Graham replied. 'What do you want?'

'They are trying to kill me, *senhor*,' came the nervous reply. 'Please, you must help me.'

'Who's trying to kill you?' No reply. 'Caldere, are you still there?'

'I am still here. I cannot talk on the telephone. We can meet, yes?'

'Not until you give me some answers . . .'

'They are following me. If you help me, I can tell you where to find the folders. Please, Senhor Graham, you must help me. I will meet you at the grain dock in half an hour. There is a warehouse with a white roof. You cannot miss it. I will wait for ten minutes at the entrance, then I will leave. Please do not call the police. They will kill me.'

'What do you mean? Are you saying they're in on this?'

The line went dead. Graham slowly replaced the receiver and raked his fingers through his hair. What the hell was he supposed to make of it? Everything pointed to it being a trap. But what if it wasn't? Could he afford to take that chance? Picking up the receiver again, he rang Rust's room. 'Of course it's a trap,' Rust said once Graham had recounted the conversation to him in person.

Sabrina turned away from the window. 'And what if it's not, Jacques? What if Caldere is on the level?'

'I phoned the duty officer at the Special Forces Brigade's HQ after Mike rang me. According to the surveillance team watching the bar, Caldere's still in there.'

'At this time of night?' Graham said in surprise.

'He has a special extension on his licence which allows him to keep the bar open after normal closing time. Not only that, the Special Forces Brigade have been monitoring his phone and the duty officer insists that no calls have been made from there for the past three hours.'

'You think Yemenkov's up to his tricks again?' Graham asked.

'Why not? He was convincing enough to fool Morales this afternoon. And he was impersonating someone Morales had known for years. You've heard Caldere's voice once. It has to be a trap.'

The telephone rang. Graham, who was the nearest, answered it. He held the receiver out towards Rust. 'It's the Special Forces Brigade for you.'

Rust took the receiver from Graham and a look of concern flashed across his face as he listened to the voice on the other end of the line. 'No, don't do anything,' he said at length. 'Thanks for letting me know. I'll get back to you again as soon as I've discussed it with my team.'

'What is it, Jacques?' Graham asked anxiously after Rust had replaced the receiver.

'The duty officer had the surveillance team take a closer look at the bar after I'd called him. The front door's unlocked, but Caldere isn't there. In fact, the whole place is completely deserted.'

'So how did he manage to slip past the surveillance team unnoticed?' Sabrina asked.

'He could just have put on a hat and a different jacket to the one he'd been wearing and walked out through the front door,' Graham replied. 'The surveillance unit wouldn't have suspected a thing, not if the lights were still on inside the building.'

'Which would imply that he knew he was being watched,' Sabrina said.

'And how would he know that unless he'd been tipped off?' Graham added.

'What are you suggesting, Mike?' Rust asked. 'That someone in the Special Forces Brigade tipped him off?'

'Well, I'm sure it wasn't one of us, which only leaves the Special Forces Brigade,' Graham retorted. 'It only confirms a suspicion I've had ever since the fiasco at Vila do Conde yesterday afternoon. It surprised me then just how quickly the Russians managed to get to the caravan site after we'd been given the location fix on the Fisiers. Now I'm convinced that they must have been tipped off by someone close to the heart of the operation.'

'Morales?' Sabrina said suspiciously.

'It could have been any of the men at the Command Centre. But right now that's not important.' Graham crossed to the window. 'Caldere's out there somewhere. Question is, is he on the run or is he trying to lure us into a trap?'

'There's only one way to find out,' Sabrina replied.

'Agreed,' Graham said, looking at his watch. 'We've got twenty minutes to get to the docks.'

'You realize that, if this is a trap, it'll have been set well in advance of the phone call,' Rust said to them.

'We've got to go, Jacques,' Graham said. 'What if Caldere was telling the truth? What if he is running scared? We can't pass up a chance like this, not if there's even the slightest possibility that it could lead us to the folders. You know that just as well as I do.'

'I agree, but I think you should take a back-up team in with you in case there is any trouble.'

'If I'm right about there being a mole in the Special Forces Brigade, I don't want any of them near me until the culprit's been weeded out,' Graham shot back.

'This mole theory of yours is all hypothetical, Mike,' Rust replied tersely. 'You can't just go around making these unsubstantiated allegations without any kind of proof to back them up.'

Graham turned to Sabrina. 'It's your call. Do you want the Special Forces Brigade in on this?'

'No,' came the blunt reply.

'Listen, *chérie* –'

'If Mike's hunch is right, then I want someone I can trust to watch my back when we get to the warehouse,' she cut in quickly.

'OK, I'm prepared to go along with you on this one, but just make sure you keep in touch,' Rust said, gesturing to the two-way radio on the bedside table.

'We will,' Graham replied, crossing to the door. 'And not a word of this to the Special Forces Brigade, at least not until we get back. Agreed?'

'Agreed,' came the reluctant reply. 'Good luck.'

'Thanks, Jacques,' Sabrina said with a quick smile, then followed Graham from the room, closing the door behind her.

Ed Miller stifled a yawn and looked at his watch. Another hour to go before his shift was over. When he got home all he wanted to do was curl up in bed and sleep through the whole day. The thought of doing just that was all that had kept him going through the boredom of the past four hours. He reached for the coffee on the dashboard and screwed his face up in disgust when he took a sip from the mug. The coffee was cold. Spitting it out, he opened the window and tossed the contents of the mug out on to the pavement.

He shivered as the wind whipped through the car and, closing the window quickly, he took the thermos flask from the glove compartment and was about to pour himself a refill when the side door of the hotel opened and two figures emerged, their hands dug into the pockets of their leather jackets, their heads bowed against the wind. He felt a surge of excitement through him – although he couldn't see their faces, he recognized Graham by the New York Yankees baseball cap he was wearing. Discarding the thermos flask, he reached for his camera and took several shots of them crossing to their car. Then, placing the camera carefully on the seat beside him, he waited until their car had disappeared around the nearest corner before starting up his own car and following them at a discreet distance.

Graham parked the car in a dimly lit cul-de-sac off the Rua João Evangelista, close to the waterfront, and killed the engine. 'OK, so where exactly is this grain dock from here?' he asked, gesturing to the map in Sabrina's lap.

'According to this, it's dead ahead, about two hundred yards,' she replied. 'It's enclosed by a fence with the main entrance on the other side of the cul-de-sac.'

Graham looked at his watch. It was almost four o'clock. He checked his Beretta, slipped it back into his shoulder holster, and climbed from the car. Sabrina got out of the passenger side and followed him through a narrow walkway which emerged on to a deserted parking bay. The wooden perimeter fence, topped with barbed wire, was situated on the far side of the parking bay. Graham estimated it to be at least twelve feet high. Maybe more. They followed the fence until they came to the entrance: two battered metal gates with the words *Doca do Trigo* painted across them in faded black lettering. Graham pushed the gates but wasn't surprised to find that they were locked from the inside.

'We're going to have to scale the gates,' Sabrina whispered.

Graham cast a despairing look up at the night sky as the

first drops of rain began to fall. He glanced round furtively then, grabbing on to the metal frame, hauled himself up and peered cautiously over the top of the gate. Although there was a light on in the hut below him, he couldn't see anyone inside. That, at least, augured well for them. Securing a better footing, he looked around him slowly. To his left was the harbour station and the customs house. Both were in darkness. A couple of hundred yards ahead of him was the quay where two tower cranes loomed like futuristic predators over a bulk carrier which wallowed forlornly in the murky water. To his right was a row of drab grey granary sheds, but there wasn't a white-roofed warehouse anywhere in sight . . .

'Do you see it?' Sabrina hissed underneath him.

He was about to reply in the negative when he caught sight of a lone building beyond the customs house. Was its roof off-white, or grey? It was impossible to tell from where he was. There was also something written across the roof, but he couldn't make out the lettering. It had to be the warehouse. Where else could it be? He gave Sabrina a thumbs-up sign, then pulled himself over the top of the gate and jumped to the ground. His Beretta was already in his hand when he straightened up and hurried across to the temporary sanctuary of a cluster of rusting drums which had been discarded behind the hut. He could see into the hut from where he was crouched. An open magazine and a thermos flask were on the table, but there was no sign of the night-watchman. Graham knew that, if it were a trap, the night-watchman would already have been dealt with to allow those who lay in wait to reach the warehouse unchallenged.

Moments later Sabrina scrambled over the gate and landed nimbly on the ground. She ran to where Graham was crouched and ducked down behind the drums. 'Where's the warehouse?' she asked, peering into the semi-darkness around her.

'I think that's it over there,' Graham said, pointing to the building at the far end of the complex.

She shielded her eyes from the rain and stared at the building for some time before finally nodding her head. 'Yes, that's it.'

'We'll split up and approach the warehouse from different directions,' Graham told her. 'That way we'll minimize the damage if this does turn out to be a trap. You stick to the perimeter fence. It'll bring you out at the back of the warehouse. I'll take the front. We'll meet up on the quay-side in, say, five minutes?'

'Agreed.' Sabrina put a gloved hand lightly on Graham's arm. 'Be careful, Mike.'

Graham patted her hand then broke cover and zig-zagged his way across a stretch of open ground until he reached the nearest of the tower cranes on the quayside. He paused to catch his breath then sprinted the hundred yards to the foot of the second crane. Only then did he crouch down and slowly look around him, his eyes screwed up against the driving rain. He could see the harbour station and part of the customs house from where he was, but not the warehouse. He scanned the length of the Panamanian-registered bulk carrier moored against the wharf not thirty yards in front of him but, like the surrounding quayside, it too seemed deserted. Satisfied, he ducked out from under the crane and ran, doubled-over, to the harbour station. Pressing himself against the whitewashed wall, he held the Beretta close to his face then swivelled round, the automatic now extended at arm's length. It was then that he saw the huddled figure standing in front of the warehouse, hands in pockets, a hat pulled down to partially obscure the face. Graham wiped the rain from his eyes, but it was too dark to be able to tell whether it was Caldere or not. Staying close to the building, he edged his way forward, the Beretta clenched tightly in both hands. He reached the only window facing out on to the quayside, but, deciding against taking any chances, ducked down to pass underneath it.

The sudden movement caught the figure's eye and, as he looked round, Graham recognized Caldere's face underneath the brim of the fedora. Caldere immediately looked around furtively, then hurriedly gestured Graham towards him. Graham straightened up slowly and edged his way forward, the Beretta now trained on Caldere.

'Senhor Graham,' Caldere said nervously, 'I did not think you would come. You did not bring the police?'

Graham said nothing.

Caldere cupped his hands over his mouth, blew into them, then rubbed them together before stepping out from the shelter of the overhanging roof. A bullet hit the wall behind him, narrowly missing him. Graham dropped to the ground, the Beretta fanning the piles of crates on the quayside from where the bullet had been fired. He couldn't see anything. Caldere, his face twisted in terror, kicked savagely at the door behind him. The flimsy lock broke under his weight and, wrenching open the door, he disappeared into the warehouse. Graham managed to get himself behind a pillar which supported the awning over the entrance to the customs house, but although he could now see the crates clearly, he still couldn't see the gunman. He knew he couldn't go after Caldere for fear of being hit. At least there was some consolation in the fact that the gunman couldn't pursue him either, not without exposing himself. All Graham needed was one shot to put the bastard down. But who was it? One of the Russians? A policeman? Caldere had said they were trying to kill him. The mole in the Special Forces Brigade? If, in fact, there was a mole, he was quick to remind himself. He looked at his watch. The five minutes were up. Sabrina would have heard the shot, but would she be able to get round behind the gunman without being seen?

Two bullets cracked out from the other side of the warehouse. One of the crates was knocked over, and for a moment Graham thought Sabrina had hit the gunman, but then his crouched figure backed out from behind one of the crates, body tensed, his automatic aimed in the direction from where Sabrina had discharged the two bullets. The gunman, apparently realizing suddenly that he had left himself open on the flank, was still swinging the automatic towards the customs house when Graham's bullet took him in the leg. Graham heard his cry of agony and saw the automatic slipping from his grasp as he fell to the ground. The weapon had come to rest inches from the edge of the quay. Clutching his injured leg with one hand, the gunman began to drag himself slowly towards it, his fingers raking the ground as he sought desperately to reach it before he was overpowered. Graham wasted no time. Darting out from behind the pillar and sprinting across to the crates, he kicked the automatic into the water before the gunman could reach it. Suddenly Sabrina appeared beside him, her Beretta trained on the gunman. Graham quickly frisked him. He was clean. Graham brought the butt of his Beretta down sharply behind the man's ear, then turned the unconscious figure over on to his back. Neither of them recognized him, but there would be time to question him later. Graham found a length of frayed rope lying on one of the crates and used it to bind the man's hands and legs.

'Was Caldere here?' Sabrina asked.

'Yeah, the shot was obviously meant for him,' Graham told her. 'He's in the warehouse. I just hope there's not another way out of there or we could have lost him. I think after this little episode tonight he'll be more than willing to talk to us if we can convince the authorities to give him protection.' Graham led the way to the broken door where he took up a position beside the open doorway. 'Caldere?' he called out. 'It's Graham. You can come out now. You're safe.'

No reply.

'Caldere, we've dealt with the gunman,' Sabrina shouted to him in Portuguese. 'It's safe now. We can protect you if you're willing to talk. Caldere, can you hear me?'

'I am scared,' Caldere shouted back in English. 'They will kill me if I come out.'

Graham cursed under his breath and looked across at Sabrina. 'I'll have to go in and get him. Keep an eye on the door.'

'I'll get him,' Sabrina said, holding up her hand before Graham could reply. 'If he's scared he'll feel more comfortable speaking his own language. It'll be easier to coax him out that way.'

Graham accepted her reasoning without comment and gestured towards the door. She stepped through the doorway and paused to get her bearings. The warehouse was in complete darkness. 'Caldere?' she called out. 'Caldere, where are you?'

Silence.

'Caldere!' Graham yelled from the doorway, the anger now evident in his voice. 'Caldere, you can come out now. Caldere!'

Sabrina patted the adjacent wall until her fingers touched a light switch. She flicked it on. Nothing. Sensing they'd walked into a trap, she was about to call out a warning to Graham when two gunshots echoed across the darkness. Both bullets thudded into Graham's chest, punching him back against the wall. He crumpled to the ground without a sound.

'Mike?' Sabrina cried out in horror, rushing across to where he lay.

'Leave him, Miss Carver,' a voice barked from somewhere inside the darkened warehouse. 'I put both bullets through his heart. He's dead.'

Sabrina swung round, fanning the darkness with her Beretta. The voice was refined, the English delivered with only the slightest hint of an accent. It had to be one of the Russians. Whoever it was must be using night-vision goggles, she thought to herself as she peered helplessly into the darkness.

'Drop the Beretta, Miss Carver,' the voice called out again, this time from a different section of the warehouse. 'I can see every move you make. Please, drop the gun.'

She knew the rules. No UNACO operative was ever to surrender their weapon in the line of duty. But if she didn't, he'd certainly shoot her as well. And she would have more of a chance if she played by his rules. Sometimes the rules had to be bent to accommodate the situation. She tossed her Beretta on to the floor.

'Kick it away from you,' the voice commanded.

She did as she was told.

'Switch on the lights,' came the order in Portuguese.

The warehouse was suddenly bathed in light. Hundreds of wooden containers were stacked in neat rows and interspersed by a maze of narrow corridors designed to admit the cluster of forklift trucks parked by the door. Sabrina eyed her Beretta which had come to rest in the nearest corridor, but she knew it was too far for her to try and make a grab for it. Then a movement caught her eye and she looked up at the catwalk above her. A man was leaning on the railing, a twisted smile on his face as he appraised her body. He was armed with a Skorpion machine-pistol. She'd never seen him before. On the wall behind him was an open fuse box. It had been that simple to trap them.

The man was still leering down at her when Graham raised his Beretta and pumped two bullets into him. The man stumbled backwards against the railing behind him and his momentum carried him over the side and he landed with a sickening crunch on the floor below.

Graham hurled himself into the corridor after Sabrina in the second before a fusillade of bullets peppered the floor where he'd been lying. He slumped back against a container and rubbed his chest gingerly. 'It still hurts like hell,' he hissed through clenched teeth.

'You wouldn't be feeling anything right now if you weren't wearing your body armour,' she replied, retrieving her Beretta from the floor.

'Yeah, I know,' he said, carefully scanning the catwalk above them. It was deserted. 'There's at least two of them in here that we know of. There could be more.'

A sudden burst of gunfire shattered the uneasy silence. It seemed to have been directed towards the entrance of the warehouse.

'They're already closing in on us,' Graham said, scrambling to his feet. 'Whoever fired that burst isn't far from here. We have to keep moving; it's our only chance. We'll split up and cover the warehouse from different angles. It's the only way we'll be able to cover the whole area.'

Sabrina moved cautiously to the end of the corridor where she paused, her back against a container, the Beretta held upwards, inches from her face. Graham gave her a thumbs-up sign. She nodded then swivelled round, Beretta extended. Then she was gone, disappearing into the adjacent corridor.

Graham ducked through a narrow gap between two rows of containers and rolled out low into the adjoining corridor. It was deserted. Raising himself on to one knee, he was about to continue when he saw a shadowy movement at the end of the corridor. Then it was gone. For a moment he thought his eyes could have been playing tricks on him. But he knew he couldn't afford to take that chance. He quickly ducked back into the gap and crouched down, his back pressed against a container, listening breathlessly for the sound of footsteps which he assumed would now approach from one of the corridors on either side of him. Not a sound. Then a thought suddenly occurred to him. What if it had been Sabrina's shadow? Or what if it had just been a trick of the light? It left him in a dilemma. Should he stay where he was, or should he risk a confrontation? The thought of a confrontation, especially if it turned out to be with one of the Russians, was a challenge he relished, but he also knew that, without the element of surprise on his side, he would only have a split second to take them out. It didn't take him long to make up his mind. He chose confrontation. And if there was nobody there, no harm had been done. It sure as hell beat squatting on his haunches, waiting for something to happen.

Wetting his dry lips with his tongue, he tightened his grip on the Beretta and was about to roll out into the corridor when a shadow fell across the containers stacked opposite him. Gritting his teeth, he eased himself down on to one knee and raised the Beretta, his finger curled around the trigger. The shadow loomed closer. He bit his lip and blinked irritably as the sweat trickled down his forehead and into his eyes. Then the shadow stopped. Graham estimated that the figure was only a few feet away from him now. He knew he'd have to shoot the moment the figure appeared. What if it turned out to be Sabrina? The thought caught him off guard, but he assured himself that he could pull back from firing if it was her out there. He doubted it was, anyway. She'd be covering another section of the warehouse. Still the shadow hovered only feet away from him.

Come on, you bastard, Graham urged. He found that he was smiling faintly to himself. He was ready for the son-of-a-bitch. Then, abruptly, the shadow receded, and a moment later it was gone. Graham cursed furiously to himself. It left him with the one option he'd hoped to avoid. He'd have to go out into the corridor, knowing that whoever was out there might be waiting to ambush him. The odds were suddenly against him. But there was no way out of a confrontation now. Wiping the sweat from his eyes, he pressed himself against the container behind him then swivelled round, Beretta extended, finger tight on the trigger.

The man stood at the end of the corridor, his back to Graham. He was wearing camouflage trousers and a flak jacket. Graham immediately recognized Yemenkov from the cropped blond hair. It only took a second for Yemenkov to realize that there was someone behind him, but by then the advantage was back with Graham.

'Don't even think it, Yemenkov!' Graham snapped when

he saw the Russian's fingers tighten around the Makarov pistol in his hand. 'Throw it down, then turn around slowly with your hands in the air.'

Yemenkov turned his head slowly, his eyes instinctively going to the two bullet holes in Graham's jacket. Then his body was turning too, the pistol already arcing towards Graham. Graham fired twice. The first bullet hit Yemenkov in the stomach, spinning him round, and the second slammed into his ribcage. Yemenkov cried out in pain and stumbled backwards, his face contorted with pain, then disappeared behind a row of containers. Graham cursed furiously and immediately went after him. He reached the end of the corridor and swivelled round to fan the adjacent corridor. A bloody palm-print was stamped on the nearest container, but there was no sign of Yemenkov. Graham followed the blood spoor into another corridor. It too, was deserted. Yemenkov's resilience amazed Graham. Two bullets in the stomach and he was still moving fast enough to evade detection. The trail of blood led to the end of the corridor. Graham paused to get his bearings at the last stack of containers overlooking the corridor. More blood on the bottom container. Yemenkov must have stumbled there and grabbed on to the container to prevent himself from falling. He'd gone right. Graham checked behind him. The corridor was clear. Positioning himself with his back against the containers, he was about to swing round into the adjacent corridor when he caught sight of a movement out of the corner of his eye.

'Drop the gun, Graham,' a voice barked, and Caldere stepped out from behind the containers at the other end of the corridor. 'I said drop the gun.'

Graham was standing in an awkward position to fire on the turn. If he missed, Caldere wouldn't, not from that range. He thought about taking a dive and firing as he came up from the first roll, but again it was a difficult shot with no certainty of success.

'Drop the gun!' Caldere snarled, moving slowly towards Graham.

Graham was still weighing up his options when Sabrina suddenly ghosted out from behind the containers, her Beretta trained on Caldere's back. Graham's eyes didn't waver from Caldere's face as Caldere came towards him.

'No, you drop *your* gun,' Sabrina snapped at Caldere in Portuguese.

Caldere froze, his expression one of horror and surprise. He'd heard nothing. With Graham's Beretta now trained on him as well, Caldere had no choice. Slowly he lowered his pistol.

Sabrina quickly disarmed him. 'How many of you are there?'

'Only four.' Caldere saw the uncertainty in Graham's eyes. 'I swear it, *senhor*.'

'You're going to lead the way out of here,' Graham told him. 'So if there are any little surprises left, you'll take the first bullet.'

'What was that shooting I heard earlier?' Sabrina asked Graham.

'I put two bullets into Yemenkov but he still got away,' Graham replied. 'God knows where he is now.'

'Dead with some luck,' she said.

'Don't count on it.' Graham scanned the deserted corridor. 'You watch Caldere, I'm going after Yemenkov.'

Caldere waited until Graham had turned away, then suddenly lashed out at Sabrina, catching her on the side of the face with his clenched fist. By the time Graham swung round, Caldere had already ducked out of sight.

A lone shot rang out across the warehouse. Sabrina dived low into the adjacent corridor and, as she came out of the first roll, her Beretta was already trained on the figure at the other end of the warehouse. It was Yemenkov. She raised herself on one knee, her finger taut on the trigger. But she didn't shoot. Yemenkov stood with his back against the wall, his chin resting on his chest, the Makarov now hanging loosely in his hand. The front of his flak jacket was soaked in blood. Pressing his left hand against his ruptured stomach, he gritted his teeth in agony as he slowly slid to the floor, leaving a diagonal smear of blood on the wall above him.

'Mike, check on Caldere,' she ordered without taking her eyes off Yemenkov, then, getting to her feet, she moved slowly towards the Russian, the Beretta aimed at his chest.

Only then did Yemenkov look up at her. His eyes were glazed over, his breathing ragged and uneven. He went into a violent coughing spasm and the blood bubbled on to his lips and trickled down his chin.

'Put the gun down,' she commanded.

Yemenkov spat contemptuously on to the floor, then raised the pistol towards her. Both she and Graham opened fire simultaneously. The bullets ripped through Yemenkov's chest, snapping his head back against the wall. The pistol slipped from his bloodied fingers and his lifeless body toppled sideways on to the floor. Sabrina hurried across to where he lay, kicked the pistol away from him, and checked for a pulse. She shook her head.

'Caldere's also dead,' Graham said, indicating the body which was slumped against one of the containers. 'But it wasn't the bullet that killed him.'

'What do you mean?'

'His death has all the signs of cyanide poisoning,' Graham told her. 'It's my guess that Yemenkov was using cyanide-tipped bullets. *Spetznaz* assassins have been known to use them in Afghanistan.'

'So even a flesh wound would kill the victim?'

Graham nodded. 'Caldere was only hit in the shoulder. He'd still be alive if it weren't for the cyanide.'

'But why would Yemenkov want him dead?' Sabrina asked.

'He obviously knew too much; Yemenkov couldn't risk that information falling into our hands.'

'Did he say anything before he died?' she asked.

'Yeah, it sounded something like *"samba dancerino"*.'

'*Samba dancarino* means "samba dancer" in Portuguese.'

'That makes a lot of sense,' Graham retorted.

Sabrina paused for a moment, her brow furrowed in thought. 'Could it have been *Sambra Dancarino*?' she asked eventually.

'Yeah, it could have been that. What does it mean?'

'Shadow Dancer,' she replied. 'And if my memory serves me correctly, UNACO used to have an operative in the Middle East called "Shadow Dancer".'

'How the hell would a two-bit hood like Caldere know about him?'

'I don't know,' Sabrina replied defensively. 'I guess it could also be a codeword, perhaps for one of the Russians. Or it may not have been that at all . . .' She smiled at Graham. 'At least we've got one live prisoner. Let's see what he has to say.'

'I wouldn't count on getting too much out of him. I think you'll find that he was only brought in for tonight's job.'

'It's still worth a try,' she said, heading for the entrance.

'Anything's worth a try right now,' came the despondent reply.

Sabrina froze as she reached the door. 'Mike, get over here.'

'What is it?' Graham called out.

'Just get over here,' she replied tersely.

Graham hurried across to where she was standing clear of the doorway. A body was sprawled outside on the wharf, close to the door. Graham estimated that two bullets had struck the man in the face. One had entered the left eye, the other had blown away most of the nose. Although he couldn't see the mutilated face under the mask of blood, Graham could tell from the clothes that it wasn't the gunman they'd encountered earlier.

'There could be another gunman out there,' Sabrina said, eyeing the doorway suspiciously.

'The shots didn't come from out there,' Graham replied. 'Look at the position of the body. The bullets obviously hit him in the face and the force knocked him back off his feet. If he'd been shot from outside the warehouse, he'd be lying face down. No, the shots came from in here.'

'Of course, that burst of gunfire we heard just after you'd taken out that guy on the catwalk,' Sabrina concluded. 'I thought it strange at the time that they would fire so wide of us, especially when they knew where we were. Now it makes sense.'

'But who is he if he's not one of them? He sure as hell isn't the night-watchman, not dressed like that. He looks like he's just come off a golf course with that jacket.'

Sabrina ducked out into the rain and, crouching over the body, slipped her hand into the inside pocket of the dead man's jacket. Finding a wallet, she returned with it to the warehouse.

'Well?' Graham asked after she'd opened it.

'Oh God, no,' she said in horror.

Graham grabbed the wallet from her. A card was displayed prominently in the window section but the typescript was in Portuguese. 'What does it say?' he demanded, tapping the window with his finger.

'It's a press card in the name of Edward Miller, a free-lance journalist based here in Lisbon.'

Graham stared at the body for several seconds, then thrust the wallet back into Sabrina's hand. 'Call Jacques on the radio and tell him what's happened. That bastard out there's going to talk. One way or another, he's going to talk.'

Sabrina grabbed Graham's arm. 'I think it would be best if I were to get the prisoner and bring him back here.'

'Let go of my arm, Sabrina,' Graham hissed angrily.

'OK,' she said, releasing her grip. 'Go ahead. Beat the hell out of him if it'll make you feel better, because that's exactly what you're going to do, isn't it?'

227

Graham didn't reply as he stared at the drenched body lying on the wharf.

'We screwed up, there's no denying that,' Sabrina went on quietly. 'We should have picked up on Miller long before we got here; but we didn't, and we're going to catch hell for it. But by taking your frustration out on the prisoner, you'll only make things even worse for us. It's just not worth it, Mike.' She put her hand back lightly on his arm. 'Let me handle it. OK?'

Graham finally nodded his consent. 'I'll report in to Jacques. He's going to blow a fuse when he finds out about Miller.'

'Can you blame him?' Sabrina replied dejectedly as she disappeared out into the night.

'Why don't you just have Reuters fax every newspaper around the world with the news that UNACO are currently on a top secret assignment in Portugal?' Rust thundered after Graham and Sabrina had briefed him on the events at the warehouse that night. 'Why confine the exclusive just to the *New York Sentinel*? Why not let every other newspaper in on the story as well?'

'And of course you never made any mistakes while you were in the field?' Graham shot back, stung by Rust's biting sarcasm.

'Sure I made mistakes,' Rust retorted. 'One of them left me in this wheelchair. But I've always tried to learn from them. It's obvious, though, that neither of you has learnt from your mistakes. Not only has this Katherine Warren managed to tail you around New York, she's also been keeping tabs on you ever since you arrived in Lisbon. Now we've got her colleague's body lying at the mortuary, gunned down while out covering a supposedly clandestine UNACO operation, and a very agitated Katherine Warren demanding to know from the Special Forces Brigade what exactly happened at the warehouse tonight. She's got all the ingredients for a world exclusive right at her fingertips. Every cable station in the US will be vying for the rights to turn this whole damn fiasco into a mini-series. Perhaps we could all play ourselves, because the moment that story hits the streets, UNACO will be finished and we'll all be out of a job.'

'We took every possible precaution to shake Warren once we knew she'd followed us from New York,' Graham retorted.

'Well, obviously they weren't good enough, were they?'

'You could have had us replaced by one of the other Strike Force teams once we knew that she was here in Lisbon,' Graham snapped. 'That way none of this would ever have happened, would it?'

'You were kept on the case because Strike Force Three was regarded as the best team in the organization.'

'Then I suggest you bring in your next "best team" to replace us and we'll return to New York, tender our resignations, and save the organization any further embarrassment,' Graham shot back.

'Is that what you want?' Rust challenged.

'Is it what *you* want?' Graham countered.

'What I want are those folders returned to UNACO intact and, despite this latest setback, I still believe that you two are our best chance of getting them back. So does the Colonel for that matter.'

'You've already spoken to him?' Sabrina said from the window, entering the conversation for the first time.

'Yes, I caught him just as he was about to turn in for the night. I doubt he's going to get much sleep now.'

'What did he say?' she asked.

'He wants you both to remain on the case, but from now on we're to work hand-in-hand with the Special Forces Brigade.'

'Come on, Jacques, it's even more obvious after what happened tonight that Zlotin's got a man inside the Special Forces Brigade,' Graham cut in.

'Not to me, it isn't,' Rust replied irritably.

'We know from the prisoner that Caldere contacted him well before midnight to arrange the ambush at the docks,' Graham told him. 'Yet the Special Forces Brigade insist that Caldere only made two telephone calls last night, both to his wife at home. Then there's Yemenkov. He must have contacted Caldere sometime last night. But he didn't use the phone. Why? Because they both knew it was being tapped by the authorities. And how would they have known that unless they'd been tipped off in advance by someone with access to that information.'

'They could have *assumed* that the phone was being tapped,' Rust answered, then held up a hand before Graham could argue the point. 'Major Inacio was absolutely livid when he learnt about what happened at the docks tonight, especially as the Special Forces Brigade will now have to bear the brunt of the responsibility just to keep UNACO's name out of it. He made his feelings pretty clear to Colonel Philpott who, in turn, made *his* feelings pretty clear to me. I took a lot of flak for letting the two of you go off without first informing the Special Forces Brigade. So from now on we play it strictly by the book.'

'In other words, from now on we're going to have a chaperon wherever we go?' Graham said with a disgruntled scowl.

'That's it exactly. And if you don't like it, you'll be replaced by Strike Force Eight. Those were the Colonel's exact words.'

Graham punched the wall angrily then swung round on Rust. 'You know my hunches are usually right, Jacques –'

'I don't want to hear it, Mike,' Rust interrupted, stabbing a finger of warning at him. 'You've been given an order and, if you don't like it, Strike Force Eight will be flown out to replace you. As you would say, it's your call.'

'Some call,' Graham muttered.

'It doesn't look as if we've got much choice in the matter,' Sabrina replied for both of them. 'So what happens now?'

'First thing we have to do is leave the hotel,' Rust replied.

'Where are we going?'

'A safe house in Estoril which belongs to the Special Forces Brigade. That way Katherine Warren won't know where you are, so at least that problem will have been eliminated. Naturally you won't be visiting Sergei any more, but after the last stunt he pulled, perhaps it's just as well.'

'What's going to happen to Warren?' Graham asked.

'The Special Forces Brigade will mount a twenty-four-hour surveillance on her, so she won't be able to go anywhere without them knowing about it.'

'I just hope the surveillance is better than the one they mounted on Caldere,' Graham said sarcastically.

'Major Inacio has already initiated an internal investigation into how Caldere slipped through the net. He's promised that, if any of his surveillance units are shown to have been negligent in their duties, he'll immediately institute disciplinary measures against them.'

'A lot of good that will do,' Graham snorted.

'When do we leave for the safe house?' Sabrina asked.

'As soon as you're ready,' Rust replied. 'I've already settled the accounts. Captain Morales is waiting in the foyer to drive us over to the house. So the sooner you're packed, the sooner we can move out.'

'What about our car?' Graham asked.

'It's been taken out of service until after we've gone,' Rust replied. 'Warren will certainly have made a note of the registration number and, even though it's highly unlikely that she'd be able to trace the car to the safe house, there's no point in taking any unnecessary chances. There'll be another car for you when you get to the safe house.'

'Come on, Mike, let's get our things together.'

Graham crossed to the door then looked back at Rust. 'The Colonel was actually prepared to replace us with Strike Force Eight?' he said, shaking his head incredulously.

231

'Every other Strike Force team is currently on assignment. You and Strike Force Eight were the only two teams available when this broke.'

'They might be able to help an old lady across a deserted street, or find a blind cat in an alley, but this is a bit out of their league, wouldn't you say?'

'OK, so they've made some mistakes in the past, but right now I don't think you're in any position to judge them, do you?'

'*Touché*,' Sabrina said at Graham's elbow.

Graham scowled, then followed her from the room.

Estoril, a cosmopolitan resort on the Portuguese Riviera, is located fifteen miles west of Lisbon. A haven for exiled monarchs and deposed dictators, it's also an established rendezvous for the international jet-set since first becoming fashionable at the turn of the century.

The safe house, with its pastel blue walls and red tiled roof, was situated on the outskirts of Estoril. Hidden from the coastal road by a grove of oak trees, it stood on a hillside with a breathtaking view of the town and its environs stretching out below it as far as the eye could see.

'Back in the States, a safe house would be a log cabin hidden away in some Pennsylvanian backwater,' Graham said, opening the sliding door which led directly from the lounge out on to a covered patio. 'This would be most Americans' idea of a dream house.'

'It once belonged to a film star,' Morales said, stepping out on to the patio after him.

'Yeah, anyone famous?' Graham asked, gazing out across the Atlantic.

Morales shook his head. 'He only ever appeared in Portuguese films. We bought the house from the estate after he died.'

'It's ideal for a safe house,' Graham said, sitting in one of the wicker chairs. 'A single approach road, visible from the

232

house, and a wall surrounding the entire property. It would be pretty hard getting in here unnoticed.'

'Or out,' Morales said with a knowing smile.

Graham nodded in agreement, then knocked on the glass door behind him. 'Bulletproof?'

'All the windows are bulletproof,' Morales assured him.

Sabrina emerged on to the patio and sat down on the chair beside Graham. 'I bet this is a real sun-trap in summer,' she said, eyeing the ominous dark clouds that were already gathering over the Atlantic.

'It is, but right now it looks like another storm's heading this way.' Morales leaned back against the railings, his arms folded across his chest. 'I was meaning to ask you, did you learn anything useful from that gunman you caught at the docks this morning?'

'Nothing of any real use to us,' Sabrina replied. 'We handed him over to your people, but I doubt they'll get anything else out of him. He was obviously just a hired gun, that's all.'

'Who hired him?' Morales asked.

'Caldere. He hired both gunmen.'

'Presumably on Yemenkov's orders,' Morales said.

'Presumably,' she agreed.

'How did Yemenkov get to the dock? Boat? Helicopter?'

'Your people found a motor cruiser moored close to the warehouse,' Sabrina replied. 'It was hired from a firm in Lisbon a couple of weeks ago by someone matching Zlotin's description.'

Morales got to his feet. 'Well, I'd better be going. There's a briefing at headquarters in just over an hour. All senior officers have been ordered to attend.'

'Any more news on Katherine Warren?' Sabrina asked as Morales crossed to the door.

'Only that she's been causing a lot of waves since Miller was killed. Major Inacio's been dealing with her, but I'm sure I'll hear all about it at the briefing. I'll call you later with any news. And if you hear anything, you know where to get hold of me.'

Graham waited until Morales had left, then got to his feet and moved to the railing. 'He seemed very interested in what the gunman may or may not have told us earlier this morning.'

'What exactly are you getting at?' Sabrina asked.

'He's suggesting that, if Morales is the mole, he could have had some contact with either Caldere or the gunmen in the past which could incriminate him,' Rust replied from the lounge, knowing that they could talk freely amongst themselves: Sabrina had already swept the house for bugs and found it to be clean.

Graham looked round at Rust. 'You can dismiss the mole theory if you want, Jacques, but I'm not.'

'I'm not dismissing it, I'm just keeping an open mind,' Rust said, wheeling himself out on to the patio. 'I'm the first to admit that some of your hunches have been crucial in solving cases in the past, but I'm also well aware that others have left the organization with egg on its face. Both the Colonel and I have had to apologize on more than one occasion to members of foreign intelligence services for your slanderous accusations.

'We're skating on very thin ice after this morning's débâcle at the warehouse, Mike. The last thing we need right now is for you to be making unsubstantiated accusations of corruption against the Special Forces Brigade. Do I make myself understood?'

'Perfectly,' Graham retorted.

'Good,' Rust said.

'But I know I'm right,' Graham added quickly.

Rust shot him a dirty look, then wheeled himself back to the sliding door. 'I've got some calls to make. I'll see you both later.'

'You want a coffee?' Sabrina asked Graham once Rust had gone.

'Yeah, why not?'

Sabrina went through to the kitchen and made a fresh brew of coffee in the percolator. When she returned carrying two mugs of steaming coffee, she found Graham in the lounge, the sliding door leading out on to the patio now closed against the chill wind which had whipped up in the last few minutes.

Sitting forward on the sofa, his elbows on his knees, his hands cupped over his face, Graham was staring pensively at the carpet. He hadn't noticed her entering the lounge and crossing the room to where he sat. It was only the smell of the coffee that finally brought him out of his reverie. 'Sorry, I was miles away,' he said, taking the mug from her.

'So I noticed. What's on your mind?' she asked, sitting down next to him.

He placed the mug on the table beside him, then sat forward again and clasped his hands together. 'I was just thinking that Katherine Warren's going to be even more determined now to publish her article after what happened to Miller at the warehouse this morning.'

'And Colonel Philpott's going to be even more determined to stop her,' she replied.

'What if he can't? What if the "Dirty Pool" don't come up with something to make her drop the story?'

'They will,' she assured him. 'They always have done when UNACO's been threatened in the past. It's one of the main reasons why the organization's managed to remain under wraps all these years.'

'They haven't come up with anything yet, have they?' he shot back.

She took a sip of coffee and placed the mug at her feet. 'This isn't just about Katherine Warren, is it? You know as well as I do that the paper would have printed her story irrespective of what happened earlier this morning. What's really bugging you, Mike?'

'If we don't find Zlotin before the folders are decoded,

then we'll have to take full responsibility for the consequences both to ourselves and to the other field operatives, won't we?'

'Agreed,' she replied hesitantly.

The uncertainty in her voice wasn't lost on him. 'But on the other hand, we've got no control whatsoever over the events leading up to Warren's story should it ever go to press. We're working on a case with one hand tied behind our backs.'

'In other words, you're not in control of what's happening around you any more,' she deduced.

'Neither one of us has been since I first came across Warren in New York. That's just the way it's turned out. Sure, the "Dirty Pool" may still come up with something to discredit her, or the paper, but it's still out of our hands. That's what makes me so uneasy.'

'You're falling back on that mistrust you felt towards your men at Delta after Carrie and Mikey were kidnapped, aren't you? You know now they weren't to blame in any way for what happened to them. You've got to start learning to trust your colleagues again, Mike. You trust me, don't you?'

Graham stared at the carpet but said nothing.

'Are you saying that, after all we've been through together, you still don't trust me?' she demanded.

'I do trust you,' came the reluctant reply.

'You don't sound very convinced of it.'

'I trust you, damn it,' Graham retorted. 'But you've earned that trust. I don't know any of these guys in the "Dirty Pool", and now I find that I'm having to put my life in their hands. Because that's what it boils down to, isn't it? If they can't prevent Warren's exclusive going to press, then you can be sure there will be contracts out on us long before the story ever hits the streets.'

'If the story ever breaks, UNACO would be finished. There wouldn't just be contracts out on us. Everyone would be at risk.'

'The revelations would certainly damage UNACO, granted, but it wouldn't destroy it. Why should it? She's got no real evidence to prove that the organization actually exists, so you can be sure that the moment the story breaks, UNACO will close ranks, leaving us on the outside. The Colonel has to put UNACO first if the organization's to have any chance of surviving. Now perhaps you can understand why I feel so uneasy about the whole situation.'

'This is all hypothetical, Mike.'

'It's a hunch, that's all, based on what I'd do if I were in the Colonel's shoes. What else could he do under the circumstances?'

'We'd be given the necessary protection if it came down to it. You know the Colonel would see to it that we were given new identities and relocated away from New York. By the time he'd finished, nobody would ever be able to find us.'

'And that makes it all right?' Graham shot back. 'We'd end up like a couple of criminals on the Witness Protection Program, constantly looking over our shoulders for the rest of our lives. What about our families? I know I'd never see my mother again. You'd never see your parents again. Is that what you want?'

'We both knew the risks when we joined the organization,' she said softly.

'Being injured, even killed, in the line of duty is a risk I can accept. But being publicly exposed by some two-bit hack out for personal glory isn't part of the deal.' Graham got to his feet and moved to the window. 'I actually considered hiring a private detective to dig into Warren's life, if only to give me peace of mind, but the more I thought about it, the more I realized that, if our people, with all their contacts, can't come up with anything, then what chance would some peeper have on his own?'

'We can only do our job out here to the best of our ability, and hope that the "Dirty Pool" *can* come up with

237

something that will put the brakes on Warren's story,' Sabrina said.

'We haven't exactly excelled ourselves so far, have we?' Graham retorted. 'And not hearing anything from C.W. since he left Marseilles hasn't helped matters either.'

'I just hope nothing's happened to him,' she said, a sudden anxiety creeping into her voice.

'We're talking about C.W. here. The guy's a human talisman. He's UNACO's longest-serving field operative and the worst that's ever happened to him in over ten years of service has been the occasional tear in one of his designer suits.' Graham looked out to sea as the first rumble of thunder rolled across the darkened sky. 'No, don't worry about him. He'll outlive us all, you can be sure of that.'

Whitlock had come to the inevitable conclusion that the Russians were going to kill him once the time came for them to leave the island. It now seemed the only logical outcome under the circumstances . . .

It was almost as if he were as much a prisoner as the two women he was supposed to be guarding. He used the word 'guarding' very loosely because, other than preparing food for them (the Russians saw to their own meals), his only other duty was to accompany them twice a day to the inspection hall where they were allowed fifteen minutes with the two cryptologists before being returned to their cells. These were basic duties that the Russians could easily have incorporated into their own shifts. So why had he been recruited for thirty thousand pounds if all he had to do was sit around idly in his cell for most of the day? He was in no doubt that Jannoc had genuinely wanted to repay him for saving his daughter's life, but why hadn't the Frenchman just paid him off and put an end to the matter? Why bring in a complete outsider on such a delicate matter? And certainly the most baffling question of all as far as he was concerned: why had Zlotin agreed to go along with the deal in the first place?

Whitlock had initially put it down to the fact that Zlotin needed him to assist with the abduction of Gunther and Lisl Auerbach but, the more he'd thought about it, the more he'd come to realize that the Russian could have pulled it off by himself. None of it made any sense to him ...

Then there was the question of Berger's death. Why had he been killed? And more ominously for Whitlock, if Berger was regarded as expendable, then presumably the Russians would feel the same way about him. A point borne out by Zlotin's refusal to allow him to carry a weapon while he was on the island. Obviously it would be that much easier to kill him if he were unarmed.

With that in mind, he'd checked the contents of the makeshift kitchen in the adjoining cell earlier that morning for a utensil that could double as a weapon in an emergency. All he'd found were three plastic spoons, a plastic spatula and two dozen paper plates – all useless to him. There were the two lightweight alloy saucepans, but the idea of him creeping up undetected on one of the Russians and hitting him over the head with a saucepan rightly belonged to the realms of slapstick farce. Then he'd set about scouring every cell in the wing looking for a discarded section of piping, a length of rope, a shard of broken glass; anything that could be converted into a lethal weapon but still be small enough to be concealed about his body. Again he'd come away empty-handed.

It was obvious that the Russians had left nothing to chance. When the time came he knew that they would deal with him, and their four prisoners, in the same cold, clinical way that they'd approached the operation from the start ...

'Viktor, wake up,' Zlotin snapped, shaking Rodenko's shoulder violently. 'Viktor!'

Rodenko was awake in an instant and sat up in bed. 'What's wrong?' he asked anxiously.

'I've just received word from the mainland that Valentin was killed at the warehouse earlier this morning.'

'What about Graham and Carver?' Rodenko asked, swinging his legs off the bed.

'Both still alive,' Zlotin hissed angrily.

Rodenko crossed to the basin in the corner of the room and splashed cold water over his face. Reaching for a towel, he dried his face then turned back to Zlotin. 'Yemenkov had it all planned down to the last detail before he left for Lisbon. What went wrong?'

'Graham's what went wrong. I warned Valentin not to be overconfident after he'd managed to outsmart Graham at the caravan park yesterday, but he obviously decided that he knew better. Had he listened to me and followed orders, none of this would have happened.' Zlotin paced the floor angrily, then stopped abruptly in front of Rodenko. 'I should never have agreed to let Valentin go over there in the first place. I should have gone myself.'

'If you'd gone it could be you in the mortuary now, not Yemenkov,' Rodenko told him.

'I wouldn't be so sure of that,' Zlotin retorted sharply. 'I know how Graham operates. We're complete opposites, and that's what I find so fascinating about him. He's not a tactician of any real merit, he rarely plays by the book, and there are endless lists of examples of where he's completely disregarded the orders of his superiors and used instead a combination of streetwise mentality and sheer bravado to achieve his objective.'

'You make him sound infallible,' Rodenko said, pulling on his flak jacket.

'Far from it,' Zlotin was quick to reply.

Rodenko reached under the bed for his boots and was about to slip them on when he paused to look up at Zlotin. 'Are you going after him?'

'No, we've already lost the element of surprise. We've also lost a valued member of the team. We can't afford to

240

take any more chances, not now that we're so close to achieving our goal.'

Rodenko finished tying his boot-laces then got to his feet. '*Your* goal, Nikolai. Yemenkov's death doesn't change anything. Once those folders have been decoded and Jannoc's handed over the money, I'm gone.'

'You know I can't complete the operation by myself,' Zlotin said bitterly.

'Use your new recruit,' Rodenko said disdainfully. 'Let him work for his money instead of sitting around idly all day.'

'He stays where he is,' came the sharp reply.

'I still don't understand why you let Jannoc persuade you to bring him in on this, especially if you're not even going to use him as a cover for Yemenkov.'

'I have my reasons, Viktor, let's leave it at that.'

'In that case, your only alternative is to ask your superiors back home to send you out a replacement.'

'There's no time to call up a replacement, not at this late stage in the operation,' Zlotin retorted.

'There's time and you know it,' Rodenko shot back. 'The only reason you won't contact your superiors is because you don't want them to find out that you're having problems out here. It's always been the same, hasn't it? The great Nikolai Zlotin can never admit to failure, can he?'

'I'd watch my tongue if I were you!' Zlotin thundered furiously.

'Or what? You'll have me court-martialled for insubordination? That may have worked with Yemenkov but it doesn't hold any water with me.' Rodenko's eyes followed Zlotin's hand as it came to rest on the holstered Makarov pistol on his belt. 'Go on, Nikolai, shoot me. After all, it wouldn't be the first time that you'd shot one of your own officers for daring to speak his mind, would it?'

Zlotin let his hand drop to his side. 'What's it going to cost for you to see the operation through to the end?'

'You make me out to be –'

'How much?' Zlotin snapped.

'Well, Yemenkov won't be needing his share of the money any more, will he?' Rodenko said after a moment's thought.

'It's yours,' Zlotin replied without hesitation. 'That would double your money. Three hundred thousand dollars.'

'And a good Communist like yourself won't have any use for two hundred thousand dollars,' Rodenko said with a cunning smile. 'The full half a million and you can count me in. For what you're going to make on those folders, together with the fact that your superiors need never know what really happened at the warehouse this morning, I'd say you've got yourself a bargain. But it's up to you, of course.'

'You've got yourself a deal,' Zlotin said coldly.

'Well, I believe it's my shift,' Rodenko said, slipping his holstered pistol on to his belt which he then secured around his waist. He paused at the door to look back at Zlotin. 'For what it's worth, Nikolai, I'm sorry about Yemenkov. I know you thought a lot of him.'

'UNACO haven't heard the last of this,' Zlotin replied softly. 'I promise you that, one way or another, they'll pay for the death of Captain Valentin Yemenkov.'

10

Larry Ryan, the editor of the *New York Sentinel*, sat silently in the back of the white Mercedes as it sped through the empty New York streets in the early hours of the morning. The two men in the car with him both wore black stockings over their heads to conceal their faces. Although he was pretty sure he knew who they were working for, he didn't know their names, nor did he know where they were taking him . . .

The telephone had woken him at home just before three o'clock that morning. It had been Katherine Warren calling from Lisbon with the news of Ed Miller's death. He'd transferred the call to his study, so as not to wake his slumbering wife and, after a lengthy conversation with Katherine, he'd gone through to the kitchen to make himself some coffee. It was then that he'd received the second call. An anonymous caller had wanted to meet with him to discuss the implications of the story Katherine Warren was currently working on in Lisbon. At first he'd suspected that the caller might have been an innovative reporter from a rival paper who'd found out that she was on assignment, but when the names Mike Graham and Sabrina Carver were mentioned, he'd quickly realized that the caller was either someone inside UNACO, or else someone with an intimate knowledge of the organization. How else could the caller have known about Graham and Carver, or that the newspaper intended running an exclusive on them? Either way, it was too good an opportunity to pass up, even though he knew only too well that he could be walking into some kind of carefully planned trap . . .

The instructions had been simple enough. The two men in a white Mercedes, who had been waiting for him outside the house, would take him to the rendezvous. He wasn't to call in to his night editor to tell him about the meeting, nor was he to conceal any listening devices on him. If either of these conditions were breached, the meeting would be called off . . .

Their final destination turned out to be a small Catholic church in Greenwich Village. The car pulled up at the back of the church and one of the men jumped out and looked around him slowly. Satisfied that they hadn't been followed, he gestured for Ryan to get out. The driver remained behind the wheel, his hand resting lightly on a concealed revolver under his blouson.

Ryan zipped up his jacket against the biting wind as soon as he got out of the car and followed the man through a semi-circular arch to a thick oak door. Again the man looked around him then gave a coded knock on the door. There was the sound of a bolt being drawn back and the heavy door creaked open. Ryan was ushered inside and the door was immediately closed again behind them, the bolt slid back into place.

The man who'd admitted them was also wearing a black stocking over his head. His jacket was open, revealing a holstered Heckler & Koch pistol on his belt. He took a debugging receiver, no bigger than a cigarette packet, from his pocket, using it to scan Ryan's clothes for any hidden microphones. The red light remained inactive. Then he ordered Ryan to turn out his pockets, and finally gave him a thorough body search. Apparently satisfied that Ryan was clean, he switched off the receiver and nodded to his colleague.

'Come with me,' the first man said, leading Ryan down the dimly lit side aisle until they reached the confessional.

'You guys have got it all worked out, haven't you?' Ryan said with grudging admiration. 'No wonder UNACO's remained a secret for so long.'

The door was opened and the man gestured for Ryan to enter. Once inside the confessional, the door was closed again behind him. Ryan sat down slowly, but when he tried to peer through the grille he discovered that a black cloth had been draped over the other side, making it impossible for him to see into the adjoining stall.

'I must apologize for the theatrics, Mr Ryan, but it was necessary if we were to meet in private,' a voice announced from behind the grille.

'I quite understand,' Ryan replied. 'Tell me, is that accent Irish or Scottish?'

'I'm sure you're a busy man, Mr Ryan, so let me get straight to the point,' came the sharp riposte. 'Does your newspaper still intend to go ahead with this story on Mike Graham and Sabrina Carver after what happened to Edward Miller in Lisbon earlier this morning?'

'You're damn right we do,' Ryan retorted. 'Ed Miller was a fine journalist who died covering a story for the paper. If nothing else, we owe it to his memory to see that the finished story goes to press.'

'And I suppose it doesn't matter to you that by exposing UNACO you'd not only be putting the lives of all its personnel in jeopardy, but you'd also effectively destroy its credibility as an undercover agency?'

'If there's a clandestine anti-crime organization working out of the United Nations, then the public have a right to know about it,' Ryan replied.

'The standard newspaper reply, "the public have a right to know",' came the disdainful retort. 'Why don't you just admit it: you don't give a damn about what the public thinks, just as long as you can splash some exclusive across the front page which is guaranteed to boost your circulation figures. Am I right?'

'I'm sure you didn't bring me here to talk about our circulation figures,' Ryan said with a wry smile to himself.

'No, I didn't. I brought you here this morning hoping to try and reason with you, but obviously that isn't going to work. That brings me to my second option. I'm prepared to offer you an in-depth interview into the workings of UNACO, but in return you'll agree to drop the story you're planning on Graham and Carver.'

'No deal,' Ryan shot back. 'This kind of story only comes along once in a lifetime. Two undercover agents mixed up in a web of murder and intrigue while on a top secret assignment in Lisbon. One's a handsome ex-football player haunted by a tragic past, and the other's a stunning blonde with the kind of looks that could melt the Brooklyn Bridge in the middle of winter. Do you honestly expect me to give that up for some "Deep Throat" type interview with someone I've never even seen?'

'You'd see me if you agreed to the deal. In fact, you'd know my name, my rank, and you could take as many photographs of me as you wanted. I could give you details of operations we've been involved in over the years, all authenticated by dates and locations. My only other condition would be that no UNACO operative would be mentioned by name. Only by their code names. Admittedly, you wouldn't have Carver's face to adorn your front page, but by the time I'd finished you'd have more than enough information to spread your scoop over a whole week. Think what that would do for your circulation figures.'

'This doesn't make any sense. Why are you prepared to sell out your colleagues just to save Graham and Carver?'

'I wouldn't be selling them out. You've obviously made up your mind to run a story on UNACO, and we both know that there's nothing I can do to stop you printing it. I see

246

this more as a damage-limitation exercise which would be beneficial both to your newspaper and to my organization. So you see, I'd actually be protecting my people. I'd also be protecting you and your family for that matter.'

'What's that supposed to mean?' Ryan demanded.

'Just as you've obviously done your homework on Graham and Carver, so we've also done our homework on you and your family as well. Actually, I've got the folder here with me. You've got a very attractive wife and a couple of lovely daughters. How old are your daughters again? Ah yes, here we are. Six and four. You're really lucky, Ryan. You've got it made, you really have. I'd hate it if anything were to happen to them.'

'Are you threatening my family, you bastard!' Ryan hissed, his face now pressed up against the grille.

'Of course not,' came the quick response. 'The problem is that Graham got someone to fax the contents of this dossier through to him in Lisbon yesterday. He wouldn't admit it to me in so many words, but it's my guess that he may already have decided to target you if you went ahead and blew his cover. An eye for an eye – he's that kind of person. And if he can't get to you, he might even resort to using your family to draw you out. Naturally you and your family would be given protection if it came to that, but frankly a couple of NYPD patrolmen wouldn't be any match for him. We're talking about Mike Graham here.'

'I can see what you're trying to do,' Ryan hissed, already picturing the excited faces of his two daughters as they'd opened their Christmas presents the previous morning. What if something did happen to them as a result of his printing the story? He could never live with himself after that. Nothing's going to happen to them, he was quick to reassure himself. You're the editor of one of the leading newspapers in the country. You have an obligation to publish this story. But still he couldn't seem to shake those innocent faces from his mind . . .

'Think about what I've said, Ryan, and I'll get back to you in the next couple of days for your answer.'

'There's nothing to think about,' Ryan replied, hoping the anxiety he was feeling hadn't come across in his face. 'I've already made up my mind to print the story on Graham and Carver, and you can be sure that this conversation's going to be included in the article as well.'

'I'll call you anyway in case you should decide to change your mind after you've had a chance to reflect rationally on what's been said here today. At least then I'll know that I've done everything possible to protect you and your family. Good morning to you, Mr Ryan.'

'Now you listen to me –' Ryan started, but the door was yanked open and the masked man indicated that it was time for him to leave. Ryan reluctantly emerged from the confessional, his eyes instinctively going to the closed door which led into the other half of the stall. If only he could get a glimpse inside . . .

'I wouldn't advise it, Mr Ryan,' the masked man said in a soft, menacing tone.

Ryan didn't reply as he was led back to the side door which had been used to enter the church.

'My colleagues will drive you back to your house,' the masked man said. 'I hope for your sake that we never meet again.'

The second man opened the door and Ryan followed him down the stairs to the waiting car. Moments later the car pulled out of the driveway and disappeared down the road.

The masked man closed the door again, bolted it, then hurried back to the confessional and rapped on the door. 'You can come out now, Colonel Philpott. He's gone.'

The door opened and Philpott emerged. Smoothing down his jacket, he gestured to the stocking mask. 'You can take that off as well, you know.'

The man pulled the stocking off his head, revealing a

sallow face and cropped brown hair. Danny Lowell, a former officer in the military branch of the American Secret Service, was team leader of Strike Force Eight. He reached through the open door and removed the black cloth and a small microphone which had been positioned discreetly underneath the grille.

'Did you get everything down on tape?' Philpott asked, making his way towards the side door.

Lowell nodded. 'He didn't go for your compromise, did he, sir?'

'No, but then I never expected him to,' Philpott replied.

'I'm not with you, sir,' Lowell said with a frown. 'I thought the whole point of the exercise was to try and persuade him to drop the story about Mike and Sabrina.'

Philpott stopped abruptly and looked round at Lowell. 'Do you honestly think I'd actually have put this whole organization at risk by giving out classified information to a newspaper?' he demanded angrily.

Lowell shifted uneasily on his feet and looked down at the floor, unable to hold Philpott's piercing stare. 'I don't know, sir,' he stammered. 'I thought perhaps the Secretary-General –'

'What's the Secretary-General got to do with it?' Philpott cut in sharply. 'Who runs UNACO, Danny? The Secretary-General or me?'

'You, sir,' Lowell was quick to reply. 'It's just that Strike Force Eight weren't briefed about your meeting with Ryan here this morning. All I know about the operation so far is what I heard when we were monitoring your conversation with Ryan in the confessional.'

'You mean you weren't briefed by the duty officer before you arrived here this morning?' Philpott enquired sharply.

'There wasn't time, sir,' Lowell replied apologetically. 'Everything happened so quickly. We were only called out an hour ago. We just had enough time to pick up the microphone from stores before we had to meet you here.'

Philpott sat down on the back pew and outlined the case briefly to Lowell.

'They'd be marked the moment the story reached the streets,' Lowell said in horror once Philpott had finished.

'Don't you think I don't know that, Danny?' Philpott retorted. 'I've already drafted in extra personnel to help try and dig up something on either Ryan or Warren which could be used to force the paper to drop the story, but so far they haven't come up with anything. And after what happened to Miller in Lisbon last night, I had the feeling that Ryan might decide to print Warren's story sooner rather than later. That's why I set up the meeting with him here this morning. Ryan may not have taken the bait, but it's certainly got him thinking. That much was obvious in his voice. He's a seasoned newspaperman who knows all the tricks in the book, and you can be sure that he's already planning some devious way of getting hold of my so-called exclusive as well as being able to keep the story on Mike and Sabrina. And that's exactly what I'm counting on, because the longer I can play him on the end of my line, the more time it'll give the "Dirty Pool" to work on him and Warren.'

'Why did you tell him that Mike might go after him if he went ahead and printed Warren's story?' Lowell asked. 'Were you trying to frighten him?'

'I'd prefer to think I made him feel uneasy. Larry Ryan has one real Achilles' heel. His daughters. He absolutely dotes on them. So by hinting that they could possibly become targets as a direct result of the story, it may cause him to think twice before he gives the final go-ahead for it to go into print. I doubt that it'll make him change his mind, but at least it might make him hold back just long enough for us to find something that could be used against the paper. Again, it's delaying tactics. And quite frankly, that's all we've got going for us at the moment.' Philpott got to his feet and moved to the door. 'Come on, we'd better get out of here before Ryan sends round one of his hacks to check out the place.'

Katherine Warren got in to JFK Airport that afternoon and drove straight over to the *New York Sentinel*'s head office on West Forty-third Street where Ryan was waiting for her.

'Welcome back,' Ryan exclaimed when she entered his office. 'You look like you could do with a good night's sleep,' he added, indicating the dark rings under her eyes.

'Why did you pull me off the story, Larry?' she demanded, glaring at him.

'I thought it best under the circumstances to bring you home,' Ryan replied in a placating tone. 'I certainly haven't pulled you off the story, if that's what you think.'

'What use am I sitting around here when Graham and Carver are still over in Lisbon?' she snapped, then got to her feet and crossed to the percolator in the corner of the room and poured herself a coffee.

'You said yourself that Graham and Carver had mysteriously checked out of the hotel within hours of Miller's death,' Ryan countered. 'They're on to you, Katy. Your cover's been blown.'

'Ed had contacts in Lisbon. I could have used them to pick up the trail again.'

'The trail's dead, Katy,' Ryan said softly. 'They wouldn't have let you get anywhere near them again. You're more useful to me here than chasing around after shadows out there.'

She took a sip of coffee then removed a folder from her shoulder bag and dropped it on to the glass table in front of Ryan. 'That's the dossier I compiled on them while they were in Lisbon. Photographs, locations, dates, times. It's all there.'

'Great,' Ryan said with a quick smile, but made no move to pick it up.

251

'That's it? Great. Aren't you even going to look at it?'

'All in good time,' Ryan replied.

'OK, out with it, Larry. Something's bugging you, isn't it?'

Ryan explained about the incident at the church that morning.

'Did you have the place checked out?' she asked once he'd finished talking.

'I sent one of the night staff round as soon as I got home, but they were already long gone. The local priest said that he didn't know anything about the church being used this morning, but he'd obviously been paid to play dumb. We weren't going to get anything constructive out of him.'

A faint smile tugged at the corners of her mouth. 'The whole thing smacks of desperation on their part. I reckon we've got them on the ropes, Larry.'

'Possibly,' Ryan replied thoughtfully.

'Come on, Larry, you don't honestly think that UNACO would give us an exclusive about their tactics and operations? It's obviously a ploy on their part to try and persuade you to drop the story on Graham and Carver.'

'And if it's not?' Ryan replied, then held up his hand before she could say anything. 'I agree, it has all the hallmarks of an intelligence scam, but what if he is on the level? It's something we've got to consider, no matter how suspicious it may seem. We've got the background details and more than enough photos of Graham and Carver which all point towards them being part of the UNACO set-up, but what we still don't have is any concrete evidence to support the story. We can still run the article on what we've got, but imagine what a difference it would make to the story as a whole if we had actual proof of UNACO's existence to back up our claims. And it wouldn't just be hearsay, it would be from a named source within the organization itself.'

'I still say it's wishful thinking, Larry,' Katherine said from the window.

'So do I, but there's no harm in playing along with him. Frankly, it doesn't matter whether the story goes to press this week or early in the New Year. It's not as if any of our competitors are running the same story, is it?'

'I guess it wouldn't do any harm to wait for his call. I'd like a couple of days to polish up the article anyway before I do submit it,' she told him. 'I also want to put together a piece on Ed to accompany the story.'

'Fine.' Ryan crossed to a pile of folders on his desk, found the one he was after, and handed it to Katherine. 'Details of Graham and Carver's immediate families. It makes fascinating reading. I had it compiled while you were away.'

'Do you want me to try and get an interview with them?' Katherine asked, opening the folder.

'Why not?' Ryan countered. 'Carver's father's a former American Ambassador to Canada and the UK. But better still, Graham's father-in-law is the former right-wing Republican senator, "Hawk" Walsh.'

Katherine opened the folder and scanned the details on the page in front of her. 'Carver's parents live in Miami and Walsh lives in Seaford, Delaware. I'll be able to see them over the next couple of days.'

'Carver's parents live in Miami, but every December they come up to New York to spend Christmas with their daughter,' Ryan told her. 'They're here at the moment.'

'Better still,' Katherine said, closing the folder. 'I'll head over to Manhattan later today and see what George and Jeanne Carver can tell me about their little girl.'

'You do that.'

She moved to the door where she paused, her hand resting lightly on the handle. 'What about this veiled death threat you got this morning? Are you taking it seriously?'

'I've got to take it seriously. Having said that, it's not the first death threat I ever received, and I'm sure it won't be the last one either. It's all part of the business.'

'Are you going to tell Louise about it?'

'The last time I told her that someone had threatened to kill me she was seeing assassins behind every tree. It's not worth going through that kind of aggravation again.'

Katherine smiled. 'OK, I'll keep mum about it as well.'

'Thanks, I'd appreciate it.'

She opened the door then looked round at him again, her face suddenly serious. 'You know Graham's capable of it, don't you?'

'Don't worry, Katy, we're going to publish and there's nothing that UNACO can do about it.'

Graham looked up briefly at Sabrina when she entered the lounge, then turned his attention back to the television set in front of him.

'Anything exciting?' she asked from the doorway.

Graham's eyes didn't leave the screen. 'A soccer match,' he said.

Sabrina raised her eyebrows in an ironic gesture that was lost on Graham. 'Gee, that is exciting,' she said in a deadpan voice.

'Yeah,' came the absent reply.

'Where's Jacques?' Sabrina tried again to engage his attention.

'He's in the study,' Graham said, gesturing vaguely in the direction of the door.

She crossed to where Graham was sitting on the sofa. 'So what's the score?'

'The score?' he replied, squinting up at her.

'You know – as in, how many goals have been scored so far by each team?' she said with gentle sarcasm.

Graham pondered the question, then reached for the remote control and switched off the set. 'You know, I've been sitting here for the last twenty-five minutes and I couldn't even tell you who's playing, never mind the score.'

'I know what you mean. I found an old paperback in my bedroom, but after I got through the first twenty pages

I realized I hadn't a clue what I'd just read. That's when I decided to come down here to see what you and Jacques were doing.'

'Jacques's been catching up on his paperwork for the last hour.'

'At least he's got something to take his mind off this waiting,' Sabrina replied with a sigh. 'I've just made a fresh brew of coffee. Want some?'

'Yeah, sounds great,' Graham said, getting to his feet and following Sabrina into the kitchen.

She poured the freshly percolated coffee into two mugs and placed one of them on the table in front of Graham, then took a carton of milk from the fridge behind her and handed it to him.

'Ah, *café*,' Rust said from the doorway, wheeling himself into the room.

'So what brings you out of hibernation on a day like this?' Graham asked, adding milk to his coffee.

'I've just finished talking to Colonel Philpott on the phone.'

'Jacques?' Sabrina said, holding out a mug towards him.

'*Merci, chérie*,' Rust said, taking it from her.

'So what did the Colonel have to say?' Graham asked.

Rust explained about Philpott's meeting with Ryan earlier that morning.

'So the Colonel's now admitted to Ryan that UNACO actually exists,' Sabrina said sharply. 'Was that absolutely necessary?'

'It's a risk the Colonel had to take if his plan is to have any chance of working,' Rust replied. 'If you think about it, he was only confirming what Ryan already knew. There's nothing Ryan could do with the information other than to say that it had come from an unknown source; that would only serve to dilute the sensationalist value of the story. More to the point, though, if the "Dirty Pool" do come up with something to discredit either him or Warren in the next couple of days, even that disclosure would never be made public.'

'So the "Dirty Pool" are still bumbling about in the dark?' Graham said bitterly. 'What the hell are they doing over there?'

'They're pulling out all the stops on this one, Mike,' Rust retorted angrily. 'You may not think a lot of them but they've been working double shifts these last two days trying to dig up something to save your skin. Just remember that before you start criticizing them.'

'Well, at least Warren's out of our hair,' Sabrina said, quickly changing the subject, sensing the sudden tension between the two men.

'Not quite,' Rust replied, turning to her. 'The Colonel received a call from your father shortly before he rang me.'

'My father?' Sabrina shot back in amazement. 'What did he want with Colonel Philpott? And how did he know where to contact him?'

'It seems that your father still has some influential friends left on Capitol Hill,' Rust told her. 'He made it known that he wanted to speak to the Colonel. Word got back to UNACO and the Colonel contacted him. It turns out that Katherine Warren was at your flat earlier today.'

'I suppose I shouldn't be surprised,' she replied with a despondent shrug.

'She wanted an interview with your parents for her article, but your father told her very diplomatically exactly what she could do with her story.'

Sabrina smiled. 'Daddy always did have a way with words.'

'If the paper's already tried to interview Sabrina's parents, then there's every chance that they'll send someone to see your mother at the retirement home in Santa Monica as well, Mike,' Rust said. 'But the Colonel's already taken steps to deal with that possibility. If Warren, or any reporter, arrives at the home, they'll be told that your mother is recovering from surgery and isn't to be disturbed.'

'They wouldn't get anything out of her anyway,' Graham said softly.

'Haven't you told your mother about UNACO?' Sabrina asked.

Graham turned the mug around slowly on the table then shook his head. 'My mother suffers from Alzheimer's disease. Some days she's completely lucid and other days . . . hell, she doesn't even know who I am.'

'I'm sorry, Mike, I had no idea,' Sabrina said softly, putting her hand gently on his arm.

'I know I've never mentioned it before, but I guess there's just some things you don't talk about,' Graham said, shifting uncomfortably on his chair. 'Perhaps that's the wrong attitude to take, I don't know.'

'Does your mother still think you're with Delta?' Rust asked.

'No, she knows I left after what happened to Carrie and Mikey. I can still remember the day I went up to Santa Monica to break the news to her that I'd resigned my commission from the unit. She didn't say a word, she just sat at the window holding her favourite picture of Mikey in her hands. I guess it was then that I realized just what she'd been through all those years when I was with Delta. That's why I've never told her about UNACO. I couldn't put her through that kind of pain again. She actually thinks I'm now a freelance security consultant with an office in New York's financial district.'

'It's probably for the best,' Sabrina said.

'She knows about you though,' Graham said, casting a sideways glance in Sabrina's direction.

'She does?' Sabrina said in surprise. 'How?'

'She found a picture of us when she last came to stay with me at my cabin up at Lake Champlain. You know, the photo C.W. took of us outside La Grenouille restaurant last year when the three of us went out for a meal together?'

'Of course I know it. So what did you tell her? That I was a client of yours?'

'I would have, if I'd had more time to think about it,'

Graham replied. 'I just had to say the first thing that came to mind. I told her that you were my secretary.'

'How original,' she retorted facetiously.

'She still asks after you, on her good days,' Graham said with a half-smile, then looked across the table at Rust. 'No, you don't have to worry about my mother, Jacques, she can't tell them what she doesn't know. And "Hawk" Walsh won't tell Warren anything either if she travels down to see him. There's only one thing he despises more than me, and that's the press.'

Rust smiled, then turned to Sabrina. 'You realize, of course, that you won't be able to return to your flat if we still haven't blocked the story by the time you're ready to fly back to New York. The worst thing we could do now is let Warren pick up the scent again.'

'In other words, I'll be shunted off to some hotel, is that it?' she retorted.

'What about me? Am I going to be holed up in some hotel as well?'

'I'm afraid so, Mike,' Rust replied. 'We don't know whether the newspaper has already found out about your little retreat at Lake Champlain, but we can't afford to take any chances. You'll both be put up at a hotel in the city, and the Colonel's already indicated that, once you've been debriefed, you'll be given extended leave so that you can both get out of New York for a while.'

'And if the story goes to press, it'll become indefinite leave,' Graham said, getting to his feet and moving to the window.

Rust finished his coffee and replaced the mug on the table. 'Well, if you'll excuse me, I've still got a mound of paperwork to get through before my head hits the pillow tonight.'

'Anything we can do to help?' Sabrina asked hopefully.

'No, *chérie*, it's all work I've brought with me from Zürich. It's the only consolation about this infuriating waiting game – at least I can catch up on my paperwork.' Rust looked from one disconsolate face to the other. 'I know that you must both be on edge right now, but until we've got a positive lead to go on, all we can do is stick it out here as best we can.'

'And what if we don't get another lead?' Graham asked, looking at Rust's reflection in the window. 'Are we just supposed to sit around here and wait for the hammer to fall?'

'Don't you think the frustration is getting to me as well, Mike?' Rust retorted. 'But there's nothing we can do until either we hear from C.W., or else the Special Forces Brigade locate Zlotin's hideout.'

'In that case, we've got nothing to worry about, have we?' Graham retorted sarcastically.

'Don't push it, Mike,' Rust snapped, stabbing a finger at Graham.

'Come off it, Jacques, don't you think that if C.W. could have contacted us, he'd have done so already? And as for the Special Forces Brigade finding the hideout . . .' Graham tailed off, shaking his head.

'I'm getting a little tired of these continual digs at the Special Forces Brigade,' Rust said angrily. 'They're one of the finest anti-terrorist units in Europe, and they've gone out of their way to give us their full support on this operation.'

'I wasn't having a dig at them. Zlotin's no fool, Jacques. He'll have made sure that their hideout is well off the beaten track. That's obviously why C.W. hasn't been able to contact us. I know the Special Forces Brigade are pulling out all the stops to find the place, but it's the proverbial needle in a haystack, isn't it? They could bring in the military and the air force and still not come close to finding it.' Graham turned away from the window, his face grim. 'We had our chance of finding Zlotin through Caldere and we blew it. So unless C.W. can work some kind of miracle, I reckon our only chance of getting those folders back now is when they eventually turn up on the black market, presuming that is what Zlotin intends to do with them once they've been decoded.'

'In other words, UNACO would have to buy them back,' Rust concluded.

'What other choice would we have?' Graham said, draining his cup.

Rust pondered the question for a moment before disappearing out into the corridor without venturing an answer.

'We couldn't be sure of getting all the individual documents back even if they did turn up on the black market,' Sabrina said, breaking the silence.

'It would be the worst possible outcome for UNACO, I agree, but the way things are looking at the moment, it may be all that's open to us now.'

'Zlotin could still make a mistake, especially now that he's lost one of his men,' she said.

'I wouldn't count on it. If anything, I think it'll only serve to make him even more vigilant than ever. He can't afford to lose anyone else, not when there's only the two of them left now to see the operation through to its conclusion.'

'Unless he drafts C.W. in to replace Yemenkov?' Sabrina said.

'Which is where the miracle would come in,' Graham said. 'But even if Zlotin were to bring in C.W. as Yemenkov's replacement, I still think it's very unlikely that he'd let him anywhere near the folders. It's all a question of trust, and C.W. certainly won't have gained Zlotin's trust in the space of a few days.'

'We could certainly do with some Divine intervention right now,' she said, rolling her eyes heavenward.

'I'd gladly settle for a pact with the devil if it would solve our problems,' Graham replied.

'I know what you mean,' she said with a sigh then, grinning wryly at Graham, indicated the empty mug on the table in front of him. 'Can I get you a refill?' she asked. 'That must be part of my secretarial duties, surely?'

Graham pushed his mug towards her without comment, but she was amused to see that he had the grace to blush as he did so.

11

'They've cracked the code.'

Zlotin discarded the paperback he'd been reading and hurried over to where Rodenko was standing in the doorway. 'Have you brought the key with you?'

Rodenko took a sheet of paper from the top pocket of his flak jacket and handed it to Zlotin. 'It looks like we're finally in business, Nikolai.'

'There's only one way to find out,' Zlotin replied, gesturing to the two aluminium cases on the table in the corner of the cell.

One of the cases contained a portable word processor and laser printer, the other a memory unit. Zlotin used an interconnect cable to link them up, then Rodenko plugged the two mains leads into an extension reel which had a cable secured to a power point in the corridor.

Rodenko watched as Zlotin inserted a floppy disk into the word processor and moments later a display menu appeared on the VDU. 'How long did it actually take Yemenkov to copy the UNACO folders on to that disk?'

'A couple of nights,' Zlotin replied.

'That's good going considering the size of those two UNACO folders.'

'Valentin was one of the new breed of *spetznaz* officers,' Zlotin said. 'Computers were second nature to him.'

261

'Well they're not to me,' Rodenko retorted. 'I'm not even sure what you're doing here.'

'The memory unit contains a program which will unscramble Silverman's code once I've fed the cryptologists' key letters into the word processor,' Zlotin replied, tapping out the details from the paper as he spoke. 'Then once the memory has all the relevant information, it shouldn't take long for it to substitute the coded letters back into the original text. Then we'll know whether the key they gave us is genuine, or whether they've substituted one of their own to try and trick us.'

'In that case, why couldn't we have used the computer to do the actual decoding instead of bringing in the cryptologists?' Rodenko asked.

'For one this memory's far too small to contain a sophisticated decoding program,' Zlotin replied. 'And even if it did have such a program, it would be useless to us unless it already contained samples of Silverman's codes. You have to remember, Viktor, that although a computer has the capacity for a memory, it still doesn't have a mind of its own. It can only work within the parameters of the information that's been programmed into it.'

Rodenko just nodded. He crossed to the bed, where he picked up the paperback Zlotin had been reading, glanced at the cover, then tossed it aside and moved to the door. Digging his hands into his pockets, he peered the length of the deserted corridor then turned back to Zlotin. 'When will it start printing?'

'When it's ready,' Zlotin retorted irritably.

Rodenko crossed to the word processor, tapped his foot impatiently on the floor as he waited for it to print, then snorted in disgust and returned to his vigil by the door.

'What's wrong with you?' Zlotin demanded. 'You're pacing up and down in here like an expectant father.'

'You know I don't trust those things,' Rodenko retorted, gesturing in the general direction of the word processor.

'You don't trust them because you don't understand them.'

'Exactly,' came the blunt reply.

Then, as if on cue, the first page slipped silently from the mouth of the printer. Zlotin picked it up and carefully read through the plaintext.

'Well?' Rodenko asked anxiously from the doorway.

Zlotin scanned the next few pages of plaintext before finally looking across at Rodenko. 'Radio Jannoc in Marseilles and tell him that the code's been broken.'

Whitlock emerged from his cell on hearing the sound of approaching footsteps outside in the corridor.

'Here's two more for you to look after,' Zlotin announced, waving the pistol in his hand to indicate Auerbach and Fisier.

Whitlock looked at the two cryptologists but said nothing. Using his key card, Zlotin activated the door of the cell where Marie Fisier and Lisl Auerbach were being held and gestured for the two men to enter. He closed the cell door again behind them.

'Have they decoded the documents for you?' Whitlock asked, although he'd already guessed the answer the moment he'd seen the two cryptologists standing in the corridor.

'Yes.'

'So what happens now?'

'If all goes according to plan, we should be out of here by tomorrow morning. Once we reach the mainland you'll be paid the balance owed to you, then you'll be on your own.'

'Why can't we leave now?'

'Because I still have some unfinished business to attend to,' Zlotin replied as he headed towards the door at the end of the corridor.

'What about the antidote?' Whitlock called out after him.

'It'll be administered to the two women before we leave the island,' Zlotin replied as the door slid shut behind him.

Whitlock returned to his cell and sat down on the bed.

He'd been thinking a lot about the so-called 'antidote' over the last twenty-four hours. If he was right about the Russians killing the prisoners before leaving the island, then why would they need an antidote to combat the effects of the virus? And if that were the case, why bother with the virus in the first place? What if the contents of the syringe Zlotin had administered to Lisl Auerbach in Leipzig had been, in fact, nothing more than a harmless tranquillizer? Zlotin had told Auerbach that a sedative had been incorporated into the solution, and Lisl Auerbach had certainly slept during the flight to Madrid.

It was with these factors in mind that he'd finally come up with what he considered to be a viable plan to break out of the wing. Well, as viable as could be expected given the limited resources at his disposal. He had intended to implement the plan that morning, but now that he knew they wouldn't be leaving the island until the following day, he'd decided to hold back until later that night when the whole prison complex would be shrouded in darkness. Ideal conditions for a plan which would rely heavily on the element of surprise if it were to have any chance of succeeding . . .

Zlotin entered the adjoining cell which doubled as their operations room. It housed a powerful radio transmitter; a short-range radar system, connected up to a fuel generator, which could detect any movement on the water or in the air within a five-mile radius of the island; and two reinforced steel cabinets which contained the small arsenal which the Russians had insisted on having at the outset of the operation. All the equipment had been supplied by Jannoc as part of the deal and delivered clandestinely to the island by a passing freighter.

'Did you get through to Marseilles?' Zlotin asked Rodenko, who was sitting in front of the radio transmitter, his back to the door.

Rodenko swivelled round in the chair and grinned at Zlotin.

'I spoke to Jannoc personally. He was very excited by the news.'

'Is the money ready?' Zlotin asked.

'Ready and waiting.'

Zlotin pulled up a wooden chair, turned it round, and sat astride it. 'Did he say when he'd be flying out here?'

'Jannoc's not coming out in person,' Rodenko replied. 'Saisse will be delivering the money for him.'

'Saisse,' Zlotin snorted disdainfully. 'So when's he expected to get here?'

'He's been in Lisbon for the past two days waiting for the word from Marseilles to deliver the money to us. According to Jannoc, we should have the money within the next couple of hours.'

'Excellent,' Zlotin replied. 'That means I'll be able to start negotiating the sale of the UNACO folders as soon as he's gone. So, all being well, I should be back in Russia by the end of the year.'

'I'll spare a thought for you freezing to death in sub-zero temperatures while I'm stretched out on some deserted beach – a cocktail in one hand, half a million dollars in the other.'

'I'm sure you will,' Zlotin retorted contemptuously, then got to his feet and crossed to the door. 'And just so that there can be no misunderstandings, the money will remain locked in the safe in my cell until the operation's over.'

'Why don't you just come out and say what you mean, Nikolai?' Rodenko shot back angrily. 'You don't trust me any more, do you?'

'I don't trust you any more because you've changed so much since we arrived here. Suddenly everything you do has to have a price. You were never like this before, Viktor. What's happened to you?'

'For the first time in my life I'm doing something for myself and not for the beloved socialist cause. And what was that wonderful cause, other than a bunch of faceless dinosaurs, steeped in corruption, who lived like royalty while the rest of us struggled to make ends meet? The same dinosaurs that you want to see back in power. You're still living in the past, Nikolai. I'm not, and that's the difference between us now.' Rodenko tossed the headset on to the table and got to his feet. 'But you don't need to worry about me. I gave you my word that I'd stick with this to the end and, whatever else may have changed, my word's still my bond.'

'For your sake, I hope so,' Zlotin retorted coldly, then turned on his heels and disappeared out into the corridor.

'Helicopter approaching,' Rodenko announced, appearing in the doorway of Zlotin's cell.

'Saisse?' Zlotin asked, looking up from his paperback.

Rodenko nodded. 'I've already spoken to the pilot over the radio and given him permission to put down on the helipad. They should be landing shortly.'

'Let's go then,' Zlotin said, grabbing the attaché case off the table beside the bed and hurrying after Rodenko.

They made their way through to the inspection hall, up a flight of metal stairs and into a long, windowless corridor. The walls and ceiling were charred and blackened from the intense heat of the fire which had swept mercilessly through the upper levels of the prison. There was an open security door at the end of the corridor. They passed through it and a second security door twenty yards further on before coming to another flight of metal stairs which led directly up on to the helipad.

Zlotin eyed the stairs suspiciously. 'Are you sure these are safe to use now? I nearly broke my neck the last time I went up there.'

'They're perfectly safe now,' Rodenko assured him. 'There were only a few corroded treads on the staircase, obviously damaged as a result of the fire. I've since removed them. All the remaining treads are now quite solid. I should know,

I've been up and down here several times since I carried out the repairs.'

'Then you won't mind leading the way,' Zlotin said, gesturing with a sweep of his arm towards the stairs.

'That makes a change,' Rodenko said with a faint smile of satisfaction. 'Nikolai Zlotin having to follow in someone else's footsteps.'

'I prefer to call it common sense,' Zlotin replied.

Rodenko went first, carefully stepping over the occasional missing tread as he made his way towards the security door at the top of the stairs. He stopped after completing three-quarters of the distance, and pointed to where he'd had to remove two treads in a row. Not that Zlotin needed any reminding of where he'd almost crashed through the staircase when the treads, both badly corroded, had given way under his weight on the day they'd arrived on the island. Had he not grabbed on to the railing as he lost his balance, he knew he would have certainly fallen to his death. He peered over the railing – nothing but a sheer drop of two hundred feet to the concrete floor below.

On reaching the top of the stairs, Rodenko used his key card to activate the door and stepped out on to the helipad. The helicopter, which had been used to bring the Fisiers to the island, stood in the faded yellow circle in the centre of the helipad. It was concealed underneath camouflage netting to make it indistinguishable from the air. It was a standard Westland Scout helicopter, which Jannoc had managed to acquire through one of his numerous under-world contacts on the Continent, and which Rodenko had since modified to his own personal requirements. He'd removed the anti-tank missile pods from the fuselage pylons then, after reinforcing the helicopter's undercarriage, he'd mounted a 30-mm calibre chain gun directly underneath the cockpit which was capable of firing up to 625 rounds per minute. He'd yet to unleash its devastating firepower on anything more substantial than a couple of wooden crates which Yemenkov had placed strategically in the water for him, but the fact that it had tested successfully was all that really concerned him.

'There he is,' Zlotin shouted above the wind, pointing into the distance.

Rodenko squinted up into the overcast sky, following the direction of Zlotin's finger. Although he could hear the faint rumble of an engine in the distance, it was still several seconds before he finally saw the hazy silhouette of the approaching Bell JetRanger. Rodenko remembered how Zlotin's uncanny ability to detect even the slightest movement with the naked eye had come to the fore during the Afghan campaign where the Mujahedin rebels regularly ambushed vulnerable Russian convoys as they made the perilous journeys through the narrow mountain passes to deliver supplies to their battle-weary troops. *Spetznaz* units had quickly been drafted in to act as advance scouts to protect the convoys, their unenviable task being to pinpoint the concealed Mujahedin positions and pass the information on to the accompanying MIG-27 fighter bombers who would then flush out the rebels before the convoys reached the intended ambush site. Zlotin had led a total of seventeen advance missions and, relying only on his guile and phenomenal eyesight, every one of those convoys reached its destination without ever coming under attack. His one hundred per cent record remained un-equalled by any fellow *spetznaz* officer in the history of the campaign.

The pilot brought the Bell JetRanger down gently on to the helipad, careful to keep a safe distance between the rotors of the two helicopters. Saisse, who was seated beside the pilot, was the only other occupant in the helicopter. He immediately drew his finger across his throat, signalling that he wanted the pilot to shut down the engine. The engine was switched off.

Saisse unbuckled his safety belt then pushed open the

door and screwed up his leathery face as the cold wind whipped through the warm cockpit. His eyes went to the attaché case in Zlotin's hand, but he made no move to get out of the cockpit. Finally he met Zlotin's unflinching stare and gestured for the Russian to approach the helicopter.

Zlotin made his way slowly across to the helicopter and, ducking under the decelerating rotors, pulled open the rear door and climbed inside. The pilot glanced round at him but said nothing.

'Do you have the money with you?' Zlotin asked.

Saisse picked up a battered hold-all which had been lying at his feet and placed it in his lap. 'You get the money once I'm satisfied that the key to break the UNACO folders is genuine.'

'No, you throw the money out on to the helipad first,' Zlotin replied. 'Then you get the case.'

Saisse reluctantly dropped the hold-all on to the helipad. Zlotin beckoned Rodenko towards the helicopter and waited until he'd taken the hold-all and withdrawn again before handing the attaché case to Saisse.

'I decoded the first page for you so that you'd be able to see that the key is genuine,' Zlotin said, handing a sheet of paper to Saisse.

Saisse unfolded the paper and opened the top folder to the corresponding page. Zlotin had copied out the first page by hand on to every alternate line and substituted the key letters above each of the coded letters to decode the text. Saisse read through it carefully then picked another page of text at random to satisfy himself that Zlotin wasn't trying to double-cross him with a spurious set of key letters. He then chose a page at random from the second folder and again checked for any discrepancies. Finding that the key again translated the coded text into legible English, he closed the folder and returned it to the attaché case, which he then locked and placed at his feet. He looked across at Rodenko who was crouched beside the open hold-all, counting one of the bundles of used fifty-dollar notes. Each bundle contained one thousand dollars. Dropping the money back into the hold-all, Rodenko removed another bundle and began to count it.

'Is he going to count it all now?' Saisse asked irritably.

'No need,' Zlotin assured him. 'If it's short we know where to find you.'

'It's not short,' Saisse snapped back indignantly.

'So now that you've got the key to decode the UNACO folders, Jannoc will finally know who was responsible for his brother's death. It just goes to prove that revenge can be a dangerous – and costly – obsession if you allow it to get the better of you.'

'If it wasn't for Monsieur Jannoc's "obsession" as you call it, you and your colleagues would be rotting in some Russian jail. Now you have your freedom and half a million dollars in cash to share between you. Remember that before you start passing judgement on Monsieur Jannoc's motives for wanting to avenge his brother's death.'

'How could I possibly forget his generosity?' Zlotin replied facetiously, then climbed from the helicopter and closed the door behind him. 'But it works both ways, Saisse. Without us, Jannoc would still be no closer to the truth.'

'Don't overestimate your importance in the operation,' Saisse retorted disdainfully. 'You and your colleagues were only the hired muscle, that's all.'

'I hardly think Jannoc would have gone to all the trouble of getting us out of Russia if he was only after hired muscle. He used us because he knew that we were professionals who could do the job for him, and I think we've justified his faith in us by turning the situation around after Berger's bungling incompetence almost cost us the operation. No, if he only wanted hired muscle, then he wouldn't have had to look any further than you and your inept right-hand man, Berger, would he? It's strange that he never considered either of you to spearhead the operation, isn't it?'

Saisse glared furiously at Zlotin, then slammed the door shut and gestured to the pilot to start the engine. Zlotin crossed to where Rodenko was standing and they watched in silence as the helicopter slowly built up enough r.p.m.s for it to lift off the helipad. Once airborne, the helicopter banked sharply away from the island and headed back towards the mainland.

'Aren't you forgetting something?' Zlotin said once the sound of the helicopter's single turboshaft engine had faded into the distance.

Rodenko reluctantly handed the hold-all to Zlotin, who took it down to his cell and locked it in the safe beside the bed. He then went through to the operations room and sat down in front of the radio transmitter.

'Can we talk?' Rodenko asked, appearing in the doorway behind him.

Zlotin hooked the headset over the back of his neck, then swivelled round in his chair to face Rodenko. 'What's on your mind?'

'You haven't told me what you're going to do with the folders. Do you already have a buyer lined up, or do you intend to put them up for sale on the black market?'

'Let me put it this way, I already have a buyer in mind,' came the reply.

'Who?' Rodenko asked.

'UNACO.'

'That's crazy,' Rodenko shot back in amazement. 'They'd arrest you the moment you showed your face.'

'And blow the one chance they have left of getting their folders back intact?' Zlotin replied. 'No, I don't think so. I'll be perfectly safe as long as I'm the one holding all the aces.'

'But you're not. All you have to bargain with now is a copy of the decoded text. Jannoc has the original UNACO folders and the cryptologists' key to decode them. That undermines your theory straightaway.'

'Jannoc has the key, granted, but he doesn't have the original UNACO folders. I do.'

'What are you talking about?' Rodenko asked in surprise. 'You gave the UNACO folders to Saisse. I saw him using them to check the authenticity of the key against the coded text.'

'What I gave Saisse was a copy of the coded text, the one that Valentin typed into the computer. He printed it out after he'd finished and had the pages bound professionally by a contact of his in Lisbon. It's not as if either Saisse or Jannoc would even know it's a copy, for the simple reason that they've never actually seen the original UNACO folders.'

'I still don't see the point,' Rodenko said. 'The fact still remains that Jannoc will have a copy of the UNACO folders.'

'If UNACO were to intercept the folders before they actually reached Jannoc, that would strengthen my hand considerably when it came to negotiating a deal with them, wouldn't you agree?'

'Yes,' Rodenko replied hesitantly. 'But how would they know where and when to intercept the folders?'

'Because I'll tell them,' Zlotin replied. 'When I was in Marseilles I overheard Jannoc and Saisse talking about how they'd conduct the handover once the folders had been decoded. Jannoc knew that UNACO had him and his organization under close surveillance, so it was decided that the folders would be decoded somewhere outside Marseilles, then left in a locker at the station to be picked up by one of his lieutenants at a later date. If UNACO staked out the station, not only would they recover the folders, but they'd also have more than enough evidence to send both Jannoc and Saisse to jail for the rest of their lives.'

'What if Jannoc fingers us when he's arrested?'

'By the time UNACO have arrested Jannoc and Saisse, we'll be long gone from here. And neither of them will know where we've gone, will they? So what could they possibly tell the authorities that could affect the outcome of our negotiations with UNACO? Don't worry, Viktor, the plan's foolproof.'

'As long as UNACO agree to stick to your script,' Rodenko replied.

'What choice will they have?'

Rodenko pondered Zlotin's reply momentarily, then nodded. 'As usual, you've obviously worked it all out down to the last detail. Who are you going to contact to set up a meeting? Graham?'

'Graham's a small fish. The only way to get something done is to go straight to the top. In UNACO's case that means their director, Colonel Malcolm Philpott.' Zlotin slipped on the headphones. 'I think the time's come for me to make my opening gambit.'

'Checkmate.'

Graham stared at the chessboard in dismay, then slumped back in the chair and looked at Sabrina who was sitting on the floor on the other side of the table. 'That's the fifth game in a row you've won.'

'And you owe me fifty bucks,' she replied with a demure smile.

'Where the hell did you learn to play chess like that?' he asked enviously.

'My father taught me when I was a kid,' she replied, then extended her upturned palm towards him. 'Fifty bucks. Cough up.'

'We'll settle any outstanding debts when we've finished playing,' he replied, waving away her hand.

'You've been saying that for the last four games,' she said, wagging a finger at him. 'Now come on, pay up.'

'Mike! Sabrina!'

The urgency in Rust's voice had them hurrying from the lounge and down the corridor to the study.

'What is it, Jacques?' Graham asked anxiously from the doorway.

'Come in,' Rust said, gesturing to the sofa. 'Sit down. I've been on the phone to the Colonel in New York. Zlotin's just contacted him over the radio in the Command Centre and told him that Abe's code was finally broken earlier today. Now he wants to sell the folders back to us. Or, as he put it, he's prepared to give us first refusal on the deal.'

'What did the Colonel say?' Sabrina asked.

'He agreed to the meeting of course,' Rust replied. 'It's a godsend. We thought the folders would go straight on to the black market. Naturally we won't pay the ransom, knowing as we do now that the money would be going towards financing a right-wing coup in Russia, but we have to make him think that we would be willing to negotiate for the return of the folders. If he suspected for one moment that we already knew about the planned coup, he'd call off the deal and we'd never see the folders again. We have to play along with him to give ourselves time to work out how best to take him down and recover the folders intact.'

'When's the meeting due to take place?' Sabrina asked.

'Four o'clock this afternoon. That's in less than two hours from now. He'd originally wanted to meet with the Colonel, but of course that would have been impossible at such short notice. So he's agreed to meet with me instead.'

'Where are you meeting him?' Sabrina asked.

'Here.'

'Here?' she said in surprise. 'I don't think the Special Forces Brigade are going to be too pleased when they find out that the Colonel's disclosed the location of one of their safe houses to the enemy.'

'It wasn't the Colonel's idea,' Rust replied.

'But how could Zlotin have known . . . ?' She trailed off as the realization suddenly dawned on her. 'Inside information.

So Mike's hunch was right all along. Zlotin must have a contact in the Special Forces Brigade.'

'OK, so you were right,' Rust said, feeling Graham's eyes burning into him.

'Thank you,' Graham said. 'Now that we know that Zlotin does have an inside man in the Special Forces Brigade, we can deal them out of any further action until the culprit's been unmasked.'

'They can't be dealt out, Mike, not after what happened at the warehouse,' Rust replied. 'The Colonel gave his word to Major Inacio that we would keep them fully informed on any future developments in the case, and that's exactly what I intend to do.'

'Future developments?' Graham said suspiciously. 'What are you implying, Jacques, that you're not going to tell them about the meeting with Zlotin?'

'Of course I am, but only after Zlotin's gone,' Rust replied. 'Zlotin made it very clear to the Colonel that he didn't want the Special Forces Brigade in on this. He specifically asked to meet with me alone. So what the Special Forces Brigade don't know won't hurt them. We know the house isn't bugged, and Major Inacio has already called off the surveillance unit which was out front when we got here. So there's no way they could know about Zlotin.'

'Inacio only did that as an act of good faith after the Colonel's assurance that we'd co-operate fully with them from now on,' Sabrina said.

'I'm prepared to take the heat for this,' Rust said, 'but right now the last thing we want to do is antagonize Zlotin. What if I were to tell the Special Forces Brigade about the meeting only for them to tail Zlotin when he leaves here? There's every chance he'd spot the tail and call the deal off. It's our necks on the line here, not theirs. I think it's best that they don't know, at least not for the time being.'

'I'm with you on that,' Graham assured him.

Sabrina nodded her agreement as well. 'You said he

wanted to meet with you alone. What about Mike and me? Do you want us to make ourselves scarce?'

'You're not going anywhere,' Rust told her. 'God forbid that there should be any trouble; I want you both here as back-up.'

'You got it, Jacques,' Graham said, getting to his feet and moving to the window. 'I have to say I'm certainly looking forward finally to coming face to face with the great Colonel Nikolai Zlotin.'

'You just make sure you stay in line this afternoon, Mike,' Rust warned him. 'I know how much you've come to despise Zlotin over the years, but if we blow this now, we're dead and buried.'

'Don't worry, Jacques, I'll be on my best behaviour,' Graham replied, looking out to sea thoughtfully. 'You can count on it.'

The intercom at the main gate buzzed moments after the wall clock had chimed four o'clock.

'He's punctual, if nothing else,' Rust said, picking up the remote control from the lounge table. A miniature television screen was built into the device which was linked to the closed circuit television camera mounted on the wall beside the gate.

'As are most soldiers, Jacques,' Graham said.

'With some notable exceptions,' Rust said, casting a side-long glance in Graham's direction. Satisfied that the sole occupant in the Ford was Zlotin, he activated the gates and waited until the car had entered the grounds before closing them again. 'He's on his way. Mike, I'm sure you'll want to meet him personally at the door.'

'My pleasure,' Graham replied, getting to his feet.

'And remember –'

'To stay in line,' Graham finished. 'Yes, Jacques, so you keep reminding me.'

'Go on,' Rust said, dismissing Graham with a wave of his hand.

Graham made his way to the front door where he paused to take a deep breath before opening it and stepping out on to the porch.

Having already parked the Ford close to the archway at the entrance to the gravel courtyard, Zlotin took an attaché case from the back seat, then climbed out of the car and crossed to the porch. 'So you're Graham. I recognize you from your *spetznaz* dossier. I've heard a lot about you from several colleagues of mine who've come up against you in the past. They all seem to hold you in very high esteem.'

'Yeah?' Graham replied indifferently. 'Are you carrying?'

'Of course,' came the immediate response. 'As I'm sure you are as well. But I hope you're not expecting me to surrender my weapon to you?'

Graham left the question unanswered and gestured for Zlotin to enter the house. He followed him inside, closing the door behind him. 'This way,' he said brusquely over his shoulder, already making his way towards the lounge.

'I was sorry to hear about what happened to your family, Graham,' Zlotin called out after him. 'How ironic that it should have turned out that they were killed by your own side.'

Graham said nothing.

'So it's true after all,' Zlotin continued. 'I read in one of our files that you'd finally come to terms with the loss of your family, but after all the rumours I'd heard about your volatile temperament, I wasn't sure whether to believe it or not.'

'I presume you read all this before you were stripped of your rank and thrown out of *spetznaz*,' Graham said coldly.

They had reached the lounge. Graham stood by the door and gestured for Zlotin to enter the room. Zlotin glared icily at him then stepped tentatively into the room, looking around him slowly. His eyes finally settled on Sabrina who

277

was standing in front of the patio door. She stared back unflinchingly at him. He finally turned his attention to Rust. 'My understanding with Philpott was that I'd meet with you alone.'

Rust looked across at Sabrina. 'You and Mike wait outside. I'll call if I need you.'

She nodded, then crossed to the door. Graham followed Sabrina out into the corridor, closing the door behind them.

Zlotin leaned forward to study the remaining chess pieces on the board on the table in front of the sofa. 'Philpott told me that you'd be negotiating on behalf of UNACO for the return of the folders. I take it he also told you not to contact the Special Forces Brigade about our meeting here this afternoon?'

'Yes, he told me,' Rust replied tersely. 'I'm intrigued to know how you found out that we were staying here.'

'Checkmate for white in eight, at most nine, moves,' Zlotin concluded after a few seconds. 'I have my sources,' he finally said, looking up at Rust.

'In the Special Forces Brigade?' Rust asked, watching Zlotin's face carefully for any reaction. Not surprisingly, his face remained expressionless.

'As I said, I have my sources. Let's leave it at that.' Zlotin cleared a space on the table for his attaché case before sitting down on the sofa. 'Well, shall we get down to business?'

'By all means,' Rust replied, wheeling himself over to the table.

'Let me first say that there are two copies of the coded text currently in circulation. I have the original UNACO folders in my possession, as well as a copy of the decoded text. A copy of Silverman's code, together with the key letters to break the code, are now on their way to Jannoc in Marseilles. I would estimate that they should be in his possession sometime tomorrow morning.'

'Double jeopardy,' Rust said tersely.

'On the contrary, I can tell you exactly where the folders are to be left for Jannoc once they've been decoded.'

Rust frowned suspiciously. 'I thought you and Jannoc were working in tandem.'

'That's what I've led Jannoc to believe. As far as he was concerned, my part in the operation was supposed to have ended when I handed over the UNACO folders and the key letters to him in return for a sum of money.'

'So if we were to intercept the folders before they reached Jannoc, that would leave you with the only set, which would automatically increase their value,' Rust said.

'You catch on quickly, *monsieur*,' Zlotin replied, removing an envelope from the attaché case and handing it to Rust. 'In there are the details of where the folders are to be left once they've been decoded. Let's just call it a gesture of goodwill on my part.'

Rust took the envelope, slit it open, and removed the sheet of paper. 'Locker 17, Gare St Charles, Marseilles.'

'I'm sure that was picked up on one of your microphones,' Zlotin said, slowly looking around the room as if trying mentally to pinpoint the obvious locations of the concealed bugs.

'I'm sure it was,' Rust replied, pocketing the sheet of paper.

Zlotin took a cardboard folder from the attaché case and placed it on the table. 'This contains copies of half a dozen pages of coded text with the corresponding pages of decoded text. Please, feel free to look through it.'

Rust picked up the folder and opened it. He ignored the coded text – it meant nothing to him anyway – and concentrated instead on the decoded pages. He only needed to read through a couple of paragraphs on each page to realize that they were genuine. Closing over the folder, he replaced it on the table. 'How much do you want?'

'I like a man who comes straight to the point. Fifty million dollars.'

'What?' Rust shot back in amazement.

'Each,' Zlotin was quick to add. 'Fifty for the coded text and fifty for the decoded text. A total of one hundred million dollars to be paid in uncut diamonds. UNACO has three days to comply with these demands. I'll contact Colonel Philpott at exactly 4 P.M. on 30 December with details of where and when to make the drop, assuming of course that UNACO agrees to pay the ransom. If not, or if you should be foolish enough to try and intercept the courier at the drop, the deal will be off and I'll take my custom elsewhere.'

'Do you honestly think that UNACO has a hundred million dollars to put up for the return of the folders?' Rust asked, still stunned at the figure involved.

'No, but the forty-seven signatories on the original UNACO Charter could easily come up with that kind of money.'

'And what makes you so sure they'd agree to these outrageous demands?'

'I haven't had a chance yet to read through all the relevant sections since the text was decoded, but one that did catch my eye was UNACO's detailed accounts of, shall we say, criminal misdemeanours accredited to certain member states of the United Nations over the past ten years. It makes fascinating reading, and you know as well as I do that those revelations would be damaging enough to topple a number of major international governments if they were ever made public. That alone should be incentive enough for them to agree to pay their share of the money.'

'And what's the alternative if we don't agree to pay the ransom?' Rust asked. 'The black market?'

'I could probably get as much on the black market if I were to break down the contents of the folders into individual sections and sell them off like that.'

'So why are you offering the folders to us instead of putting them up for sale on the black market?' Rust asked suspiciously.

'Quite simply, time,' Zlotin replied. 'This way I can get the ransom quickly, but if I were to put them up for sale on the black market, it could take months to complete the various transactions. But don't get me wrong, I'd certainly have no qualms about doing it if UNACO were to refuse to meet my demands.'

'I've no doubt you would,' Rust replied angrily. 'Even if we were to agree to your demands, what guarantees would we have that you wouldn't double-cross us once the ransom had been paid? After all, if you've already made one copy of the decoded material, what's to stop you making more and putting them up for sale on the black market as well?'

'No guarantees at all,' Zlotin replied, slipping the folder back into the attaché case. 'But then you don't have much choice in the matter, do you?'

'Tell me, Zlotin, what does a fanatical Communist like yourself want with a hundred million dollars?'

'What I want with the money is of no concern either to you or to anyone in your organization. You just make sure that you pass on my demands to Philpott. As I said, he'll be contacted in three days' time for his answer. I'm sure –' Zlotin stopped mid-sentence as the radio transmitter on his belt suddenly emitted a shrill beep. The transmitter was linked to an infra-red sensor attached to the side of the car which he'd activated before entering the house. The beam had just been broken ...

'What's that?' Rust demanded as Zlotin quickly silenced it.

Zlotin didn't answer as he hurried to the patio door. Pulling open the door, he stepped out on to the patio and peered down cautiously into the courtyard. Three men, wearing black balaclavas and armed with assault rifles, had slipped silently into the courtyard and were making their way towards the house. When Zlotin swung round to face Rust, his Makarov pistol was already in his hand.

'What's going on?' Rust demanded, his eyes riveted on the pistol.

'I warned Philpott what would happen if he tried to double-cross me,' Zlotin snarled, levelling the pistol at Rust. 'I warned him.'

Rust was still clawing for the Beretta he kept strapped to the inside of the chair when Zlotin shot him twice through the heart. The force of the bullets slammed Rust back in the wheelchair, then he slowly slumped forward and toppled out on to the carpet.

Quickly, Zlotin ran to the door leading to the corridor, locked it, then took two smoke grenades from inside the attaché case. Removing the pins, he tossed them into opposite corners of the room before hurrying out on to the patio. He heard Graham's agitated voice calling from the corridor; this was followed by frantic banging on the door, and moments later the door was obscured by a billowing cloud of black smoke. Zlotin closed the patio door behind him. Glancing swiftly around him, he rushed to the table that stood on the terrace and ducked down under it, out of sight of the courtyard below. He called up Rodenko on his two-way radio.

'How long will it take you to get to the house?' Zlotin hissed, his eyes constantly darting around him.

'Two, three minutes at the most,' Rodenko replied.

'I'm pinned down on the patio,' Zlotin snapped. 'I won't be able to hold out here for much longer.'

'I'm on my way,' Rodenko replied, breaking the transmission.

Zlotin clipped the radio back on to his belt and kept the pistol trained on the patio door. He took some comfort from the fact that the door was bulletproof, so he was quite safe as long as it remained closed. And if either Graham or Carver were to reach it through the dense black smoke, he'd be able to pick them off the moment they emerged out on to the terrace. He also knew there was a chance that the masked men he'd seen in the courtyard might attempt to storm the patio from the ground, but he'd be ready for them the moment the grappling hooks appeared over the side of the railing. His only fear was that he wouldn't be able to stave off a sustained assault launched from inside the house, especially if automatic or semi-automatic weapons were used. He wiped the sweat from his face and looked down at his watch. Where was Rodenko? What was keeping him?

Then he heard the sound of splintering wood from inside the lounge. The door was being broken down. Wetting his dry lips, he held the Makarov in both hands, waiting for the patio door to open. A burst of gunfire suddenly strafed over his head, peppering the wall. It had come from the courtyard. Could they see him from down there after all? Another fusillade was sprayed across the patio and a bullet ricocheted off the railing and slammed into the wicker chair behind him. Again he checked the time. Two minutes had already elapsed since he radioed through to Rodenko. So where was he?

A volley of bullets suddenly ripped through the wooden floorboards and Zlotin had to fling himself out of the way to avoid being hit. Someone was firing from underneath the balcony and he knew there wasn't anything he could do to counter the gunfire without being seen from the ground. He wiped his forearm across his sweat-streaked face and his eyes darted from the patio door to the splintered bullet holes in the floor around him. Gritting his teeth, he braced himself for the next volley . . .

Then, like some insidious bird of prey, the Westland Scout helicopter suddenly loomed into view from behind the grove of oak trees on the verdant hillside directly in front of the house. The chain gun opened fire from the helicopter's reinforced undercarriage, scything a deadly fusillade low across the courtyard. Zlotin heard a lone scream emanate from underneath the balcony, then the chain gun fell silent. The helicopter was being skilfully manoeuvred; now it was hovering directly above the covered patio and a rope ladder was being dropped out through the passenger door.

Zlotin made a grab for the ladder as it brushed against the railing, but a gust of wind swept it away from his outstretched hand. He waited until it swung back towards him, and was about to loop his arm through the rungs when the patio door was suddenly thrown open and the smoke began pouring out into the dark, overcast sky. Spinning round, Zlotin fired a concentrated burst through the smoke-filled doorway, then grabbed again for the ladder. This time he caught it, and he gestured wildly with his free hand for Rodenko to lift him clear of the patio. The helicopter was rising, lifting Zlotin up, but suddenly Graham burst through the smoke and, hurling himself at Zlotin, managed to wrap both arms around the Russian's leg, pulling him back down again towards the balcony. Zlotin lashed out with his foot and, although he caught Graham painfully in the stomach, he couldn't shake him loose. Cursing furiously, Zlotin lashed out with the pistol, catching Graham a glancing blow on the side of the head and stunning him. Zlotin kicked out again, bringing his foot down savagely on to Graham's shoulder. Graham lost his balance and fell heavily on to the patio.

The helicopter had already banked away sharply from the house when Sabrina dived low out on to the balcony and came up fast on to one knee, her Beretta trained on Zlotin who was still hanging precariously to the rope ladder as it was drawn slowly towards the open cockpit door. She could have taken him out from that distance, but they needed him alive, at least until they had recovered the folders. Holstering her Beretta, she crossed to where Graham was still struggling to get to his feet. She winced when she saw where Zlotin's pistol had opened a gash above his left eye. The blood streamed down his face and on to the front of his blood-spattered shirt.

'Have you found Jacques yet?' he asked anxiously,

wiping the blood irritably from his face with the back of his hand.

'No, the smoke's still far too thick in there,' she replied, helping him to his feet.

He shrugged her hand off his arm angrily. 'If you haven't found him yet, then what the hell are you doing out here?'

'You said you were going after Zlotin, so I came out after you in case you needed back-up,' came the sharp riposte.

'I specifically told you to stay in there and look for Jacques. For once in your life, why the hell can't you just do as you're told?' Graham snapped, then brushed past her and disappeared back into the smoke-filled lounge.

She bit back her anger and hurried after him. They both called out to Rust but there was no response. The smoke was already beginning to dissipate when Graham stumbled across Rust's wheelchair. It was empty. Already fearing the worst, he dropped to his knees and began methodically patting the surrounding carpet. Suddenly his fingers brushed against something. It was a shoe. He felt his way up the motionless body and instinctively pulled his hand back when he touched the blood-soaked shirt. 'Sabrina?' he called out. 'I've found Jacques. He's bleeding badly. I'm going to take him out on to the patio. I can just make out the door from here.'

'I'll meet you there,' she called back through the smoke.

Graham slipped his hands gently underneath Rust then, struggling to his feet, carried him carefully across the room and out on to the terrace. He could see that Rust was dead even before he checked for a pulse. Removing his baseball jacket, he draped it over Rust's face, then looked round slowly at Sabrina who had appeared in the doorway behind him. She stared at the body, then crossed to the railing and hugged her arms tightly across her chest as she stared out to sea. A tear escaped from the corner of her eye, but she brushed it away quickly with her fingertips.

'You OK?' Graham asked softly, putting his hand lightly on her shoulder.

'Sure,' she replied in a hollow voice.

'I know –' he broke off abruptly and pulled his Beretta from his shoulder holster as he ducked down, pulling Sabrina down with him.

'What is it?' she asked anxiously.

'I thought I saw a movement over there,' he replied, gesturing towards a section of undergrowth beyond the courtyard.

Sabrina unholstered her Beretta and followed the direction of Graham's pointing finger. She scanned the thicket then shook her head. 'I don't see anything. Are you sure you saw something?'

'Pretty sure,' he replied.

'That's good enough for me. Let's check it out.'

They returned to the lounge where the smoke had diffused sufficiently for them to make out the doorway on the opposite side of the room. They kept their backs pressed against the wall when they emerged into the hall, and made their way cautiously to the front door. Once in place, Graham gestured to the door. Sabrina pulled it open and Graham swivelled round, fanning the courtyard with the Beretta. It was deserted. He crossed to where a black-clad figure lay sprawled at the foot of the steps. An assault rifle lay nearby. Graham estimated that at least a dozen bullets had struck the man in the back. He checked quickly for a pulse. Nothing.

Sabrina darted out from the doorway and zig-zagged her way across to the safety of the fountain in the centre of the courtyard. It was then she saw the bloodied body of a second man, also dressed in black, crumpled against the bullet-scarred wall directly underneath the patio. Graham ran, doubled over, to where she was crouched and looked across at the second body.

'Who are they?' Sabrina whispered.

'Judging by the weapons, I'd say Special Forces Brigade,' Graham replied.

'It doesn't make any sense. Why would they be here?'

'That's what I'm hoping to find out,' Graham said, stabbing his finger towards the undergrowth. 'If there is another one of them in there, he could still be alive.'

'You go first; you know where you think you saw him,' she said.

Graham darted out from behind the fountain and sprinted to an oak tree on the edge of the courtyard. Holding the Beretta in both hands, he swivelled round, fanning the undergrowth. The man was slumped against the foot of a tree, his shattered left leg twisted grotesquely underneath him. He'd removed his balaclava and was using it to try and stem the flow of blood from the gaping bullet wound in his side. He saw Graham as he stepped out from behind the tree, but made no move to grab the assault rifle which lay beside him.

Graham lowered his Beretta and moved towards the man. 'Special Forces Brigade?'

The man nodded through the pain.

'Sabrina?' Graham called out over his shoulder, then crouched down next to the man. 'You're going to be OK, buddy. We'll get some back-up out here and you'll be on your way to hospital in no time at all.'

'I've already called for back-up,' he hissed through clenched teeth. 'It's on its way. My two colleagues . . .'

Graham shook his head. 'They're both dead. I'm sorry. What the hell happened out here?'

'The helicopter had a gun mounted on the undercarriage,' the man said, gritting his teeth against the pain.

'Who gave you the order to come here?'

'Captain Morales.'

'Son-of-a-bitch,' Graham snarled, then looked round when Sabrina appeared beside him. 'Did you hear that?'

She nodded. 'And you think Morales is Zlotin's inside man?'

'Don't you?' Graham replied.

'We can talk about it later,' she replied. 'But right now this guy needs medical attention. I'll go back to the house and call for assistance.'

'It's already on its way,' Graham told her.

Sabrina slipped her jacket around the man's shoulders, then eased the balaclava gently from his hand and gave him a clean handkerchief to use in its place. Knowing there was nothing else either of them could do for him without proper medication and dressings, she was still trying to make him as comfortable as possible when she heard the sound of a car heading up the approach road towards the house.

'Seems like the cavalry's finally arrived,' Graham said, getting to his feet. 'You wait here and I'll go and get help.'

'Mike?' Sabrina called out after him. 'You do anything stupid now and the Colonel's going to crucify you.'

'Hey, all I'm going to do is get some help for this guy,' came the defensive reply.

'And confront Morales if he's there. We still don't have any solid evidence to link him to Zlotin. You've got to bite the bullet until we've got all the facts at our disposal.'

Graham didn't wait to hear her out. Emerging from the undergrowth, he crossed the courtyard to where two black Mercedes were parked in front of the house. 'Leave him, he's dead,' he shouted to a paramedic who was crouched over the soldier lying at the foot of the porch steps. 'There's an injured man back there in the undergrowth. His leg's shattered and he's taken a bullet in the ribs. He's obviously in a lot of pain.'

The paramedic looked to the man standing by the car, his back to Graham. The man nodded and the paramedic immediately picked up his bag and ran towards the undergrowth.

The man turned to face Graham. It was Morales. 'We got here as quickly as we could. What happened?'

Graham grabbed Morales and slammed him back against

the car. 'Jacques Rust is dead, you son-of-a-bitch, that's what happened.'

A soldier, who had been standing guard at the front door, hurried down the steps, his assault rifle trained on Graham.

'*Não*,' Morales snapped, gesturing for the man to lower his weapon.

The soldier looked from Morales to Graham then slowly lowered his weapon and returned to his vigil by the door.

Morales held up his hands towards Graham. 'I'm sorry about your colleague, I really am. I had reservations about sending in a team without any kind of back-up, but I was merely carrying out orders.'

'Who told you to send in the team?' Graham demanded.

'Major Inacio. Had it worked, he'd probably have been given a commendation. But it didn't and now he's going to have a lot of explaining to do once the dust has settled.'

'You're not wrong there,' Graham replied, stepping away from Morales.

Sabrina hurried across to where the two men were standing. 'Mike, I told you –'

'It's OK,' Graham cut in quickly. 'Inacio gave the order to send them in.'

'Major Inacio?' Sabrina said in surprise, looking at Morales.

'Yes,' came the tight-lipped reply.

'How did he know that Zlotin was here?' she asked.

'The house was under surveillance,' Morales told her.

'But I thought Major Inacio had agreed to withdraw the surveillance teams after he'd spoken to Colonel Philpott in New York,' she said.

'On the condition that UNACO would co-operate fully with the Special Forces Brigade after the incident at the warehouse yesterday morning,' Morales replied. 'He wasn't convinced that UNACO would stick to the agreement. Obviously he was right.'

'What the hell did you expect us to do?' Graham

demanded angrily. 'Zlotin made it clear that the deal would be off if the Special Forces Brigade were involved. This was our last chance to get the folders back intact. We had to go along with him. And now Inacio's really blown it for us.'

'If you'd confided in us in the first place, there's every chance that all this needless bloodshed could have been avoided. After all, it's not as if Zlotin could have known if you'd told us about the meeting.'

'That's where you're wrong,' Graham replied, and his eyes instinctively went to Sabrina, fully expecting her to intervene before he could say any more. She remained silent.

'How could he have found out?' Morales challenged.

'I think Inacio was Zlotin's man inside the Special Forces Brigade,' Graham replied. 'I know I don't have the kind of evidence that would stand up in a court of law, but just answer me this: how did Zlotin know about this place?'

'I . . . just assumed that you told him,' Morales replied hesitantly, a hint of uncertainty creeping into his voice.

'It was his suggestion that we meet here when he contacted the Colonel in New York,' Sabrina told him.

'OK, let's just say for argument's sake that Major Inacio is working with Zlotin,' Morales said. 'Why would Zlotin suggest meeting you here knowing that it would be sure to point the finger of collaboration at someone inside the Special Forces Brigade? It doesn't make any sense.'

'I think it makes perfect sense,' Graham was quick to reply. 'I said Inacio *was* Zlotin's inside man in the Special Forces Brigade. Past tense. It was obvious from what Zlotin said this afternoon that he's now working freelance. He's already given us enough information to put Jannoc away for life. So if he doesn't need Jannoc any more, he's not going to need any of his other cronies either, is he? So by suggesting that we meet here, he's said in so many words that he found out about the safe house from someone inside the Special Forces Brigade. Why else would he have insisted that we keep the Special Forces Brigade out of the deal? He knew that if his contact found out that he'd been double-crossed, he'd be likely to send in the troops to even the score.'

'I assume these three were on surveillance duty when Zlotin arrived at the house,' Sabrina said, indicating the dead soldier at the foot of the steps.

Morales nodded. 'They recognized Zlotin straightaway from the photographs we had of him on file. That's when they radioed through to headquarters.'

'Was Inacio there at the time?' Graham asked.

'No, I was the duty officer. I contacted Major Inacio straightaway and that's when he gave me the order to send them in.'

'Obviously he couldn't risk waiting for back-up to be sent out here in case Zlotin had already gone by the time it had arrived,' Graham concluded. 'What exactly were his orders?'

Morales stared at the ground, still struggling to come to terms with what he now considered to be conclusive proof of Inacio's involvement with Zlotin.

'What were his orders, Captain Morales?' Graham repeated.

'Shoot to kill,' Morales replied in a barely audible voice.

'And because of that, three men are now dead,' Graham said bitterly.

'What do you want me to do?' Morales asked.

'Nothing. It's out of our hands now,' Graham told him. 'I still have to contact Colonel Philpott in New York and tell him about Jacques' death. He'll make the necessary arrangements with the authorities out here to have Inacio investigated, but whether they'll be able to make any of the charges stick is open to question.'

'And you're still no closer to getting the UNACO folders back,' Morales said, looking across as two soldiers emerged from the undergrowth carrying their now sedated colleague on a stretcher.

'Today was the closest we were ever going to come to getting them back,' Graham replied. 'Zlotin's not going to make the same mistake twice, you can be sure of that.'

* * *

'You did well today,' Zlotin said, entering Rodenko's cell.

'It's what you're paying me for,' Rodenko replied from the bed where he was busy cleaning his dismantled Makarov pistol.

'The voice of the mercenary,' Zlotin snorted contemptuously.

'Sneer all you want, but it's not my plans that have been thrown in disarray after what happened this afternoon,' Rodenko said without looking up from the recoil spring he was wiping.

'It's a temporary setback, nothing more,' came the indignant reply.

'So what are you going to do now?'

'I've already contacted my superiors back home,' Zlotin told him. 'They've agreed that I should go ahead and sell the folders on the black market. Admittedly it's now going to take a lot longer to raise the capital we'll need to finance the coup, but that's just something we have to accept.'

'Why don't you push up the price and offer the folders to UNACO again? I think you might find that they'll be more receptive to negotiation next time.'

'The UNACO deal is off,' came the blunt reply.

'It was just a suggestion, that's all.'

'I've been given new orders to rendezvous with my brother-in-law, Major Koslov, in Oran, Algeria. He'll be my new partner.'

'You mean you don't need me any more?' Rodenko said.

'Not after tomorrow. A Cessna's already been hired for me from a firm in Porto, and they've got the necessary clearance for a flight plan to Algeria. All I need you to do is fly me to the mainland in the morning. Then you're on your own.'

'What time do we leave here?'

'First light,' Zlotin replied, moving to the door.

'I'll be ready,' Rodenko called out after him, then went back to cleaning his pistol.

* * *

Graham didn't know how long he'd been standing on the balcony when the loud knocking brought him sharply out of his reverie. Crossing to the door, he peered through the spy-hole, fully expecting to see Sabrina in the corridor. It was Kolchinsky. He opened the door, the surprise still mirrored on his face. 'Sergei, what are you doing here? The doctor said you weren't due to be discharged from hospital until the middle of next week.'

'I discharged myself an hour ago,' Kolchinsky replied. 'The doctor wasn't too pleased, but I'll be fine just as long as I take it easily.'

'You look real pale. Are you sure you're all right?'

'I will be when you finally get around to inviting me in,' came the dry riposte.

Graham stood aside to let Kolchinsky enter the room. 'You want a coffee?'

'Yes, thank you,' Kolchinsky replied, rubbing his hands together. 'Why have you got the balcony door open on a night like this? It feels like Siberia in here.'

'I was out on the balcony when you knocked. To be honest, I didn't even notice the cold until you mentioned it. I guess my mind's still preoccupied with other things.' Graham closed the sliding door then looked round at Kolchinsky. 'I assume you've heard the news about Jacques?'

'Why do you think I'm here? The Colonel briefed me over the phone earlier this evening,' Kolchinsky said, easing himself into an armchair. 'How's Sabrina taken Jacques' death?'

'She's been very quiet ever since we left the safe house. I don't think she said a word in the car on the way over here, and after we'd checked in she announced that she wanted to take a long bath. That was well over an hour ago.'

'She obviously wants time to herself,' Kolchinsky concluded.

'Yeah, that's how I read it,' Graham replied, handing the cup of coffee to Kolchinsky.

'It's understandable. After all, he was once her partner.'

'It was more than just that, though,' Graham said, sitting on the bed. 'She always looked on Jacques as the big brother she never had. You remember how she and I used to be constantly at each other's throats when I first joined UNACO?'

'Vividly,' Kolchinsky replied, peering at Graham over the rim of his cup.

'Did you know that at one point she used to call Jacques in Zürich and talk to him about it?'

'No, I didn't know that,' Kolchinsky replied.

'It only happened three or four times in the very beginning, just until we'd found our feet as partners, but I remember I was well pissed off about it at the time. If she had a problem, why didn't she go to C.W.? He was team leader, not Jacques.'

'I've always wondered why you resented Jacques; now I know why,' Kolchinsky said.

'I never resented Jacques,' Graham shot back defensively. 'I had the greatest respect for him. He was always a real pro. One of the best in the game, you know that as well as I do.'

'I know you respected him on a professional level, but you were never comfortable socializing with him, were you?'

'I'm not comfortable socializing with most people,' Graham replied, raking his fingers through his hair. 'Jesus, all I did was pass a harmless comment and suddenly you're reading all kinds of Freudianisms into it.'

'OK, subject closed,' Kolchinsky said, then gestured to the telephone. 'Call Sabrina. I've got something I want to discuss with the two of you.'

Graham rang her room and she promised to be over right away. When she arrived, Graham ushered her into the room.

'How are you feeling, Sergei?' she asked.

'Still a bit weak but I'll be fine,' Kolchinsky assured her.

'I thought the Colonel was flying out to take charge of the operation himself,' she said. 'That's what he implied when Mike rang him earlier today.'

'That was his intention, but with seven other Strike Force teams currently on assignment as well, he can't afford to leave UNACO headquarters right now. That's why he asked me if I felt up to handling the operation in his absence.'

'For UNACO, or for the KGB?' Graham asked.

Kolchinsky looked round sharply at Graham who was standing by the sliding door. His eyes narrowed uncertainly. 'What's the KGB got to do with this?'

'You're taking over as the new Director early next year, aren't you?' Graham replied. 'Or should I call it by its new title, the Russian Intelligence Service?'

'How did you find out about this?' Kolchinsky asked.

'Jacques told us,' Sabrina told him.

'Yes, it's true,' Kolchinsky said at length. 'I have accepted the Directorship of the new RIS, but I'm still the Deputy Director of UNACO, and will continue to carry out my duties in that capacity to the best of my ability. I hope that clears up the situation, but if either of you still doubt my loyalty to this organization, then now's the time to speak up. And if that is the case, I'd rather step down than jeopardize this operation. We can't afford to work in an atmosphere of suspicion and uncertainty, not with so much at stake.'

'I don't doubt your loyalty to UNACO, Sergei,' Sabrina was quick to assure him.

'Michael?' Kolchinsky said, looking at Graham.

'We're wasting time,' Graham said, sitting on the bed next to Sabrina. 'Let's get on with the briefing.'

'It's hardly going to be what I'd call a briefing,' Kolchinsky said, reaching for the attaché case on the floor beside him. Opening it, he removed a folder. 'In fact, there is only one bit of information I have to pass on to you. Michael, it seems as if your hunch about Major Inacio was right after all.'

'Has he been arrested?' Graham asked quickly.

'He's disappeared,' came the reply.

'What do you mean, "disappeared"?'

'Just that, Sabrina,' Kolchinsky replied, taking a sheet of paper from the folder. 'His wife confirmed that he'd left the house at around the time the order was phoned through to Captain Morales to send in a team to assassinate Zlotin. She said he had a hold-all with him, but she doesn't know what was in it. And that's the last anyone has seen of him.'

'Did he tell his wife where he was going?' she asked.

'No, but then she was used to him taking off without saying anything. It was all part of the job. An APB has been put out on him, but so far the authorities haven't come up with anything.'

'How long after he left the house was the APB issued?' Sabrina asked.

'A couple of hours,' Kolchinsky replied.

'So in theory he could already have skipped the country?' she concluded.

'In theory, yes,' Kolchinsky was reluctant to admit.

'He may already be dead,' Graham suggested. 'Suicide has to be a possibility, Sergei. He must have known that the trail would eventually lead back to him, so what if, in a last act of revenge, he tried to settle the score by having Zlotin killed before taking his own life?'

'It is another possibility, I agree, and one that's already been put forward by some of his colleagues, but unless a body's found, we have to assume that he's still alive.' Kolchinsky finished his coffee then closed the folder and slipped it back into his attaché case. 'Well, if you'll both excuse me, I've still got to read through all the reports Jacques wrote up on the case.'

'Are you staying in the hotel?' Graham asked.

'Yes, I'm on the second floor, although I must say my room doesn't have nearly such a spectacular view of the gardens as you have from up here,' Kolchinsky said, getting to his feet and crossing to the sliding door.

'It's a small luxury afforded to the condemned man,' Graham said behind him.

'This isn't over yet, Michael,' Kolchinsky shot back.

'You could have fooled me,' Graham snorted.

'The Colonel's already contacted the heads of all the major intelligence agencies to warn them that Zlotin may attempt to sell the folders on the black market. They, in turn, have alerted their operatives in the field, so should any of the documents reach the black market, we'll certainly know about it.'

'Then what?' Graham asked.

'We'll put in a bid, albeit through a second party, and in doing so we'll hopefully be able to pinpoint where Zlotin's operating from and take the necessary steps to recover them.'

'It's a long shot to say the least,' Graham shot back disdainfully.

'I said it wasn't over yet; I didn't say it was going to be easy recovering the folders. On the contrary, I think Zlotin's going to be extra cautious after what happened at the safe house this afternoon. Long shot or not, if he's still got the folders, then there's still a chance that we can get them back. What we have to prevent at all costs is any of the decoded documents, however trivial they may be, being passed on to a third party, because then they could be used to prove UNACO's existence. That in itself would almost certainly signal the end of the organization as we know it.'

'It's a bit late for that with the *New York Sentinel* planning their own big UNACO exposé sometime in the next few days,' Graham said.

'The Colonel's still stalling them over the story he promised Larry Ryan. As long as Ryan thinks he can get his hands on a double exclusive, he's likely to keep the whole project on hold.'

'He'll only keep it on hold for so long,' Graham was quick to point out. 'The guy's already got the scoop of the year on his hands. He's hardly going to want to keep that kind of story under wraps, is he?'

'I'll admit that time's beginning to run out for us, but right now every extra hour is vital if we're to find something to prevent the story from ever reaching the streets. And you know as well as I do that UNACO has been renowned in the past for pulling a disadvantageous situation around to suit its own needs. The organization's continued existence is testament to that, isn't it?'

'Up to now,' Graham said at length. 'I know you mean well, Sergei, but if there were any dirt on Ryan or Warren, it would have come to light by now.'

'I only hope you're wrong,' Kolchinsky replied as he picked up his attaché case and left the room.

Graham closed the door behind him then turned back to Sabrina. 'You were very quiet just now. You OK?'

She nodded. 'I was thinking, that's all.'

'Jacques?'

'No, I was actually thinking about C.W. I just wish there was some way he could get in touch and let us know that he's all right. We haven't heard a thing from him since Christmas Eve, and after what happened at the safe house this afternoon . . .'

'I've told you, the guy lives a charmed life,' Graham said, trying to reassure her. 'Don't worry, he'll get in touch with us when he's good and ready.'

'You're probably right,' she said softly.

'Would I lie to you?' he asked in a mock-serious tone.

'It has been known,' she replied with a smile.

'Yeah, well, not this time. Trust me.' Graham looked at his watch. 'It's gone eight and I'm starved. You know, I haven't eaten a thing since breakfast. You up to a meal in the restaurant?' He noticed the hesitation in her eyes. 'I can understand if you want to be alone right now. I know you and Jacques were pretty close.'

'Jacques was a good friend,' she replied after a thoughtful silence.

'I know,' Graham said softly.

'Come on,' she said, getting to her feet. 'You're not the only one who's starving.'

'You sure you don't want some time to yourself?'

'I had some time to myself earlier, and I feel a lot better for it. Now I'm ready to come back into the fold.' She noticed the uncertainty lingering in his eyes. 'Would I lie to you?'

'It has been known,' he muttered as he grabbed his jacket from the wardrobe and followed her out into the corridor.

12

Whitlock looked at the illuminated dial on his watch. 12.20 A.M. It was time to put his escape plan into action . . .

Picking up the torch from beside the bed, he crossed to the cell door and paused to listen for any sound from the cell further down the corridor where the prisoners were being held. All was quiet. He slipped silently into the adjoining cell which housed the makeshift kitchen; only after he'd closed the door did he switch on the torch. The beam illuminated the items he'd left beside the butane gas cylinder the previous evening: an alarm clock and a small vanity mirror, both of which he assumed had belonged to Berger; a candle stub, a box of matches, and two pieces of electrical wire of roughly equal length which he'd found in one of the cells. He'd earlier prised off the glass façade from the front of the alarm clock, and prepared the two pieces of electrical wire by removing a section of insulation from each end, leaving the bare strands exposed.

He crouched down beside the gas cylinder and lit the candle. Once the flame had caught he switched off the torch and, unscrewing the lens cap, removed the small, bulb-shaped glass envelope which encased the delicate tungsten filament. This was going to prove the hardest bit of all – breaking the envelope without damaging the filament inside. He began to twist the cover gently between his thumb and forefinger, trying to loosen it just enough to be able to dislodge it from its base, but still leaving the filament intact. After several minutes of continuous kneading, he felt the envelope beginning to give and, gritting his teeth, he gingerly worked it back and forward like a child would a loose tooth, until finally it came away from the base. He wiped the sweat from his eyes, then eased the envelope carefully over the filament before pulling the candle closer to the torch to check that the filament was still undamaged. Peeling back the torch's outer rubber membrane, he attached one end of the electrical wire to the exposed negative switch contact, and the other end to the minute hand of the alarm clock. He then attached the second piece of wire to the positive switch contact and to the hour hand of the alarm clock.

Taking three matches from the box, he snapped them in the middle so that they each formed an L-shape, and balanced them carefully in front of the torch with the heads touching the filament. Then, moving the hour hand to six o'clock and the minute hand to twenty past the hour, he blew out the candle and got to his feet. There was now only one thing left to do – open the valve on the gas cylinder. As it was a new cylinder, he'd already estimated that it would take about five minutes for all the gas to escape into the room. When the two wires touched on the face of the clock, the contacts would be activated, switching on the torch; then the heat from the naked filament would ignite the matches . . .

His eyes had already become accustomed to the dark by the time he left the cell. After discarding his padded jacket on the floor close to the cylinder, he secured the door again behind him and made his way silently to the cell nearest to the security door. Taking the mirror from his pocket, he propped it against the foot of the open door and adjusted it until he was able to see the length of the dark, deserted corridor. Now he could monitor the Russians' every move without being seen from the corridor; the moment they disappeared into the cell to inspect the damage, he would be able to slip out into the inspection hall unnoticed.

He was well aware of the numerous mishaps which could still befall his plan if the Russians didn't stick to his carefully scripted scenario. What if Zlotin left a guard at the security door? What if they closed the security door behind them? What if one of them remained in the corridor? But, despite his reservations, he was still adamant that it was the best he could have done with the limited resources he had at his disposal.

He knew that if the Russians caught him they'd kill him, but then he was certain that they intended to kill him and the hostages anyway before they left the island later that day. This way he still had a chance. He had nothing to lose, not any more . . .

The whole prison seemed to shudder with the force of the explosion. Zlotin, who had been asleep in his cell, yanked his pistol from the holster on the table beside the bed and ran through to the operations room.

'What's going on?' he demanded of a bewildered Rodenko who was staring anxiously at the radar screen.

'It could have been a long-range missile,' Rodenko replied. 'Nothing's showing up on here. Whoever's firing at us is obviously out of range.'

'I don't think it was a missile. The authorities aren't going to risk firing on the prison without first knowing the exact location of the hostages.' Zlotin unlocked the armoury and removed two pairs of night-vision goggles and two AK-47s. He handed one of each to Rodenko, then moved to the door. 'Come on, let's go.'

Rodenko pulled the goggles over his face then hurried after Zlotin, who made straight for the wing which housed the hostages. They took up positions on either side of the security door and Zlotin gestured for Rodenko to use his key card to activate it.

Zlotin swivelled round the moment the door slid open, fanning the corridor with the AK-47. He immediately saw the buckled cell door lying at the far end of the corridor. 'Royce?' he bellowed and, receiving no reply, ignored the impassioned cries and loud banging which were now emanating from the hostages' cell and ran straight to Whitlock's cell. It was empty. Stepping over the demolished door, he peered cautiously into the adjoining cell where the kitchen had been situated. Part of the wall opposite the door had been blown out by the sheer force of the blast; crossing tentatively to the gaping hole he was able to see and hear the waves as they crashed against the foot of the rock face below him.

A section of wall which had been loosened by the explosion suddenly collapsed and fell away into the darkness. Zlotin stepped swiftly back from the wall; as he did so his heel caught on something lying on the floor. The twisted remains of a gas cylinder.

'Had it been a missile, the wall would have imploded, not exploded, wouldn't it?' Zlotin said when Rodenko appeared in the doorway.

'So what was it?' Rodenko asked, peering through the gaping hole in the wall at the sea below.

'Get away from there!' Zlotin hissed angrily. 'The wall's unsafe. It could come down at any moment.'

Rodenko crossed to where Zlotin was crouched over the gas cylinder. 'What's that you've got there?'

'The cause of the explosion,' Zlotin replied, standing up. 'A gas leak.'

'And now Royce is missing,' Rodenko said, picking up a shred of fabric from the floor, all that remained of the jacket Whitlock had left behind in the cell. 'It's possible that he could have left the valve open on the cylinder by mistake last night. Perhaps he smelt gas from his cell and when he came through to investigate he created a spark which ignited the trapped gas. The door could have caused the spark. He wouldn't have stood a chance.'

'If the door caused the spark, then he'd have been blown outwards, wouldn't he?' Zlotin retorted, hurrying out into the corridor. It was deserted. He looked round at Rodenko. 'So where's the body?'

'It was a theory, that's all,' Rodenko replied. 'Perhaps he was already in here when the gas blew. The force of the explosion could have blown him out into the sea. Whatever happened, he couldn't have survived it.'

'Not unless he staged the whole thing to make it look as if he'd been killed in the explosion,' Zlotin replied.

'Why would he do that?' Rodenko asked in amazement. 'As far as he was concerned, we were going to pay him the balance of the money owed to him before we left here in the morning. He couldn't have known that we were going to kill –'

'Of course, the operations room,' Zlotin cut in sharply, snapping his fingers. 'That's got to be it.'

'That's got to be what?' Rodenko retorted, but Zlotin was already sprinting towards the security door.

Rodenko hurried after the retreating Zlotin, using his key card to lock the security door again behind him. He ran across the inspection hall to where Zlotin had already taken up a position outside the open doorway which led into the illuminated wing where the operations room was housed.

'What's going on, Nikolai?' Rodenko hissed at Zlotin.

'There isn't time for explanations now,' Zlotin shot back, pulling the night-vision goggles up on to his forehead. 'If he is in there, I want him taken alive. Is that understood, Viktor? Alive.'

Rodenko just nodded.

Zlotin was first through the doorway and he made straight for the operations room. Rodenko was close behind him, watching his back. Reaching the wall adjacent to the operations room, Zlotin swivelled round to fan the cell with his AK-47. It was deserted. 'Check the rest of the wing, he could be hiding in one of the cells,' he said when Rodenko appeared in the doorway behind him.

Using his key card again, Rodenko locked the security door before carrying out a thorough search of all the cells in the wing. He found nothing. When he returned to the operations room it was empty. 'Nikolai?' he called out. No response. 'Nikolai?' he repeated, a sudden anxiety creeping into his voice.

Zlotin emerged from his quarters, the fury evident on his face. 'My key card's gone. It was on the table next to my bed. It's my guess he'll use it to get out on to the helipad and sabotage the helicopter. It's the only way he can keep us on the island.'

'The helicopter's locked.' Rodenko took a miniature transmitter from his pocket. 'This activates the locks.'

'We still need to check it out.'

Rodenko locked the security door behind them then grabbed Zlotin's arm. 'I don't know what's going on here, Nikolai, but you've got some explaining to do once we've found Royce.'

Zlotin glared at Rodenko. Jerking his arm free, he pulled the night-vision goggles back down over his eyes and ran to the metal stairs on the other side of the inspection hall. He bounded up them two at a time, then sprinted down the long, windowless corridor, through the two open security doors, only pausing to catch his breath when he reached the foot of the second flight of metal stairs which led up to the helipad. The security door at the top of the stairs was locked. Rodenko arrived breathlessly behind him. Cautiously they made their way up to the security door, careful to avoid the missing treads on the stairs under their feet.

'If he has got into the helicopter, could he use the chain gun?' Zlotin asked once they reached the top of the stairs.

'No. Yemenkov installed a small computer in the cockpit for me. It controls the chain gun and all the instrumentation. Royce couldn't activate anything inside the cockpit unless he knew the codes for the program.'

'Good.' Zlotin gestured to the key card in Rodenko's hand. 'Open the door, I'll go out first.'

Rodenko wiped the sweat from his forehead, then slid the key card into the slot. Zlotin swivelled round, the AK-47 trained on the helicopter. The camouflage netting had been pulled aside to reveal the passenger door, and he could see Whitlock bent over the controls in the cockpit, but it wasn't until they hurried across to the helicopter that Whitlock looked up and saw them. Zlotin gestured with his assault rifle for Whitlock to get out of the helicopter.

Whitlock looked from Zlotin to Rodenko to the two AK-47s. Realizing the futility of his situation, he slowly opened the cockpit door and jumped out on to the helipad. He tossed a tangled mass of wires on to the ground at Zlotin's feet, then slowly raised his hands above his head. 'I'd have done a better job if I'd had more time,' he said ruefully.

'Search him,' Zlotin snapped.

Rodenko slammed Whitlock up against the side of the helicopter and frisked him. He found a screwdriver tucked into the back of Whitlock's trousers – the one he'd left in the operations room the previous day. That explained how Whitlock had managed to force the passenger door and prise open the protective casing in the cockpit to get at the intricate circuitry which controlled the steering system.

'I assume that you've already contacted your colleagues over the radio,' Zlotin said to Whitlock. 'Why else would you have sabotaged the helicopter unless you had a reason for keeping us here?'

'Colleagues?' Whitlock replied with a frown.

'Your colleagues at UNACO,' Zlotin said. 'Mike Graham and Sabrina Carver.'

'I really don't know what you're talking about,' Whitlock replied. 'My name's –'

'Clarence Wilkins Whitlock,' Zlotin cut in quickly. 'The team leader of UNACO's Strike Force Three.'

'He's with UNACO?' Rodenko said in amazement. 'How long have you known that?'

'I've known his real identity ever since I hired him in Marseilles,' Zlotin replied. 'The photograph was an ingenious idea, Whitlock. Obviously the brainchild of your Colonel Philpott. And it would have succeeded as well, but for the fact that UNACO's mole in *spetznaz* works for me. Actually, he has done ever since UNACO first recruited him.'

Whitlock knew it would be pointless to keep up the pretence that he was Frank Royce. Zlotin had been on to him from the start. 'So by recruiting me, not only were you able to keep tabs on me, you were also able to effectively remove me from the operation itself.'

'That's it in a nutshell,' Zlotin replied.

'Why didn't you just kill me in Marseilles?'

'I couldn't take the chance that UNACO wouldn't have pulled in Jannoc if you'd turned up dead in Marseilles. Jannoc's weak, and if UNACO had sweated him long enough, he'd probably have ended up telling them about the island. It wasn't worth the risk. And as you so rightly pointed out, this way I was able to take you out of circulation. You've been useless to UNACO, haven't you? Well, at least until now. As I said, I have to assume that you have already called for back-up over the radio. But don't worry, we'll be able to repel any attack from here. After all, this is a fortress.'

'Just the two of you? I assume it is just the two of you now. I haven't seen Yemenkov around for the past couple of days. I take it his disappearance has something to do with the motor cruiser leaving here on Christmas night. Having a cell close to the landing bay does have its advantages. Strange thing is, I never heard it return.'

'Captain Yemenkov was killed while on assignment,' came the terse reply.

'My condolences,' Whitlock replied coldly.

'His death has already been avenged. A friend of yours, I believe? Jacques Rust. I killed him myself.'

Whitlock was still lunging at Zlotin when Rodenko brought the butt of his AK-47 down viciously on to the back of his head. Whitlock crumpled in an unconscious heap at Zlotin's feet.

'My condolences,' Zlotin said disdainfully, looking down at Whitlock.

'If he's already contacted UNACO, it'll only be a matter of time before they start swarming all over here,' Rodenko said anxiously.

'I would estimate an hour, two hours at the most.'

'I'll never have the helicopter fixed by then,' Rodenko shot back.

'You don't know that until you've tried, do you? So instead of standing here whining, why don't you get on with it?'

'What are you going to do?' Rodenko demanded, stung by the sarcasm in Zlotin's voice.

'I'm going to put our friend in a safe place,' Zlotin replied, effortlessly lifting the unconscious Whitlock over his shoulder. 'If you still haven't managed to repair the helicopter before the authorities descend on the island, then we may need him to buy us some time if we're to have any chance of getting away from here in one piece.'

'Nikolai?' Rodenko called out after Zlotin. 'Why didn't you tell me about Whitlock before?'

'It's all a matter of trust, Viktor,' Zlotin retorted then, adjusting his grip on Whitlock, crossed to the security door and disappeared down the stairs.

Sabrina was awake within moments of the telephone ringing. Sitting up in bed, she switched on the light and picked up the receiver. 'Hello?' she said, checking the time on her watch. It was 2.17 A.M.

'Sabrina, it's Mike. Sergei's just called me. He wants us in his room right away for an urgent briefing.'

'Did he say what it was about?' she asked, unable to conceal the excitement in her voice.

'No, but it must be something pretty important if he wants to see us at this time of night.'

'I'm on my way.'

Replacing the receiver, she pulled back the sheets and swung her legs out on to the floor. She was already wearing a grey tracksuit and, after slipping her feet into a pair of plimsolls, she grabbed her key card off the dresser and hurried from the room. Ignoring the lift, she made straight for the fire exit and bounded down the stairs to the second floor. She arrived breathlessly at Kolchinsky's door and was about to knock when she heard the lift 'ping' behind her. The lift doors parted and Graham stepped out into the corridor. He crossed to where she was standing, hands on hips, still struggling to catch her breath, and appraised her with a bemused smile before knocking on the door.

Kolchinsky opened the door and ushered them into the room. 'Sit down,' he said, clearing an area of the folder-strewn bed for them. 'I think we've finally hit the jackpot. A few minutes ago, C.W. contacted the duty officer at the Command Centre.'

'Did he say where he was?' Graham asked.

'Is he all right?' Sabrina added anxiously.

'Yes and yes. We know it was C.W. because he identified himself by his UNACO ID number. He told the duty officer that he was in an abandoned prison called *A Fortaleza* on an island situated somewhere off the Portuguese coast. He didn't know its exact location. The hostages are all safe and well. He said that he'd managed to give the Russians the slip but that he expected them to be on to him shortly. It didn't make any sense but he wouldn't elaborate, saying that he still had to disable the helicopter so that the Russians wouldn't be able to leave the island before you got there. That's when the transmission ended.'

'*A Fortaleza*. The Fortress?' Sabrina translated. 'Has the duty officer found out where it is?'

'No, but when I rang Captain Morales at the Special

Forces Brigade he told me that it's situated off the coast of Porto. It was closed down some years back after a fire damaged much of the building's infrastructure.'

'It's the perfect location,' Sabrina said, making no attempt to conceal the admiration in her voice.

'When do we go in?' Graham asked tersely.

'Once you've seen the architects' plans of the prison,' Kolchinsky replied. 'Captain Morales is on his way over here with them now.'

'Did you tell him about C.W.?' Sabrina asked.

'Yes. I know I could have given him some spiel to explain how we'd found out where the Russians were holed up, but I thought it best to come clean and tell him the truth.'

'How did he take it?' she asked.

'Not too well at first. He was angry that the Special Forces Brigade hadn't been told earlier that we'd infiltrated the opposition's nest, but he seemed to calm down after I'd pointed out that, had Major Inacio known about C.W., he'd certainly have fed the information back to Zlotin. I didn't need to say any more. It seems that Major Inacio's a very touchy subject with them right now, especially as there's still been no trace of him since his apparent disappearance yesterday afternoon.'

'So you don't think they're going to kick up a fuss about UNACO withholding information from them once this is over?' she asked.

'Considering that Jacques' death came about as a direct result of Major Inacio's treachery, I think you'll find that the Special Forces Brigade will be more than willing to forgive and forget once the dust has settled.' Kolchinsky looked across at Graham who was standing by the patio door, arms folded tightly across his chest. 'What's bothering you, Michael?'

'I don't see why you had to bring in Special Forces Brigade on this,' Graham replied bitterly. 'We could have handled it ourselves.'

'Jacques mentioned your antagonism towards the Special Forces Brigade in his notes,' Kolchinsky said. 'In fact, it seems to have cropped up several times during the course of this operation.'

'You said yourself that you hold Inacio responsible for Jacques' death. I'd say that was reason enough not to trust them,' Graham shot back.

'One rotten apple doesn't necessarily taint the whole barrel,' Kolchinsky was quick to point out.

'I'd say that all depends on how long the rotten apple's been allowed to fester in the barrel, wouldn't you?' Graham retorted.

'What are you suggesting, Michael? That Inacio may have accomplices in the Special Forces Brigade who are still passing information on to Zlotin?' Kolchinsky demanded. 'Is that it?'

'I'm not suggesting anything, Sergei,' Graham replied. 'I'd just feel a lot safer if Sabrina and I could go in alone.'

'I'll bear your comments in mind, Michael, after we've had a chance to see the plans.'

When Morales arrived he had a copy of the architects' plans of the prison complex. Removing the plans from their protective cover, he spread them across the bed; several bulky UNACO files were used to pin down the edges.

'I've had a chance to study these on my way over here,' Morales told them. 'As far as I can see, there are only two ways into the prison. The first is through the main entrance, which leads off from the landing stage, and the second is through the entrance on the helipad on the roof of the building. Both entrances are protected by security doors which the Russians will almost certainly have activated since they arrived on the island.'

'You seem pretty sure of that,' Kolchinsky said.

Morales removed a key card from his pocket and handed it to Kolchinsky. 'We found this on Yemenkov's body. It's an electronic passkey which is compatible with the prison's security system.'

'It could certainly come in useful,' Kolchinsky mused, turning the key card around slowly in his hand before giving it back to Morales.

'There is a third way into the prison,' Sabrina said without looking up from the blueprint she was studying.

'I think you'll find you're mistaken, Miss Carver,' Morales told her. 'Those are the only two entrances both in and out of the prison complex. That much is obvious from the accompanying text.'

'It also says in the accompanying text that the prison was built on the site of an old castle dating back to the mid-seventeenth century which was later destroyed in 1809 by the French fleet during the War of National Liberation.'

'Yes, I read that as well,' Morales replied. 'But I don't see what you're getting at. As you said, the prison was destroyed during the War of National Liberation. It was never rebuilt.'

'Granted, but it also says in the text that two of the castle's original dungeons were discovered almost intact while the prison was being built. The only reason they're thought to have survived the French bombardment was because they'd been built below the waterline.'

Graham crouched beside Sabrina and rested his arm on her shoulder. 'I'm sure this is a fascinating story, but could we skip the history lesson and get to the point?'

'That's the point,' she said, tapping a word on the blue-print. '*Comporta*.'

Morales peered more closely at the diagram. 'I didn't see that,' he admitted guiltily.

'I hate to break this up, but would someone tell me what the hell this *comporta* is?' Graham barked in frustration.

'*Comporta* is the Portuguese word for a sluice-gate; according to this, there was one built into the dungeon's wall,' Sabrina explained. 'If we could get in through the dungeon there's a flight of stairs leading up to what was once the medical wing of the prison. There is a security door between the stairs and the wing, but I doubt the Russians would have bothered to lock it. And even if they have, we've now got a passkey to open it.'

Graham studied the plan for some time, then got to his feet and, digging his hands into his pockets, crossed to the patio door where he stared out thoughtfully across the night sky.

'May I see that?' Kolchinsky asked from the armchair, gesturing to the blueprint on the bed.

Sabrina took it to him and pointed out the relevant details to him.

'So what exactly do you have in mind?' Kolchinsky asked.

'We could try and blow the sluice-gate from the outside and get into the prison that way,' she told him.

'It's certainly a possibility,' Kolchinsky admitted. He looked across at Graham who was still standing pensively by the patio door. 'Michael, I know that scheming look only too well. What is it this time?'

'I think blowing the sluice-gate would be a good idea, in theory,' was all Graham would venture.

'Meaning?' Sabrina asked suspiciously.

'Meaning that if we know about the sluice-gate, then so will the Russians. If we're to have any real chance of getting into the prison undetected then we have two possible means of entry – the main entrance and the dungeon. Forget about the helipad, the Russians would hear an approaching helicopter long before it got anywhere near the island. I suggest we use both options because, by splitting up, there's less chance of Sabrina and me being compromised once we're actually inside the prison.'

'Makes sense,' Sabrina admitted.

'And where exactly do we come into this little scenario?' Morales queried. 'Or are we just expected to tidy up again after UNACO like we did at the warehouse?'

'There are four hostages on the island, Captain Morales,' Kolchinsky replied. 'I can assure you that Nikolai Zlotin wouldn't have any qualms about using them as human shields if he thought that some kind of attack was imminent.'

'He used human shields in Afghanistan,' Graham said. 'Children as young as three were tied to the front of Russian tanks which were escorting troop convoys through the rebel-held mountain passes. It's a fact that no convoy was ever attacked while under his command. I'd say that goes a long way to explaining why, wouldn't you?'

Morales remained silent.

'Our best bet would be to adopt a softly-softly approach. Sabrina and I could bring out the hostages unharmed then, once we'd melted into the background, the Special Forces Brigade would be left to take the accolades. Imagine what that would do for the image of your unit, especially in the light of the Inacio affair.'

'We'd also be the first to take the flak if the operation were to fail,' Morales was quick to point out.

'That's also true, but I can tell you now that if the Special Forces Brigade were to try and storm the island, you'd have four dead hostages on your hands,' Kolchinsky said as he rolled up the blueprint and handed it back to Morales. 'You may kill Zlotin and Rodenko in the process, but that would be scant consolation when the accusations started to fly. I know that UNACO has no real jurisdiction here, and as a senior officer in the Special Forces Brigade you have every right to overrule me, but I hope you'll see that what we're saying does make sense.'

'Let's say I was to go along with you, what exactly would this "softly-softly" approach entail?' Morales asked.

'We'd have to approach the island by boat,' Graham told him. 'I'd suggest using SDVs – swimmer delivery vehicles. That way we'd be less likely to be detected.'

'And once you were inside the prison?' Morales asked when Graham fell silent.

'We'd have to improvise,' Graham replied with a shrug.

'It's just another way of saying that we'd be living off our wits as we went along,' Sabrina said when she saw the look of uncertainty cross Morales' face. 'Sure, if we knew exactly where the prisoners were being held then we'd be able to plan our strategy in advance. But we don't, so we will have to improvise.'

'How much time would you need to complete the operation if you went in by yourselves?' Morales asked.

'That's a hard one to call given that we don't know where the hostages are being held,' Graham replied. 'We'd need at least thirty minutes to get into place, and another thirty minutes to undertake a search of the prison. That's assuming that we don't come across any unexpected setbacks. Of course we may find the hostages a lot sooner than that but, to be on the safe side, I'd say we'd need at least an hour and a half.'

'Sixty minutes,' Morales said at length.

'It's cutting it fine –'

'And you'd guarantee that they'd be going in alone?' Kolchinsky was quick to cut across Graham's protestations.

Morales nodded. 'But if they're not out of there within an hour, then we move in and take over.'

'This isn't some kind of race to see who can get the quickest results,' Graham snapped at Morales. 'There're hostages' lives at stake here, in case you'd forgotten. And our colleague may now be a hostage as well. If we are to go in by ourselves, then we've got to do it professionally, and we can't do that if we're constantly having to check our watches to see how much time we've got left before the cavalry comes charging in.'

Morales took a sheet of paper from his pocket and handed it to Sabrina. 'You can read Portuguese, Miss Carver. It's a communiqué I received from my superiors as I was about to leave headquarters to come over here. I know I shouldn't be showing it to you, but maybe it'll help you to understand the predicament I'm in right now.'

Sabrina unfolded the paper and read the telex in silence.

'Well?' Graham prompted.

'Captain Morales has been given orders to lead an assault team on the prison and take it by force if necessary.' Sabrina folded up the communiqué and handed it back to Morales. 'The orders are to be carried out without delay.'

'Now perhaps you can understand why I can only give you an hour,' Morales said to Graham. 'As it is, I'll probably be hauled up in front of a court martial for insubordination. But if you're right about Zlotin, then I could be leading a suicide squad to the island. We've already lost five men during this operation, and you can imagine what that's done for morale. If there's a chance that you can bring the hostages out without further bloodshed, then I've got to risk it, even if it means disobeying a direct order.'

'OK, an hour,' Graham said finally. 'When do we leave?'

'There's a helicopter on standby at a military air-base on the outskirts of the city. My team should already be there. If you can prepare a list of what you need, I'll have the pilot order it for you over the radio. It'll be waiting for us when we reach Porto.'

'You'll have it,' Graham assured him.

'I just need to grab my Beretta and a jacket from my bedroom, then I'll be ready,' Sabrina announced, crossing to the door.

'Yeah, me too,' Graham said, going after her.

'I'll meet you both down in the lobby,' Morales told them.

'Michael?' Kolchinsky called out after him. 'I want a word with you and Sabrina before you leave the hotel.'

Graham nodded, then hurried after Sabrina who had already left the room.

'There seems to be a good rapport between them,' Morales said to Kolchinsky after Graham had closed the door behind him.

'They trust one another implicitly. I think that goes a long way to explaining the bond that exists between them. They also seem to have an uncanny ability to know exactly what the other's thinking, especially when they're in pressure situations. That, to me, is the real strength of their partnership. Yet their personalities are complete opposites. Strange, isn't it?'

'They do say opposites attract,' Morales said, returning the blueprints to their protective cover.

'Yes, they do,' Kolchinsky replied diplomatically.

Morales smiled. He could take the hint. 'Well, I need to contact the air-base to let the men know we're on our way. We'll talk again when I get back.'

Kolchinsky shook hands with Morales, then went back to the armchair to wait for Graham and Sabrina. When they returned, he gestured them into the room and had Graham close the door behind them.

'What did you want to see us about, Sergei?' Graham asked, perching beside Sabrina on the edge of the bed.

'I would have thought that was pretty obvious, Michael,' Kolchinsky retorted sharply. 'You may have been able to hoodwink Captain Morales, but then he hasn't seen the memo the Colonel sent to me last night, has he?'

'What did you want me to tell him? That the Colonel found out from a contact in France that Saisse bought a radar system and two sonar buoys on the black market the day before you and Abe were attacked at the airport? Do you think he'd have been so quick to let Sabrina and me go in alone if he'd thought that these devices had already been installed on the island?'

'I'm sure he wouldn't,' Kolchinsky replied.

'Why didn't you tell Captain Morales about the memo, Sergei?' Sabrina asked. 'I thought that the UNACO hierarchy had agreed to co-operate fully with the Special Forces Brigade after the incident at the warehouse.'

'I intend to tell him, but exactly when will depend on the viability of Michael's plan. It's obvious that he left out certain details when Captain Morales was here.' Kolchinsky turned back to Graham. 'I assume there are some missing pieces to this plan of yours and that you don't just intend to "improvise" your way into the prison?'

'I do have a plan in mind, Sergei,' Graham told him.

'But if the Russians have already installed the radar and the sonar buoys, we won't be able to get into the prison without being detected,' Sabrina was quick to point out.

'*You* won't,' Graham said, patting her arm.

'Why do I get the impression that I'm about to be set up here?' she said, eyeing Graham suspiciously.

'No, it's Zlotin who's about to be set up,' Graham countered with a satisfied smile. 'You'll be fine as long as you stick to the plan.'

'We'll be able to judge that for ourselves once you've told us what you have in mind,' Kolchinsky said, folding his arms across his stomach. 'Now, Michael, let's hear your plan.'

13

'How much longer before the helicopter will be ready for take-off?'

'Thirty minutes at the most,' Rodenko replied without looking round at Zlotin who had opened the cockpit door behind him. Picking up the torch from the seat beside him, he concentrated the beam on the rewiring he'd completed. Satisfied with his work, he nodded to himself. 'Yes, I'd say about thirty minutes. The damage wasn't as bad as I'd originally thought.'

'Good, because we've got company,' Zlotin said.

Rodenko's eyes narrowed suspiciously. 'UNACO?'

'I don't know yet,' Zlotin replied. 'The radar's picked up two unidentified craft heading towards the island.'

'By air or sea?'

'Sea,' Zlotin replied. 'They're approaching from the east which would suggest that they originated from the mainland.'

'What are you going to do?' Rodenko asked.

'First I need to know who's actually out there,' Zlotin said, patting the pair of second-generation image-intensification night-vision binoculars he had hanging around his neck. 'Then I'll be able to decide on the best course of action to take.'

Rodenko scrambled out of the cockpit, turned up the collar of his blouson against the biting wind, and followed

Zlotin to the wire fence which formed the perimeter of the helipad. Digging his hands into his pockets, he crouched down beside Zlotin, who slowly arced the night-vision binoculars across the dark waters beyond the island.

'There they are,' Zlotin announced at length, focusing the binoculars on the approaching craft. 'Two amphibious inflatables, each with a single occupant. They're still three or four miles away but closing fast.'

'Graham and Carver?' Rodenko suggested.

'I can't see their faces, but it's my guess it's them.'

'They obviously don't know about the radar,' Rodenko said.

'Obviously.'

'There's a rocket launcher in the helicopter,' Rodenko said. 'Do you want me to set it up? We can take them out the moment they get into range.'

'No,' Zlotin replied, lowering the binoculars. 'If we were to blow them out of the water now it would only bring in the reinforcements. The longer we can play this out, the longer you'll have to work on the helicopter.'

'What are you going to do?' Rodenko asked.

'Nothing,' Zlotin said.

'You're going to let them come to the island?'

'That's exactly what I intend to do, Viktor. There are only two ways they can get in here: through the main entrance or by blowing the sluice-gate in the dungeon. The landing stage's already covered by infra-red motion detectors and closed-circuit television cameras, so even if they do have Valentin's key card, they won't be able to get near the door without triggering the alarm. But if I know Graham like I think I do, he'll send Carver in through the main entrance. He had something of a reputation as an explosive expert when he was with Delta, so it's my guess that he'll want to blow the sluice-gate himself. And when he does, he'll flood the dungeon.'

'Drowning Whitlock in the process,' Rodenko said with a knowing smile.

'And Carver,' Zlotin was quick to add.

'Assuming you can take Carver alive and get her down to the dungeon before Graham blows the sluice-gate,' Rodenko observed.

'Assuming I can take Carver alive?' Zlotin snorted in disgust. 'She's good, for a woman, but I hardly think she'll be any match for me, do you?'

'I wasn't suggesting that she was,' Rodenko replied defensively.

Zlotin eyed Rodenko coldly before continuing. 'What Graham won't know is that there's a metal grille bolted to the rock face over the outside of the sluice-gate. I don't know exactly when it was put there but it certainly doesn't appear on any of the original plans. I only saw it when I checked the area outside the sluice-gate as part of the security programme when we first arrived on the island. It'll take him some time to dislodge the grille and, by the time he's ready to blow the sluice-gate, Carver will already be in the dungeon.'

'Why not just kill her?'

'Carver's the one person Graham really cares about since he lost his family. So imagine what it'll do to him when he realizes that he's been directly responsible for her death! He's always blamed himself for what happened to his wife and son, and at the time the guilt nearly broke him. This time it *will* break him.'

'You almost make it sound personal,' Rodenko said.

'I suppose in a way it always has been personal. I've followed Graham's career closely ever since he first came to prominence at Delta. Now there isn't anything I don't know about him. And vice versa, I believe. Graham and I are two of a kind, Viktor, only on different sides. And what better way to destroy your arch enemy than by letting him destroy himself?'

'You seem very sure that Graham will play into your hands,' Rodenko said.

'He will,' Zlotin replied, looking out into the darkness. 'Believe me, he will.'

The unique British-designed Subskimmer, now in operation with many Special Forces units around the world, can be transformed from surface craft to a completely self- contained, submerged swimmer delivery vehicle within the space of sixty seconds.

It was the obvious choice of craft when Graham had compiled his list of requirements. These had been radioed ahead to a Special Forces Brigade contact in Porto after the helicopter had lifted off from the air-base outside Lisbon. The two Subskimmers, together with the other items on his list, were waiting for them by the time the helicopter landed on a secluded beach somewhere between Porto and the industrial town of Matosinhos.

Graham and Sabrina quickly changed into their figure-hugging neoprene wetsuits and closed-circuit oxygen breathing apparatus then, after smearing their faces with camouflage cream, they followed Morales to where the two sixteen-foot Subskimmers were rocking gently in the shallow water.

'Synchronize watches,' Morales said, peeling back the sleeve of his black sweatshirt. 'I make it . . . 3.47.'

'Check,' Graham agreed straightaway.

'Check,' Sabrina chorused.

'One hour,' Morales reminded them. 'If we haven't heard anything from you by then, we're coming in with the helicopters.'

'By then we'll be ready to break open the champagne and toast a successful operation,' Graham told him.

'I'll drink to that,' Sabrina said, crossing to the nearest Subskimmer.

'*Boa sorte!*' Morales called out after her.

'*Obrigado*,' she replied with a quick wave.

'Good luck,' Morales said to Graham.

'*Obrigado*,' Graham rejoined, then put on his passive night-vision goggles and moved to the second Subskimmer.

Morales smiled, then nodded to the two soldiers standing beside him. They hurried forward to help push the Subskimmers into the water. Once the Subskimmers were afloat, Graham and Sabrina climbed aboard, switching on the eighty-five horsepower outboard motors. They gave each other a thumbs-up sign, then Graham took the lead and sped away from the beach. Sabrina followed closely behind him.

They'd both had previous experience of the Subskimmer, having undergone rigorous training in them as part of recent UNACO manoeuvres off the Newfoundland coast, but it was the first time that either of them had been called upon to use the craft during an actual operation.

A biting, blustery wind whipped across the restless sea, but the rain which the meteorologists had predicted the previous evening had yet to materialize. Judging by the clouds which were gathering ominously overhead, though, they both knew it would only be a matter of time before the deluge came. Sabrina, following closely in the wake of Graham's Subskimmer as it bounced across the water, found that she was having continually to wipe the spray from the lens of her night-vision goggles and, in frustration, she finally swung out from behind him and remained abreast of his craft until he eventually cut his engine when they were less than a mile away from the island.

Switching off her engine, she manoeuvred her Subskimmer alongside his craft. 'Can you see the helicopter?' she asked as he scanned the island through a pair of powerful night-vision binoculars.

'No,' Graham replied, lowering the binoculars. 'But then only part of the helipad's visible from down here anyway. The helicopter's probably hidden under camouflage netting and parked on the far side of the helipad.'

Sabrina took the binoculars from him and focused on the helipad. She couldn't see any sign of the helicopter either. Then she slowly panned the binoculars across the face of the dark, foreboding façade. 'It looks like a location set from one of those old Boris Karloff movies,' she concluded, handing the binoculars back to Graham.

'OK, you know what to do?' Graham asked, checking his Beretta.

'I should do by now,' she replied. 'We've been through the plan enough times since you first hatched it back at the hotel.'

'And you're sure you're comfortable with it?'

'How many times do I have to tell you, Mike, I trust your judgement. If you say I'll be OK as long as I stick to the plan, that's good enough for me.'

'Yeah, you will,' Graham assured her.

'Mike, remember when you told Sergei in the hospital that you wouldn't kill Zlotin if he was unarmed. Do you still feel that way after what happened to Jacques?'

'Jacques had a gun,' Graham reminded her.

'That doesn't answer my question.'

Graham held her stare momentarily, then gestured to her Subskimmer. 'You submerge first. I'll call Morales and tell him that we're about to move in.'

She swapped her night-vision goggles for a face mask, then turned her attention to transforming the Subskimmer into a wet SDV. First she sealed the outboard's exhaust, then she activated the suction-pump which was situated in the centre of the Subskimmer. It began sucking the air from the side tubes; within seconds they collapsed and the craft quickly flooded with water. She was already seated behind the swivelling motor tube when the Subskimmer dipped below the waves and, switching on the two electric propulsion units which were situated on either side of the bow, she was able to move the craft to the right or to the left, or up and down, depending on how she chose to turn the tube.

Getting her bearings from the compass on the cross tube in front of her, Sabrina started out towards the island. With a maximum speed of only two and a half knots, the Subskimmer's progress was always going to be slow, and she purposely kept the craft close to the surface of the inky, nigrescent water to avoid the perilous outcrop of rocks that littered the seabed which she was able to detect on the echo sounder, another of the instruments on the cross tube. There could be no margin of error on her part, otherwise the operation would be doomed to failure . . .

It took her twenty minutes to reach the mouth of the cavern where she secured the Subskimmer underneath the landing stage. Then, silently breaking the surface of the water, she discarded the face mask and closed-circuit breathing apparatus and slipped on the night-vision goggles which she'd brought with her. Removing her Beretta from a waterproof pouch clipped to her belt, she eased herself out from under the landing stage, and trod water as she slowly took in her surroundings. Her attention was immediately drawn to the closed-circuit television camera mounted on the rock face above the locked security door. She had to assume that the Russians had reconnected it again but, from the angle of the lens, she'd only be visible once she tried to approach the door. Then there was the infra-red motion detector on the packing crate at the far end of the landing stage. It had obviously been recently installed, and she was in no doubt that it was functional. She knew it would detect her the moment she set foot on the landing stage, but she was confident that a single bullet would incapacitate it. She guessed that a second infra-red motion detector was likely to have been placed behind the small hut on the landing stage close to the cavern entrance. Not that it mattered – the Russians would already have picked up the Subskimmers on the radar and would be lying in wait for her inside the prison. But it was vital to Graham's plan that she take out the infra-red motion detectors before she went through the security door.

She swam to the ladder which was bolted to the side of the landing stage, then slowly climbed the rungs until her head appeared above the level of the deserted platform. Her eyes flickered from the closed security door to the infra-red motion detector then, resting her wrist lightly on the top rung, she lined up the detector's glowing red eye in the Beretta's sights and gently squeezed the trigger. The bullet scored a direct hit, smashing the eye and knocking the shattered detector off the crate. Then, turning the Beretta on the camera, she shot out the lens before scrambling up on to the platform where she crouched down and looked across at the hut. Was there an infra-red detector hidden behind it? There was only one way to find out, she thought, and got to her feet.

'Impressive shooting, Miss Carver,' a voice echoed across the cavern.

She dropped down on to her haunches again, the Beretta fanning the landing stage. It was then she saw the rusted horn speaker mounted on the far wall. Underneath it was another closed-circuit camera. Whoever was operating the Tannoy system had obviously been monitoring her every move ever since she had first stepped on to the platform.

'I assume that you do have Captain Yemenkov's key card on you,' the voice boomed out again over the speaker. 'Please, feel free to come inside. Unarmed, of course.'

'Go to hell,' she hissed coldly and put a bullet through the centre of the camera lens.

'If you try –' the voice was cut off abruptly when a volley of bullets thudded into the loudspeaker.

She snapped a new clip into the Beretta, then moved cautiously towards the security door; but as she passed the hut, she activated the infra-red motion detector concealed behind it. Wincing at the piercing shrill emitted by the alarm, she waited until she'd reached the wall adjacent to the security door before turning the Beretta on the detector and silencing it with a single shot.

So far, so good, Sabrina thought to herself, but then that had been the easy bit. She suddenly remembered what Mike had said to her back at the hotel: *I know that Zlotin would see it as a personal triumph if he managed to kill me, and what better way than if he were able to use you to lure me into some kind of trap? So if you were to show up by yourself at the main security door, I know he'd make sure that you were taken alive. I've said all along that his one weakness is that he can be predictable, and now we can use that predictability to our advantage. Of course there's going to be a certain amount of risk involved, but you've got to trust me on this, Sabrina . . .*

Now it was time to put that trust to the test. Not that it worried her. She trusted Mike implicitly. She smiled to herself. The whole plan was steeped in danger and that's what made it all the more exhilarating for her . . .

She unzipped one of the pockets in her wetsuit and removed the key card. Then, pressing her back against the wall, she slipped it into the slot next to the door. There was a metallic click and the door slid open. Silence. Not that it surprised her. These were highly trained *spetznaz* operatives, not a couple of trigger-happy amateurs. She guessed that they would be lying in wait for her somewhere close to the door, biding their time until she came to them. Of course there was always the chance that they already had their weapons trained on the doorway, ready to open fire the moment she committed herself to entering the building. Possible, but unlikely. It was a risk she had to take. Taking a deep breath, she launched herself low through the doorway, the Beretta already fanning the corridor as she rolled across the floor.

The corridor was deserted. Raising herself on to one knee, she looked around slowly, making mental notes of all possible areas where the Russians could be concealed. To her right was the waiting room. The door was ajar. There were two more rooms further down the corridor but both doors were closed. She knew she'd have to check all three rooms.

She took up a position beside the waiting-room door, and eased it open gingerly with her fingertips before swivelling round, the Beretta extended at arm's length as she fanned the dank-smelling room.

The two men were sprawled face-down in the centre of the room. Suspecting some kind of trap, she trained the Beretta on them and slowly moved across the wooden floorboards to where they lay. She was only a few feet away from them when the rancid odour stopped her abruptly in her tracks. She knew the fetid stench of death only too well. Screwing up her nose, she crouched beside the nearest body and reluctantly reached out a hand to turn it over. It was Abe Silverman. Rigor mortis had already set in, and the skin had turned a sickly bluish-grey colour. She estimated that he'd been dead for several days. She turned over the second body and recognized Helmut Berger from the photograph in his UNACO file. The deep, jagged wound on the left side of the stomach was consistent with the type of injury inflicted by a survival knife; judging by the angle of penetration, she estimated that the blade had been forced up through the ribcage and into the heart. Death would have been almost instantaneous. She suddenly sensed someone behind her, but as she turned she felt a sharp needle prick in her neck. She fired blindly, but the shadowy figure had already disappeared out into the corridor. She tried to get to her feet but found that her legs were unsteady and she had to grab on to the back of a wooden chair to prevent herself from losing her balance. Pulling the small tranquillizer dart from her skin, she tossed it angrily on to the floor and pushed the chair away from her, but when she took a step towards the door her legs buckled underneath her and she stumbled and fell, landing directly on top of Berger. She reeled backwards, lashing out with her feet as she desperately tried to push the body away from her. The room was already beginning to haze and distort around her, but when she tried to tear the night-vision goggles off her face she found that her fingers were numb and unresponsive. The Beretta slipped from her hand and clattered noisily to the floor.

Then nothing.

When Sabrina came round she found herself in a dank, gloomy room. She assumed that she was in one of the dungeons underneath the prison. Although she was able to stand on the stone floor, her arms were stretched above her and a pair of rusted manacles had been clamped tightly around her wrists. The manacles were connected at each end to a short chain which was looped through a metal ring embedded in the wall. A dull ache throbbed incessantly through her head and this only added to her mounting frustration, but the more she tugged angrily at the chain holding her, the more the pain seemed to pound through her head. She finally gave up and slumped back against the wall.

'Sabrina, are you all right?' a familiar voice suddenly called out to her.

'C.W., is that you?' she replied, peering into the darkness from where she thought the voice had originated.

'Yes,' Whitlock replied. 'Can you see me? I'm about thirty yards to your right.'

'I can't see anything in here at the moment,' came the bitter reply. 'It's those damn night-vision goggles. Once you take them off you're virtually blind until your eyes have managed to adjust to the dark again.'

'Are you all right?' he repeated.

'Right now my head feels like it's being used as a punch bag, but apart from that I guess I'm OK. What about you? Are you all right? We were beginning to get really worried about you. We hadn't heard from you in days; we thought that something might have happened to you.'

'That's because I've been locked away with the hostages ever since I got here.'

'How did you get out?' she asked.

'It's a long story, I'll tell you about it when we get out of here. Zlotin knew who I was right from the start. It turns out that our man in *spetznaz* has been working for him ever since Colonel Philpott first recruited him.'

'I can't say I'm surprised,' Sabrina replied. 'Did Zlotin bring me down here?'

'Yes. You were unconscious, but he gave you an injection, obviously to bring you round, then disappeared back into the prison. I'm sure we'll have the pleasure of his company again, though, even if it's only to gloat over his success in having caught two UNACO operatives in his little net.' There was a sudden pause. 'It is only two, isn't it?' Whitlock asked, an anxiety creeping into his voice. 'Mike wasn't with you, was he?'

'No.'

'Thank God for that . . .' Whitlock trailed off when he thought he heard the sound of approaching footsteps. 'Sshh. I think Zlotin's coming back.'

Moments later a shadowy light fell across the cell. It was only then that Sabrina realized they were in an oubliette. The only means of access was through the top of the dungeon. She noticed that the floor sloped upwards from the wall which housed the sluice-gate: it had been customary in many medieval castles to construct the floor in this way as a means of forcing a confession out of a prisoner. The psychology behind the idea had been simple. The prisoner would have been placed in the chains furthest from the sluice-gate and a relative, usually a wife or child, would have been chained beside the sluice-gate, which would then have been opened, allowing the water to enter the oubliette. The prisoner would have been left with a stark choice. Confess the crime or watch their loved one drown in front of them. The psychology invariably worked but often the jailers, having extracted their confession, let them both drown anyway. Sabrina's main concern was that she was the one nearest the sluice-gate.

Zlotin climbed down the ladder into the dungeon. He was dressed in a pair of baggy camouflage trousers, a blue-and-white hooped T-shirt and an unbuttoned flak jacket. He was carrying two lanterns with him. 'I'm glad to see that you're back with us again, Miss Carver. No ill-effects, I hope?'

'Not until you appeared,' she retorted, eyeing him contemptuously.

Zlotin's cold smile never reached his eyes. 'I can understand your bitterness. I'm sure you must still be smarting over the way I reeled you in with such ease. So much for you being one of UNACO's finest.'

'Two out of three isn't bad, Zlotin, but you still haven't got Mike yet,' she replied triumphantly. 'He is UNACO's finest.'

'So I've heard, but then I've no intention of "getting" him, as you put it,' Zlotin replied, hanging the lanterns on the wall above them. 'The helicopter's ready for take-off so I see no reason to remain here any longer than is absolutely necessary.'

'What happens to us?' Whitlock asked.

'I'd say that was entirely up to Graham,' Zlotin replied. 'I know it's his intention to enter the prison by blowing the sluice-gate, but if he knew that you were already in here, he might think twice about risking your lives. He'd then have to swim around to the landing stage and enter through the main door instead. But that would mean wasting valuable time, and you could both be dead before he actually got to you. What a dilemma to be in. I only wish I could stay around to see how he resolves it.'

'How will he know that we're in here?' Whitlock demanded.

'He should be able to see you through the opening in the sluice-gate,' Zlotin replied, crossing to the ladder.

'Opening?' Sabrina called out suspiciously after him, her eyes automatically going to the sluice-gate not five feet away from where she stood.

Zlotin climbed back up on to the landing above the oubliette, then crouched down beside a wheel situated directly above the sluice-gate. He tried to turn it. It wouldn't budge.

'What the hell are you doing, Zlotin?' Whitlock shouted in horror as Zlotin continued to struggle with the wheel.

Ignoring Whitlock's outburst, Zlotin gritted his teeth as he summoned up all his strength to dislodge the wheel. After several seconds of sustained pressure the wheel finally gave. At first only a trickle of water entered the dungeon, but the more he turned the wheel, the more the water began to seep through the aperture. When he was satisfied with the flow of the water, he got to his feet and peered down into the dungeon where Whitlock and Sabrina were already tugging furiously at their chains.

'You're crazy, Zlotin,' Whitlock yelled.

'I don't know why you're complaining, Whitlock. The cant of the floor's in your favour. You'll have the perfect vantage point to watch your colleague drown. Who knows, if Graham hurries he might just get here in time to save you. But then I wouldn't hold my breath.' Zlotin smiled faintly at the irony of the phrase.

'You can't leave us here to die,' Sabrina screamed up at him.

'You did say that Graham was UNACO's finest. Well, now's the time for him to prove it. *Dozvydanya.*'

Zlotin pulled in the ladder and left it on the landing before making his way up a flight of stone steps and through two open security doors into what had once been the prison's medical wing. He slipped on his night-vision goggles, then returned to his own quarters where he removed the hold-all and attaché case from the safe in the corner of the cell. The hold-all contained Rodenko's pay-off, and the attaché case the UNACO folders. He still had one thing left to do before he departed the island. He crossed to the wing where the four prisoners were being held and placed the two cases beside the security door. The cryptologists had kept to their side of the bargain; he'd make their deaths quick . . .

'Going somewhere?' a voice called out behind him.

Zlotin's hand automatically dipped towards his holstered Makarov pistol on his belt.

'Try it and you'd be dead even before you'd unclipped the holster,' the voice hissed threateningly behind him.

Zlotin's mind was racing as he slowly extended his hands away from his body. It was Graham – he'd recognized the voice straightaway. Graham must have slipped in through the main entrance after he'd taken Carver down to the dungeon. It was the only explanation. Why had they both risked using the same route to enter the prison? He knew that Graham was unpredictable, but it still seemed to have been a huge gamble to take, especially with so much at stake. It didn't make any sense to him, but there would be plenty of time to reflect on that later. His only concern now was to get to the helicopter so that Rodenko could put as much distance as possible between them and the island before the reinforcements arrived to take the prison by force. He knew he would have to move fast, but at the same time he couldn't afford to make the slightest mistake. Not with someone like Graham . . .

'Turn around!'

Zlotin did as he was told.

Graham, who had been concealed in the entrance of one of the wings, crossed the inspection hall to where Zlotin was standing. He was wearing a pair of night-vision goggles and was armed with a Beretta. 'Put your right hand on your head and use the thumb and forefinger of your left hand to take the pistol out of the holster. And do it very slowly.'

Zlotin clasped his right hand on his head and, without taking his eyes off the Beretta, gingerly opened the flap on his holster and removed the Makarov with his thumb and forefinger. He held it out towards Graham.

'Drop it on the floor and kick it over to me,' Graham ordered.

Zlotin dropped the pistol and, using the side of his foot, swept it across the floor to within inches of Graham's feet.

'Now get up against the wall and assume the position,' Graham ordered, kicking the pistol under the stairs.

'I'll make a deal with you, Graham,' Zlotin said, standing his ground. 'You let me go –'

'No deals!' Graham cut in angrily. 'Assume the position.'

'I'd hear me out if I were you,' Zlotin told him. 'It might just save Carver's life.'

'What are you talking about?' Graham demanded.

'Carver and Whitlock are down in one of the dungeons. The sluice-gate is already open and at the rate the water's entering the dungeon, I'd estimate that Carver has, at most, five minutes left before she drowns. Let me go and I'll give you the keys to unlock their chains.'

'I'm going to count to three, Zlotin,' Graham said in a barely audible voice. 'If you haven't given me the keys by then, I'll kill you and take them myself. I swear I'll kill you. Now give me the keys!'

'It's not that simple,' Zlotin replied calmly. 'I don't have them on me. They're in my quarters.'

'Where are your quarters?' Graham demanded, his breathing becoming increasingly ragged as he struggled to control the anxiety which was tightening in a knot in the pit of his stomach.

'Throw down your gun and I'll tell you,' Zlotin replied.

'No deal,' came the terse reply.

'Then she'll die,' Zlotin said with an indifferent shrug.

'And so will you,' Graham retorted.

'Death doesn't frighten me, Graham. You should know that. What I will do is show you to my quarters if you agree to let me go. Deal?'

Graham hated himself for negotiating with Zlotin, but

what choice did he have? Sabrina's life depended on it. 'Show me,' he snapped tersely.

Zlotin knew this would be his only chance to take Graham. It was obvious that Graham was on edge, having allowed his personal feelings to encroach on his professional judgement. A mistake Zlotin would never have allowed himself to make, irrespective of the circumstances . . .

Zlotin feigned to turn to the right and, as Graham made the mistake of starting to move with him, Zlotin lashed out with his fist, catching him painfully on the side of the head. Losing his balance, Graham landed heavily on the floor, the Beretta flying out of his hand. Zlotin looked to his own pistol but it was out of reach underneath the stairs. He unsheathed his lightweight German Eikhorn survival knife, which he'd had concealed at the back of his camouflage trousers, and moved in on Graham who was clawing desperately for his Beretta. The gun lay just beyond his outstretched hand. At last Graham managed to curl his fingers around the automatic but, as he raised it to fire, Zlotin slashed the serrated knife down across his forearm, ripping through Graham's wetsuit and slicing a deep wound in his arm. Graham howled in agony and dropped the Beretta, which spun away from him. Graham was still struggling to get to his feet when Zlotin caught him agonizingly in the ribs with the tip of his steel-capped boot. He cried out in pain but forced himself to his feet, knowing that he would be dead if he were to lose his footing.

Zlotin circled him slowly, the knife gripped tightly in his hand. He stabbed at Graham who had to jump back to avoid the tip of the blade cutting him again. Graham was already holding his bloody arm against his injured ribs as he watched Zlotin's knife hand sway from side to side, preparing for the next lunge. Zlotin feigned to the left but this time Graham didn't fall for it. Instead he parried the incoming thrust, grabbing Zlotin's wrist as he did so. Zlotin reacted quickly, clamping his free hand over his knife hand to try to force the blade towards Graham's stomach. The blood on Graham's hands was acting as a lubricant; he couldn't get a grip on Zlotin's wrist and he was continually having to concede ground just to keep the blade at bay. His back touched the wall, Zlotin increased the pressure, and Graham knew he couldn't sustain a defence for much longer. He had to improvise. Fast. Then it came to him. He shifted all his weight to his left leg, forcing Zlotin to overbalance, and the knife shot forward and gouged an uneven scar across the wall. In that instant Graham hooked his fingers underneath the Russian's night-vision goggles and ripped them off his face.

Zlotin suddenly found himself completely blind in the darkness. Taking advantage of Zlotin's confusion, Graham clamped both hands around the knife and rammed the blade deep into Zlotin's stomach. 'That's for Jacques Rust,' he hissed.

Zlotin stumbled back against the wall, his hands clasped over his stomach as the blood pumped through his fingers. The surprise was still mirrored on his face when his legs buckled under him and he crashed to the floor.

Graham checked for a pulse. Nothing. Knowing that Rodenko was still somewhere on the island, he took the precaution of hiding the attaché case and hold-all in one of the cells before setting off at a frantic pace towards the dungeons, hoping desperately that he wasn't too late to save Sabrina. Having already memorized the layout of the prison complex from the blueprints he'd studied on the helicopter, he was able to weave his way through the labyrinth of corridors until he finally arrived breathlessly at the entrance to the medical wing. It was then he heard Whitlock and Sabrina shouting for help. Relief flooded through him. He wasn't too late! He sprinted the length of the corridor, through the waiting room and the surgeon's parlour, before emerging into a second corridor. The security door leading to the dungeons was at the end of the corridor. He ran through the open doorway, bounded down the stairs, and finally came out on to the landing overlooking the dungeons.

Whitlock and Sabrina were in the dungeon furthest from

the stairs. Whitlock was already waist-deep in the water, but Graham was horrified to see that only Sabrina's head and upstretched arms were now visible above the waterline. He knew he'd have to act fast if he was to have a chance of saving her.

'Mike, close the sluice-gate,' Whitlock yelled when he saw Graham on the landing above them.

Graham hurried across to the wheel and tried to turn it. Nothing happened. Cursing under his breath, he wiped the blood from his hands and tried again to turn it. Still it wouldn't move.

'Have you closed it yet?' Sabrina shouted up to him as she struggled to keep her head above water.

'It's jammed,' Graham replied as he tried for a third time to close the sluice-gate. Still the wheel wouldn't budge.

'Mike, for God's sake do something,' she screamed up at him.

'What do you think I'm trying to do?' he yelled back at her. Rubbing gravel on to his bloodied palms, he took a firm grip on the wheel, his arms shuddering with the effort as he tried to force it. After several seconds of sustained pressure, the pain from the deep laceration on his right forearm finally became too much to bear. 'I can't shift the damn thing,' he called to them. 'I'm coming down there. I'll have to pick the locks on those chains.'

'Mike, whatever you're going to do, just make sure you do it quickly,' Sabrina shouted. 'Another minute and I'm going to be underwater.'

Graham discarded his night-vision goggles then lowered the ladder into the dungeon. He climbed down until he reached the water, then swam across to Sabrina. She'd already been forced to tilt her head back to try and evade the rising water which was beginning to lap at her chin. Treading water, Graham removed the Mauser Officer's knife from his pocket and inserted the blade gently into the keyway of one of the manacles which held her arms above her head.

He eased it carefully from side to side, but he couldn't get the tip of the blade to activate the lock.

'Mike, hurry up,' Sabrina urged, spitting the first drops of water from her mouth. 'I'm already standing on tiptoe.'

'I'm doing my best,' Graham retorted, inserting the blade again and twisting it carefully inside the keyway. Still the lock wouldn't give.

She began spluttering as the water streamed into her nostrils.

'Mike, she's gone under,' Whitlock screamed in horror as Sabrina's head dipped under the water.

Graham locked his arms around her waist and, gritting his teeth as the pain seared through his injured forearm, hauled her up until her head appeared again above the waterline. 'I've got to pick the locks before the level of the water reaches the manacles.'

'I know,' she said softly. 'I've managed to hold my breath underwater for two minutes at the Test Centre before. I should be able to do it again now.'

'Don't worry, I'll have you out of those damn things by then,' he promised her.

She took a deep breath then nodded for him to release her. He watched her head disappear under the water and knew the stark reality facing him: unless he was able to pick the locks on both manacles within the next couple of minutes, she would drown . . .

Carefully he inserted the blade into the keyway of the other manacle and, biting his lip with such venom that it drew blood, he began to trace the tip inside the aperture, willing it to open. Nothing happened. Cursing furiously, he looked at his watch. It was already coming up to a minute since she'd gone under. He prodded the tip of the blade back into the keyway and twisted it gently. Still nothing. He punched the wall in frustration then tried again.

Suddenly the blade snagged on something inside the

key-way. He tickled the blade delicately inside the aperture, ever fearful that the rocking motion of the water would dislodge the blade and he would have lost the incentive. Then he felt the lock give and he gave a shout of delight as the manacle came away from her wrist. But his joy was short-lived. Sabrina's limp arm splashed into the water and sunk from view. Was she unconscious? Or dead? No, she wasn't dead, he chided himself angrily. She was one of the best underwater breathers amongst the field operatives. So what had happened? For a moment he was tempted to try and haul her head above water, but he knew it would only waste more valuable time. The level of the water had already reached her forearms. This was his last chance. If he couldn't pick the lock within the next thirty seconds, the manacles would be underwater. And she would die.

With renewed determination, and wiping the sweat from his forehead with the back of his hand, Graham inserted the blade into the keyway. For what seemed an eternity nothing happened, but just as he was beginning to fear the worst, the tip of the blade penetrated the lock. Turning the blade gently inside the lock, he heard a distinctive metallic *click* and the manacle sprang open.

He grabbed her wrist and yanked her up until her head was clear of the water then, clamping his arm across her chest, he swam backwards towards the ladder.

'Mike?' Whitlock called out to him.

Graham looked round sharply at Whitlock, startled by his voice. He'd been so caught up in trying to free Sabrina that he'd all but forgotten that Whitlock was there too. He was horrified to see that the water had already reached Whitlock's chest. 'Hang in there, buddy, I'll be with you as soon as I can, but first I gotta try . . .' He trailed off and gestured towards Sabrina.

'Give me the knife, Mike,' Whitlock said. 'I should be able to pick the locks myself.'

'Yeah, sure,' Graham replied absently and, cradling Sabrina's head carefully with his good arm, he reached out and pushed the knife into Whitlock's hand.

Whitlock noticed the blood streaming from the deep laceration on Graham's right forearm but didn't mention it. There would be time for questions later.

Graham reached the ladder, then ducked underneath Sabrina and levered her limp body across his shoulders in a fireman's lift. He carried her up on to the landing where he laid her out gently on the floor. He felt the side of her windpipe for a pulse in her carotid artery. Nothing. He extended her neck by tilting her head back, then eased the cap off her head and unzipped the wetsuit at her throat. Then, pinching her nose, he breathed hard into her mouth, forcing her chest to rise. He took his mouth off hers to allow her chest to fall again. He went through the motions a second time then checked for a pulse. Still nothing. Her only chance now were ECCs, external cardiac compressions. He quickly unzipped the wetsuit down to her navel then, locating her breastbone, interlocked his hands and placed them on her exposed skin, the heel of his lower hand resting on her sternum. He pushed down hard with the full weight of his body behind him, forcing her breastbone towards her spine, then removed his hands to allow her chest to recoil. He repeated it fifteen times, pausing after every five compressions to check her pulse. There was still no response.

'Come on,' he shouted at her. 'Don't quit on me now.'

He went through the motions again – two mouth-to-mouth resuscitations to fifteen ECCs. Still no sign of a pulse.

Whitlock, who had managed to pick the locks on the manacles, climbed silently up the ladder and crouched down beside Graham. 'You give her mouth-to-mouth, I'll apply the chest compressions.'

They went through the routine twice, but at the end Graham still couldn't detect a pulse.

'What the hell went wrong?' Graham asked, staring down into the oubliette where Sabrina had been manacled to the wall. 'She should have been able to hold out longer than she did.'

'She can't have got over the effects of the tranquillizer Zlotin gave her before he brought her down here,' Whitlock said softly, putting his hand lightly on Graham's shoulder. 'It's no use, Mike, she's gone.'

'No,' Graham snarled, shrugging off Whitlock's hand. 'We do it again. And again. I don't care how many –'

'Mike,' Whitlock cut in. 'She's dead.'

Graham shoved Whitlock aside and again gave her mouth-to-mouth resuscitation. 'Breathe, damn you,' he yelled at her as he pumped the heel of his hand down on to her sternum. 'Breathe!'

'You've done everything you can for her,' Whitlock said gently. 'It's over, Mike. She's gone.'

'It's not over,' Graham snapped as he continued to push down savagely on her breastplate. 'She wants to breathe. I know she does. Come on, Sabrina, you can do it. Breathe, Goddammit. Breathe!'

Whitlock was about to pull Graham away from her when he saw her chest move. Had it just been a reaction to the pressure Graham was applying to her sternum? Then her chest moved again. He pressed his fingers against her windpipe and felt a faint pulse in her carotid artery. 'Jesus Christ, she's alive.'

Graham inhaled deeply then pinched her nose and blew hard into her mouth. Her chest rose with the influx of air. For a moment nothing happened. Then, as her chest fell, she began to cough. At first it was a weak, choking sound, but when Graham placed her in the recovery position the coughing became more violent and her body shuddered as she vomited on to the floor.

'You just don't know when to quit, do you?' Whitlock said with a nervous chuckle as he realized just how close they had actually come to losing her.

'Story of my life,' Graham replied gruffly, then turned back to Sabrina who was now lying on her side, her face

341

twisted in pain as she clutched her stomach. 'How are you feeling?'

'Stupid question,' she hissed, and vomited again.

Whitlock got to his feet. 'You stay here with Sabrina. I'm going after Zlotin and Rodenko, if they're still on the island.'

'Zlotin's dead,' Graham replied.

'And Rodenko?'

'I haven't seen him.'

'I think I know where he'll be,' Whitlock said, picking up Graham's night-vision goggles. 'Where's your gun?'

'I dropped it when Zlotin cut me. I guess it must still be somewhere in the inspection hall.' Graham watched Whitlock cross to the stairs. 'C.W., be careful.'

'You bet,' Whitlock replied, then disappeared through the open doorway at the top of the stairs.

Rodenko eased Zlotin over on to his back. He didn't need to feel for a pulse. It was obvious that Zlotin was dead. What had happened? Zlotin had contacted him on the two-way radio ten minutes earlier to say that he was going to pick up the attaché case and hold-all from the safe and for him to start up the helicopter. The minutes had dragged past and, when there was still no sign of Zlotin, he'd begun to get worried. He'd finally shut down the engine and, taking a Kalashnikov AK-47 from the back of the helicopter, had gone in search of Zlotin.

Rodenko knew he had to get off the island as quickly as possible if he were to have any chance of self-preservation. That's all that was left to him now. He'd thought about taking one of the cryptologists with him as a hostage but he'd quickly dismissed the idea – it would only waste time. The money? Had Zlotin picked it up from the safe before he'd been killed? Or was it still there? There was only one way to find out ...

Rodenko hurried to the wing where they had been quartered. He was wearing a pair of night-vision goggles, so there was no need to advertise his presence by switching on any lights. Making his way cautiously down the corridor, he paused outside Zlotin's quarters then swivelled round and fanned the cell with the AK-47. He cursed angrily when he saw that the safe was open. And empty. If, as he suspected, Graham had killed Zlotin, then the hold-all could be anywhere. There certainly wasn't time to try and locate it. He would have to cut his losses and get off the island before he was discovered. There was always the rendezvous with Koslov to fall back on . . .

Whitlock had been on his way to the helipad when he'd come across Rodenko crouched over Zlotin's body in the inspection hall. He'd also seen that Rodenko was armed with an AK-47. Whitlock knew he couldn't possibly have covered the distance without being cut down. He'd decided to bide his time. He waited until Rodenko had disappeared through the open security door and followed discreetly behind him. Now, taking up a position inside the cell nearest to the doorway, he waited for Rodenko to make his next move . . .

He heard Rodenko curse loudly, then the sound of approaching footsteps as the Russian strode back towards the security door. Whitlock crouched down like a predator against the wall, ready to spring the moment Rodenko appeared. It was the only way he could be sure of catching Rodenko by surprise. The footsteps grew progressively louder. As Rodenko passed in front of the doorway, Whitlock leapt out, slamming him up against the opposite wall. The AK-47 fell to the floor, skidding out of reach of both men. Rodenko, momentarily winded, quickly regained his composure and brought his elbow down sharply on to Whitlock's shoulder. Grunting in pain, Whitlock dropped to one knee. Rodenko caught him with a jarring punch to the side of the head and Whitlock sprawled to the ground, landing within a couple of feet of the fallen AK-47. Rodenko was reaching for his holstered Makarov when Whitlock snatched up the assault rifle and swung it on him. Rodenko hurled himself through the doorway as Whitlock fired.

Whitlock scrambled to his feet, his head still ringing from the punch, and moved carefully to the doorway, the AK-47 held tightly in both hands. A bullet thudded into the wall inches above him, forcing him to duck back inside the corridor. He heard the sound of retreating footsteps. Then silence. He waited a few seconds, then launched himself through the doorway and rolled across the floor, coming up on one knee behind an overturned crate. The hall was deserted. There was always the possibility that Rodenko was hiding in one of the wings, waiting for him to commit himself, but Whitlock thought it far more likely that he was already on his way to the helipad. A sudden thought flashed across his mind. Rodenko would be sure to lock the security door behind him once he'd reached the helipad. Whitlock patted his shirt pocket – the key card he'd found in Zlotin's cell wasn't there now. He checked his other pockets. It wasn't in any of them. Zlotin must have removed it, which meant it must still be on the body . . .

Satisfied that it was safe to come out from behind the crate, he darted across to where Zlotin's body lay and found the key card on him. He slipped it into his pocket, then ascended the stairs and made his way cautiously along the fire-scarred corridor, through the two open security doors, finally emerging at the foot of the stairs which led up to the helipad. The security door at the top of the stairs was locked.

Having scanned the length of the deserted corridor behind him, he made his way slowly up the stairs, careful to step over the missing treads as he went. He paused once he'd covered three-quarters of the distance and, grabbing hold of the railing with his free hand, jumped nimbly over the two missing treads which had left a gaping hole in the stair-case and a sheer drop of two hundred feet to the concrete floor below. Reaching the top of the stairs he pressed himself against the wall and slipped the key card into the lock.

The sound of the helicopter's engine roared through the open doorway and he could hear that it had almost reached the r.p.m.s necessary for lift-off. He knew he would have to move fast if he were to prevent the helicopter from leaving the island. Gripping the AK-47 tightly in both hands, he swung round into the open doorway. The Westland Scout helicopter was parked in the faded yellow circle in the middle of the helipad, and he could see Rodenko frantically at work behind the controls in the flight deck. He fired a burst at the engine housed directly behind the cabin. The bullets made no impression on the reinforced steel plate Rodenko had inserted in front of it when the Russians had first taken possession of the helicopter. Then he turned the AK-47 on the flight deck, but the bullets only left a row of dimpled scars across the bulletproof glass.

Suddenly the helicopter rose up from the helipad and swivelled around as if on an invisible axis, and in that moment Whitlock realized what was about to happen. He flung himself through the doorway as Rodenko opened fire with the 30-mm calibre chain gun. The bullets chewed harmlessly into the sloping wall above the stairs. Whitlock landed awkwardly, lost his balance, and tumbled backwards down the stairs. His heart missed a beat as he felt himself falling through the gaping aperture in the staircase where the two treads were missing. Making a desperate grab for the railing, he managed to lock his fingers around it, and for an agonizing moment, all that prevented him from falling to his death was his one-handed grip on the base of the railing. He gritted his teeth as he slowly reached up his other hand and locked it firmly around the railing as well, then, swinging his body like a trapeze artist, he began to build up the momentum: with any luck he could bring his leg up over the nearest tread and haul himself back up on to the staircase. Finally he had enough momentum to attempt the manoeuvre; he swung his leg up towards the tread but misjudged the distance and cried out in pain as he caught his knee painfully on the edge of the tread. Swallowing nervously, he could feel the sweat on his hands acting as a lubricant on the metal railing. He knew he couldn't hold on for much longer . . .

'Give me your hand.'

Whitlock looked up sharply, startled by the voice above him.

Graham was crouched over the aperture, his left hand held out towards Whitlock. 'Give me your hand,' he repeated.

Whitlock could see that Graham's eyes were glazed and his face had taken on an unhealthy greyish pallor from the amount of blood he'd already lost. 'Mike, get away from here. You could keel over at any moment. I'll try and swing myself up again.'

'Give me your hand, for Christ's sake,' Graham hissed, then wrapped his injured arm around the railing to brace himself to take the strain.

'You haven't got the strength to pull me up. Now get the hell out of here.'

Graham cursed under his breath, then reached down and clamped his hand around Whitlock's wrist. 'Now let go of the railing.'

'Mike, you're not —'

'Trust me on this one, buddy,' Graham replied in a soft, but firm tone.

Whitlock knew he had little choice but to go along with Graham. His hand was already beginning to slip down the railing. With a mounting sense of unease, he reluctantly let go. He saw Graham grit his teeth in pain as he took the full weight of Whitlock's body on his good arm. Then slowly he began to haul Whitlock up towards him.

After several tense seconds, Whitlock was finally able to grab on to the nearest tread with his free hand. He used it to lever himself up on to the staircase; once safely on it, he slumped back against the railings, the intense relief etched on his sweating face. 'I owe you, Mike,' he said, patting Graham on the shoulder.

'Like hell you do,' Graham retorted. 'Did you get Rodenko?'

'No,' Whitlock replied grimly. 'He managed to get the helicopter airborne then turned the chain gun on me. I had to dive for cover. That's when I lost my balance and fell down the stairs.'

'Well, that answers my next question,' Graham said. 'Where's Sabrina?'

'She came as far as the inspection hall with me but she obviously needs more time to recover . . .' Graham trailed off and looked up at the open doorway. 'Do you hear that?'

Whitlock listened for a moment, then nodded on hearing the sound of the approaching helicopters in the distance. 'I presume they're on our side?' he said tentatively, casting a suspicious glance in Graham's direction.

Graham looked at his watch then struggled to his feet. 'Yeah, the Special Forces Brigade. Right on time. Come on, we'd better break the news to them that Rodenko's their responsibility now. He can't have got very far though.'

'Do you want a hand?' Whitlock asked when he noticed how unsteady Graham was on his feet.

'No, I'm OK. I just feel a bit light-headed, that's all,' Graham replied, holding his injured arm protectively against his stomach. 'I'll tell you something, though. It's not my arm that hurts right now. Zlotin caught me in the ribs with his boot. It feels like a couple of them are broken. Christ, it hurts.'

'So you've been suffering in silence all this time?' Whitlock said, purposely staying close to Graham in case he were to lose his balance and fall.

'There hasn't exactly been time to discuss the . . .' Graham trailed off when he emerged on to the helipad. 'Well, I'll be damned. Perhaps I've been underestimating Morales all along.'

Whitlock frowned. Who was Morales? He pushed the thought from his mind as he stepped on to the helipad and looked up at the approaching helicopters. The Westland Scout was returning to the island, escorted by two Special Forces Brigade Alouette III helicopters which were both armed with wire-guided missiles on their fuselage pylons. One Alouette remained directly above the Westland Scout, the other stayed on its tail. Both helicopters had powerful spotlights trained on the helpless Westland Scout. There was no escape for Rodenko.

'Put down on the helipad,' a voice boomed through a loudspeaker on the undercarriage of one of the Alouettes. 'Then step out of the helicopter and lie face down on the ground with your hands on your head. You have ten seconds to comply otherwise we'll open fire on your craft.'

Whitlock pulled Graham back into the doorway as a fierce wind whipped up around them when the Westland Scout hovered momentarily over the helipad before its skids touched down on the ground. The engine was shut off and the cockpit door was opened from the inside. Rodenko jumped out on to the helipad, his hands raised above his head.

'Lie face down on the ground and put your hands on your head,' the voice thundered from the Alouette directly above him.

Rodenko peered up at the dazzling spotlight which illuminated him on the helipad, then lay down on his stomach and clasped his hands on the back of his head. One of the Alouette helicopters landed on the helipad and half a dozen men, all armed with machine-pistols, leapt from the open cabin door. Four sprinted across to where Rodenko lay and the other two approached Graham and Whitlock, their machine-pistols trained on them.

'It's me, Mike Graham,' Graham announced, stepping out from the doorway. He noticed their eyes go to Whitlock. 'Don't worry, he's one of us.'

Morales climbed from the passenger seat of the grounded Alouette and crossed to where Graham and Whitlock were standing. Like the others, he was dressed in black and his face was obscured by camouflage cream. He handed both men a blanket then his eyes went to Graham's injured arm. 'You look like you've been in one hell of a fight.'

'You should see the other guy,' Graham retorted, wrapping the blanket around his shoulders.

'Zlotin?' Morales asked.

Graham nodded. 'He's dead.'

'Where's Miss Carver?' Morales asked, looking around him.

'I left her in the inspection hall. You'd better send one of your men down to see if she's all right.'

'And whoever you send, tell them to mind the stairs back here,' Whitlock added, stabbing his thumb over his shoulder. 'They're a bloody menace.'

Morales barked an order to one of the men hovering behind him, who nodded and disappeared through the security door behind them. 'I'll have the paramedic look at that arm for you,' he said to Graham. 'He can patch it up until we can get you to a hospital.'

Whitlock took Morales to one side. 'We need to get Mike to a hospital pretty quickly. He's lost a lot of blood. You can see how unsteady he is on his feet. He's also taken a blow to the ribs. There's a possibility that a couple of them could even be broken.'

Morales spoke quickly into a two-way radio and moments later the second Alouette landed on the helipad. 'There's a paramedic on board,' he told Graham. 'Do you want a stretcher?'

'It's only a cut, for God's sake,' Graham shot back. 'You're making me out to be some kind of invalid. I think I can manage to walk to the helicopter by myself.'

Whitlock gave Morales a helpless shrug, but both men were quick to react when Graham seemed to stumble before regaining his balance again.

'I'm OK,' Graham was quick to reassure them.

'You look it, Mike,' Sabrina said from the doorway. She crossed to where the three men were standing.

'Here comes the paramedic now,' Morales said, indicating the man hurrying towards them. 'I'll leave you in his capable hands.'

The paramedic took one look at Graham's arm and gestured to the helicopter. 'We need to get you to a hospital right away.'

Graham turned to Whitlock. 'Are you staying behind on the island?'

'Yes, I'll need to show Captain Morales where the hostages are being held. Why do you ask?'

'Zlotin had an attaché case and a hold-all with him. I didn't have a chance to look inside them, but it's my guess that one of them contains the UNACO folders. I left them in C Wing. The second cell from the main door on the right-hand side.'

'I'll be sure to pick them up,' Whitlock told him.

Sabrina slipped her arm around Graham to support him. 'Come on, Mike, let's get you to the helicopter.'

'Quit fussing,' Graham said irritably, but made no attempt to pull away from her as they crossed to the helicopter.

Morales smiled to himself. 'It's true, opposites do attract.'

'What?' Whitlock said, frowning.

'Sorry, I was just thinking aloud,' Morales told him. 'I presume the hostages are still locked up?'

'Yes. We thought it best to leave them where they were. At least they weren't in any immediate danger.'

'You lead the way,' Morales told him, and beckoned to two of his men to accompany them into the prison.

'I wonder how they're going to take to finding out that I'm actually one of the good guys?' Whitlock said with a thoughtful smile. 'Well, I guess there's only one way to find out, isn't there?'

14

'So there never was a virus,' Philpott said once he'd finished reading through Whitlock's case report.

'No, sir,' Whitlock replied as they sat in his office on the twenty-second floor of the United Nations building in New York. 'When I challenged Rodenko to produce the antidote, he said that Zlotin had invented the story about the virus to make sure that Professor Auerbach and Dr Fisier would be more compliant when it came to decoding the folders. Naturally we had Lisl Auerbach and Marie Fisier checked by a toxicologist as soon as we got back to the mainland, but he couldn't find any traces of any foreign substances in their bloodstreams. It seems that they were only injected with a harmless sedative.'

'That's certainly a relief.'

'It was once Zlotin's deadline had passed without incident,' Whitlock told him. 'I don't think any of them were really at ease until then, despite the toxicologist's assurances that neither woman was in any danger.'

'That's understandable,' Philpott replied, then sat back in his padded chair and stared thoughtfully at the report on his desk before looking up at Whitlock again. 'How did they react when they found out that you were really working for UNACO?'

'At first they were pretty hostile towards me, but when

they found out that I'd been responsible for alerting the authorities, they seemed to ease off a bit. I suppose their initial reaction was only to be expected after what they'd been through. But at the end of the day, they were released unharmed, and that's all that really counts, isn't it?'

'What did you make of Professor Auerbach?' Philpott asked.

'I didn't have much contact with him while I was on the island, but from what I could see, he seemed to have handled the pressure a lot better than Dr Fisier. The same went for Lisl Auerbach. Her temperament never ceased to amaze me. Why do you ask?'

'We need a new head of cryptology to replace Abe Silverman,' Philpott replied.

'And you're thinking about bringing in Auerbach?' Whitlock said, then gave a nod of approval. 'You could do a lot worse, sir.'

'I'm glad you think so, because I offered him the job this morning.'

'What did he say?' Whitlock asked.

'He's due to take up his new post in early February.' The intercom buzzed on Philpott's desk. He flicked on the switch below the light. 'Yes, Sarah?'

'Mike Graham and Sabrina Carver are here, sir,' his personal secretary told him.

'Send them through,' Philpott said, activating the sliding door with the miniature transmitter on his desk. He waited until they had entered the room, then closed the door again behind them. 'How's the arm, Mike?' he asked, gesturing to Graham's right arm which was in a sling.

'It feels a lot better today, sir,' Graham was quick to reassure him.

'And the ribs?'

'Still twingeing a bit, but at least they're not broken. The X-rays showed that they were only bruised.'

'*Severe* bruising of the ribcage,' Philpott corrected him. 'I received a copy of the X-rays this morning.'

'It could have been a lot worse, sir,' Graham said, sitting down on one of the black leather sofas.

'Are those your reports?' Philpott asked, indicating the folders in Sabrina's hand.

'Yes, sir,' she replied, handing them to him.

'There is just one thing I want clarified before we start the briefing. Mike, tell me something about the background to this plan you hatched to get the hostages off the island.'

'Sergei said he'd brief you in full about it, sir,' Graham said hastily.

'He did, but I'd just like you to go over it again in your own words. What made you think that you could pull it off in the way you did?'

'Zlotin's one weakness was his predictability, sir,' Graham told him. 'He liked to play it by the book. It paid off for him ninety-nine per cent of the time but, having studied his campaigns in detail since I was at Delta, I knew that if we ever came up against each other, I would be able to out-manoeuvre him simply because I would be able to adapt more easily than he would. But to defeat him, I had first to think like him. And that's what I did. I put myself in his position and tried to work out how he'd react when he saw Sabrina and me approaching the island on our own. We weren't supposed to know about the radar or the sonar buoys, so that was already a factor in our favour. There were only two possible routes for us to get into the prison: through the main entrance and through the dungeons. Two individuals, two options. The perfect scenario for someone like Zlotin. He would have known that I was a demolition expert at Delta, so obviously I'd be the one who'd blow the sluice-gate. I let him think that he was right by sending Sabrina in through the main entrance. She shot out all the infra-red detectors and the closed-circuit TV cameras, which then allowed me to cross to the security door undetected after she'd already entered the prison. I knew that as there were only two Russians on the island, one would have had to remain either in their ops room or on the helipad

353

to monitor the possibility of an air attack. That left one of them, which I assumed would be Zlotin, to lie in wait for Sabrina when she entered through the main entrance.

'I knew he wouldn't kill Sabrina. She would be far more important to him alive, at least until he'd used her to lure me into some kind of trap. So I gave him five minutes then went in myself. That's when I came across him and, well, you know the rest.'

'The rest being that you came within a whisker of losing your partner,' Philpott shot back. 'Or was that also part of the plan?'

'Sir, that's not fair –'

'It's OK,' Graham cut in quickly, putting a reassuring hand on the indignant Sabrina's arm. 'The Colonel has every right to be angry. I realize that I overlooked the fact that he'd open the sluice-gate, and that almost cost Sabrina her life. That's something I'll have to live with for the rest of my life. But having said that, sir, I still wouldn't change a thing if I had to do it over again.'

'We all know the risks involved when we undertake an assignment,' Sabrina told Philpott. 'We accept it as part of the job. And if Mike asked me to go through it all again tomorrow, I'd do it without hesitation. We got the hostages out unharmed and that could never have been achieved if the Special Forces Brigade had tried to take the island by force. That alone vindicates Mike's plan.'

'I'm glad we both agree on that then,' Philpott said, looking straight at her.

'You mean you'd have sanctioned the plan as well, sir?' Graham asked in surprise.

'I did,' Philpott replied. 'Sergei rang me as soon as you'd left the hotel. I knew there were bound to be risks involved, but I had no hesitation in giving it the green light. As Sabrina rightly pointed out, you'd never have got the hostages off the island alive had the Special Forces Brigade gone in with guns blazing.'

'What would have happened if it hadn't worked, sir?' Graham asked suspiciously.

'It worked, so let's leave it at that,' Philpott replied.

'Where's Sergei, sir?' Whitlock asked, quickly changing the subject. 'He told us he'd be back today in time for the briefing.'

'He was due to fly back this morning, but last night Rodenko agreed to co-operate with the investigation on the condition that it was Sergei who questioned him. So Sergei will be staying on in Lisbon until he's finished interrogating Rodenko. That could take another couple of days if Rodenko knows as much as he's letting on.'

'Smart move,' Graham said thoughtfully.

Sabrina's eyes flickered between Philpott and Graham. 'Why is it a smart move?' she asked hesitantly.

'Every recruit has to sign a document when they join *spetznaz* promising never to reveal anything to the enemy either about themselves or about the organization,' Graham told her. 'The punishment for violating the code is death. Rodenko knew that he'd be sure to face a life sentence when he was handed back to the Russian authorities, so his only chance of weaselling out of it would be to plea-bargain. In other words, a reduced sentence in return for turning state's evidence. But had he waited until he was back in Russia before blowing the whistle on his former colleagues, there are still more than enough hard-liners within the security services to ensure that he'd never have lived to testify at his trial. What better way to save his own neck than by agreeing to talk to Sergei, a liberal expatriate Russian with powerful connections inside the Kremlin? So if Sergei were to put in a good word for him, who knows what kind of deal he could make with the Russian authorities?'

'Reduced sentence or not, he's still going to wind up in a Russian jail,' Sabrina said.

'Not if he's smart,' Graham replied, looking across at Philpott. 'What exactly were his terms for agreeing to turn state's evidence, sir?'

'He's agreed to give the Russian authorities the names of all his co-conspirators in return for dropping all outstanding charges against him.'

'Have they gone for it, sir?' Whitlock asked.

Philpott nodded. 'Yes. He's already named over a dozen politicians in Russia's supreme legislature, the Congress of People's Deputies, as well as several top-ranking officers in the armed forces as being the masterminds behind the proposed military coup which was to have taken place within the next couple of months. He's prevented what would have turned out to have been a very bloody and very costly civil war in Russia. Those individuals named by Rodenko have already been arrested and, according to a source of mine inside the Kremlin, a considerable amount of incriminating evidence was seized as well. I think you'll agree that accepting Rodenko's terms was a small price to pay for netting the big fish behind the conspiracy.'

'He's not going to be allowed to walk, is he, sir?' Sabrina asked in horror.

'Not likely,' Philpott retorted. 'He was responsible for the murder of at least two members of the Special Forces Brigade and of Hardin, the American who was working at Caldere's club. That alone will get him three life sentences in any Portuguese court of law.'

'He'll still be out in fifteen years,' Graham snorted.

'With a new identity,' Philpott added. 'That's already been agreed with the Russians. He knows that he became a marked man the moment he began collaborating with the authorities.'

'Did he confirm that *spetznaz* were behind the attack on the convoy taking them to the military prison outside Moscow?' Sabrina asked.

'Yes,' Philpott replied. 'Koslov masterminded the operation using a team of *spetznaz* officers sympathetic to the cause, although he wasn't actually there when it was carried out. The three of them were then given false papers and smuggled out of the country on board a fishing trawler bound for Sweden. They were met in Sweden by Saisse and taken on to France. The authorities have already arrested Koslov in Algeria. He's to be sent back to Russia to face trial with the other conspirators.'

'Talking of conspirators, any news of Inacio?' Graham enquired.

'Nothing so far,' Philpott said, shaking his head. 'It's very unlikely that he'd still be in Portugal though. Interpol's been alerted, so it should only be a matter of time before he's picked up.'

'The Colonel was telling me before you got here that Saisse has also gone missing,' Whitlock told them.

'Missing, sir?' Sabrina said suspiciously.

'Acting on Zlotin's tip-off, we were able to intercept the folders when they were delivered to the main railway station in Marseilles. The French police then launched simultaneous raids on all of Jannoc's business premises, and over fifty of his men have been arrested. The *gendarmerie* told me that they were confident of smashing the entire Jannoc organization by the end of the year. That includes impeaching members of local and national government who were in his back pocket.'

'Was Jannoc arrested?' Graham asked.

'He was arrested at his main casino, *Le Boudin*. We've now got enough evidence to put him away for life.'

'But no sign of Saisse?' Sabrina said.

'He hasn't been seen since he handed over the folders to a courier in Nantes. Jannoc's refused to say anything since his arrest, but the word is among some of his men that he actually suspects Saisse of setting him up. It seems that the two of them haven't exactly been seeing eye to eye since Jannoc's brother was killed. Jannoc openly accused Saisse of having ambitions on his organization and Saisse, in turn, blamed Jannoc for making several bad deals which has left the organization on the verge of bankruptcy.'

'Could there be some kind of link between Saisse and

Inacio?' Graham queried. 'It seems strange that they should both have disappeared at roughly the same time.'

'There's a team of analysts in the Command Centre working on that theory right now,' Philpott said. 'But so far they haven't come up with anything.'

'Rodenko might know something, sir,' Whitlock suggested.

'He claims that he doesn't, but then if Saisse and Inacio are in collusion, it's unlikely that the Russians would have known about it anyway. As it is, the Russians were double-crossing Jannoc and now it seems that Saisse was probably double-crossing him as well. This collusion theory is just speculation at the moment, and it'll stay that way until one or both of them have been arrested. Only then will we know the truth.' Philpott pulled another file towards him and opened it. 'I've received several enquiries about the arrangements for Jacques Rust's funeral since I broke the news of his death to the other field operatives. Sabrina, I know you specifically asked Sergei about it when you were over in Portugal. I've been in touch with his parents in France, and they've decided on a quiet family service in his home town of Dijon. Naturally I respect their wishes and, to be perfectly honest, I think it's for the best anyway. It would have been a security nightmare to have had so many field operatives gathered together in the open like that. It would have required a strong police presence, and that would only have intruded on the family's grief. I'm sure you understand.'

'Yes, sir,' Sabrina said quietly. 'Will there be a UNACO representative at the funeral?'

'I'll be attending the funeral on behalf of the organization,' Philpott told her. 'Sergei will be attending Abe Silverman's funeral in Haifa. I'm not sure yet of the exact dates, other than that both funerals will be held within the next week. Of course I'll let you know as soon as I hear anything definite.'

'Has anyone been pencilled in to replace Jacques, sir?' Graham asked.

'Yes. C.W.'s been officially appointed as the new Director of European Operations. He'll be flying out to Zürich to assume command early in the New Year.'

'You owe me fifty bucks,' Graham said, grinning triumphantly at Sabrina.

'That cancels out the money you still owe me after I whipped your butt at chess,' she replied with a cheeky smile.

'You guys had a wager on me taking over from Jacques?' Whitlock said in surprise.

'You were the obvious choice,' Graham said. 'Well, I thought so.'

Sabrina noticed Whitlock's eyes flicker to her and she gave him a sheepish grin. 'You tried your hand at management once before and you didn't like it. That's why I didn't think you'd take the job in Zürich if it were offered to you.'

Whitlock got to his feet and crossed the room before turning back to face them. 'You're right. I didn't particularly enjoy my stint here as Deputy Director. But the situation's changed. I guess Carmen was right when she said that I was getting too old for field work. And in any case, I have to face up to my new responsibilities now that I'm about to become a father for the first time.'

Sabrina was the first to her feet, and she hugged Whitlock fiercely. 'I'm so happy for you, C.W. Carmen must be over the moon.'

'Yes, she is,' Whitlock replied with a thoughtful smile.

'Congratulations, buddy,' Graham said.

'Thanks, Mike,' Whitlock replied.

'So if it's a boy is it going to be called Clarence after his dad?' Graham asked with a mischievous twinkle in his eye.

'Not bloody likely,' Whitlock retorted. 'A simple name will suffice, thank you.'

'Does Carmen know about Zürich yet?' Sabrina asked.

Whitlock nodded. 'Yes. We had another of our fall-outs before I left for Marseilles, so the first thing I did when I got back this morning was to have a long talk with her to clear the air. Then I rang the Colonel and asked him to put my name forward for the vacancy in Zürich. He told me that my name was already one of those under consideration, and an hour later he rang back to say that the Secretary-General had gone along with his recommendation to appoint me as Jacques' successor. Carmen was absolutely thrilled. It's no secret that our marriage has been going through a sticky patch for some time now. The move to Zürich will be the best thing to have happened to us in a long time. It's a chance to start over again. I can't wait to get out there and take up my new post.'

'I just hope it works out that way for you, buddy, because if Warren does go ahead and publish her story we can all kiss goodbye to any thoughts of a future in this organization.' Graham swung round on Philpott. 'I suppose the "Dirty Pool" still haven't managed to come up with something to use against them?'

'I was going to get round to that,' Philpott replied in an unruffled voice. 'I rang Larry Ryan last night and told him that you and Sabrina wanted to drop by his office later this afternoon to straighten out a few things with him before the story went to press.'

Graham and Sabrina exchanged horrified looks. 'I don't understand, sir,' Graham said anxiously.

'You will,' Philpott replied, sitting back in his chair. 'I've told Ryan that you'll be there at four o'clock sharp. Make sure you're on time.'

Larry Ryan scooped up the receiver after the first ring. 'Yes?'

'This is security in the main foyer, sir,' a voice announced. 'I have a Mr Graham and a Miss Carver down here who say they have an appointment with you. Only their names aren't listed anywhere on the computer.'

'They're expected,' Ryan assured him. 'Have someone show them up to my office right away.'

'Yes, sir.'

Ryan severed the connection then dialled out an internal number. 'Katy, it's Larry. Drop everything and get your butt over here. Graham and Carver are on their way up to my office.'

'I'm there,' Katherine Warren was quick to reply.

Ryan replaced the receiver, then got to his feet and removed a folder from the top drawer of the metal filing cabinet behind him. He pushed aside the document he'd been working on and placed the folder on the desk directly in front of his chair.

Moments later there was a knock on the door and Katherine entered the room carrying a folder similar to the one on Ryan's desk. 'We've really got UNACO rattled, Larry,' she said, closing the door again behind her. 'Why else would they have thrown Graham and Carver to the wolves unless they thought it would take the pressure off the organization?'

'You could be right; it could be some kind of damage limitation exercise. But then I guess we'll just have to wait and see, won't we?'

'Whatever the reason, it can only enhance the story once it hits the streets,' she said. 'Have you finalized a date yet to send it to press?'

'We're probably looking at the first week of the New Year, but we'll discuss the exact date at the next ops meeting.'

There was a sharp rap on the door. Ryan switched on a hidden tape recorder which would pick up the conversation from various concealed microphones secreted about the room, then crossed to the door and opened it. He ignored the security guard as his eyes went to Graham and Sabrina. 'Please, come in.'

They entered the room and Ryan closed the door again behind them. 'I think you already know Miss Warren?' he said, gesturing to Katherine who was standing by the window.

Sabrina eyed her disdainfully. 'The smell's certainly familiar.'

'Somehow I wouldn't have taken you for a sore loser, Miss Carver,' Katherine said with a faint smile of satisfaction.

'The game's not over yet,' Sabrina replied icily, holding her penetrating stare.

'You've obviously picked that up since Katy got back to New York,' Ryan said, indicating Graham's injured arm. 'Nothing too serious, I hope?'

'We didn't come here to shoot the breeze, Ryan,' Graham snapped angrily.

Ryan sat down again behind his desk and extended his upturned hands towards Graham. 'OK, so what's this all about? After all, you were the ones who called the meeting.'

'We're here to make a deal with you,' Graham told him.

'So deal,' Ryan said with a bemused smile. 'I just hope you haven't come here to try and persuade us to drop the story, because it won't work. It goes to press early in the New Year.'

Graham removed a videotape from the attaché case he was carrying and placed it on the desk in front of Ryan. 'So will that the moment the story breaks.'

Ryan turned the videotape around in his hands then looked up at Graham, a puzzled frown on his face. 'So what's on this tape that should have me quivering with fear?'

'How much do you know about your wife's past, Mr Ryan?' Sabrina asked.

'Louise and I have no secrets from each other,' Ryan retorted defensively. Katherine looked visibly shaken at the mention of her sister's name.

'Then you'll know that she rebelled against her parents' affluent lifestyle when she was seventeen and left home to try to make it on her own?' Sabrina continued.

'She spent a year in a commune off Times Square before realizing that her life wasn't going anywhere. She reconciled herself with her parents who then gave their blessing for her to attend drama school,' Graham added.

'I know all about that,' Ryan shot back. 'What the hell has any of this got to do with the videotape?'

'You should know if you don't have any secrets from

each other,' Graham said, sitting in one of the padded chairs in front of Ryan's desk. 'Then again, I doubt she'd have told you about the film she made while she was staying at the commune.'

'Film?' Ryan demanded, but when he looked across at Katherine he noticed that her face had suddenly gone very pale.

'It was a small budget film that was only ever released on the New York underground circuit,' Sabrina told him. 'There are those who'd doubtless call it art, but I think you'd find most people would regard it simply as pornography. But what really makes it so depraved is that there are children in it as well. We could only watch a couple of minutes of it before we had to turn it off. The tape's been spooled back to one of the scenes involving your wife.'

Ryan slotted the tape into the VCR on the shelf behind him and used the remote control to activate the television set on the opposite side of the room. He only watched a few seconds of the film before switching it off. There was no doubt in his mind that the naked figure on the screen had been that of his wife, Louise.

'Where did you get that from?' Katherine snapped furiously. 'There were only half a dozen prints of the film ever made and they were all supposed to have been destroyed in a warehouse fire.'

'We know about the fire, Miss Warren,' Graham said, looking across at her. 'We also have an affidavit from a lifer in San Quentin who gave us a very accurate description of the woman who paid him to torch the warehouse.'

'What exactly are you getting at?' Katherine snarled.

'Nothing,' Graham was quick to reply. 'We would only supply the evidence if it were ever to go to trial. It would be up to a jury to make the call.'

'Frankly, we're not that bothered about the fire,' Sabrina said. 'It destroyed thousands of this kind of cheap video nasties, so that can't be a bad thing, can it?'

'You never answered my question: where did you get the video from?' Katherine asked again.

'We didn't,' Sabrina told her. 'We have a team at UNACO whose job it is to dig up the dirt on anyone who threatens to expose the organization. Naturally they have contacts at the lowest level of the criminal underworld. That's obviously how they came up with this. I don't know how they acquired it and, to be honest, I don't want to know either.'

'So what exactly is the deal?' Ryan asked. 'If we publish the article about UNACO, you send a copy of this tape to Louise's boss, is that it?'

'If you publish the article about UNACO, we'll release copies of the video to every major TV network across the country,' Graham corrected him. 'Imagine what that would do to your wife's career as a children's television presenter? She'd never survive the scandal. And even if she were to try and ride it out, think about the effect it would have on your two daughters. You know how hurtful other kids can be at that age. Your children would come home in tears every day. That's hardly fair on them, is it?'

'Then there's your mother, Miss Warren,' Sabrina said, looking at Katherine. 'You moved back to New York to be close to her after her second heart attack. Imagine what it would do to her if she were ever to find out that Louise had made a film like that. It could kill her, couldn't it?'

'Now that we've laid our cards on the table, it's up to you to play your hand,' Graham said, picking up the attaché case at his feet. 'You'll be contacted in an hour's time for your answer. If you decide to press ahead with the story, you know what the consequences will be. If you agree to drop the story, you'll be expected to hand over all the relevant information you have about UNACO, as well as the negatives of any film taken of us, or anyone else associated with the case. And as you've no doubt taped this meeting, we'll want that cassette as well.'

'And of course you'll hold on to the original copy of the film,' Ryan said bitterly.

'That goes without saying,' Graham replied.

'You've got it all worked out, haven't you?'

'We have to protect the anonymity of our organization any way we can, Miss Warren,' Sabrina said, following Graham to the door. She opened the door, then looked back at Katherine. 'It was a good try. Better luck next time.'

Katherine had to restrain herself from slamming the door behind them. 'Damn bitch,' she snarled, slumping down into one of the armchairs.

Ryan switched off the tape recorder, ejected the cassette, and tossed it in the top drawer of the desk. 'When did you first find out about the film?'

'Louise told me shortly after she'd finished making it. She was strapped for cash at the time and she was too damn proud to ask our parents to help her out. I know she regretted making it as soon as it was finished, but by then it was too late. God, she could be incredibly naïve at times.'

'Who paid the arsonist?' Ryan asked softly. 'You or Louise?'

'Come on, Larry, you don't really think –'

'Who paid him?' Ryan thundered.

Katherine brushed a strand of hair nervously from her face. 'I did. I had to protect her. You must understand that. I thought I had but obviously I was wrong.'

'Does Louise know about the fire?'

'She knew that the warehouse went up in flames, but she doesn't know that I arranged it. She still seems to think it was some kind of fortuitous twist of fate. But then Louise was always the innocent in the family. That's probably why she gets on so well with kids.'

'I'm sure it is,' Ryan muttered sarcastically.

'Are you going to confront her about the film?'

'What good could that possibly do? No, some things are better left unsaid.'

'I think that's a wise choice,' Katherine replied. 'It could only harm the marriage in the long term.'

'And you don't think this has harmed it?' Ryan snapped back. 'Marriages are supposed to be built on trust. But then again perhaps I'm just expecting too much. I should have realized at the time that she couldn't have been as perfect as she made herself out to be when I first met her.'

'I know you're hurting, Larry, but you've got to remember that it was one stupid indiscretion she made when she was still a teenager.'

'And that makes it all right?' Ryan slammed his fist down angrily on to the desk. 'It's given UNACO the perfect ammunition to use against us, and there isn't a damn thing we can do about it.'

'It would have been one hell of an exposé though, Larry,' Katherine said after a thoughtful silence. 'We'd have been the toast of the town. The envy of every newspaper across the country. We were that close, weren't we?'

'Yeah,' Ryan replied, picking up the folder on the desk and leafing through the contents. 'What could have been, Katy. What could have been.'

Whitlock left the United Nations with mixed emotions that afternoon. The excitement of the challenge facing him as the new Director of European Operations in Zürich was over-shadowed by the deep sorrow he was feeling at the loss of his friend and former Strike Force Three partner, Jacques Rust. The guilt still lingered on in his mind as he thought back to his fateful decision the previous day to wait until after dark before setting up the explosion in the prison. Had he decided to go ahead and do it that morning, as originally planned, the authorities would have reached the island earlier and Rust might still be alive. On the other hand, the dark-ness had been his only ally, and had he attempted the same plan during the day, he might have been killed, leaving the hostages to the mercy of the Russians. It was a dilemma without a solution, and he knew it would always be there to haunt him for the rest of his life . . .

Then there was the opportunity for him to start over again with Carmen, rebuilding their marriage around the joy of their first child, which would be offset by the sadness he already felt about finally being retired from the field. But it wasn't the actual field work he'd miss: he was the first to admit he was already getting too old to be chasing around after villains half his age. No, it was the camaraderie which had existed within Strike Force Three that would be impossible to replace once he took up his new post in Zürich. Finally, the last of UNACO's original field operatives was being put out to pasture. The end of an era? No, he preferred to see it rather as the beginning of a new era that he hoped would one day lead him back to New York as the new UNACO Director. And he knew that's what Philpott already had in mind . . .

It was already dark by the time he reached his apartment block in Manhattan. He drove his white BMW down the ramp of the basement car park and parked in his reserved space. The adjoining space was empty. Carmen wasn't home yet. He crossed to the lift and was about to use his personal ID card to activate the doors when a figure emerged from behind a pillar close to the lift. It was Fabien Saisse. Saisse was holding a newspaper across his stomach. He moved it aside to reveal the Heckler & Koch P9S in his hand.

'Open the doors,' Saisse snapped in his thick French accent.

Whitlock inserted the key card into the slot and moments later the doors parted. Saisse followed him into the lift and pressed the button for the seventh floor. The doors closed.

'What's this all about?' Whitlock demanded.

'That will become apparent in due course, *Whitlock*,' Saisse replied sarcastically. 'Or would you still prefer to be called Royce?'

Whitlock said nothing. His mind was racing as he weighed

up his chances of reaching the pistol before Saisse could pull the trigger, but he quickly realized that the odds were stacked too heavily against him. No, it wasn't worth it. He'd bide his time and wait for the right moment . . .

The doors parted on the seventh floor and Saisse gestured for Whitlock to step out of the lift. Saisse concealed the pistol behind the newspaper again and went after him. Whitlock paused outside the apartment door and slipped his hand into his pocket.

'You had better be reaching for your keys,' Saisse hissed threateningly behind him.

Whitlock eyed him coldly, then slowly withdrew the keys from his pocket. The door opened directly on to the lounge. Saisse pushed him into the apartment and quickly closed the door again behind them.

'Give me your gun,' Saisse ordered, gesturing to Whitlock's chest.

'I'm not armed,' Whitlock told him.

'I will not ask you again,' Saisse snarled, levelling the pistol at him.

Whitlock tore off his jacket and tossed it on to the chair. He held up his arms to show Saisse that he wasn't concealing a weapon. 'We only carry when we're on assignment. The weapons are all returned to the arsenal when the assignment's over. It's standard procedure. You should know that if you've read through our folders. The procedure's in there.'

Saisse frisked him thoroughly then pointed to the chair nearest the door. Whitlock sat down.

'Are you going to tell me now what it is you want?' Whitlock demanded.

'Information,' came the reply.

'And once I've given you this information, then you'll kill me,' Whitlock snorted disdainfully. 'Is that the deal?'

'If you refuse to give me the information, I will kill you,' came the chilling reply. 'That is the deal.'

Saisse's history of violence was well documented in his

UNACO dossier, and Whitlock knew that the Frenchman would almost certainly kill him after he had the information he wanted. But he also knew that Saisse couldn't risk killing him before he got the information. Whitlock found himself in a dilemma. His only chance would be to stall for as long as possible and hope that Saisse would make a mistake which he could turn to his advantage. But the longer he held out, the more chance there was of Carmen arriving back at the apartment. He desperately wanted to keep her out of this, especially in her condition. But for the moment it was Saisse who was holding all the aces . . .

'How did you know who I was?' Whitlock asked. 'There weren't any photos in the folders.'

'I only knew you as a name from the UNACO files. I found out where you lived and I have been watching the building since daybreak. I first realized that you were Whitlock when I saw you leave the underground car park this morning.'

'So this has got nothing to do with me being Royce?' Whitlock said suspiciously.

'Nothing,' Saisse replied contemptuously.

'OK, so what exactly is this information you want?'

'You and your former partner, Jacques Rust, were assigned to an operation in Cairo four years ago involving UNACO's top contact in the Middle East at the time. He was only ever known by his code name: Shadow Dancer.'

Whitlock remembered the operation in question. It had all started with a tip-off from Shadow Dancer to his handler at the Command Centre that a major drugs deal was due to go down in Cairo. A shipment of high quality heroin, worth in the region of fifty million dollars, was to be transported under heavy guard from the Lebanon's Bekaa Valley through to Cairo, where the representatives of a European consortium would pay for it in the equivalent value of gemstones. Philpott had dispatched Whitlock and Rust to Cairo to liaise with Shadow Dancer. It was the first time that either of them had worked with him, and what they had found when they got to Cairo was a middle-aged man riddled with the anxiety of having lived on the fringes of betrayal for too long. He'd agreed to help UNACO one last time, then he wanted out. Philpott had agreed.

Shadow Dancer already had a plan in mind. They wouldn't get near the heroin shipment, it was too well protected. The weak link was in Cairo. No gemstones – no deal. Shadow Dancer had assured them that his team of handpicked men could snatch the gemstones at the prearranged rendezvous minutes before the deal was due to go down. In return, he wanted half a million pounds in cash, and safe passage for him and his family out of the country. Whitlock and Rust had had their doubts about the plan, but Philpott had castigated them both for doubting Shadow Dancer's loyalty to UNACO. Shadow Dancer *would* carry out his part of the deal.

And he had. Although neither Whitlock nor Rust had been there when the gemstones were taken in what proved to be a bloody gun battle, Shadow Dancer had arrived shortly afterwards at their hotel where a jeweller had been on hand to authenticate them. The money had been paid to Shadow Dancer, who had then flown back to his home town of Beirut to finalize the details of his move abroad. That same evening he was dead, killed instantly when his car was involved in a head-on collision with a lorry. A subsequent UNACO investigation was to prove beyond any reasonable doubt that the fatal crash had been nothing more than a tragic accident . . .

'He double-crossed UNACO, *n'est-ce pas*?' Saisse asked, his voice breaking Whitlock's train of thought.

Whitlock recalled how Philpott had called in several favours by getting the then head of the Egyptian police to leak an anonymous rumour back to the Lebanese underworld that Shadow Dancer had been the sole mastermind behind the heist and that it was obvious he'd already hidden the gemstones before his untimely death. Whitlock and Rust had been sworn to silence on their return to New York and the amended version of the events was subsequently entered into the official UNACO files. Not that Whitlock had any idea what had really happened to the stones after they were handed over to Philpott in New York . . .

'So that's what this is all about,' Whitlock said. 'You read about the operation in our files so you think that because I was one of his contacts in Cairo at the time, I must know something that could lead you to the stones. I'm sorry to disappoint you, but as you said, he double-crossed us as well.'

'We have known all along that UNACO were behind the heist,' Saisse said as if it were unimportant.

'*We?*' Whitlock asked suspiciously.

'Do you think that I just happened to stumble across the details of the Cairo operation in your files and flew over here on the off-chance that you might know something about the location of the missing stones?' Saisse snorted. 'This is the culmination of over three years of precision planning.'

'You still haven't said who "we" are,' Whitlock said, struggling to keep his composure as he realized that all his preconceived ideas about Saisse being little more than an opportunist had been wrong. This was a professional scam and he desperately needed to know more about it if he were to have any chance of outwitting the Frenchman.

'There were initially five of us, now there are only two left. We met in the Lebanon. I was stationed there three years ago as part of a United Nations peacekeeping force. So was my adjutant, Heinrich Berger. The Portuguese also had a unit there.'

'Which included Inacio and Caldere?' Whitlock concluded.

'João Inacio and Luis Braga,' Saisse corrected him. 'Once we had agreed to pool our resources it was decided that, on his return to Portugal, Braga would resign from the army and change his name to Caldere, in case any connection

371

was made between him and Inacio. Inacio was already being tipped as future head of the Special Forces Brigade. We could not afford any slip-ups.'

'Smart move,' Whitlock concluded. 'So when Mike asked Inacio for information about Caldere, Inacio was only too pleased to oblige, only first he edited out anything that could have incriminated him.'

'As I said, we could not afford any slip-ups. Not with fifty million dollars at stake.'

'And the fifth conspirator?' Whitlock asked.

'UNACO's main contact in the Lebanon, Nazir Barak,' Saisse replied with a triumphant smile.

'I can't say I'm surprised,' Whitlock shot back scornfully. 'Barak worked for anyone who paid him. He was a wealth of information, but he was never trustworthy. So how exactly did he find out about the gemstones?'

'Barak knew Shadow Dancer. He didn't know his real name; just knew him by one of the many aliases he used. They were never friends, but there seemed to have been some kind of bond between them because of the nature of their profession. That was why Shadow Dancer went straight to Barak's house when he returned to Beirut after the heist. He knew it would be the one place he could hide until it was safe for him to leave the country.

'Of course he never mentioned anything about the heist to Barak, but he did have a key with him, and when Barak asked him about it, he was told that it was for a safe deposit box in Cairo. A box that he had rented out under his own name. A clever twist. At the time Barak thought nothing of it, but it was only after Shadow Dancer was killed that the rumours reached the Lebanon that he had been the mastermind behind the gemstone heist in Cairo. Naturally Barak put two and two together and realized that he was on to something big. After all, he was the only person who knew about the key. He found it amongst Shadow Dancer's belongings, which were still in the house, but it was useless to him unless he could find out Shadow Dancer's real name. All his subsequent enquiries came to nothing.'

'How did the four of you get in on the deal?'

'Barak was an inveterate gambler who had outstanding debts right across Beirut. Many of those debts were spread among the French and Portuguese troops who were in the Lebanon at the time. He was beaten up on more than one occasion for not paying his markers on time. Then some of the troops threatened to kill him if he did not hand over the outstanding money. That was when he came to see us. Inacio and I both used him as an informer while we were stationed in the Lebanon. He wanted protection. He was very frightened and in his nervousness he let slip that he would be able to pay off all the debts once he had located the gemstones. We pressured him into telling us everything he knew about the heist, and he agreed that, in return for our protection, he would bring us in on the deal. It was as simple as that.'

'Was he still under your protection when he was gunned down by a mysterious assailant in his house?' Whitlock asked disdainfully.

'His death was no great loss,' Saisse replied with a dismissive shrug. 'The key was already in a safe place, that was all that really mattered to us. It was after his death that we hatched the operation to get the UNACO files. Inacio found out about the anti-terrorist conference in Lisbon at least a year before it was due to take place. But we had to deflect suspicion from him, so I made it look as if we had received the information from Jannoc's contact inside UNACO, Professor Marcel Toure.'

'And Jannoc knew nothing of this plot?' Whitlock asked.

'Nothing. We only needed him to finance the operation. I knew the only way he would go along with it would be if I could convince him that he needed the files himself.'

'Of course,' Whitlock said, nodding his head to himself. 'You had Christian Jannoc killed, then made it look as if he'd been caught up in a gun battle with one of our Strike Force teams. That way you were able to persuade Jannoc to finance your operation so that he could avenge his brother's death. It's ingenious, Saisse.'

'I killed Christian Jannoc myself,' Saisse replied with a chilling smile. 'No slip-ups, remember?'

'Whose idea was it to bring in the Russians?'

'Mine. I first heard about them through their lawyer in Moscow. They wanted out of Russia, we needed a slick team to spearhead the operation. An ideal partnership. Of course Jannoc went along with it from the start. The rest I think you know.'

'And you think I know Shadow Dancer's real name?' Whitlock said.

'I know you can find out,' Saisse replied. 'According to your file, you have a computer here in the apartment which is linked to the main computer in the Command Centre at UNACO headquarters.'

'Shadow Dancer's real identity was known only to a handful of senior personnel within the organization,' Whitlock said. 'Any information on him will be classified, and I don't have the necessary authorization to access those programmes.'

'You are beginning to test my patience, Whitlock,' Saisse snapped, his finger tightening around the trigger. 'I know from the files that you have a Grade A classification which entitles you to access all UNACO documents.'

'OK, I'll get the information you want,' Whitlock replied in a placating voice, then gestured in the direction of the hall. 'The computer's in my study.'

'Get up slowly and put your hands –' Saisse stopped abruptly when he heard the sound of a key being inserted into the front door.

Whitlock's eyes went to the door. Carmen. It was the moment he'd been dreading. He had to warn her. The door opened but, before he could call out to her, Saisse anticipated his reaction and brought the butt of the pistol down sharply on the back of his head. Whitlock stumbled forward and fell to his knees. By the time he'd cleared his head, Carmen was already standing in the doorway, her eyes wide and fearful as she looked from her stricken husband to the pistol in Saisse's hand.

'Leave him!' Saisse snapped when she made towards Whitlock.

'I'm OK,' Whitlock was quick to reassure her. 'Just do as he says.'

'Very sensible,' Saisse replied with a sneer. 'Now close the door and come over here.'

'Your business is with me, Saisse,' Whitlock said. 'Leave my wife out of it.'

'Come here,' Saisse ordered, levelling the pistol at her head. 'I will count to three. One.'

'She's pregnant, for Christ's sake,' Whitlock yelled furiously. 'I told you I'd get the information you want. Just leave her alone.'

Saisse lowered the pistol until it was trained on her stomach. 'Two.'

'What kind of animal are you?' Whitlock screamed at him.

Carmen swallowed nervously, then closed the door and crossed to where Saisse was standing. He immediately pulled her to him and, locking his arm around her throat, pressed the Heckler & Koch against the side of her head. 'Whitlock, put your hands on your head and walk slowly to the study. Any heroics, and I kill your wife.'

'Just take it easy, Saisse,' Whitlock implored him, struggling to his feet.

'Put your hands on your head,' Saisse barked.

Whitlock clamped his hands on top of his head and began to move slowly towards the study, his mind racing as he desperately sought a way to disarm Saisse. What frightened him most of all was that he couldn't come up with a viable plan, not while Saisse had Carmen as a hostage . . .

'Oh God,' Carmen gasped, clutching her stomach.

'Carmen!' Whitlock cried out in horror and moved towards her.

'Stay where you are!' Saisse yelled at him.

Carmen's legs buckled under her, but she managed to regain her balance. 'I feel dizzy, I have to sit down,' she pleaded. 'Please, I must sit down.'

'No,' Saisse snarled in her ear.

'I told you, she's pregnant,' Whitlock hissed at Saisse. 'Let her sit before she falls down.'

Saisse cursed furiously, but at the same time he knew she would be useless as a hostage if she were to faint in his arms. He pulled her back with him towards the nearest chair. She tilted her head to the side, easing the pressure from around her throat, then stamped her stiletto heel down savagely on to his instep and felt the metal rip through his flesh. His agonized howl choked in his throat as she brought her elbow up sharply into his Adam's apple. He stumbled away from her, his fingers clawing at his throat as he gasped for air.

Whitlock lunged at Saisse and, grabbing his gun hand, slammed it against the wall, forcing him to drop the pistol. He hammered two vicious body punches into Saisse's stomach and, as the Frenchman doubled over in pain, he delivered a jarring rabbit punch to the back of his neck. Saisse was unconscious before he crumpled to the floor. Whitlock, his features contorted with rage, hauled Saisse up by the collar and began punching him repeatedly in the face.

Carmen rushed forward, but when she tried to pull him away from Saisse he just brushed her aside, continuing to rain down more punches on to the bloodied face. 'Stop it!' she screamed.

Whitlock looked up sharply, startled by the sound of her

voice, then gazed around the room in bewilderment before his eyes finally settled on Saisse's battered face. For a moment he was transfixed by the horror of what he saw then, lowering Saisse to the floor, he sat down slowly on the sofa and buried his head in his hands, struggling to come to terms with what he'd just done.

Carmen sat beside him and put her arm gently around his shoulders. 'It's OK,' she said softly.

Whitlock raised his head slowly, the disbelief still mirrored in his eyes. 'I don't know what came over me. I mean . . .' He trailed off with a helpless shrug.

'I do,' she said. 'You were just protecting your family.'

'My God, the baby,' he said anxiously. 'Is the baby –'

'The baby's fine,' she was quick to reassure him.

'Are you sure?'

'I'm sure,' she insisted gently.

'I have to call Colonel Philpott,' Whitlock said, indicating the telephone. 'He'll arrange with the NYPD to have Saisse taken into custody.'

'I'll see what I can do for him until he can get proper medical attention,' Carmen said, getting to her feet.

'The cops will see to him,' Whitlock said brusquely.

'You know as well as I do that I took an oath when I graduated as a doctor, and that means I have a duty to treat Saisse, irrespective of my feelings towards him.'

Whitlock knew it was futile to argue with her, and reached for the telephone to call UNACO headquarters.

'So the jigsaw's finally complete,' Philpott said after Whitlock had briefed him.

'We still haven't got Inacio yet, sir,' Whitlock reminded him.

'He'll be picked up soon enough,' Philpott replied. 'Saisse and Inacio may have been partners in crime, but you can be sure that they were only in this caper for themselves. Saisse won't take the rap by himself. It's not in his nature.'

'No, I guess not,' Whitlock replied, then got to his feet and pointed to the empty glass on the table beside Philpott's chair. 'Can I tempt you to a refill, sir?'

Philpott held out the glass. 'Just a small one for the road. I'm due back at the UN in an hour to brief Strike Force Ten on their latest assignment.'

'It wouldn't do for you to arrive for the briefing the worse for drink, sir,' Whitlock said, quickly putting his hand to his mouth to hide the smile as he tried to imagine Philpott in a state of intoxication.

'No, it wouldn't, would it?' Philpott replied with a smile of his own that told Whitlock that his deception had been tumbled.

'If only Caldere had managed to say more than just "Shadow Dancer" to Mike before he died,' Whitlock mused thoughtfully as he poured a short measure into Philpott's glass.

'It would certainly have saved us a lot of trouble,' Philpott agreed with a disgruntled shake of the head. 'When I first received Mike's report I tried every way possible to tie in Caldere to UNACO's "Shadow Dancer", but each time I came up a blank. At the time there seemed to be absolutely no connection whatsoever between the two of them.'

'You couldn't have known, sir, not without more information to go on,' Whitlock said, handing the tumbler to Philpott. Then, resuming his seat, he picked up the cold compress from the table and applied it gingerly to his skinned knuckles.

'How is the hand?' Philpott asked.

'It still hurts like hell,' Whitlock replied with a grimace.

'I can imagine, if Saisse's face was anything to go by,' Philpott said sternly. 'He was barely conscious when the police took him away. You certainly did a good job of working him over.'

'I know I was out of line, sir,' Whitlock said, staring guiltily at the offending limb. 'I don't know what got into me. I guess

I just snapped when I realized how close I'd come to losing Carmen and the baby. I know that if I'd given Saisse the information he wanted, he'd have had no qualms about killing her.'

'Or you,' Philpott was quick to point out. 'I understand why you did it, C.W., but that doesn't mean I condone it. UNACO operatives are expected to uphold the law, not transgress it.'

'No, sir,' Whitlock replied contritely. 'I realize that there could be repercussions if Saisse were to lay a charge against me.'

'That's the least of our worries,' Philpott told him. 'Saisse will be far too busy trying to weasel out of a life sentence to be bothered about any charges against you. No, it's the Secretary-General that concerns me. You know how agitated he gets when he hears about field operatives taking the law into their own hands.'

'You don't think this could affect my promotion, sir?' Whitlock asked, the sudden consternation evident in his voice.

'Not in the slightest. After all, I'm the one who has the final say on any appointments within the organization, not the Secretary-General.' Philpott looked round and smiled at Carmen when she entered the lounge. 'How are you feeling, my dear?'

'A lot better than Saisse must be feeling right now,' she replied, sitting down on the sofa and pulling her feet up underneath her.

'That wouldn't be too difficult, I imagine,' Philpott said, glancing disapprovingly at Whitlock. 'C.W. told me how you took on Saisse by yourself.'

She shrugged as if it were nothing. 'C.W. taught me the basics of self-defence soon after we were married so that, if I were ever attacked, I would be able to defend myself. I couldn't do anything when I was sitting down, but when Saisse forced me to stand up I feigned a dizzy spell. At first I thought he wasn't going to buy it, but he must have known that I would have been useless to him if I had fainted. I made my move when he began pulling me back towards the chair.'

'It must have taken a lot of nerve to have pulled it off,' Philpott said, draining the tumbler and replacing it on the table.

'You don't think of it that way when you're protecting your family,' she replied, smiling gently at her husband.

Philpott reached for his cane and got to his feet. 'Well, you'll have to excuse me. As I told C.W., I've got a meeting back at the UN. And C.W., I'll expect a full report on my desk no later than ten o'clock tomorrow morning.'

'You'll have it, sir,' Whitlock replied, walking Philpott to the door.

'When exactly are you leaving for Zürich?' Philpott asked as Whitlock opened the door for him.

'We're booked on a Swissair flight out of JFK on the third of January,' Carmen called out from the sofa. 'I can't wait to get out there and start decorating our new house.'

'Colonel, there's been something I've been meaning to ask you,' Whitlock said. 'Whatever did happen to those gemstones after I handed them over to you?'

'Have you ever wondered where we got the money from to build our European headquarters in Zürich?' Philpott replied, then patted Whitlock on the arm. 'Good night, C.W.'

'Good night, sir,' Whitlock said with a smile, and closed the door behind him.